A Man Apart

JAN RABIE

A Man Apart

TRANSLATED BY THE AUTHOR FROM
THE ORIGINAL AFRIKAANS

Collins
ST JAMES'S PLACE, LONDON
1969

First published in South Africa
by Human and Rousseau under the title
Waar Jy Sterwe

© Jan Rabie, 1966
© in the English translation, Jan Rabie, 1969
Printed in Great Britain
Collins Clear-Type Press
London and Glasgow

. . . For whither thou goest, I will go; and where thou lodgest, I will lodge: thy people shall be my people, and thy God my God:

Where thou diest, will I die, and there will I be buried: the Lord do so to me, and more also, if ought but death part thee and me . . .

Foreword

Originally the African sub-continent was peopled by small yellow-skinned hunters, the Bushmen. When the first Dutch settlers arrived in the 17th century, however, they found that the fertile coastal area had already been taken over by another yellow-skinned people, the Hottentots, and that the Bushmen had been driven into the dry interior. Throughout the 18th century white settlers, often intermingling racially with the Hottentots whom they had overrun, and reinforced by French Huguenot immigrants and slaves from India, Indonesia, Madagascar or Angola, advanced ever farther along the East coast and into the hinterland. To meet them from the North-East came the black Bantu tribes, known to Europeans as the Kaffirs. A clash between these two expanding and aggressive powers became inevitable.

In 1795, as a by-product of the Napoleonic Wars in Europe, British forces occupied the Cape. They found the Dutch divided between 'Orangists,' supporters of the Dutch royal house, who were in favour of collaboration with the British, and 'Patriots' who, inspired by the French Revolution, dreamt of freedom from the European yoke. Profiting by the unrest, many of the Hottentots and half-castes turned on their Dutch masters, first as servants of the British, later more and more as allies of the Bantu tribesmen.

It is against this background of simmering discontent and growing racial tension that Jan Rabie has set his story.

Part One

Part One

I

On a hilltop overlooking the public road to the east, high above the deep canyon of the Gouritz River, partly hidden behind tree aloes, three horsemen sat looking down, watching a dust cloud approaching. They had been watching it for a long time. Now they could distinguish the blue and red uniforms of the British dragoons, and the helmet plumes of the officers nodding as their horses strained down the last slope to the water. Farther back followed a straggle of men with red uniforms and striped trousers, the Pandours, struggling to control a milling mass of pack animals and relay horses. The three Patriot burghers frowned whenever their eyes returned to these Hottentot soldiers in the service of the British.

One of the burghers, a field-cornet from Graaff-Reinet, grimaced defiantly:

'Let the English come. The people won't let them pass!'

With a gesture fitting the words, he took a tricoloured national cockade from his pocket and pushed it into the band of his felt hat. Far below, where horses and soldiers now formed a long bright-coloured rim along the mud-brown riverbank, the hot south-easter from time to time ironed out the British flag. Fiercely, the burgher added:

'If you men from Swellendam and Stellenbosch do your duty and stand by the Patriots of Graaff-Reinet, if you don't betray our country like the Orangist turncoats from the Cape, then these foreign tyrants won't rule us for long.'

'But surely the English will give the Cape back to the Hollanders, once they've made peace with Napoleon?' one of the others countered.

The burgher from Graaff-Reinet laughed.

'And what about this accursed oath, the oath of loyalty to the British King?'

For a while they were silent. A horse stamped now and again, and a vague tumult rose in gusts from the deep Gouritz valley.

'Now they are using the Hottentots against us too.' Thomas Muller, a young swarthy-faced burgher also from Graaff-Reinet spoke bitterly. When the two older men remained silent, he tightened the rein of his white-starred mount, and said impatiently:

'Well, General Vandeleur seems in as much of a hurry as I am. I'd better ride on if I want to pass the Longkloof before them.'

For a while the three burghers followed the wagon road between Cape Town and the eastern frontier, churned to dust by a century of trekking pioneers. When they caught up with two heavily laden ox-wagons, they drew in their horses.

'Supplies for the troops. Sent ahead to be in time at Mossel Bay.'

There were four yellow-skinned Hottentots with the wagons: two drivers and two team-leaders. They greeted the newcomers, glancing uneasily at the three horsemen riding so purposefully beside their wagons.

Scheepers asked the driver of the hindmost wagon for whom they were riding transport, and where they were going. He asked his questions in the commanding voice a white man normally used to a Hottentot, and the driver answered with the usual friendly respect. He did not know what was under the canvas covers, the soldiers had loaded it themselves and the Government baas had told him not to touch it.

The horsemen suspected that there would be barrels of gunpowder, lead and flints, precisely what the rebels needed most since all transport of ammunition out of Cape Town had been prohibited. But at any moment a cloud of dust might arise behind them so it was hardly a moment for violence. Something else attracted young Muller's attention: the foremost driver had climbed on to the box of his wagon, as if he wanted to escape attention.

The burghers spurred on their horses to the front of the wagon. Scheepers repeated his questions more harshly this time. The driver was still young and less subservient than the others, but he answered readily that he had been commandeered to ride transport for the Government and that his name was Douw Prins.

'Douw Prins! That's no Hottentot name!' Muller exclaimed.

Something about the driver's face was not Hottentot either; a lighter skin-colour accentuating a black mole beside his nose, straighter hair, a firmer chin, and an awkwardly sullen look of pride. He stayed silent, however, looking at the white man who was about his own age. For some reason or other this made young Muller angry:

'You Hottentots are getting conceited these days, heh? Who told you to fawn on the English? Who's your baas, heh?'

The young driver had trouble in answering calmly:

'I have no baas, Mynheer . . .' Then his face crumpled out of control as he stuttered: 'I'm a free man! This is my wagon and my oxen! I can ride where I want!'

'Stop when a Christian speaks to you!' Muller ground out, shouting to stop the oxen which were still plodding along.

But the driver sprang to his feet, raised his long whip and let it resound with a thunderous crack, setting the horses rearing away and the oxen once more tautening their traces. Again and again the whip slashed the air, swiftly flicking here and there over the heaving shoulders of the red and black team.

Muller seemed on the point of attacking the insolent driver, but his older companions restrained him. Their faces showed the same uncertain annoyance as when they had watched the Pandour troops, an emotion very like that which had wrestled with Douw Prins's features.

'You bastard, I'll remember you, I'll let you know you're in this world!' the swarthy young man called over his shoulder, as he swung his white-starred mount away.

The horsemen had hardly gone when Makman, the second driver, and Douw's own team-leader, Lafleur, came running up to him:

'Haitsa, man, what are you making trouble for? Hell, man, can't you see these whites are poisonous?'

Douw's hands still trembled, though clenched firmly on the whip. He himself seemed bewildered at his outburst.

Makman dug out his pipe and filled it with tobacco before he said with his usual indolence:

'It's not worth the trouble to stick out one's neck before it's time. One just has to wait till the English have tamed the rebel Dutchmen. Then the Child of Man will be able to raise his voice again.'

His slit eyes narrowed behind puffs of strong tobacco:

'Heh, shouldn't one be clever like a jackal, and wait till the right time comes?'

Beside him Lafleur nodded his pepper-corn skull in sly agreement:

'Heh, Douw? Walk softly, and then jump out on the baboon-haired whites?'

Suddenly the young driver rolled up his whip and pushed it through the hooks outside the wagon-tent. He no longer trembled, but when he faced the two Hottentots, he was angry once more:

'I won't wait to become a man another day! I'm a man already, today!'

2

Far behind another trek of two wagons came crawling along the churned-up road.

While soldiers, supply-wagons and dispatch riders hurried past towards the turbulent frontier districts where war threatened, and occasional fleeing colonists or wagons with loads of agricultural produce for the Cape passed in the opposite direction, this trek lingered for days at the first aloe-covered hills this side of the Breede River, or the plant paradise near Swellendam ... The Swedish botanist, Bengt Lindstrom, had time to spare, for he had undertaken a great expedition to investigate the famous botanical wealth of the Cape of Good Hope.

Ten days after General Vandeleur's troops had marched past, Lindstrom's trek stood beside the Vet River. During the twilight hour he sat at the collapsible table in his tent. Before him lay the journal of his travels, his sketch book, and a rare *Amaryllis* and *Stapelia* which he had dug up earlier that day.

Lindstrom smiled as his eyes strayed away to the activities of his camp and the stately view of the Langeberg mountains draped in evening blues, and then back to his diary where he had just written:

'6 March, Anno Domini, 1799. The variety of life-forms in this vast, wide land is unbelievable. In the four months since I disembarked at Cape Town, I have found literally hundreds of varieties of animals, birds and insects that are unknown even in specialist writings. But it is the wealth of plants and flowers that most astounds me. Sparmann, Thunberg and Le Vaillant did not begin to prepare me for the abundance that awaits one here.

'It is as if the space and sunlight and the many different climates continually create new forms; as if even plant families have run wild, just like, if the far-fetched comparison is admissible, the Cape Colonists in their expansion and diffusion across this wide, empty land. What fascinates me, too, the farther I penetrate the country, is how many shrubs and trees use thorns to protect—I might even say to isolate—their flowers or berries . . .'

Outside the tent the dogs started barking. Lindstrom tried to collect his thoughts while he sharpened the tip of his goose quill. He was on the point of rising to light the candle, when Barend, his half-caste camp foreman, came to call him to the fire. There were visitors.

Unusual visitors, Lindstrom understood from the attitude of his people around the fire-side. All were simultaneously asking questions in a mixture of Hottentot, Cape-Dutch and even Malay which Lindstrom, with his correct Dutch, found hard to understand. He, too, was surprised by the arrivals: an old grey-headed dwarf of a man, a young girl and an old woman on top of an unusual mount, a riding-ox, as well as another ox so laden with bundles that only its horns and tail were showing. Behind followed a long-horned cow and her calf. But it was the three travellers who drew his attention: all three wore worn-out European clothing and looked more or less Hottentot, but all showed definite racial differences. The little yellow man with a rough, home-made violin over his shoulder, looked indeed not so much a true Hottentot as a shrunken Bushman. The girl was dark, as if one of her parents had been a black slave, but with a mixture of other blood which made her look delicate and exotic. The old woman, who sat in so stately a fashion on her riding-ox, had long, straight hair and a pale face eloquent of white blood. Only when Lindstrom stood before her, did the old woman greet him:

'Mynheer, pardon us if we disturb you. I want to ask you a favour. Could we please follow you to Mossel Bay, close to your trek? People sometimes trouble us, especially my adopted daughter, Ruth. We won't be in your way. But we'll be very grateful to you.'

Lindstrom remained silent for a moment, surprised by the character and—was it patient dignity?—revealed by her voice. She grew up with white people, he found himself thinking. Then he hastily nodded:

'But of course.'

'Thank you, Mynheer,' the old woman said quietly, adding: 'Call me old Katryn. And this is Speelman. He will make music at any time.' Then she slapped her ox's neck. Before she could ride off, Barend asked, with the suspicion Lindstrom was by now used to in half-castes:

'Why do you travel around the world all on your own?'

'I'm looking for my grandson, Douw Prins, who left to ride transport for the Government. Did you perhaps see him? I hear there are two wagons together. He's got a mole by his nose and his complexion is light.'

Two of Lindstrom's Hottentots, Slinger and Esau, reacted at once. Yes, yes! They had seen him the evening they had spent by the Breede River pontoon. He had kept very much to himself. It seemed as if Lindstrom's whole company remembered this young Hottentot half-caste, including a young burgher from Stellenbosch, Tielman Roux, who added that he remembered Douw because he had refused drink and tobacco when he, Tielman, had offered him some in a friendly way. The young burgher seemed surprised by it, even now.

' "I do not drink or smoke," that's what he said.'

Half an hour later some kind of hut made of sticks and plaited mats stood beyond the camp fire, with skin blankets spread inside as bedding. Old Speelman put a kettle of water on one side of the camp fire, but otherwise the three arrivals stayed apart and made no further demands on hospitality. They refused all offers of food. The old woman sat upright and apparently motionless on her blanket. Lindstrom found that he was making no progress with his notes. Eventually he rose and did the round of the camp to see if everything was in order. He passed the hut and stopped nearby.

The old woman did not move. It was the dark girl who reacted. Lindstrom saw her big eyes gleam as she stretched over to touch the old woman and whisper:

'Ouma Katryn . . . Ouma Katryn . . .'

Lindstrom was a man in his prime who had retained his respect for old age. 'Ouma Katryn,' he used the girl's form of address, too, but with some embarrassment, 'you want nothing from us, but here is a small present for you.' And he handed her a snuff-box from the supply of knick-knacks which he had brought along to win the favour of the natives.

'Many, many thanks, Mynheer,' the old woman said, from a far, sad distance as it sounded to Lindstrom. She let the snuff-box fall on to her lap. He remained standing. These people did not beg shamelessly like the ordinary Hottentots, nor was their aloofness the sullen pride of the normal half-caste. Least of all the old woman.

'Ouma Katryn, why are you looking for your grandson? Isn't he busy with a job? Won't he return after it's over?'

'He doesn't want to return, he's running away. He was hurt in his pride, where it hurts a man most. Ruth and I have to go and help him.'

The old woman sighed before she added, seemingly confused:

'Our Dear Lord knows I'm getting old, I have to bring my grand-children together before I breathe my last.'

Behind him the Swede heard footsteps. It was Tielman Roux. Tranquilly the old woman continued:

'Mynheer, I can hear you're a Dutchman from another nation, and perhaps you do not know these things. In this country the Dutchmen have the right to indenture a Hottentot or a half-caste till his twenty-fifth year. If he marries and has children before his twenty-fifth year, the Dutchman may claim the children too and indenture them in their turn to their twenty-fifth year. The parents stay on to be near their children, as is right and human. So, even though we are not slaves, our people are never free until they're old and incapable of earning a living. But, Mynheer, a spirit of restlessness has come over the land, and has affected us, too. When my grandson, Douw, got the first down on his chin, his baas gave him a big beating. Douw decided he wanted to go and work somewhere else, and so he ran away over the dry Karroo, to the north. But his baas caught him and punished him severely. The day Douw became twenty-five, he left his baas's farm. But in all the years of his youth he never looked at a girl. He absolutely refused to marry.'

In the dull glow from the fire behind him Lindstrom could see how the girl fidgeted before she lay down, her face disappearing abruptly into the darkness of the hut.

'He saved every stiver of his earnings,' Ouma Katryn went on, 'so as to be able to buy his own wagon and oxen and be independent. Then he went to Baviaanskloof mission station to learn to read and write like a Dutchman. There he started doing transport work to earn a living. Now he'll never return to the Boland.'

Before Lindstrom could speak, the young burgher, Tielman Roux, cut in irritably:

'We burghers are not unjust or evil. We are law-abiding citizens who have to civilise the raw heathen and teach them not to live like idle loafers. Discipline is essential; otherwise this country of ours will go to the devil!'

Bengt Lindstrom remembered that this law-abiding young

burgher had been locked up in the Castle prison for months, because he had refused to sign the oath of loyalty to Britain and that his father had saved him from perpetual banishment only by going on his knees to Lord Macartney. In his bitterness he also was leaving the district of his birth, just like Douw Prins.

Still dignified, Ouma Katryn answered: 'Yes, it is true. The Hottentot people have become very bad. The old leaders are dead, and the new paths are full of thorns.'

Lindstrom promised that he would do his best to help her find her grandson, but when she did not seem to hear, he stood up to go. At the entrance to his tent he looked back. Ouma Katryn was still sitting upright, as if she was facing far horizons from the back of her riding-ox.

Lindstrom did not feel like sleeping. He took his copy of Le Vaillant's *Voyage dans l'Intérieur de l'Afrique* from his document trunk, and re-read what the French savant had written sixteen years before, in 1783, about the Cape half-castes:

'I want to describe a kind of men who compose what one might call a *composite race*, a race which is now only a century old. I believe no traveller has mentioned them before ... I mean the illegitimate children of white men and Hottentot women, or Hottentot women and negro men. They are usually called Bastaards, half-castes, although this designation generally refers to the former, because the latter are less numerous. Hottentot women do not give themselves easily to negroes whom they despise; for why, the women ask, do black men allow themselves to be sold like animals? On the other hand they feel honoured to have intercourse with whites and to be considered their concubines. It is the race originating from these unions which is to be met with ever more frequently and which is multiplying. They are free, like the Hottentots, but consider themselves superior, though they are looked down on here in the Cape and it is not even the custom to have them baptized. These white half-castes take more after the Europeans than after the Hottentots: they are braver and have more energy than the latter, and are not afraid to work. On the other hand they are not only more lively and enter- prising, but also more vindictive ... the impetuous race of white half-castes is continuously gaining ground, and one may predict that one day it will dominate the Cape of Good Hope . . .'

Lindstrom closed the book. For a while he sat looking at the yellow flame round the black wick. Outside in the night an animal howled—a jackal or an African wolf, he still had to learn how to distinguish these animals—and closer by vague rustlings came and went as if bats were ecstatically hunting. Lindstrom set his jaw, pulled his diary nearer and wrote:

'What a naturalist may establish about the great variety of plants and animals, also applies to the human inhabitants of the Cape. Nowhere else on earth have I seen such variety, such a melting pot of different races and languages, so many social divisions and cross-breedings. It is a second Babylon, with at least half a dozen languages, all of them, it sounds to me, murdered and spoken brokenly.

'It is as if this vast land imposes disintegration on its human inhabitants, as if people have to become isolated as lonely individuals, as if too much isolation must necessarily lead to division. A need for greater unity will probably only come later. There are already signs that history is starting to force the colonists to look to their friends. All over the country a national feeling is awakening amongst the burghers, directed against the British Occupation, and against the invading Kaffirs on the eastern frontier. But what is the place of the Hottentots and the fast-growing numbers of Bastaards of mixed blood? Where will they finally find communal solidarity . . . ?'

3

In a little dip on the Kleinberg flats the hindmost wagon, the kitchen wagon, stuck fast, and the thongs of the back yoke broke twice in succession. Every delay gladdened the Swedish savant's heart, because he could wander off into the veld to his heart's content while his people struggled with extra teams and such things as strops, yokes and loose spokes. They, not he, had to worry about the length of every stage and where the oxen were to get their next pasture and water in this dry year.

Tielman Roux was not supposed to help with the wagons and, anyway, the half-caste was so competent that the young burgher was able more and more to act as the trek's official hunter. In this way he could satisfy the urge for adventure in the wilds felt by many a young man who lived in the settled Boland, and which had grown in him irresistibly while he was in prison. This morning he rode in a wide circle around a herd of bonteboks, shooting one ram and three pheasants. Ample meat for the eight people in Lindstrom's trek; no, eleven, he decided, when he looked round to where Ouma Katryn's little group still faithfully followed.

But this morning Tielman only wanted to move ahead faster. In front of them the land was shelving, the hills becoming round and hairy, suddenly to kneel before the great blue plain of the sea.

Great blue smile of the sea, it seemed to Tielman and to the other tired and dusty travellers. The whips of the drivers resounded more gaily over the two teams of oxen and the dogs came out from the shade under the hind wheels to add their boisterous barking to the new feeling in the air. Only Lindstrom remained impervious; once he even made the wagons stop so that he could make a rapid drawing of some wonder plant or other which looked like a mere rubbishy weed. At this point the half-caste rebelled and said that they had to hurry on to pitch camp and look for wood and water. This very evening, too, the three hind wheels had to be taken off to shorten the spokes. Lindstrom tranquilly agreed that Barend should go on ahead, only leaving him a horse. This horse Tielman had to hold for a long quarter of an hour, before the big blond man consented to mount. Then the two white men rode down to Mossel Bay; rode slowly, for Tielman's wish that rare plants would prove to be really rare was constantly frustrated.

Yet his heart sang within him. For the first time since the

Boland and his humiliation in prison his spirit soared to meet the open distances ahead of him, free and therefore yearningly one with the blue-green crescent where sea and land met, stretching ever farther and hazier to where the farthest mountain peaks met the sky. Was that last, wispy pinnacle Formosa peak ... nearly half-way to Kaffirland ... ten days on horseback? A whole new, mysterious world he had never yet seen ...

On the last downhill stretch Tielman shouted joyously to the phlegmatic Swede: 'Come, Mynheer, let's see who gets down first!' Digging in his heels, beating with his hat, he raced his bay horse, Vonk, madly down the sandy road, across the beach, and, gun above his head, right into the wet, green sea.

That afternoon there was quite a to-do underneath the milkwood trees where visiting wagons parked beside the sea.

When the animals had drunk their fill, Barend and Esau started working on the hind wheels; Kassiem began preparing the fat pheasants for a royal burial in a rice-and-butter stew; while the other Hottentots strengthened an old kraal with branches to serve as protection for the animals at night. They would have to stay at least a week in Mossel Bay if the wheels were to be properly adjusted. Lindstrom, too, had much to do. Next day Landdrost Faure would arrive, with the Auditor-General, John Barrow, to address a meeting of farmers about the shortage of grain. Lindstrom would be able to ask for a permit to cross the mountains into the interior, and to meet Barrow as well, a geographer and savant in his own right. Tielman Roux was looking forward to meeting the local burghers and hearing their opinion on the revolt in Graaff-Reinet.

But first there was Kassiem's lovely rice-stew swimming in spices and butter, and tonight, too, a tot of Pontacq wine for all those eager to rinse the dust from their throats. Barend Ockers, foreman of the camp, shared out in the hierarchic manner that was taken as a matter of course: the best portions, on china plates, for Mynheer Lindstrom and Tielman; a china plate only slightly cracked for the half-caste; a new tin plate for the Malay cook; old tin plates for the three Hottentots; an old pot lid for the small Bushman. Mynheer Lindstrom decreed that Ouma Katryn,

Ruth and old Speelman should be considered members of his trek and get food, too. They could not live off their cow's milk, griddle cake and a handful of raisins. His own supper was served in his tent beside a tangle of plants and writing materials.

When the evening thickened to golden-grey varnish over the bay, camp fires started flickering; many farmers from Outeniqualand and still farther away had already arrived so as to be in time for the next day's meeting, or to exchange shop wares for timber, skins or butter at Murray's brand new store on the beach.

Everywhere people were greeting each other, inquiring after the health of uncles or cousins, or, in Tielman's case, trying to establish which local families might be related to him on his father's or mother's side. A certain Marthinus Botha remembered that Tielman Roux had been one of the four young men who had refused to sign the oath of loyalty and had consequently nearly been banished from their country; this meant that the ubiquitous debate about the Graaff-Reinet revolt could safely be allowed to flare up in his presence. Tielman heard that Rautenbach was waiting at Coega with two hundred men to ambush the English and that Coenraad Buys was busy collecting another thousand burghers. Rumour added that ten thousand warriors of the black king, Gaika, were also rallying. Now was the moment at which Swellendam's burghers had to decide if they wanted to join the uprising or not. In Stellenbosch Tielman had heard of resistance but seldom of revolt; now he became so fiery that if someone had proposed it he would have grabbed his gun and horse to race to the east. But it got no further than talk—rebellion against the superior power of the British authorities was a serious matter. Many of the burghers had seen the strong British forces trek past three weeks ago.

When Tielman rose at last from Botha's camp fire, the Southern Cross hung aslant the sea. He pulled off his shoes to walk over the cool, wet beach; filled with a seething, sea-born surge of patriotic love, then cautious fear, then surrender again to reckless impulse.

Beyond Lindstrom's camp fire burned a smaller fire where a grey hump, old Speelman, sat bowed over his fiddle's strings; later, when other Hottentots collected, to change to his bow-stringed ghoera and send out ancient, drawn-out notes above the sighing breath of the sea. The two women, the old with a black shawl over long, silver hair and the young with be-ribboned bonnet pulled low over her frizzy curls, sat so that they could watch the road. On the few occasions that a wagon rumbled along on the other side, Ouma Katryn told Ruth to go and see who it was.

Later still, when the half-caste had left for his bed in the kitchen wagon, the Hottentots already lay snoring and the young white man returned with his shoes in his hand, the two women still sat by the fire-side. Tielman clambered on to his mattress in the back of the wagon. Too wide awake to sleep, he got down again, looking to where a candle still burned in Lindstrom's tent and then towards the fire where Ouma Katryn sat talking slowly and softly. No, not talking, she was reading from a book. From the Bible, he saw, as he approached.

He could hardly believe it. Was she carrying a heavy bible in those bundles on her pack-ox's back? As a white man Tielman had mixed feelings about Ouma Katryn, whom he could not consider a typical serving-maid, and whom, like everyone else, he called Ouma Katryn. He convinced himself that his feeling of respect was no more than curiosity and went nearer to ask:

'So you can read, Ouma Katryn?'

The old woman put her finger on the line she had reached and answered, gently: 'Yes, Mynheer. I bought this bible for my grandson, Douw, who learnt to read from the German missionaries.'

Over her shoulder he saw she was reading from the Book of Ruth, and asked with a smile:

'Is that where you got your adopted daughter's name?'

'Yes, Mynheer. She's a bit faint-hearted and so I read this to make her remember.' Without another word, she bent her head to the Bible held slanted towards the fire, and read the passage in a halting voice: '. . . For whither thou goest, I will go; and where thou lodgest, I will lodge: thy people shall be my people, and thy God my God:

'Where thou diest, will I die, and there will I be buried: the

LORD do so to me, and more also, if ought but death part thee and me . . .'

The girl Ruth had a timid gentleness that made her attractive. Tielman's eyes shied away from the bowed bonnet and he stood still till the old woman had finished. In the ensuing silence he tried with embarrassment to find something to say. It came out flippantly:

'Ach, but your Ruth doesn't need to marry into another people.' Aren't you all half-caste Afrikaners? his tone of voice really wanted to imply.

Ouma Katryn slowly closed the Bible and raised her eyes to look at the young white man. There was dignified reproof in her voice:

'Mynheer Roux, you know our country is full of people of many kinds. There are not only white and brown people, there are also many kinds of people with mixed blood. And we are being thrown together whether we want to be or not. My own dead husband was a white-skinned Bastaard just like me, and yet some of my grandchildren and great-grandchildren are today as dark as Ruth and others are so white that they are counted as white people. They no longer want to know me or the other members of the family, yet they are still my own, my family.'

After the fiery debate about the struggle against the English it was as if Tielman had suddenly to think of something that had always been near to him but which he had never recognised and which, in his confused irritation, he did not want to recognise. Peevishly he raised his voice:

'And so? What's the point of trying to bring together this . . . this difficult family of yours?'

Ouma Katryn's left hand rose slowly to wipe away something like a tremble from her cheek; her voice was still firm when she said:

'Aie, Mynheer, aren't they blood of my blood?'

Tielman was uneasy: he had enough problems of his own and now only wanted to get away. He felt relieved when Lindstrom cleared his throat behind them. The botanist came striding along with a piece of paper on which a dried twig had been pasted and with another small green twig in his hand.

'I'm glad you're still up,' he babbled contentedly, 'you may perhaps be able to tell me how I should classify this *Rhus*. I mean, do you have one name for these two shrubs, or is it only one kind?'

All eyes turned to look at it.

'But this is toughbush!' Tielman exclaimed. 'Yes, that's it. They're both toughbush, or krintang, as the Hottentots call it.'

'Yes, krintang bush, like we find on the dry plains,' Ouma Katryn agreed. 'This green one from beside the sea only looks a little different, a little more curly.'

'That's what I thought!'

The scientist was so innocently overjoyed at their unanimity that his audience smiled with an amused good-will which quickly ended the tension.

* * * * *

Next morning the two white men walked along the shore to the Postholder's house and the gigantic, empty wheat-shed. These were the only buildings at Mossel Bay, not counting the few fishermen's huts and Murray's shop half an hour farther on where the roads to Attaquaskloof and Outeniqualand met. On a board on the stoep, the veranda typical of the South African homestead, some government proclamations had recently been stuck up. A score or two farmers had collected to read them; some grumbling, others nonchalantly ignoring the half-dozen British soldiers in their impressive uniforms. An eager group formed around the representatives of the authorities, Landdrost Faure and Auditor-General John Barrow, consisting mainly of Orangists, loyal to the British. One of the fieldcornets was assuring Barrow that, if the Graaff-Reinet rebels ever came that way, they would form a commando to drive them back.

Tielman Roux's dislike of any British soldier or official, made him stand with Marthinus Botha and other patriotic burghers. When Bengt Lindstrom had finished talking Scandinavian with the Danish Postholder and had got a chance to talk with John

Barrow, Tielman wanted to go and listen but, after a glance at his companions' faces, he did not dare. It was clear that they especially disliked Barrow, a sturdy, energetic man who talked in such a swift, omniscient, conceited way that the interpreter could hardly keep up.

'This is the man who knows for sure that our dear earth is more than six thousand years old,' an elderly burgher said, with a shake of his head. 'He's supposed to have seen it in the stones. And in our faces he saw that we are the worst and cruellest people on earth.'

'Do you know him?' Tielman cautiously asked.

'Yes, cousin, we know him. He passed through some time ago on a journey round the country. One has to be very careful when one speaks to him. He's nothing but an English spy who has had many a burgher arrested if they said the slightest thing which sounded like loyalty to Holland. Even if he had no proof except the gossip of run-away Hottentots.'

'Yes, those rascals are now looking for new masters!' a man with a heavy beard angrily remarked.

'Really?' the young burgher asked in surprise. 'Where I come from we know the Hottentots only as faithful and obedient workers . . .'

'You people from the Boland have too soft a life, you don't know what's happening out here,' the man interrupted him. And with a suspicious nod he went on to ask:

'Cousin, why is your plant doctor so friendly with Barrow? Are you sure he's not just another spy who only pretends to be an innocent?'

Already irritated and fiercely loyal to the calm, innocent Swede, Tielman exclaimed: 'What nonsense! Mynheer Lindstrom is a decent, honest man only interested in his work! He told me he wanted to ask Barrow about the lichens in some cave beyond the headland! That's what they're talking about now!'

He had spoken so loudly that some of the bystanders took fright and moved away while a group of the Orangists came nearer.

'Careful, cousin, here come some rotten eggs,' Botha hissed from the corner of his mouth. The conversation continued on other matters, chiefly about the quota of grain that every farmer thought he could deliver in the coming season. This, too, was the main theme of the meeting that started shortly afterwards under the chairmanship of Landdrost Faure. Barrow made swift notes, visibly impatient at the leisurely tempo of the proceedings: early that afternoon he wanted to set off with two fresh horses to catch up General Vandeleur. He wanted to enjoy the sight of the Graaff-Reinet mutineers surrendering, a burgher with sharp ears and some knowledge of English told the others.

While the negotiations about wheat and barley went on, other thoughts smouldered unspoken amongst the collected burghers: the turncoats and toadies wooing government favour, the dull, ordinary protagonists of law and order and the rebel Patriots, dreaming of revolution and a republic like that of glorious France. A death-like silence reigned when the Landdrost read a new proclamation: The prohibition of all travel over the frontiers of the district of Swellendam and, additionally, stern punishment for anyone who harboured or even received in his home anyone from Graaff-Reinet.

When a burgher dared to ask: 'Even though they may be blood relations?' the Auditor-General flung up his chin as though the flag of sedition had been hoisted by the devil himself.

'Yes. Those are the orders of His Excellency, the acting Governor, General Dundas himself . . .'

After the meeting Tielman and Lindstrom went to the tiny sandy bay where Diaz and his sailors had landed in 1488, the first white men to tread the soil of Southern Africa. Past a broad milkwood tree flowed the stream where the Portuguese sailors had filled their water-casks three centuries before. Tielman tasted the brackish water and walked restlessly around while Lindstrom stood with his hand on the coarse trunk, deep in thought.

'Tielman, I'm going to change my route. No longer across the mountains to the interior but along the coast through the forests. Towards Plettenberg Bay.'

The young burgher stopped in his tracks, dismayed:

'Mynheer, is it . . . is it because you could not get permission to cross Attaquaskloof?'

The Swede nodded.

'They refused an innocent visitor like you? Is it ... perhaps because I'm with Mynheer's trek?'

'Possibly. Faure and Barrow know about you. No, wait,' he checked Tielman, 'listen. It's all the same to me which areas I see first. This state of emergency won't last for ever, and then we can cross the coastal mountains to the east. No, no, Tielman, I've made up my mind. I, too, have my pride. I won't let myself be separated by force from a pleasant travelling companion. I'd rather travel with you than without you.'

However much Tielman argued, a problem facing him was in this way solved or rather postponed, namely where and when he was to leave the naturalist's trek. In Stellenbosch he had impulsively joined Lindstrom's expedition without any definite plans, a young man of twenty-one who wanted only to be away for a while from a district where he felt cooped up and humiliated. For him too it mattered little along which route they travelled so long as it was eastwards, in the direction of the turbulent frontier districts of whose dangers and adventures he had heard so much.

As they were walking along they saw a horseman galloping, not along the public road, but straight down a coastal hill. When they reached the wagons, there was a great commotion. Men were thronging around the young rider who was still holding his white starred mount, ready at any moment to leap into his saddle and race away.

Tielman ran forward. The horseman was a certain Muller from Graaff-Reinet. He brought an urgent message from Rautenbach: Men of Swellendam, come and help us before it is too late. General Vandeleur's forces had joined up with the soldiers from Algoa Bay. On March 13 the English had begun to march inland with this overwhelming force. Rautenbach was awaiting them at Coega with a hundred and fifty rebels but they would have to fall back. They were too few, they could not fight alone. Graaff-Reinet was full of turncoats and traitors who only deserved contempt. Even worse, the Hottentots were now stealing their masters' horses and guns and running away in their hundreds to join the enemy. Faithful burghers were so discouraged that they were leaving for home to protect their wives and children. If the men of Swellendam did not come at once, all would be lost. In God's name, help.

The young burgher looked completely exhausted and disheartened: today was the 17th, so he must have ridden the three hundred and fifty miles in four days. Within three or four days Graaff-Reinet would fall.

It was quiet around him. The messenger had arrived so quickly and unexpectedly that the Patriots had had no time to prevent some of the Orangists from being present too.

The faces around Tielman showed that everything was lost already.

'Rebels of the Coward Republic,' one of the English faction sneered. When the Orangists turned away, a burgher sprang forward to face them. He was angry as a bull which had seen red.

'Don't increase your shame by blabbing to the authorities!' he threatened. 'Don't trample your own blood farther into the dust! Let this man ride away in peace. If one of you tries to take his horse, I'll shoot him!'

The men remained standing, most of them looking at the ground.

'Ride, cousin, ride,' Botha said at last. 'We'll see what we can do.'

The messenger from Graaff-Reinet put his foot into the stirrup, swung on to his saddle and looked at the circle of silent men. He would have once more to risk by himself the wild, uncharted wilderness over the mountains. 'God help our people!' he nearly sobbed. Then he dug in his heels, racing back the way he came, not once looking round.

Tielman had to clench his teeth not to follow him. He felt Lindstrom's hand on his arm and knew that he was walking by his side as the other burghers also turned away, one by one, to their horses and wagons. He suddenly saw an old, sallow face framed by strands of grey hair billowing from a bonnet. He was so ashamed of himself that he could look nobody, not even Ouma Katryn, in the face. He turned his face away but heard her ask Mynheer Lindstrom what the horseman's name had been and the Swede answer: 'Thomas Muller.' Vaguely he wondered why she stood there, sounding so out of breath.

*   *   *   *   *

Next morning Barend and the others abandoned their work on the wagons for a spell of fishing. Fish, even dried, would be a welcome variation on the menu where meat three times a day was the general rule. A team of slaves from a neighbouring farm, commanded by a Madagascar half-breed, had arrived with a rowboat and a drag-net; schools of fish were reported to be swarming close inshore.

The sea was calm with lazy green wavelets hardly breaking on the shore and a darker spot could clearly be seen where a school of fish was milling, sometimes breaking the surface in a silvery rustle. Hastily they rowed the boat around it and dragged the net back to the beach in a wide half-circle. Some men threw off their breeches to wade into the water. They managed to trap a large part of the school of mullet and laughed and strained to get the catch ashore.

Ouma Katryn and Ruth had been sitting on a nearby dune but, when Tielman looked again, they had gone. Though his attention was mainly on the fishing, he turned and saw that a wagon loaded with huge yellow-wood beams had stopped nearby and that Ouma Katryn was hurrying towards it with Ruth following more slowly behind. A little later he looked again and saw Ruth returning, while the old woman stood gesturing before a yellowish Hottentot, or was he perhaps a half-caste? Would this be the long-awaited grandson, Douw Prins, and was the meeting with his family disagreeable to him? Why did the young girl come up to the row of straining men and also start pulling at the net, tugging as if her life depended on it?

The harvest from the generous sea rustled and flapped on the beach. Men jumped around on the seaward side of the net to grab the long silvery fish and throw them on to the sand. When pulling the net was no longer necessary, Ruth, too, gathered escaping fish. She ignored the half-naked men. A laughing black slave snatched the red turban off a companion and, tying it round his loins, started to imitate a Hottentot smacking his feet in a triumphant dance on the wet sand. Boisterously, Tielman, Barend and others encouraged them. Then someone brought knives. Ruth, the dark girl, crouched down at once to clean the fish. She still looked only at her hands when Ouma Katryn arrived, to say with a sigh:

'He's riding to Swellendam with a load of wood for the new church. But he's coming back, Ruth; he's coming back.'

When Douw and his team-leader, Lafleur, set off later on the afternoon stage, Ouma Katryn went to speak to Lindstrom. The old half-caste told him that her grandson had ridden transport for the Government as far as Plettenberg Bay and returned with a load of timber from a man called Joubert. He would be back in a week. Then Douw would most likely return to the Outeniqua forest, earning more money to pay for the gun which he had bought. She and Ruth would wait here for him.

Kind-hearted Lindstrom at once proposed that he should hire Douw, so that his empty wagon could be of use through the Kaaimansgat. He had heard that it was a steep and difficult ravine to cross and Douw, by now, knew it well. He would pay Douw as much as for a full load. His own trek would stay here where there were more than enough plants to keep him busy: the oxen anyway needed a long rest.

Ouma Katryn was glad of this proposal and promised to talk Douw round. She went to tell Ruth. The girl still hardly spoke but, whereas at first she had shyly kept to one side, she now bustled all over the camp with wood, water, fish and even a broom of toughbush branches. Everything had to be spotlessly clean. Tielman thought that the young maid had suddenly decided to work herself to death.

4

Since Douw had joined the foreigner's trek, he was constantly busy, without time to talk to Lafleur or anybody else. At the ford over the Great Brack River, where they had to wait a while for low tide, he occupied himself greasing the axles of his wagons and mixing a new supply of tar and fat in his grease-bucket. He felt like joining Tielman and Barend in shooting something for the pot on the lake teeming with flamingoes, pelicans and water-fowl, but he kept to himself. When his grandmother came to fetch his coarse blue shirt so that Ruth could mend the torn sleeve, he pulled it from his lean sinewy torso, without a word.

The sun was still high when they reached the White-Els River.

'Hookaai!' The driver pitched his voice over his oxen, following it up with a long-drawn whistle which brought them to a stop. On the opposite hill a farmer's house was visible, still a mile away, but Douw made Lafleur unharness the oxen while he walked over to the other wagons. Lindstrom did not care much where the evening camp was to be; anyway he was still some way behind where the bees were buzzing around the late summer flowers. So Douw told Barend and Tielman that it was best to camp there for the night, and cover the last stage to Outeniqua in the morning. The half-caste shared Douw's reluctance to spend the night on a farm and be humiliated by the white man's double standard of hospitality. Only the young burgher looked sadly at the house across the valley; he had once declared, with a laugh, that he was on this trek to inspect all the girls along the road and to select the loveliest.

'There are strange pot-holes with waterfalls lower down the river,' Douw told the sky next to Tielman's head. He avoided directly addressing this white man who was five or six years younger than himself. He was reluctant to call him Sieur or

Baas like any other subservient Hottentot, whereas he readily addressed the Swede as Mynheer.

The young man, who was often bored on his own, impulsively turned to Douw, meaning to suggest that he should go with him, to hunt or swim. But when he looked at Douw, he found that he became as stiff and awkward as the latter. Douw gave him no second chance; he left at once. He had chosen to camp here for another reason.

The two women went to wash themselves in a pool of coffee-brown water surrounded by tall rushes. As soon as the dark girl came back from the river, Douw called her. He pointed higher up in the valley:

'Lafleur and I are busy with the animals. You go and tell Jakobus Cloete that I've brought his stuff. It's the farm round the bend, it's not far. Jakobus isn't some nasty Dutchman, he's a Hottentot farming his own land.'

The girl nodded but did not go. It was the first time Douw had addressed her. He had not looked at her, though, as if wary of her glowing face. Her hands started to rub convulsively against each other and she burst out in one desperate, breathless sentence:

'I know you think nothing of me but now you must know the worst of me, too, Douw; I waited so long for you, I felt so terrible when you left just like that, I went to throw myself away, Douw, I shamed myself with young baas Piet, with Salomon . . .'

'I don't want to hear!' Douw ground out, with his arm raised to strike. And when she blindly ran away:

'You whore! Why do you follow me!'

'Because I asked her, my child,' Ouma Katryn said behind him. 'I'm old, I need her help.'

Douw swung on his heel, jerked his gun from the wagon, whistled to his dog, and strode away towards the lake where Lafleur had driven the oxen to graze.

In the twilight, when he came back tired with a buck over his shoulder, Jakobus Cloete and two other Hottentots were waiting with a calabash of honeybeer which they had brought along. Cloete was dressed like a farmer, in a waistcoat, corduroy trousers, veldschoen and a broad-rimmed hat with a low crown. The other two were barefoot herdsmen: one wore tattered trousers, and the other a dirty skin blanket over his shoulders.

Douw greeted them and went to his wagon, returning with an armful of things which he had bought for Cloete at Swellendam, much more cheaply than at Murray's expensive shop. In a halting voice he spelled out their prices: 2 lbs. tobacco @ 7 schellings the lb.: one rixdollar and 6 schellings; one lb. tea: one rixdollar and 3 schellings . . . altogether 14 rixdollars and 5 schellings.

'Just the price of a good draught ox,' Douw said.

But Cloete dug into a skin pouch.

'No, I'd rather pay cash. I lost too many cattle during last winter's lamb-sickness. Thanks a lot. Here you are. And I'll send you a fat sheep for your trouble tomorrow.'

With this Douw was content. Cloete and his men remained seated, however, filled their pipes, handed the calabash around and shifted their feet while they looked distrustfully at the white men's fire the other side of the road. When Douw refused the honeybeer Cloete asked in a whisper:

'Man, have you heard of the great trouble?'

Douw turned at once to old Speelman, who was bringing another stump of wood to the fire:

'Uncle Speelman, please go and play some music over there so that nobody comes to disturb us. We've got things to talk about.'

He glared at Ouma Katryn and Ruth who were busy roasting an eel on a grid of green twigs. The two women did not stir or look up. Then the Hottentot farmer started to tell his story:

'Yes, man, these days our people are the first to hear of new troubles brewing. Well, one of the woodcutters who works for Joubert came down the forest path from Longkloof. Yesterday, that was . . .'

'Would that be the Joubert who lives near Kaaimans?'

'Himself. Well, this fellow brought the news that the English had taken Graaff-Reinet, Tuesday of last week. Now the Dutchmen are lying low. But the English are waiting for them. And they're going to smoke them out, too, for every single Hottentot is crawling out of his hole to run after Vandeleur's flag. All of them have big mouths now, all want to become Pandours and to go and smell out and shoot the white farmers. Even here, from our side, they're streaming across the mountain, women, children and all. Man, this is the great trouble I'm scared of.'

He remained impressively silent, but Douw merely pulled the buck nearer and, holding it down with one foot, started to skin it. He wanted to stay out of this quarrel between Patriots, English, Kaffirs or anybody else. Ruth still squatted with downcast eyes the other side of the fire but Ouma Katryn, on her camp-stool, now sat silently watching her grandson's knife slipping through the buck skin. Through the purple evening Speelman's violin wheezed up and down like spasmodic breathing. Cloete started again:

'I don't mind the farmers taking a beating for once . . .'

'Haitsa, the Smooth-haired Ones have trampled us flat like dung-cakes for a long time now!' one of the raw Hottentots exclaimed.

'Yes, yes!' Lafleur concurred with a quick glance at his driver.

'. . . but I want to stay out of it. I don't want my Dutchman neighbours to take it out on me. They already want an excuse to squeeze me off my ground. No, man, I tell you, a wheel turns. And then? Most of our Hottentot people don't think. Their noses are so flat that their eyes peer at each other and don't see what's awaiting them over the hill. Today the Patriots are having a hard time. But tomorrow? Tomorrow the Kaffirs will go back over the Fish River, the English will load their soldiers back on the boats, and then our people will have to pay for their fun. Around here the white men are already so suspicious that they grab their guns if they see a strange Hottentot. No, I say this time is good only for vultures who want to eat while the sun shines. I'm scared of what comes next. I've my farm and wife and children to think of. I want to have friendly neighbours.'

Again silence fell. Douw shook the entrails out on the skin, stood back and hung the skinned buck on the hook above the hind wheel.

'Why do you tell me this, Jakobus?' he asked curtly.

Cloete glanced to right and left before he cautiously replied:

'Man, I've heard that the farmers are asking a lot of questions about you; whether you didn't steal your wagon and gun somewhere. They can't believe that a brown man could work so hard just so as to earn money for himself. They wonder if you're not planning to carry gun-powder and lead to the rebellious Hottentot captains of the Sundays River valley . . .'

Douw strode forward so violently that Cloete sprang to his feet, his palms raised in appeasement:

'Slowly now. I'm only trying to warn you in time . . .'

'I tell you it's an infamous lie! I've earned my own things by the sweat of my brow, not by helping trouble-makers. Not by slinking around like a jackal preying on other people's loss! This is not my war! I'm a free man. I have only one desire; no longer to work under a white man, to stay to one side and live my own life! So help me God!'

He still glared at Cloete.

'It is truly so,' Ouma Katryn quietly said, as if trying to calm Douw that way. 'Douw served till his twenty-fifth year on Koos Meyer's farm. Now he's working himself to death so as to be independent.'

Her grandson swung round to look at her and Ruth and then bent down to grasp the calabash and take a long swig at the honeybeer. There was a sound like a woman's suppressed gasp from across the fire, as well as a cackle of enjoyment from Lafleur who came forward to take over the calabash. Then Jakobus Cloete said with a sigh:

'Great Mercy, what's to become of us decent Afrikaner people if the white men start seeing enemies in all of us? I hear the Hottentot captains are talking of joining up with the Kaffirs, of fighting together against the Christians who are taking over the whole country. That's a bad, wrong thing. And I say no. If the Kaffirs come this way, I'll stand with the Dutchmen. Even though it may be against our own Hottentot people lusting after easy wealth. I tell you I stand for law and order. But my great headache is this, won't the Dutchmen treat all of us the same way once their trouble is over? Then the fire will burn us from both sides. Heh, Douw, man?'

Douw had no word of consolation to utter. Even his companion, Lafleur, merely mumbled darkly:

'Haitsa, this thing called man can't for ever hurt in one's shoes like a devil's thorn!'

Then Jakobus Cloete and his herdsmen got up to go.

'Don't you first want to silence your stomachs?'

'No thanks, cousin, our supper is awaiting us. Keep the honey-beer.'

Minutes later buck liver sizzled in the three-legged iron pot and supper began round Douw Prins's camp fire. Old Speelman was there too, for Douw had said that his people should not live off the charity of others. 'But we may send them a little present,' had been Ouma Katryn's opinion, whereupon she had herself taken two eels to Lindstrom's encampment.

Only the two old people spoke now and again. Ruth served and carried, her eyes on her hands. Douw's young face looked closed and bitter even while he ate. Lafleur, the Hottentot team-leader, left early to inspect the oxen and horses which were still moving restlessly between the two camp fires. Anyway, the calabash was empty. He furtively walked around to Lindstrom's tent where he begged a drink with clasped hands and a sugary voice:

'The wine is old, Sieur,
The weather is cold, Sieur.'

Ouma Katryn left her grandson alone. She waited till he put down his tin plate and burst out:

'As if a Hottentot or a Bastaard is not a man, too; capable of working for himself! I know many of them are good for nothings, but we aren't all the same!'

Then his grandmother asked him:

'Douw, you left your home without telling us anything. I can see how hard you worked, you've paid for your own wagon and your own gun. I'm proud of you. But tell me, Douw, do you want to do transport work for ever? What are you really aiming at? To go east?'

'I want to stand on my own legs,' he answered promptly, 'on my own farm. The farther one goes from the Boland, the more empty ground there is, just waiting for willing hands. I'll get myself a farm, even if I have to hack it inch by inch from the Outeniqua forest. I by myself. I have nothing in common with robbers and murderers!'

'One cannot live by oneself . . .'

'Leave me alone!' he flared up angrily. 'I ask only one thing, to be left in peace! To put this whole damned mess behind me! With all respect, Ouma Katryn, the whole world can go to the devil! I didn't ask you to come and pester me.'

Patiently the old woman tried again:

'My child, you may chase us away if you feel like it, but you can't hate the whole world . . .'

'No, Ouma Katryn,' Ruth suddenly interrupted her, 'a man must be able to hate if he wants to remain a man with his own pride.'

It was so unusual for the dark girl to join unasked in a conversation that even old Speelman raised his eyes from the embers. Slowly Douw stood up, staring at her with contempt:

'Just listen to the black servant-girl. *She* talks of pride! She, who had no shame when young baas Piet or Salomon said she must lie down! Sies!'

'It was because of you!' the girl hit back wildly. 'Douw, Douw, it was because you left without even coming to say good-bye. I hated everybody, I hated you, I wanted to drag myself in the dust. But I would have done better to drown myself in the dam, do you hear!'

Her voice broke in a raw sob but the young man replied coldly: 'Why are you still alive then?'

The girl's head sank then jerked up again. She stared at Douw and slowly walked away, to hide herself in the dark hut.

With awkward fingers old Speelman drew his violin and ghoera closer to his side. Ouma Katryn slowly got to her feet, returning a minute later with something wrapped in her dark shawl.

'Douw, my child, I sold my little flock of sheep to buy this precious gift for you. Until now I have had no occasion to give it to you.'

Her grandson stood rigid, watching her old hands unwrap the gift.

'Since you want to be alone, let the Lord go with you. Look, this is His Holy Word. Take it, it is yours now. It must go with you in your wagon-chest.'

Douw looked at the Bible. He did not move, only said hoarsely:

'Ouma would have done better to bring me gunpowder and lead.'

The old woman went on holding the Bible, her hands trembling ever more. 'Oh, my child . . .'

Then Douw came forward as if he had been pushed, took the Bible and went to put it in the chest under the front wagon-seat. He did not return to the fire-side but walked away into the night.

Old Speelman fumbled over the strings of his battered violin, but put it aside to take up the ghoera. Tonight the age-old Hottentot music had to speak for him. He bent his face to the feathered quill on the bow-string, an insignificant little old man with frizzy, ash-grey tufts of hair. Half drowned behind wrinkles and broad, knobbly cheekbones his tearful eyes peered over the sunken hollows of his cheeks. But his old mud-blue lips blew long quivery notes over the quill, hoarse from emotion, filled with the magic power of music to creep into the hearts of all who could hear and desire.

5

'Is cousin a trader?' was the first question Lindstrom heard when his wagons were being unharnessed at Outeniqua's Government Post. Ackermann, the German Postholder, a former servant of the Dutch East Indies Company, came out to greet the new arrivals, as well as the local burghers, foresters and fugitive farmers from the east who were temporarily squatting on government land. As was their custom, they brought gifts of fresh vegetables, fruit and milk. Lindstrom was grateful, but somewhat overwhelmed, and finally, annoyed by Ackermann's endless complaints about his bad house, the drought, his neighbours whose oxen had ruined his pasture, the old, sickly shoemaker who was his only assistant, Hottentots who ran away, and every other human being who arrogantly came to fell timber in the forest which was under his supervision. Also, Lindstrom's barrel of brandy was fast emptying.

Next morning the botanist shifted his camp several miles to the east, to the edge of the forest above the deep gorge of the Kaaimans River. They rode past a farm with a whole village of Hottentot huts. Soon the owner of the farm, Paul Joubert, a lively, teasing rogue of a man, came over to introduce himself. It seemed that he knew Douw Prins, for he walked over to Douw's wagon too.

Lindstrom and his people were enchanted by the encampment on the edge of the forest. Through an open grassy glade with rich grazing flowed a clear stream of water. Inland, dark-green forested slopes billowed up to the blue peaks of the Outeniqua mountains. To the south the Indian Ocean gleamed below the rust-red cliffs of coastal capes. All around stretched a real paradise for a botanist.

As soon as he could Lindstrom slung his collector's bag over his shoulder and set off to look for new varieties of plants. He started with the lianas or tree vines which the inhabitants called baboon-ropes. Tielman Roux swung exuberantly on several to see if they could really bear the weight of a big ape. Even the free-black girl, Ruth, walked with a more elastic step as they started the great cleaning up of the camp, the washing and darning and ironing of everybody's clothes, from little Boesman's leather pants to Mynheer Lindstrom's pleated chokers. Since they were going to stay several days in this lovely spot, the half-caste carefully checked the condition of the wagons. From now on they were going to encounter the worst and most dangerous roads.

Early in the afternoon Douw came to ask when they would start the crossing of the Kaaimans. Not for another week, the Swede answered, but he would compensate Douw for every delay. No, Douw preferred to earn money meanwhile by honest transport riding: he wanted to leave that very evening with a load of roof-trusses and top-beams for a new house, but he would be back within a week.

For several days Lindstrom and the young burgher from Stellenbosch wandered through the forest, into deep narrow ravines where sharp scents revealed the habitat of spicy herbs and strange kinds of flowers. Sometimes one of Joubert's Hottentots accompanied them to teach them the local names of trees and useful plants, and to help them trace the rare tree-lories, birds whose magnificent emerald and purple feathers glowed in twilight vaults of the forest. Once Tielman shot a bush-buck—like most of the colonists he rarely went anywhere without his gun—and they enjoyed a lunch of fresh liver and chops under a huge yellow-wood tree which the woodmen had not yet succeeded in reaching.

The botanist was overjoyed to be able to talk about his work, and find out everything which Tielman might know. But in the end the young man's restless energy became too much for him, especially when Tielman dragged him to that part of the forest where the woodmen's axes and saws resounded the whole day long, and teams of oxen unexpectedly came lumbering from the peaceful green with mighty logs dragging behind them, puffing and straining while whips and sjamboks rained down mercilessly on their backs. It hurt Lindstrom to see a forest giant come tumbling down, and Tielman's proposal that they go on to hunt elephants and buffaloes made him realise that he was a middle-aged man whose heart was liable to race dangerously fast.

He was actually glad when Douw's wagon returned one morning amid a noisy mêlée of dogs and Tielman walked over towards it. Were they not both young men? With a half-cynical smile he wondered how Tielman's overtures would prosper, for he had already noticed that this aloof Hottentot half-caste, who did not act like a Hottentot, had disturbed the young burgher in some way or other.

That afternoon the sky clouded over and an unseasonable

shower rustled down. Autumn was early. For two whole days the people had to shelter under tent, wagon canvas or reed matting. The oxen stood around in the veld with smoking bodies but Barend and Tielman were uneasy about the horses, who had to be rubbed dry again and again, and fed mixtures of weak vinegar, garlic and saltpetre. The dreaded horse-distemper occurred frequently in this damp, marshy area, chiefly when the rainy season started after a drought and poisonous vapours rose from the earth. Lindstrom stayed in his tent, contentedly absorbed in drawing, classifying and jotting down notes.

The sky turned radiant blue once more and Douw departed with another load of timber to some destination determined by Paul Joubert, or perhaps Jakobus Cloete who had been appointed official overseer of the Hottentot lumbermen. According to the calendar in Lindstrom's document trunk it was already April 10 —two weeks after their arrival in the Outeniqua paradise—when he realised that he had to awake from his botanic dreams and act firmly. Idleness was definitely becoming the father of vice among the people in his service.

The previous week he had paid his six men: the three Hottentots, the Bushman team-leader, the cook, Kassiem, and the half-caste Barend Ockers. Kassiem and the Hottentots had at once started a mighty drinking-bout which progressively grew worse. They wasted all their money buying wine and tobacco from the local farmers, and cannabis, locally called dagga, from Joubert's workers. This they supplemented with an evil brew made from wild forest grapes and wood ash. The easy lazing around in Lindstrom's camp had attracted Hottentots and shameless servant maids from neighbouring farms, so that there was no end to the drunken rousting, love-making and fighting.

Tielman had seemed indulgent, as if not at all surprised that Hottentots acted in such a way. The half-caste, however, had complained about the debauchery. But it was only when Lindstrom realised how it humiliated Ouma Katryn that he sternly asserted his authority. One afternoon he and Tielman returned late and heard the old woman scolding a drunk for shaming his people so filthily. The others staggered around her in a laughing

43

circle, really only aware of Ruth whose calico dress was torn around her neck.

'Ach, granny, your arse,' the drunken Hottentot swore. 'Stop keeping us from that nice bit of cunt. She's made to ride to heaven.'

Lindstrom was a big, heavy man but he reached the loose-tongued fellow in a few strides, picked him up like a loose bundle of thongs and threw him down the waterhole where Ruth had dammed up the stream for the washing.

'Wash out your mouth, dammit!'

He darted round and grabbed the next Hottentot to dump him in the water too. 'Get clean, will you!' Tielman and Barend quickly followed his example and, within a minute the pool was filled with stupefied, soggy bodies.

'Get away, all those who don't belong here!' the Swede bellowed. 'And those who work for me, behave from now on. If I find another man drinking during the daytime, I'll send him packing at once! Do you hear?'

Soon calmed down, he gave Barend orders how to act if such a thing were to happen again. The restless Tielman profited by the occasion to remark:

'It comes from all this loafing around doing nothing. It's time we moved again.'

'I think you're right ... Doesn't the real forest only begin farther away, at Knysna ... ?'

At that moment they heard an excited shout.

One of the Hottentots, sneaking away, was pointing to the road rising over the rim of the Kaaimansgat. From the bushy slope five horsemen were approaching, three English soldiers in bright uniforms, a Hottentot Pandour soldier, also in uniform, and another Hottentot, probably their guide. They were coming from the east, from Graaff-Reinet or Algoa Bay.

Without stopping to think, Tielman jumped on his horse, raced the few hundred yards down to the road, reined in before the horsemen and asked where they were coming from.

The soldiers and their horses were exhausted. Nobody answered. The lieutenant riding in front did not even look at the young burgher, only at his bay horse with Arab blood, and in passing he flicked his riding-whip in a cold, haughty way at horse and man to make them stand back. After him followed the two dragoons with tired, red-burnt faces and the two Hottentots, laughing maliciously at the discomfited burgher. Tielman swung his horse around and rode away.

Half an hour later a messenger hurried over from Joubert's farm. Baas Lindstrom please had to come and interpret English, otherwise there would be trouble. The soldiers wanted to stay the night.

When Lindstrom proposed to ride over, Tielman checked him: 'Oh no, we must walk and leave our horses behind. They have the right to commandeer fresh horses along the road. Any horse.'

On Paul Joubert's stoep a comedy was taking place that threatened to turn to tragedy. The lieutenant was barking orders in an English which was degenerating from haughty to angry. Joubert, for his part, understood only Dutch. When the Pandour took over and gave orders to Joubert in fluent Cape-Dutch Joubert replied that he did not understand Hottentot. He was indignant; had he not already fulfilled the demands of hospitality by supplying bread and coffee? Were he and Rutger Van Huyssteen, whose wife and five children were temporarily harboured under his roof, not busy weighing out the prescribed rations for travelling soldiers, right there on his stoep: one and a quarter pounds of bread and one and a half pounds of meat per man, as well as nine pounds of barley and seven pounds of chaff per horse? However hard the soldiers tried, the two burghers could not understand a single word.

The Hottentot soldier, enraged at being ignored, now yelled: 'I'm not speaking Hottentot, I'm speaking pure Dutch! You must listen to me, do you hear! Don't you know I'm English, too, now! I can do what I please with you!'

'The interpreter, the interpreter is coming,' Joubert called patiently while he struggled with the rusty pair of scales.

The English officer stood stiff as a ramrod, his face a grimace of aversion for these peasants with their uncouth manners and raw, outlandish speech. When Lindstrom and Tielman arrived, he came forward with a smile of relief at seeing a European who could speak civilised English.

'Please tell these idiots that we want accommodation for the night.'

The Swede interpreted, whereupon Joubert flung wide his arms to explain that, already, two big families were occupying the one, small house. He held up the fingers of both hands to explain how many people there were.

Lindstrom calmly interpreted back and forth and at last it transpired that there was another house, the unfinished home-stead of the Van Huyssteens, which the unexpected guests might use if they wanted to. And that was what was finally agreed upon: five coarse pallets filled with straw, candles and a barrel of water were carried over to the unfinished house some distance away. The roof was only half thatched, but it was better than nothing. The soldiers were too tired for further quarrelling.

As they walked away in the twilight, Tielman asked if Joubert had really not understood the soldiers.

'Of course I understood,' the old joker laughed grimly, 'but they should not come and act as if we were the foreigners here in our own country.'

At this stage Van Huyssteen burst out with other, bad news. Friday April 6 the burghers of Graaff-Reinet had laid down their arms before General Vandeleur. They did it in good faith, for they had not fired a single shot. But the English arrested eighteen of the leaders, including the grey-beard, Commandant Adriaan van Jaarsveld, Prinsloo and Rautenbach. All eighteen were now being sent to the Cape to be arraigned for high treason. The Pandour had triumphantly added that all of them would be hanged or banished for life. Furthermore Coenraad Buys, One-arm Botha and four others were outlawed with prices on their heads, and a mighty Hottentot army, foaming at the mouth, was now over-running Graaff-Reinet.

Lindstrom said nothing. Joubert heard a wagon approaching, and said that they should walk over to the road.

It was Douw Prins. He handed a letter to Joubert and reported that all had gone well. Joubert wanted to persuade Lindstrom and Tielman to drink with him on his stoep but the two men preferred to walk back to their camp with Douw. It was already dark. On the way the botanist told Douw that they were shifting camp to Knysna in two days' time and that his help would be most welcome. Douw only nodded, staying as politely aloof as ever.

With a frowning face the young white man kicked at the stones in his path. Suddenly he asked Douw if the two of them could not leave early next day to scout out the road ahead. They might even meet up with buffaloes or elephants.

The half-caste slowly rolled up his long whip before he refused. First, he said, he had to see if his wagon needed new bottom-boards.

The two white men witnessed Douw's joyful reception by his people. Ouma Katryn and old Speelman dropped all they were doing to meet him with open arms, and Ruth ran around the fire to stand some distance away with bright, scared eyes. The chastened Hottentots wanted to show how zealous they really were and came to help with the unharnessing. Douw himself seemed moved: he stalked stiffly around his wagon till his pride could hold out no more and he started unpacking his newly earned possessions for all to see. A big, brand-new axe, a second-hand lumber saw and chisels. He also brought out a roll of material for women's clothing which he pushed nonchalantly into his grandmother's arms.

She embraced him and radiantly inquired: 'For Ruth and me?'

Immediately sullen again, her grandson merely shrugged.

Lindstrom was surprised by Douw's attitude to Ruth. Wasn't the girl pretty, not too big or plump or big-boned, with the exotic delicacy of her Oriental blood and the soft, feminine compliance of her mother from Africa?

Late that night the botanist was still trying to finish off his classification of certain forest plants. He had reached the family of parasites, but his thoughts kept wandering away to the human forms of life inhabiting this landscape. The day's impression at last led him to write:

'It seems to me that in many respects human races and peoples also prey like parasites on each other. No real cohabitation is possible except on terms imposed by the strongest: a master and slave relationship. I am told that the Hottentots were once a proud and lively people. But now that they have lost their country and even their language, and everywhere work as subordinates to European Christians, they seem sad and listless, an impression disturbed only by their short interludes of wild drunkenness with no thought for the morrow. According to rumours from Graaff-Reinet some of them now want to throw themselves into wild revolt, blind to what may follow. The great majority, however, stay passive, loyal to their masters.

'The case of the half-castes or Afrikaner people is totally different. Whenever the blood of a white man or some black slave or Malay progenitor is added, one gets an active, independent kind of person who—as the pure Hottentots themselves say— "works hard like a white man." Douw Prins is a coloured man of this sort, a man of mixed blood. The writer is himself a Christian and European who considers his civilisation and religion to be the best for humanity, rightly awakening this country from its primitive sleep. But surely it cannot be the white blood that brings a progressive character, it must rather be the cultural striving and the social relationships; the relationship of master and parasite. When a people proves to be undeniably the weaker, it seems also to lose its courage and its will to exist. I have been assured that Hottentot women bear fewer children by their own men than formerly, but that every group of half-castes is increasing swiftly. Moreover, it is a fact that there is still a great shortage of women among the immigrants, among Europeans as well as imported blacks and Orientals. According to the latest census the ratio is five men to every three women. The Hottentots as a people therefore seem doomed, in the course of time, to disappear in a new, mixed population. But what future awaits this new hybrid people?

'To take the analogy of parasitism further . . . In the world of plants it is the smaller, weaker parasites that gradually overwhelm giant trees. It therefore seems that it would be wise for the European colonists to seek to establish a common culture with their half-castes. If, in the long run, they become too dependent upon the labour of their hosts, an inverse parasitism may come about, that of the weaker on the stronger, and the dominant Christians may lose their vitality and self-determination, while their former hosts may thrive on their ruin. . . .'

6

It was the loveliest and most terrifying ravine that Ruth had ever seen. She kept shuddering and held Ouma Katryn round her waist. The rough road twisted like a snake above the abyss. How could trees grow so densely against such terrific precipices and not fall over? Their green was nearly black and the water far below the blackest brown she had ever seen. Only ahead, in the sea-gap where the seawater fought with the river, did it become green with flecks of foam. A breathless fear nagged at her thoughts: did alligators really live in this dark water?

'Ouma Katryn,' she whispered, 'what does an alligator look like?'

The old woman shook her head vaguely. She was probably visiting her many memories or, perhaps, was too sorry for the poor oxen and wagons to think of anything to say. Half guiltily Ruth once more concentrated on the struggle of man and beast over the narrow, wretched road. All the time, as brake-shoes groaned, men shouted at the oxen, grabbing thongs and leaning over backwards to prevent the wagons from rolling down. That man Barend was really good with a wagon. And, of course, so was Douw.

He kept on running from one side of the wagon to the other to soothe or encourage the oxen. She could see the sweat patches on his shirt and how he braced his legs when he pulled at a thong. Whenever she looked openly at him a warm dizziness mounted in her, today related to the dark threat of the precipitous gorge through which the black water flowed. Now she clenched her teeth till she felt a slow shudder that once more made her quiet and attentive. She had to support Ouma Katryn, poor Ouma, who could not ride across this stretch because it was too steep. She was young and strong, she could work, she could do everything for which Ouma Katryn needed her, for which they, he . . . When she realised she had started humming a silly tune, she stopped, ashamed. How could she be happy now that everybody was suffering so?

Ruth tried to look only at the terrible road that remained to be overcome. It was funny, but now she was no longer scared of the precipices.

The road coiled down and up again, across a stream, through savage piles of rocks and trees which leant over as if to jump down on the travellers. It was a rough, scared kind of road which shied away from every obstacle and at last took steeply to its heels down to a second stream. Proudly Ruth saw that it was not the white half-caste or the two white men who took decisions, but Douw. The ford was at its lowest, the rising tide from the sea was damming it up; if they did not want to stay here at the bottom of this hole till the next morning they would have to cross at once. Ruth helped Ouma Katryn on to Douw's wagon and, getting on too, sat watching with big eyes how the red-black water churned through the spokes of the back wheels.

On the other side there was a narrow strip of open ground where the oxen could rest a while. The steepest and most difficult stage lay ahead, up the mountain side, over transverse ridges of rock that would pound the draught-beams and force the groaning men to lever from behind.

The men set to work loading the three wagons and everything was once more fastened and clamped down; Kassiem and the women looked after coffee and food; Speelman and the little Bushman guarded the horses and loose cattle.

Even when she brought him food, Douw did not look at Ruth; for a brief moment she saw that his eyes were not black-brown like the Kaimaans River but honey-brown like his granny's. He let his coffee get ice-cold before he drank it; on purpose, she knew. Afterwards he could not hurry enough to get the first wagon on the move, all thirty-six oxen harnessed before it so that the other two wagons had to wait. Even with this triple team it was a murderous venture scaling the new precipice, a screaming and a cracking of whips that echoed on and on to torture one's eardrums. The poor animals became so stubborn under this endless punishment that they had to be allowed to rest for long minutes.

Ruth stayed down by the water-side. Once again she felt so desperate that she could weep. What had he said the other night: 'Why are you still alive then?' It had been like a knife-blow. Yes, yes, but she had also seen how his face twisted as if he was tormenting himself with those hateful words. It was her fault. Every time she appeared before him, she drove him to this torture. Her fault. She was the dirty thing that had to go. ...

The water licked and whispered over the round river stones along the edge but farther in it eddied more swiftly over the greater depths. Clean, clean water; and yet the darkest water she had ever seen. Darker than her own skin. 'Just listen to the black servant-girl!' he had said contemptuously, he with his light skin. In a sudden passionate surge she knew: But I wanted to be dirty! When he left without me, I wanted to throw myself away, I wanted to be drunk and disgusting, I wanted to see everything dirty, filthy, dead! Finished! Why should she go on beating and beating herself, like a dead-beat ox, just so as to keep going.

The unholy fire of her despair shuddered once more through her limbs, so that she started to walk along the river's edge; stumbling over her long dress; following the water; downstream, like the water. It flowed faster than she could walk so she started running to keep up. Branches, stones, got in her way. Then the water spoke ice-cold to her feet. Clean and cold, the wavering gibberish of her desolation welling darker inside her.

A voice called and called; arms took hold of her and held her, gasping and staggering. 'My child, my child,' Ouma Katryn stuttered, as if it was she who had to make such a terrible effort to remain in life. Ruth turned towards the old woman and clung to her. Shuddering, without words or tears, she tried to hold Ouma Katryn upright.

Ouma Katryn stroked her as she spoke: 'Oh, my child, I need you. Douw needs you. Believe me, my baby-child, believe me . . .'

They walked slowly back to where the men were at work, too busy to ask what had happened. It was true. Ouma Katryn was a bony, old woman whose legs were weak, and Ruth had to help her.

'Come,' Ouma Katryn said, 'put on your bonnet, and help me up the hill, to where I can ride again. It's a long way up.'

Ruth deliberately walked the whole way on foot, until the evening; a stony, churned-out track before her clumsy feet; rank, damp tunnels smelling like musty bread; trees, with long old-man's-beards and broken limbs, surrounding one like interminable rows of ghosts, the devil's many masks in gnarled humps of roots; enormous forest giants rearing up above the tiny people and their oxen. Green. Black. Leaves. Tree-trunks. Monotonously black-green later on. Tiredness. A river, and another deep gorge where she felt much too tired for fear. Then the evening camp where she could work and later slump down in a black silence of sleep.

In the morning she once more felt her young body's desire to live. But she knew that if, henceforth, she expected anything, even a mere friendly look from Douw, the torture would start afresh. She remembered what dear, wise Ouma Katryn had whispered last night in their shelter: 'Ruth, my child, if you really love him, you don't have to demand happiness. Loving is enough, even if it hurts ever so much, believe me, believe me.' She would not again look for happiness. She would avoid looking at him, at his honey-brown eyes or the silly little mole beside his nose.

When they passed a stream she often used to linger behind to scrub her face and hands with white sand, to scrub them pale with pain.

Ruth was as quiet as before but less withdrawn. She took more interest in the route; the few lumbermen's huts at clearings in the forest; the Swart River, where they had to be rowed across in a boat and the wagons unpacked and floated across on barrels; and at last Knysna's big sea-lake where the horses swam out to the islands to eat the water reeds, and where they camped at a farm with broad milkwood trees and a green carpet of grass. It was a lovely place with imposing buildings, lush farmlands, a vineyard, orchards, and red and white rambler roses covering whole fences with flowers. Here they would stay a week or so, Mynheer Lindstrom decided, after he had obtained permission from the owner.

Here, in this new paradise, where the generous autumn sun woke yet more odours from the earth, something happened to please and yet, in another way, to scare her. For some time she had been wishing that Douw would make friends with the other restless young man on the trek, young Sieur Roux. Was Douw for ever to remain embittered because of what the white men of Sandfontein had done to him? Would it not help if he could get to like another Dutchman, if he could go and hunt elephants and buffaloes in the forest as Sieur Roux wanted? Even though it might be dangerous and Douw would be gone for days?

The day Douw and the young burgher rode away together from the camp, she knelt down behind a tree and prayed: 'Oh, Lord, Ruth thanks you.' She had to learn to keep her gladness secret, to make it completely her own. Even Ouma Katryn should not know.

But the other thing was dark and evil, like the darkness which had bubbled up that time at Sandfontein and made her shamelessly look for self-abasement. It was something that came from the world's dark waters and rank, gloomy thickets.

She had felt it the afternoon that she had walked into the warm hollow between the green folds of the hills, to look at the white flowers with the sweet smell. She was drunk from the odours, like the orange and black butterflies which fluttered around the flowery shrubs. There was a tree with a high smooth stem from which hung branches of rose-red berries. She had stood wondering if one could eat them, when Lafleur crept softly up behind her and suddenly grabbed her round her waist and tried to kiss her neck. When he did not desist she struggled and slapped him. He only laughed and tried to talk her round:

'Haitsa, you lovely thing, you're just the girl for me. Flame and candle, that's what we two will be once we're far away together. We've got to leave this bunch of old women, heh, little girl? This is no life for people who want to have some fun. Heh, what do you say, you with your honey-sweet body made for love? Heh, ain't I right, don't you want to come with your Lafleur?'

At that moment he was quite different from his usual obsequious self; she felt a manly warmth radiating from him, as he gave his body, his laughter as abandoned as a yellow rock lizard emerging from a dark crack into the sunlight. And she felt her body answering, the old drunkenness, the old yearning desire to surrender everything and become free from the pain of thought. She was so tired, so tired of Douw who remained closed and remote and let only pain emerge. She gasped:

'I'm going to tell Douw.'

'Douw?' he grinned, still more cockily. 'As if he cared. You're too dark for him; he'll only look at a lighter girl. That's how Bastaards are, and you know it.'

But when he pulled her closer, fondling her with his warm hands while she strained away halfheartedly, while her half swooning eyes saw the pockmarks on his puffing nostrils, a small, bitter place within her began to swell till it shook like a tree through all her body. She broke from him and ran away: 'No, no!' Blindly and yet resolutely: 'No!' She, who could not stay faithful, was now offering this joyous pain of faithfulness to the man who had rejected her, was possessed by a new, bitter pride which made her smooth her clothes before she came within sight of the people at the camp.

It was this same faithfulness which led her to spy on Slinger and Lafleur; to follow them and overhear what they were plotting.

These two heroes wanted to go and join the rebel Hottentot captains across the Gamtoos River; to rob Dutchmen and thus achieve a life of careless wealth and ease. But for that they would have to wait till the trek reached Plettenberg Bay. Beyond, to the east, stretched only the wild forest without a single farm or road, with run-away slaves and wandering Kaffirs and armed Hottentots as the only inhabitants. Once in the Tzitzikamma wilderness nobody would dare to pursue them. In Plettenberg Bay it would be child's play to steal horses, guns and ammunition from the wagons at dark of night and run away. Lafleur and Slinger knew exactly how to get at Lindstrom's supplies of powder and lead, and they agreed beforehand on every detail of their plan.

The same evening Ruth told Ouma Katryn what they were plotting.

The old woman sighed and said, after a long silence, that they should not tell Mynheer Lindstrom alone but Douw, too. Douw was so sensitive about white men punishing Hottentots that they had better wait till he and young Roux returned.

The girl wanted to exclaim that she would tell Douw herself, but she forced her tense body to become slack and meek.

'Yes, Ouma,' she only whispered.

'Yes, Ouma, yes, Ouma.' Her thoughts lulled her into sleep, where her dreams ran unhampered like barefoot girls in a morning full of footpaths.

7

On an old overgrown path Douw pointed at a former snare-hole in which the mouldered wood had already become part of the caved-in sides.

'A *keisie*. My people used to catch elephants here.'

Douw rode in front on the bay mare, Sieraad; Tielman on the gelding, Vonk, a chestnut with a blaze. Both had gun, powder-horn and knapsack slung over their shoulders, and behind the saddle of each was a rolled-up blanket.

'My people.' The young burgher looked askance at the deep hole; only when they were some way past did he say: 'But you're no Hottentot.'

In saying that he said much more: that he had calculated that one of Douw's great-grandparents had been white and that his grandfather or father or mother had probably been white half-castes too, so that he must be something like a quarter white; and furthermore that he had asked Douw to come with him because he considered him to be totally different from a simple servant.

Douw rode on a while before he answered: 'Perhaps I'm a man.'

After that he looked guilty; he kept on making Tielman ride in front.

Stiffly and without much talk the two rode through the gorges. Douw succeeded always in addressing the young burgher impersonally, without using either his name or 'Sieur'. The white man, who was not used to associating on an equal footing with people who were not completely white, looked more embarrassed than sullen.

In places the underbrush was so dense that they had to lead their horses and even sometimes use the axe. The man whose turn it was to hack away tried not to show that the violent work was tiring him, and the other had to take the axe from him by force: it became an unspoken competition.

They looked usually for high open spaces on the ridges of hills from where they could see over the mighty green folds of the coastal forest, towards the inland mountains. They had to know where they could most quickly find another clearing and where the mountain sides would be less steep and, of course, they kept a lookout for faint Hottentot or animal footpaths leading through the forest, or perhaps a wagon trail hacked open by some pioneer or illegal woodman. Douw had heard that some such rough track started on this side of Touws River and reached the main road on the other side of Duiwelskop.

When they eventually found it, the forest seemed narrower but no less unspoilt and impressive. At first they had spoken only about necessary practical decisions, but now they pointed out to each other venerable yellow-wood giants towering above the lesser tree-tops, or stinkwood and white-pear trees with straight trunks that could supply ship's masts or beams of at least thirty feet by eighteen inches. No wood-cutter had ever been here. The only signs of life were the birds and insects and once, too, a swishing as some medium-sized animal, perhaps a bush-buck, fled through a thicket of ferns. But it was not only the untouched wealth that made Douw's eyes gleam; continually he was looking around for some soft-sloping clearing through which a stream flowed, a place for a new farm where only a farmhouse and enclosures for the cattle were needed to complete a dream.

Tielman, who by this time considered himself as good a forester as Douw, mainly had eyes for the tracks of the forest giants; the dangerous buffalo and, especially, the real king of the animals, the elephant. In one spot several heaps of elephant dung lay around, each bigger than a wooden pail even though they had been flattened by rain. He stopped excitedly, his hand instinctively clutching his gun. His companion remarked, without much enthusiasm, that his people described the elephants of the cool Outeniqua forests as the biggest elephants on earth. Again: his people.

The track mounted ever steeper against the foothills of the mountain until they could no longer ride. The green shadows became darker and the pillars and splashes of sunlight paler and more oblique. Evening was near.

Against a slope where dense brushwood, thorny shrubs and monkey ropes made any progress a painful struggle, they lost the faint path completely. They decided to take their own way, each to one side of the ridge, and to search separately for the path. It must be somewhere close by.

Tielman became uneasy as he led Vonk laboriously through the thickets and heard no more sounds from Douw's direction. He could see only a few yards around him in the greenish twilight and developed a suffocating feeling of anxiety. But a man could not call out to his companion without a proper reason . . . Tielman kept struggling upwards against the dreary slope that he hoped would soon flatten out into a grassy clearing. From the last viewpoint he had seen open mountain slopes with blue peaks rising above the sea of tree-crests. But the accursed labyrinth kept on and on, while it became dark. The stillness throttled him unbearably.

Out of breath as he was, he started talking to his horse or

singing loudly, from time to time stopping in his tracks to listen. He heard no answering noise and a sudden idea came into his head. He had noticed that Douw had never once addressed him by his name or as Mynheer or Sieur: perhaps the proud half-caste was too obstinate to call out to him? Damn it, couldn't he just call 'Hey!' or something? Well, *he* was not puffed up with pride. It was much more important to stay together than to look for an old path.

'Douw!' he called, till his throat grew sore, 'here I am, Tielman, Tielman! Answer me, where are you?'

Suddenly the forest opened before him. He burst through the last trunks and branches and found himself on a green slope of grass, below a wide amphitheatre of cliffs coloured purple by the setting sun. And there, on the other side of a fern-filled gully, the wagon track swung clearly round a slope. Tielman ran to it, hooked Vonk's reins on to the last tree where the track came out, cupped his hands and shouted at the forest beneath him: 'Douw! Douw! The track comes out here! Here! Here, where I am!'

And look, the son of a bitch walking as cool as a cucumber along the track itself. Tielman did not see relief as great as his own on the face of the exhausted Douw, he only felt his angry gladness as he called, 'Damn it, man, why didn't you answer? If you don't know it yet, my name is Tielman.'

'I turned back and looked for the road lower down,' Douw excused himself, and suddenly got such cramp in his leg that he had to sit down where he was and rub it away.

'Let's make our camp just here, heh?' Tielman decided. 'I'd rather sleep in the open where an elephant has lots of room to tread.'

'That's it. His boots are rather big.' Douw laughed so immoderately that he forgot his cramp.

In the gully a lovely trickle of water coursed underneath a roof of heath and bracken which they had first to prise open. The horses could drink, too, and graze for a while before they were tied to a tree as near as possible to the fire. The two men's food consisted only of bread, raisins, and dried meat which they washed down with water. Their conversation was disjointed and fitful, but they compensated for that by zealously hauling up logs and keeping the fire going. Even when they lay fast asleep in their skin-blankets it was still a red eye looking at the stars.

The next day was totally different; up over the last heights and then on the open roof of the world where a young man's heart could rejoice because his eyes could travel so far across the light and the blue. Tielman did feel frustrated, though, when they topped the last rise of the Outeniqua mountains and he saw how many new ranges blocked his view of the interior. Only behind those ranges and farther deep valleys did the inland roads lead on to the Longkloof. They rode over the rough, much barer plateau heights to where they could more or less see where the wagon-track must turn off behind Duiwelskop. Then their eyes turned eastwards, along the mountain crests. Without discussing it, they more and more felt their freedom from wagons and oxen and the lowland's responsibilities and continuous cares; they more and more became young men enjoying and discovering life to their hearts' content. Tielman looked for game to shoot and Douw for a corner which he could make his own. Both were startled when a herd of white-and-black striped asses burst from a thicket of giant reeds. It was the first time they had seen real mountain zebras. Excitedly they raced them for a while, till dense brushwood made them turn away.

That evening, around a fire on which roebuck chops sizzled, Douw unbent so far as to tell the young burgher about his dream of a farm of his own in this wilderness, far from the beaten track. The following day Tielman understood why his companion's eyes kept wandering around so eagerly. The afternoon of that third day they arrived at an attractive, shallow dip of land. Even after the dry summer a small stream was still flowing through good, deep black soil around an overgrown pond; all around were stretches of open grass which the last tendrils of the forest enclosed like fences: a basin-shaped paradise nearly a mile in length and half-a-mile wide. Unallocated government land belonging to nobody, with the nearest neighbours down in the Keurbooms valley probably a day's journey away.

Douw remained sitting on his horse. At first he merely looked, later he dismounted to touch the soil, to walk around impatiently, finally to stand on one particular spot in front of a hardpear tree.

Here, his glowing eyes told him, here.

Suddenly he hurried to unsaddle his horse. He grabbed his axe and chopped four spars with sharp points which he drove into the ground before the hard-pear tree, fastening cross-bars on top with monkey ropes and covering them with grass branches. A shelter made by man, a visible sign of his claim to that bit of land.

Tielman was disconcerted by Douw's passion and exclusive silence. It was clear that they were to stay the night there so he made a wide detour to the north and around the forested valley to look for game. He stared down the slopes to the east, towards the Keurbooms valley, to see if they were gentle enough to allow passage to a wagon and oxen.

At his return a fire burnt before the rough shelter. Now Douw was feverishly talkative. He held forth on the excellence of the place as a mountain farm, how he was going to build a road down to Keurbooms and, as soon as possible, drive over to Swellendam to take out a grazing licence in his own name and pay the quit-rent for a loan-farm. It would be easy to carve out some kind of wagon trail over the gradually descending slopes.

Tielman wondered whether Douw might not meet with a refusal: were new land-rights these days not granted solely to white colonists? But he kept the thought to himself. They made two more fires: wild animals had scared the horses the previous night and here there would probably be leopards, too. Tielman took out the flask of brandy which he kept for emergencies and laughingly insisted that they drink to the new farm. Deeply touched, Douw drank from the flask.

While they roasted the partly smoked haunches of the previous day's buck, the young burgher's curiosity made him ask where his companion got a name so unusual as Douw Prins.

'A Dutch teacher in our area had that name. He was an old vagabond and a drunkard, but he taught me the alphabet. I was very grateful that a white man could take that much trouble and, when he left, I took his name.'

'I wanted to ask you long ago,' Tielman went on, with a forced laugh. 'Who was it who treated you so . . . badly?'

Douw turned his roasting meat as hesitantly as his companion had spoken. Sooner or later this tension was bound to grow between them.

'Ach, I wanted to be self-supporting,' his voice sounded unnaturally indifferent, 'and that's just what my kind isn't supposed to be. There can only be one kind of boss in this country. You know.'

Tielman scratched the hot embers from his meat. His mouth was tightly shut. Now Douw felt impelled to force open the abscess which lay inside him:

'When I began to grow up the baas at the farm said I was wasting his time with all those letters of the alphabet. An indentured Bastaard belonged to his baas, body and soul. I had to work, and that was that. I stood it a year or two and then I asked his permission to go and work on another farm. For that he gave me a hiding. So I ran away. But he followed me into the Karroo and the other farmers helped to catch me. Then he had me tied up in the wagon-shed. I couldn't move for eight days. Every day I was beaten by Hottentots currying favour with the baas. He wasn't really an evil man; he only wanted to break my independence and then he would be good to me again. I only had to say "Yes, Sieur . . ." "No, Baas . . ." every time I spoke and promise never to run away again. The eighth day I couldn't hold out any more, and I . . . I . . .'

He pushed a stump on to the fire, while his voice rose raw and rebellious. 'I had to stay six more years at Sandfontein to slave for him. For that is what you Dutchmen have decided. That all other people, without their permission, may be indentured for twenty-five years like slaves. And for six long years I choked on my shame. If it had not been for my grandmother, I would have committed a murder. But she gave me new courage. For six long years I stood it. I saved up all my wages and refused to drink or smoke or have fun, however much the other labourers teased me. I fell in love with a girl but never looked at her. If we were to marry and have children, they, too, would become the property of the baas. On the last day I collected the cattle and sheep which I had earned and that same night I shook Sandfontein's dust from my feet for ever. Some of my cattle I exchanged for a wagon from butchers' agents along the road, and at Baviaanskloof mission station I worked long enough to pay for a gun and to learn to read and write. Now I'll die rather than serve another white man.'

He stood up and stared fiercely into the fire where his meat was charring. Tielman moved it to one side for him. The half-caste could not stand still; with every moment of silence his wild eyes said: Come on, just talk, you white man!

The young burgher began eating his meat before he mumbled, with a full mouth: 'You're not like other Afrikaners, that's why.'

'Damn it,' Douw erupted furiously, 'if other people are born crawling toadies, do I have to be the same? Are you Dutchmen the only people entitled to self-respect? Is the world made only for you? As true as God, this is going to lead to a bloody smash-up one day!'

Now Tielman, too, looked sullen because a half-caste glared at him and abused him. His awkward youth gave him no clue what he could do to maintain his dignity. He hardly tasted what he ate, then, at random, reproached his companion:

'And so you left the girl in the lurch, just like that? I suppose it was Ruth whom you treat like a dog these days.'

Never before had Douw so fallen a prey to violence. He thrashed desperately with his arms, as if battling against a dark stream about to overwhelm him. Then suddenly he stopped dead. Weakly and tonelessly he stuttered: 'I was ashamed of myself before her for too long. I wanted to regain my self-respect, alone. But it was a mistake . . . I forgot that she . . . that she could throw away her own self-respect. I forgot Dutchmen have the right to seduce every young woman servant on their farm. I spit on her: I spit on everyone called Sieur this and Sieur that!'

He looked as if he could weep.

Tielman could not bear it any more. He rose and said with all the dignity he could muster: 'I did not ask you to call me Sieur this or Sieur that. I asked you to call me Tielman.'

He turned away and wrapped himself in his skin-blankets.

Douw tramped around, tried to eat, dragged logs on to the fire and later went to lie down too. Inside the rough shelter. His shelter. But sleep refused to come.

Now and then Douw raised his head to look at the spot where Tielman was lying opposite the fire; motionless, though a stone was bruising his hips. No leopard or other prowling danger erupted from the black night to release them from their silence. It was long after his companion had started snoring that Douw stopped tossing and turning and fell asleep.

Without even discussing it they started the return journey in the morning. The sooner they got back to camp the better. Towards the east the land was softer, gentler and easier on the horses' hooves, but still densely overgrown. They rode in silence along the watershed, only speaking when they had to. Tielman was not even interested in the spoor of game while Douw's unhappy eyes wandered over a landscape which they hardly saw.

During the afternoon they had to cross deep gorges and a broad fringe of forest around the upper reaches of the Bietou River. They were forced to lead their horses and to rely on the confusing paths of animals. It was windless and sultry in the green half-light. Once they heard lumbermen's axes in the distance; otherwise the silence was a brooding presence.

In a maze of young trees under an umbrella of high yellow-woods they unexpectedly had trouble with the horses. Vonk and Sieraad started snorting and rearing and refusing to advance. Tielman was impatiently tugging at his chestnut's reins, when Douw stopped in his tracks and whispered, 'Tielman, Tielman...'

Softly and urgently his hand reached out to press Tielman's shoulder. Tielman, Tielman, his hand said, too.

Behind him Vonk made as if to rear up again. Tielman controlled his horse by gathering in the bridle and forcing it down, then he stood breathlessly silent. His eyes rolled, bulging from their still sockets to pierce the wall of foliage flecked with green and black. What and where was the danger which Douw had perceived? It was so quiet in front of them that he could hear a wasp flying a little way behind his head.

A Man Apart

It was only when he raised his eyes that a shudder paralysed his body from head to toe. Then only did he see the enormous upraised ears, the pale arches of the tusks pointing straight at him, the half-concealed outline of the massive body that melted so well into the obscurity of the forest that he at first thought his eyes were crazily betraying him. But no, there were three, four elephants only yards away from him, above him. He hardly breathed. His eyes stared till his eyelids felt like lead. They were too close. A man treasuring his life could do only one thing now: stand still as death.

Suddenly mighty bellies rumbled and such an ear-splitting trumpeting exploded that Vonk yanked him over backwards into a spiny shrub. Simultaneously, as if at the Day of Judgement, an uproar of trumpets rent the air, the earth thundered and trees crashed and whipped around them. When Tielman had his horse under control again and had helped Douw recapture Sieraad, the elephants had gone. The forest was once more as silent as if their encounter had been a dream.

Now that their great fright was past, they laughed hilariously at each other's grey faces.

'Old Douw, why are your trouser-legs dancing so?'

'Heh, and what about you, Tielman? You're a useless hunter! Was your gun suddenly too heavy to raise?'

'Not at all! Did you expect me to shoot so heavy an animal so far from our camp? Who would have carried him home?'

Now they really laughed, great friends.

They loaded their guns with heavy charges of powder and six-pounder bullets, but they did not really try to hunt as they pressed on southwards and late in the afternoon reached the wagon road between Knysna and Plettenberg Bay. When it was time to light the evening fire their supper of mouldy bread and dried meat seemed hardly enough for two hungry stomachs.

'Why don't we go on to look for coffee at the Knysna camp? It's only an hour on horseback.'

Without more ado they spurred their horses towards the west. Like two gaily mischievous boys they planned to approach the camp unseen; Tielman would steal the coffee kettle from the

fireside and food from the kitchen wagon while Douw would be
attracting everybody's attention with strange sounds from the
other side. Afterwards they would quietly disappear to start the
greatest hunting trip of all times.

When they topped the rise and saw the lagoon gleam under the
moon, they became quieter. The nearer they came to the normal
world with its wagons and people and divisions, the more they
grew apart from each other with a sense of oppression, a kind of
dejected regret. They knew beforehand that somebody would see
them, that their temporary friendship would end that evening.

When they came so close that the firelight began to paint a
red crust over Douw's face, Tielman sharply reined in his horse.
Already sunk back into his old bitterness, Douw did not look up.

8

On April 23 Mynheer Lindstrom shifted his camp to Plettenberg
Bay. By the middle of May he was far up the Keurbooms valley.
He wanted to be out of the humid coastal forests before the first
winter rains and to set to work exploring the vegetation of the
drier interior, moving ever closer to the frontier districts. The
mountain passes had been declared open once more and at
Graaff-Reinet and Algoa Bay garrisons kept the rebellious Patriots
quiet while their leaders remained imprisoned in the Castle
prison.

Admittedly there were rumours that the English authorities
were having trouble with their swollen rear-guard of Hottentot
run-aways, whose guns they were trying to take away, and that
the Hottentot captains now considered themselves betrayed and
were starting to plot with the Kaffirs in the Suurveld. But the
colonists to whom Lindstrom spoke expected more talk than
fight from these people and pointed out that the majority of their
Hottentot labourers had loyally sided with them. It was only the

raw scum on the eastern frontier who caused trouble. The colonists' attitude was that Hottentots who raised their hands against their former masters and sided with the Kaffirs deserved only scorn or a bullet.

The very first day at Plettenberg Bay Lindstrom experienced this unrest in his own group. As soon as his tent had been pitched and the two whites had returned from a first visit to the Post-holder, Ouma Katryn came mysteriously to ask if she could discuss an urgent matter with them, with Barend and Douw present as well. Then the old woman revealed what Ruth had discovered, that Slinger and Lafleur were on the point of stealing horses, guns and ammunition and absconding into the forest.

This story made the Bastaard break out that he had expected something like this for quite a while. The men must be punished at once. But the calm Swede silenced him. He turned to Douw who had stayed near the doorway, frowning, and asked him what he, as Lafleur's employer, proposed. Douw looked everywhere except at Tielman, who was standing beside Lindstrom, and at last said, much too loudly, that he knew what it meant to be beaten, and that he himself would never give another man a hiding. Violence was an evil thing. And who knew whether this was not merely woman's talk? He would talk to Lafleur and, if it were true, would pay him his wages and let him go.

On this Lindstrom let his employees enter one by one and asked each the same question: if they wanted to stay in his service, or to join the robbers in the forest. Without any prompting Esau and April reported that Slinger and Lafleur had tried to talk them into absconding too; Kassiem, the Malay cook, corroborated the story. The two guilty men however, violently denied it, until a quantity of lead, powder and flints which he had systematically stolen from Lindstrom's supply, was found in Slinger's blanket roll. At this stage Lafleur, Douw's team-leader, pleaded with sobs that Slinger had forced him to co-operate and said that, if Douw could forgive him, he would like to stay on.

To this Douw agreed.

'Tonight they must be made harmless.' About this Barend, the

camp-foreman, was adamant. So that night Slinger and Lafleur
slept tied to each other. Lindstrom ordered that all guns should
henceforth be kept under the mattresses of the reliable men. He
himself always slept with his pistol under his pillow.

In the morning Slinger got his wages and a skin-bag of food,
and was put on to a horse. Tielman and Douw rode on each side
of him, guns over their shoulders. They took him for two hours
on horseback, across the ford of the Keurbooms and along the
beach, to where the sea capes of Tzitzikamma rose like huge
green dunes from the sea. There Tielman ordered:

'Get off. Kaffirland is that way. But if ever you show your
treacherous face near us again, you won't get off so lightly. Get
going!'

The Hottentot who till then had maintained a sullen silence,
remained standing, glancing furiously from Tielman to Douw.
Deep folds cut into the flesh around his cheekbones and his eyes
became mere slits as he screwed up his face. Then his head jerked
up as he flung at Douw, in a whining snarl: 'You give yourself
airs like a white man, heh? Just you wait, one day you'll sob on
your knees too!'

Douw, who had reluctantly accompanied Tielman because the
young man had preferred him to foreman Barend, who was over-
zealous with a sjambok, seemed completely taken aback by this
unexpected attack.

'You impudent scoundrel, start moving!' Tielman called
angrily. He raised his gun, but the Hottentot had started off at a
trot along the beach. Behind the young burgher Douw put a
halter on the third horse before he turned his mare and raced
back beside the sea the way that they had come.

It became a thunderous gallop past avalanches of red rocks and
the foam-smacking sea before Tielman caught up with his companion. Just past the estuary of a small river Douw reined in his
horse and tied it to a washed-up tree-stump. When Tielman also
dismounted his companion stood looking at the mouth of a cave,
sixty feet up on a slope overgrown with brushwood.

'I've heard about this cave, I want to go and look at it.'

Surprised, Tielman followed him along the footpath up the

slope. Uneasiness pricked his skin, so that he carried his gun at the ready in his right hand.

The cliff side bulged upwards over the long, protected vault against which red and black daubs of colour looked like leaping buck and prowling children. Many people had lived for many years in this cave. The floor was ash-grey and flattened by countless feet; towards the back lay charred bones, shards of pots, arrow tips and splinters of stone; in front of the mouth of the cave an enormous heap of seashells pushed its rejected breast against brushwood climbing from below. Bushmen? Strandlopers? Hottentots? 'My people'.

Agitatedly Douw stood looking around, as if he himself did not know what he sought. His eyes caught and rejected every sorry remnant which they saw. Was it Slinger's poisonous words which had driven Douw to this desolation? To end the silence, Tielman broke in: 'Man, you'd better watch out for Lafleur. He's going to play you a nasty trick.'

The words rang hollow under the dome of rock.

Douw paced around, suddenly exclaiming: 'You call us frizzy-haired half-castes the Afrikaner people! Very well, I'm an Afrikaner, and I ask only to be left in peace. Your quarrels are not my quarrels. If there's to be fighting, I want to be left out of it!'

His voice was on the edge of tears like that of Slinger a little while before. His eyes on the floor, Tielman walked farther away to where the bulge of the rock face made a turn. He bit his lower lip in an effort to restrain angry words, then froze to a standstill. Before his feet was the ash of a fire over which sand had been strewn, still faintly smoking. Danger!

His eyes darted up and around and then down across the thicket, to the narrow lagoon stretching inland from the estuary, to where a foot-path along the bank disappeared under the dangling loops of monkey ropes which bordered the dark forest. Now he smelled the forest's sultry, rotting odour. As his eyes searched, his hands grabbed the powderhorn and shook out powder to prime his gun, ready for cocking the hammer.

He saw no movement anywhere. But then he heard a sound against the sea's roar behind him. Vonk neighing.

He sprang back, grabbed Douw's arm, startling his companion from his embittered meditation: 'They're stealing our horses! Come!'

As he ran he whistled high and shrill to Vonk and Sieraad. On the path he tried to move stealthily. His back felt open and naked until he heard Douw pant behind him. Then he saw them. Although it was the first time, he knew at once that they were Kaffirs. Three, four supple black-gleaming figures trotting along the lagoon path with swaying animal tails around their thighs and knees, one of them already almost at the bunch of rearing horses.

Tielman shouted: 'Leave our horses, or I'll shoot!'

Without thinking, he left it to Douw to try and stop the more distant Kaffirs, while he himself ran straight to the horses. The foremost Kaffir tried to jump on to Sieraad's back, but when Tielman ploughed to a stop to raise his gun, he let go and ran away in a wide circle towards the others. Tielman quickly calmed the frightened horses, then turned back to where Douw stood panting for breath, shouting at the half-dozen warriors: 'Whose horses are you trying to steal? You rascals, stand back, I say!'

Assegais held low, the Kaffirs came nearer, step by slow step, a black, gleaming half-moon against the white sand, while they smiled cheekily and pointed to their ears as a sign that they did not understand.

'You understand me well enough!'

The strangeness of the black men made Tielman shiver. The dark betrayal of their nearly naked bodies hid behind their relaxed muscles and friendly gestures as they slowly came closer still. It was an old tactic of theirs on the eastern frontier to overrun farms in this peaceful way and then to possess themselves of every animal on four legs by their sheer preponderance of numbers. But what were they doing here, three or four hundred miles from the frontier of Kaffirland?

Tielman prayed as he touched Douw's arm. If Douw fired a warning shot, the Kaffirs might rush them. If he killed one, it could become a criminal matter.

'I'll shoot your guts to bits!' the Hottentot half-caste suddenly shouted with rage, raising his gun. Tielman raced back, leaped on to Vonk's back, grabbed the halters of the two loose horses with his left hand, drove his chestnut forward with his knees, and pressed his gun with his right hand to his shoulder. Seconds, feeling like minutes, went past before he reached Douw again.

'Jump on, man.'

A gun shot thundered. Bellowing with pain a warrior clutched his arm. Tielman felt a moment of panic when the other Kaffirs looked like rushing them and Douw missed his stirrup before he could mount Sieraad. But then sand pelted beneath their horses' hooves and Douw got a chance to reload his gun.

The black warriors remained where they were; even from fifty yards away the two horsemen could see the red stain on the sand where the wounded man was squatting.

'Back to Kaffirland, robbers and rascals that you are!'

A warrior with strings of clinking beads round his ankles, trampled around wrathfully, shouting something in his own language. Douw cupped his hands around his ears and laughed. Then they rode away.

'They weren't afraid at all, heh?' Douw said, still laughing. But Tielman was angry: 'We could be dead. What's the matter with you? I thought you didn't want to fight anybody!'

'A thief isn't anybody, heh, Tielman?'

He still laughed as he made Sieraad race over the loose, thick sand. Without stopping, they rode to the ford over the Keurbooms, and swam alongside their horses through the black-brown water. The young burgher was now also infected by this reckless exuberance. The day had wings to its young body. They started singing a Dutch sea shanty when they saw a ship, a schooner, come sailing around Cape Seal, its sails high like great white wings that could at any moment fold down to the blue bay.

They skirted the lagoon towards the Postholder's house at the foot of the steep hill. Beside the enormous timber warehouse the Postholder, his sons and one white servant were struggling to drag a heavy flat-bottomed rowing-boat from a lean-to. The two young men dismounted to help, excited by all these naval activities. The ship had lowered a boat, and the sailors who rowed it to the land reported that a load of timber and beams were needed for the new sea-jetty at the Cape.

The poor Postholder stood almost tearing his hair because the supply of timber in the shed was so small. Piles were lying ready in the forest, cut and fashioned, but hands to transport them were lacking. Every single government servant or Hottentot labourer waited only for a chance to become independent and then disappeared into the forest to work as a lumberman. When Douw offered his wagon and oxen for transport, he was hired on the spot to carry loads of timber at six rixdollars the load. Directly after Douw's whip cracked once again; he wanted to earn enough money in a week to pay the quit-rent on 'his' farm and to buy a young but seasoned horse from a farmer.

*   *   *   *   *

Lindstrom, too, had labour problems. With the Postholder's help, however, he managed to get a new Hottentot driver, Jan Karieka, from a Hottentot kraal near the Government Post. The evening before he left Plettenberg Bay Lindstrom had an interesting conversation in the Postholder's house. Also present were James Callender, a lively enthusiastic Englishman who acted more or less as adviser to the English authorities, two farmers of the neighbourhood, Jerling and Cornelis Van der Wath, as well as Tielman Roux. The conversation turned to the troubles on the eastern frontier and, especially, recent developments with the Hottentots. After all, the Kaffirs had been an enemy for at least a generation, but the Hottentots were a new problem.

In his sober way the Postholder tried to tell Lindstrom how uncertain the existence of the frontier farmers had become since they had started colliding with the black waves of Kaffir tribes arriving from the north-east: usually starting with disputes over grazing rights for the Kaffirs' cattle. The original inhabitants, the Gonaquas or wild Hottentots, caught between the two camps and driven off their ancestral lands, were making their last stand. Their tribal system was degenerating, and they were often forced to interbreed with the blacks. The Hottentots of pure stock, who had gone to work for the white farmers, shared their masters' rough, uncertain existence, so that they were probably the poorest Hottentots in the whole of the Cape of Good Hope. As herdsmen and shepherds, it was they who were the hardest hit by the black marauders. For that reason, too, they rebelled against their misery. It was of course true that many of them were indolent by nature and that they absconded in such great numbers to the British forces in the hope of a life of ease and plenty and better wages. But they also believed that the British conquerors wanted to subjugate the Dutch colonists alone.

'All this mess was caused by the English who have not the slightest idea of the real facts of life in this country,' Van der Wath indignantly put in. 'The acting governor is letting himself be talked into folly by that hater of the Dutch, John Barrow. Just imagine: heathens used to subdue Christians!'

He did not dare say more, for Callender, an Englishman who had recently conferred with Barrow, looked sharply at him before he remarked with a smile: 'You forget the upstart republics of Swellendam and Graaff-Reinet; you forget that four years ago they rebelled against the Dutch authorities, too.'

The Postholder went on to say that General Vandeleur now wanted to disarm and disband his rearguard of Hottentots, but that the latter were scared of returning to their former masters. 'One can understand that such a state of affairs may lead to trouble.'

Shyly Tielman Roux also put in a word. He believed that the majority of Hottentots and Afrikaner half-castes were loyal upholders of the law, and cited Douw's reaction when the Kaffirs tried to steal their horses.

Van der Wath added some details about the gangs of robbers hiding in the Tzitzikamma who previously had been too afraid of organised reprisals to undertake serious raids, but were now becoming more brutal every day. It was hardly the moment for such a change in the conversation but Tielman was young and impetuous, and he shifted uneasily on his seat until he had a chance to ask: 'What is the position of a law-abiding, hard-working Hottentot half-caste who wants to farm on his own? Would he be allowed to get free land somewhere to start his own farm?'

This made the two local burghers grumble that such a farm would merely become another hot-bed for loafers, by which they really meant that labour for the colonists was already much too scarce. But Postholder Meeding gave an official's answer: each case was judged on its merits. If a Hottentot half-caste could convince the Landdrost and the fieldcornet of his ward that he was a Christian, capable of running a loan-farm, and that there was no prior claim to this new homestead, then the law would offer no hindrance. It was always the Government's policy to make friends rather than enemies.

Would testimonials from trustworthy people help?

Yes, they would.

Bengt Lindstrom looked at Tielman in surprise. Like many other big men he was passive and meek and did not expect or ask much from humanity. For that reason, he had started to seek satisfaction in the impersonal world of the botanist. He had seen the shy friendship develop between Douw and Tielman and he understood what the young burgher was driving at. Shortly afterwards, as they walked back to their camp, Tielman asked if the two of them could compile a testimonial to support Douw's application. Lindstrom gladly agreed.

Next day he left a case of completed botanical samples in the Postholder's keeping and shifted his camp farther inland. In the first week of May his trek stood on the edge of the forest, above a deep gorge beyond Paardekop.

Here he spent a pleasant evening by the camp-fire in the company of a hunter returning from the east to the Cape with two wagons, ivory, horns and skins. This man could talk entertainingly about his hunting trips and was furthermore a level-headed, frank individual who made a good impression on Lindstrom. His wife and children were on his farm near Swellendam, while the base for his hunting expeditions in the east was what he called his cattle-post in the Tarka. It had been attacked and destroyed several times by the Kaffirs, but by now he was used to starting afresh. When this pioneer farmer and hunter invited Lindstrom, if ever their paths were to cross again, to join in a trip to the distant Great River, the savant enthusiastically agreed. Schutte's plan was to undertake a new hunting trip across the frontier after sowing time, towards the beginning of summer; he promised to keep his ears open so as to hear where the botanist's whips might be cracking.

At Paardekop the two young men left Lindstrom's camp once more for a hunting trip in the mountains and for a visit to Prinshoop, the name Douw Prins had given to his prospective farm. The following week, when Lindstrom's trek had advanced as far as the upper reaches of the Keurbooms, Tielman and Douw left his trek with all their possessions, the one temporarily and the other permanently.

Tielman had found the botanist's tortoise pace much too slow for his adventurous youth; he had decided to ride ahead to visit the turbulent frontier districts, and only to return after some months. Douw's wagon, on the other hand, would turn left up the mountain to Prinshoop. Lindstrom was relieved that Ouma Katryn had had her way and that she, Ruth and old Speelman would accompany her grandson. Lindstrom did not pay Douw in cash for his services but rather in goods which he would have trouble in obtaining in the wilderness: a bag of wheat flour, packets of vegetable seeds, a few tools, and above all some gunpowder, lead and flints which he could spare from his own supply. He also handed over the testimonial addressed to the Landdrost and signed by him and Tielman.

Bengt Lindstrom was long to remember that last evening, under the mighty, stone slopes. He remembered it for the feeling of loss which any parting brings, from however chance a companion, the feeling that each new separation is a little dying, a small reminder of one's own fleeting existence. But still more he remembered it because of Ouma Katryn, who parted with such sorrow from people she had grown to know. I suppose I'm a member of her family by now, Lindstrom thought, with a smile, as he carried his campstool over to Douw's fire.

It seemed to Lindstrom as if the black girl's furtive glances at

the young burgher spoke of jealous relief at the coming separation, as if she were glad that the friendship between the two young
men would now end. Around the fire, in front of the others, it
did not look much like a friendship. Douw sat silent, dourly
staring at the fire, while Tielman shifted uncomfortably on his
seat. If it had not been for Speelman's music, the others would
have felt uncomfortable too.

Then Ouma Katryn whispered something to Ruth, and the
latter rose to return with 'a small present for Mynheer's daughter'.
The two women had made it in secret—a pair of soft gloves:
lambskin inside, rock-rabbit outside, with a pattern of coloured
beads along the seams.

'We made them a little too big, for Mynheer's little girl will be
bigger when you return to your country.'

Deeply moved, Lindstrom thanked them and expressed his
regret that he had no return gift.

'Mynheer has been much too generous already,' came at once
from Douw, the eternal independent.

Lindstrom had noticed before how the old woman needed to
express herself through religion whenever she was moved; now
it was the same, and Ruth was sent to fetch the Bible from the
wagon-chest.

'Would Mynheer like to read a bit for us? In farewell?'

Ruth held the gloves while the Swede sat with the heavy Bible
on his knees. He was embarrassed because there was no bible
amongst his scientific books, nor had Tielman a bible in his
baggage: only these 'half-heathens' practised religion in his
camp. Perplexed, he wondered what he should read. Something
to fit . . . then he knew. The passage that still fascinated him,
cooled-down agnostic though he was. Christ's message of love.
He looked up the Sermon on the Mount and read by the flickering
fire-light:

'Blessed are the meek: for they shall inherit the earth . . .',
up to the later passage:

'Ye have heard that it hath been said, Thou shalt love thy
neighbour, and hate thine enemy.

'But I say unto you, Love your enemies, bless them that curse you, do good to them that hate you, and pray for them which despitefully use you, and persecute you;

'That ye may be the children of your Father which is in heaven: for he maketh his sun to rise on the evil and on the good, and sendeth rain on the just and on the unjust.

'For if ye love them which love you, what reward have ye . . . ?'

Ouma Katryn's cheeks were wet when he stopped but Douw's eyes were fixed rebelliously on the fire. When Ouma Katryn uttered a pious 'amen', he looked up quickly: 'Mynheer Lindstrom, here in our country it is not the meek who inherit the earth. Over at Baviaanskloof our people often argued with the Moravian Brothers about this. How can we believe the Bible of the Dutchmen when it asks us to turn the other cheek and yet the worst Dutchman can do whatever he likes?'

In the silence which followed Lindstrom felt that he had to answer. Uncomfortably he was aware that he, a white man and an agnostic, was not competent to discuss such a matter in religious terms.

'Yes, one finds that kind of bad Christian the world over,' he answered calmly enough. 'But the Bible does not praise them. Listen . . .'

He turned to where Christ had been so angered by the whitened sepulchres.

'All therefore, whatsoever they bid you observe, that observe and do; but do not ye after their works: for they say, and do not.

'For they bind heavy burdens and grievous to be borne, and lay them on men's shoulders; but they themselves will not move them with one of their fingers . . .

'And love the uppermost rooms at feasts, and the chief seats in the synagogues . . .

'But woe unto you, scribes and Pharisees, hypocrites! . . . therefore ye shall receive the greater damnation.

'Woe unto you, scribes and Pharisees, hypocrites! for ye compass sea and land to make one proselyte, and when he is made, ye make him twofold more the child of hell than yourselves . . .'

Lindstrom was even more embarrassed when he stopped, and he felt he had to add:

'Sorry, Douw, that I have to silence you with the Bible, I know it is difficult for one to quarrel with it. And I know the ancient Jews were a blatantly intolerant people who exterminated others so as to take over their land. But this is precisely what Christ told those arrogant Jews.'

'This is what our Saviour tells all people,' Ouma Katryn added.

Again there was silence. Perhaps only because he had felt a kind of reproof in the last sentence did Douw put out his hand to take the Bible and read it himself. A child of hell . . .

The sight of Douw holding the Bible made the parting even more moving for the old woman.

'Oh, my children,' she murmured tremulously, 'to think we may never see each other again.'

And without warning she started, so that all of them had to sing with her:

> 'Dat's Heeren zegen op u daal,
> Zijn gunst uit Zion u bestraal . . .'

Afterwards, radiantly happy, the old woman asked if Mynheer, in conclusion, would lead them in prayer; it was not fitting for a woman to do so before men. Lindstrom could not refuse and launched into a vague, faltering prayer that God should guard them and that the people of this country should one day all be prosperous and happy.

Later Lindstrom would look back somewhat cynically on his involuntary, solemn role that evening; but mainly he would remember the faces as they gleamed around him in the fire-glow: Ouma Katryn with the pious submissiveness which, with her, was eloquent of an almost child-like inner joy; old Speelman with his bright, pitch-black eyes in his wrinkled ape-like face; dark Ruth who looked down fixedly at the fleecy gloves on her lap; Tielman, taming his youth so visibly into obedient humility; Douw, unconvinced and bitter, who sat staring at the Bible in his hand; as well as the Moslem, Kassiem, and two or three Hottentots who had approached either from curiosity or respect.

A Man Apart

In the morning Tielman, with two of Lindstrom's servants, accompanied Douw's trek up the mountain slope to help him over the first, worst inclines. Tielman did not intend to return to Lindstrom's camp but to keep straight on, across the mountain to the north, taking a short-cut along the dangerous cliff-side path to reach the Longkloof as soon as possible.

*　　*　　*　　*　　*

Next day Lindstrom trekked farther towards the Duiwelsberg. There he heard that an English lieutenant with a whole detachment of soldiers had been ambushed by the Kaffirs not far from Algoa Bay and massacred to a man, but that General Vandeleur, on the advice of the miserable Barrow, was still trying to win peace by treaties and presents. 'The barbarians are now convinced that the Christians are scared of them,' said the farmer who gave this news. But he seemed, on the whole, rather glad that the English, too, had received a blow that might wake them up.

At the beginning of June Lindstrom moved completely away from the coastal mountains to investigate a totally new kind of vegetation to be found in the semi-desert inland areas. Slowly he swung east to join up once more with the main road in the Longkloof proper. It was mid-July by the time he got so far.

At one of his camps, a farmer came to warn him that things were going wrong on the frontier. He had been hearing queer rumours about Congwa's black warriors, as well as rebellious Hottentot chiefs. To be sure, the commandos had been called into action, but the burghers were dejectedly returning to their homes because they were not allowed enough ammunition and the stupid English believed the Kaffirs' talk of peace. Could the barbarians advance from the eastern frontier right up to this area? Lindstrom wanted to know. No, it was much too far. But prudence was the mother of wisdom; Lindstrom would be well-advised not to venture any farther in that direction.

However, finding his voyage of exploration such a carefree joy, and the gentle, sunny days so lovely in that long, narrow valley between two sky-blue mountain chains, Lindstrom could not bear to turn back. On July 22, 1799, he moved on into the

Longkloof. One day's journey farther, while Lindstrom halted
at a babbling stream, two men on horseback came racing by as
if the devil were on their heels. One was a burgher, the other a
British dragoon in uniform.

'Turn back, cousin!' the burgher shouted as he thundered
past. 'Flee! The robbers are coming in their black thousands!'

Really worried for the first time, Lindstrom let the Bastaard
harness the oxen at once and turn the wagons, while he got his
gun and horse and mounted a little hill to see what lay ahead.

It was a lovely noon without any haze and when he saw thick
columns of smoke rising on the horizon he knew that disaster
was at hand. Ahead, about half an hour by horse, on the next hill,
he saw people bustling around a farmhouse. He could not make
out clearly what they were doing, it looked as if they were piling
something like a high bank of earth around the building. Nearer,
on the road, were clouds of dust where wagons and bunches of
cattle and sheep were being driven in hot haste. He could hear
the whips cracking almost interminably and once something
sounding like distant gun-fire.

When the foremost wagons approached, he could not see a
single Hottentot servant: it was white women and children who
led the teams or urged on the stock. From a frightened burgher
he heard of the approaching calamity. A tidal wave of Kaffirs and
rebel Hottentots was sweeping down the Longkloof, well armed
and on horseback. They had already murdered dozens of Christians and their faithful servants on outlying farms and captured
hundreds of horses and guns. Nothing could stop them. At
Sundays River, where a commando of burghers had tried to make
a stand, a hundred horses, sixty saddles and half a dozen men
had been lost. The Graaff-Reinet district was burning from end
to end; the entire region was desolate and empty. Every farmhouse was being burnt, every fruit-tree chopped down. 'We're
going to exterminate every Christian in the land, even though you
run as far as the Cape'—so the bloodthirsty villains had shouted
at the few women and children whose lives they had seen fit to
spare before they drove them into the barren mountains. The
unheard-of element was that the Hottentot rabble was now

banding together with Captain Congwa's black legions. They had attacked so craftily and unexpectedly that they had burst across the Gamtoos River for the first time in human memory, right into the Longkloof from where they were now threatening the whole country. 'The miserable English are to blame for this. They were asleep, and full of soft talk about things of which they knew nothing.'

'Cousin, flee back as far and as fast as you can,' the burgher urged Lindstrom, 'or go and shelter on some farm where a strong force of men has gathered. A lone traveller hasn't got a chance.'

Throughout that night Lindstrom fled back westwards; first alone, later with two and finally more families with half a dozen wagons.

By daybreak a horseman on a foam-flecked chestnut gelding had caught up with them. To their great joy Lindstrom and Tielman Roux recognised each other. The young man told Lindstrom that he had come to warn him and how, at a burning house not far away, he had barely escaped from a gang of blood-drunk villains.

In broad daylight, when the human eye could see for miles around, they had to stop to let the exhausted animals rest. From a nearby farm, where a wall of earth was being thrown up as a battlement around the house, a man came racing down. The fugitives milled around the wagons, inquiring about comrades of whom they had had no news, anxiously wanting to know how close the fire was burning on their heels, and bewailing their sorry plight and the fate of their murdered relations whose bones lay rotting in the open plain or who had had to be hurried into the earth without coffins.

A greybeard raised his arms, to call the sky to witness the injustice which the Government of His Britannic Majesty had inflicted by refusing to give them gunpowder and lead. How could they offer any resistance, deprived of ammunition as they were? 'How can we fight the barbarians with empty guns?'

Amid the general panic Lindstrom let his Hottentots harness the poor oxen once more before his wagons.

'Let's get right out of the Longkloof,' Tielman agreed, his

face a battlefield on which consternation contended with excitement at a disaster which was also an adventure. He was particularly impressed by the fact that the young burgher, Thomas Muller, whom he had admired for his courage earlier that year at Mossel Bay, was also fleeing with them, his blonde wife and baby with him on his wagon. Who could have thought that the barbarians would ever penetrate so far to the west?

Part Two

9

Days were the time of light between dawn and twilight when work could be done. Evenings were the time of firelight when urgent odd jobs could be tackled. Nights were for lying awake and planning before sleep covered all under its merciful blanket. Happiness was merely the realisation of progress while sluggish autumn crept towards winter. Happiness sometimes, too, was the recognition of faces around him but mainly of hands helping so that Prinshoop could be born.

First of all the kraal for the animals was finished with poles and branches, close to the lean-to shelter under the hard-pear tree. Then followed the cooking-shed, the enlarged lean-to shelter, and the first room in which the women could sleep. Ruth helped to fell the poles, drag them homewards, plant them and fill the spaces in between with pliant sticks and clay while Douw and Lafleur fixed the roof on top of the walls with a proper roof-ridge, trusses, supports and top-beams. Finally the floor was laid with clay from ant-heaps and smeared over with fresh cattle-dung. The proud moment came when Ouma Katryn and Ruth could carry their meagre possessions into their room and inaugurate the house. The very first piece of furniture was a bedstead of leather straps and a mattress stuffed with everlastings which Ouma Katryn had gone to collect herself. Then came a bench and a rough table of flattened slats of wood.

But attainment brought no proud surge of joy, still less repose. Every night work that had still to be done rushed down on him like a horde of wild animals. There was the timber that had to be felled and dried before the humid days of winter; the wooden tub and stone oven that were absolutely necessary; the tools he lacked; the skins that had to be tanned and cured, and shoes and thongs to be prepared; the meat they lacked because there was no time for hunting. Every night he worried about elephants which could flatten everything in their wake, or leopards which might prey on the fourteen oxen, the two cows and a calf, the solitary horse. Luckily it seemed that lions, wolves and the other big carnivores had been so reduced in numbers in the neighbourhood that they did not need to light fires every evening around the kraal.

Sometimes moments of rest did come even in his urgent haste to make Prinshoop a reality: times when he raised his eyes and could see far around him with the realisation that he was a free man, or times when he washed his sweaty body in the stream among the reeds, feeling the goodness of the water and knowing and smelling the earth under his feet. His corner of earth.

Unconsciously Sandfontein, the farm of his white baas, had become the model after which he strove. One day, when Lafleur grumbled that they were working themselves to death like white people, Douw answered that Prinshoop would not resemble some old Hottentot shanty but would be better than the farm of any white pioneer.

When the first winter rains fused the folds and heights of the mountain landscape into one universal greyness, a large pile of timber lay underneath the lean-to, closed off on its northern and western sides. He had felled mainly the smaller trees: hard-pear and stinkwood which he could prepare as wood for furniture, as well as wild chestnut, so suitable for yokes, and ironwood, which provided the best wagon-axles. For the sawing of bigger planks a team of workmen with long-saws and plank-saws would be needed; he could only manage smaller, finished articles for which axe and adze sufficed and with which he would earn more money for every wagon-load. Some of the wood warped so that Douw, in his impatience, became a worshipper of the sun.

And, by night, a worshipper of fire. Especially after the night a leopard jumped over the kraal wall. When Douw heard the cattle's wild uproar he grabbed his gun and shouted at Lafleur to bring fire-brands. Seconds later he was spread-eagled over the fence, aiming at a shadowy, spotty shape bounding away into the

86

dark, tumbling forwards among the milling animals as the random shot thundered. Only when he stood outside again, did he see that it was Ruth who had come to hold a glowing fire-brand so close to the danger. The ox, though mauled, would survive. But henceforth two fires burned the night through at the corners of the kraal. It was a blessing wood was so plentiful and old Speelman so fond of fires.

May became June, and June, July. However tired they were at night, Ouma Katryn regularly observed family prayers. Douw was present whenever he could manage. The elder trees, so late in covering themselves with bunches of creamy, sweetly scented blossom, lost their last trimmings. The nights turned bitterly cold. Lafleur sat shivering and sullen before the fire under the lean-to, deaf whenever Douw called to him. The roof leaked, a musk-cat caught one of Ouma Katryn's three hens, an ox fell ill, old Speelman doubled over with pains above his heart and in his back, finally an attack of 'flu and stomach trouble dragged down Douw's stringy body, too.

He was a bad patient. He lay under the tent of the wagon, with his face towards the other people in the yard in front of the farm: long-suffering Ouma Katryn, Ruth with eyes always lowered. Ruth he still tried violently to drive from his thoughts.

She and Ouma Katryn brought him slops of flour and vegetables and herb extracts. Ouma Katryn was still a diligent herbalist. She and Ruth had dared to smoke out a bees' nest in a hollow tree so that Douw could get a brew of honey, wild wormwood, 'horse teat' and 'Hottentot bedding'. Old Speelman was given another concoction which was supposed to be good for his heart. While she doctored the two men, the old woman kept on about some herb which she could not track down on this mountain, and followed this up with a solemn rhyme: 'Fever and pain, fever and pain, be my friend and I your enemy, so go away, in the name of the Father, the Son and the Holy Ghost.'

'It's just feebleness that makes you look like this,' she scolded her grandson. 'As soon as you get up again, you must take your gun and go and shoot some proper meat, so that you can get back some strength into your marrow-bones.'

It was Ruth who served and carried for Douw and for old Speelman on the other side of the fire under the lean-to's shelter. When he was not looking after the animals, Lafleur kept the fire going. He was full of wise-cracks whenever Ruth passed; she bore with them passively, though once or twice she laughed at his silliness. Douw could no longer bear her meekness; when she once more appeared with a mug of medicine, standing before him in her threadbare calico dress, her eyes down-cast, he muttered scornfully: 'You're a born servant. You've got the soul of a slave.'

The girl put the mug down slowly, twined her hands tightly together, then faced him to say: 'I'm not a slave, Douw, for I can choose whom I want to serve.'

He was so surprised that she should answer him, and answer him so proudly, that his lips stupidly spelled out: 'And who is it, may I ask?'

Her eyes filling with tears, she turned away.

Furious with himself, Douw lay with his head turned away. Later, when the sky cleared after the morning's rain, he softly climbed from the wagon and went to saddle his horse. Buck spoor would show up well on the wet earth. Only when evening was falling did he return, swaying with fever but with meat over his saddle.

Before his grandmother could scold him, he threw the bush-buck down in front of Ruth. 'Skin it,' he ordered brusquely.

Perhaps the potent meat soup did its work for, after two days, Speelman was up and sitting with his fiddle beside the fire while Douw, too, felt ready to use his legs once more. It was then that the old Bushman, with a sigh, told the flames: 'Ach, yes, I suppose we all run away.'

Douw had long been wondering what had made the old man leave his home to follow Ouma Katryn; now he aggressively asked: 'And what might Uncle Speelman be running away from?'

The grey head nodded to one side before old Speelman said, with a laugh: 'I suppose from my death. Over there in the Koo I had become too old to swing a spade. Nobody needed old

Speelman any more. So I sold my few animals and went away with Ouma Katryn to follow new paths. But now my old legs see the shadows that stay by the side of the road.'

A silence followed in which could be heard Lafleur's axe and the women's voices down by the marsh. Douw asked: 'And I, uncle Speelman, what am I running away from?'

'You should know better than I do, Douw.'

This reply angered the young man, but he remained silent. What did the old devil mean by talking of running away?

Later he returned to the charge: 'Only a coward grovels before others. I'll never again allow a white man to order me around. Here I stand fast, here on Prinshoop. I want to stay my own master.'

Opposite him the old grey-head's attention was now entirely on the fire. 'Ach, yes, we have enough wood,' he mumbled, on his own tack, 'but in summer the Children of Men do not need to stoke so much.'

Next day Douw was up and busy with the sick ox whose numb hindquarters had to be rubbed with tar. Next the garden fence had to be enlarged and raised: he wanted to put in barley and wheat to see if the grain would do well so high up the mountain. But sometimes he caught himself brooding over this idea of his having run away. As if he were running away! He had simply had to leave Sandfontein to retain his self-respect as a man!

The sick ox died and he had a fierce clash with Lafleur; it did not look as if the Hottentot would stay for long. This was no life, he grumbled, without women or even a tot or a plug of tobacco. Lafleur could go to the devil, there was enough cash in the wagon-chest to pay him the eight stivers a day he was due since last February. Let him go!

Two evenings later he thought otherwise. After supper and prayers around the rough table Ouma Katryn announced: 'Douw, you must start thinking where we can be most help, for in the spring Ruth and I and Speelman are moving on. If I don't go now, I'll never see my family again. I know. And the inland summer is not good for an old person like me.'

Douw had never had to face the fact that he had become

accustomed to the presence of the others and had grown dependent on them. The chill of loneliness folded around his heart. He would be alone, here in the mountains, without friend or neighbour. Alone. Was that what he wanted?

The wintry wind outside the small room made the candle flicker so that the four faces round him billowed away into the darkness: Ruth—he found he could not look at her; Ouma Katryn —her grey lips moved without making any sound. Was she praying? Then the old woman said out loud: 'If the Lord preserves us, we'll come back.'

'No, I'll manage,' he said firmly enough. But he felt such bitterness and futility that he was ready to jump to his feet and curse God and life.

When Lafleur and Speelman had left he still sat before the small yellow candle with its even yellower flame. His hands kept turning the pages of the Bible and his eyes caught tiny black fly-trails: *Thus sayeth the Lord . . . children of Israel . . . Land of Egypt . . . And Joshua . . . Have mercy on me . . .*

It was the first time Douw had looked so chastened and, when the old woman spoke once more, it was the first time that she had rebuked him like a sorrowing mother: 'Douw, my child, I'm very, very sorry for you. You had no real youth. You were always a strange, quiet child who never laughed. That was why I loved you so much. But now that you have become a man, you have hardened your heart. You make it unpleasant for others to be near you. You are afraid of people, Douw, you are afraid of soft, friendly words . . .'

You run away, old Speelman had said.

'One can never really hate the whole world, but you try to act as if you did. I know one must be hurt before one can learn and you have been hurt bitterly, in your pride. But a hurt person who refuses to learn, him one may as well cast away . . . He will burn himself away like an old rag that smoulders without ever bursting into flame . . . Douw, my child, why do you work so hard without ever . . .'

'Stop preaching at me!' he shouted, suddenly violent. 'You're a Bastaard yourself! You know yourself that we Bastaards are children from hell! How do you know that I don't want to throw myself away like an old rag? What do you know of the devil that drives a man when . . . when he . . .'

His milling arms sank. Ouma Katryn had always been like a mother against whom he had had to assert himself stubbornly when he became a man. Now his thoughts were an impotent darkness.

'Yes,' he brought out bitterly, 'I ran away from Sandfontein to start a new life but sometimes I feel that I might just as well be dead.'

Ruth, who had busied herself with the bedding in the half-light behind them, suddenly came up to Douw.

'Don't talk like that, please, please,' she begged. Her dark skin looked grey and the lower half of her face trembled while her eyes kept on blinking.

From so near, her big dark eyes looked like funnels of despair, endlessly caving in. Douw stared into them for only an instant but it was long enough to shake him out of himself and to recognise his own distress in her: the same chaotic, intolerable desolation as was trying to break down his strength of will into utter surrender. It was as if, from his very bowels, he felt her say: Please don't, Douw, for your self-respect is my self-respect and your pride is my pride.

He felt the violence within him become quiet and numb with pain.

'I'll be glad if you'll stay on till I've been to the Landdrost at Swellendam,' he said, and turned away.

Work, shelter from the rain, more work till he could sleep like a log. That was what the days brought. He could do much; for the skies did not bring torrential waters but drizzle and low clouds of mist and the miserable damp steaming from the forest when the sun shone again. Half-finished timbers warped and the brown horse started to hang its head as if it were getting horse-sickness. How could that possibly be? Wasn't it high and healthy here on the mountain, and didn't horse-sickness occur only during the summer months?

At the same time Ouma Katryn and old Speelman got it into

their heads that the frogs in the marsh were croaking very queerly at night. And why had the dogs howled so sadly on Thursday evening? Could these animals sense wandering spirits?

*   *   *   *   *

July 28 was a Sunday. Douw could not work and so he saddled his horse to explore the countryside around Prinshoop. In the early spring he would have to take the wagon down with a load of yokes and axles and would need to find an easier road, for the way he had come up in the autumn had been much too steep and dangerous. First of all he rode around the edge of the forest above the valley, considering the long, shallow inclines that led down to the inhabited world below.

As he stood on a green slope, looking over the fantastically creased and eroded valley of the Keurbooms, it struck him how quiet it was. He could not hear a single lumberman's axe sounding far below. Could that be because it was Sunday? He had heard that the lumbermen down there were a wild, Godless lot.

He did not stay long on the eastern side, because he was mainly interested in the rough road crossing the coastal mountains to the west of Prinshoop. He would try and find a way to join up with the pass which he and Tielman had followed. One did not sell timber in Plettenberg Bay but to the west, where the forests had been exhausted, or to the north, in the dry, treeless interior. It was a long, long ride along the roof of the world, mounting slowly towards the west with sudden deep dips into dense scrub which exhausted his horse. To the south, patches of cloud clung to the flanks of the Outeniqua mountains and the blue-and-silver sea, but northwards the sun was baking the earth which, even now in winter, quivered barren and brown. It was not till the next day that he reached Duiwelskop and the narrow pass where wagon wheels had cut grooves into the rock. This route would be quite passable on its northern side. If only it had not been so far from Prinshoop.

As his eyes looked down over the broad ledge along which the old road mounted to the pass, he saw people coming towards him. All on foot, three men, half a dozen women with children, and some cattle, fat-tailed sheep and goats. They were already quite near.

His first reaction was to withdraw to where they could not see him and to hide his horse behind a rocky knoll. He was in no way eager to let strangers know that he was living up here. But his curiosity kept him watching them.

There was something strange about this trek. The man in front drove the pack-oxen before him and carried a muzzle-loader over his shoulder. He was a sallow, yellowish Afrikaner like Douw. But the two men behind him, wearing coarse clothes and pistols and boots like the British troops, were no half-castes but whites with sun-reddened faces. Douw had heard of the many war-weary deserters from the British army hiding on distant farms or at Hottentot kraals, and he knew at once that these were two of them. Behind followed a bunch of Hottentot women with young children. Several were pregnant. Much farther to the back followed a half-grown boy of eleven or twelve, with the cows and small livestock. Douw recognised him as a young Bushman—a member of that piteous nation harried, by Dutchman, Kaffir and Hottentot alike, from their shelters in the mountain and the wilderness: the older ones to be killed, the children to serve as cheap labour.

Douw wondered why such a trek could be coming this way. Around here farms were close to each other and British troops were patrolling the roads. Were they fleeing? If so, from whom? Behind them the landscape was quiet and empty. Only far to the north-east tiny clouds of smoke rose white and grey against the blue wall of the mountains. Could those be bush fires so late in the year?

When the man with the pack-oxen emerged on the pass, Douw moved closer to his horse. But these people were too exhausted to have any suspicions about possible spies; they staggered to the first big protea bush to sink down in its pool of shade. Soon the women and children were at the crest as well. Douw did not want to attract any attention to himself and Prinshoop, and wondered whether he should show himself at all. Now he could hear the two white men's broken Dutch and the women's shrill voices as they quarrelled while dividing the food. Fierce aversion made

Douw stay where he was. Yes, go on, make some more little Bastaards, he thought, some more children from hell who belong nowhere.

But the boy . . . It was just such a little herdsman that he needed on Prinshoop. Then Lafleur might as well go . . . Douw opened his knapsack and took out bread and dried meat and the big knife he had made himself at the mission station.

Meanwhile the animals were arriving and also looking for shade. The boy did not join the group under the protea. Eyes to the ground he walked around looking for mountain onions and other wild roots or berries. In this way he came round the rocks where Douw sat.

Douw smiled. 'Are you hungry? Here you are.' And he threw the boy a hunk of bread, as well as a slice of biltong.

For a long moment the little Bushman stood motionless, rigid like a wild animal ready to flee. Then his broad nostrils quivered in his yellow face, and his quick eyes darted to where the food lay. But he did not pick it up. This was a boy who had known many beatings and little generosity.

'Where do you come from, heh?'

The boy took one step nearer to the food. All at once he stooped and grabbed it. Then he stood motionless as before. Only when Douw did not move did he put his stick under his arm so that both hands could be free to bring the food to his mouth. He was thin but sinewy, nearer thirteen than eleven. He carried all he possessed slung over his shoulders: his loin skin, a skin knapsack, and a sheepskin blanket.

'What's your name, heh? My name is Douw.'

Abruptly Douw felt such pity that he was ashamed to be sitting there like any covetous burgher, possessed by the unholy desire that this poor child should come and work for him. He stood up, leaving the remainder of the bread and the dried meat lying where it was.

'I'm going to talk to your people.'

As Douw moved off with his horse, the boy showed that he had understood the question:

'I Tkanna!' he called, and pointed at his chest.

94

A Man Apart

Under the protea tree the men were reaching for their weapons.

'Good day, cousin!' Douw started talking to the half-caste from far away, 'what is cousin's name? I'm Douw Prins.' And airily: 'You'd better eat the sheep at once before the spotted cat gets them.'

Very suspicious, the three men still held their fire-arms.

'Where do you come from?' the Bastaard wanted to know, while his eyes probed the plain behind Douw. He did not even introduce himself. Their shirts open to the navel, the two deserters sprawled in the shade under the protea, their bleary eyes seeming to ask little of life.

'I'm just hunting. I live over that way towards Plettenberg Bay. I was wondering what could be wrong down there, that you had to come up the mountain so fast.'

'Don't you know about the war?'

When Douw shook his head, the Bastaard surlily told him:

'The whiteskins were asleep and the wild Hottentots and Kaffirs tackled them simultaneously. It's the biggest war there has ever been. All over the east there isn't a farm where the smoke isn't rising. Now the devil's children are swarming like locusts down the Longkloof. For Dutchmen and Bastaards they have no mercy at all. Flight is the only hope, or standing together as one commando in a strong place.'

Upset, Douw wanted to know more.

He heard that the Kaffirs and 'Captain' Stuurman's ruffians were everywhere, perhaps even on the seaward side of the Outeniqua mountains. They had thousands of guns and horses. Woe betide the man who showed his face.

'And where are you fleeing to now?'

'There are some caves I know of in the hills behind here. We'd rather lie low till the swarm of bees has passed.'

The half-caste said no more, but added frankly: 'If I were you, I'd ride home hell-for-leather. If your home is still standing, that is.'

The grim way in which the men still held their guns convinced Douw more than their words. Without more ado he said good-bye and left.

Lafleur. He would not tell Lafleur of this.

For a moment the boy's eyes drew his attention away from this new worry.

''Bye, Tkanna, my boy!'

Ride. Ride. But burn down Prinshoop, he thought; ridiculous!

*　　*　　*　　*　　*

At twilight next evening the dogs began barking. In the purple dip by the side of the blue-black forest a horseman came racing towards them. Douw chased the women into the house and stood waiting, his hand on his gun. When he recognised Tielman Roux on Vonk, he felt so glad that he ran forward.

'Evening, Douw, man!'

'Evening, Tielman; evening, man!'

'Good gracious, but you've worked fast! Prinshoop looks like an old homestead already!'

'Yes? We've tired ourselves out. But we've only begun, you know.'

The animals were already in the kraal, and it was time to sit by the fire and have supper. Lafleur could not be prevented from hearing the shocking news. Tielman held forth at length about the murders and destruction and also said that Mynheer Lindstrom had fled back to Cornelis Van der Wath's farm near Plettenberg Bay. Quite a number of colonists with all their livestock had collected together on this farm which was being organised as a kind of fortress for the whole neighbourhood. He was living there, too, and the younger men were patrolling as much of the area as they could. Meanwhile everybody was desperately waiting for the English to relent and to let ammunition through from the Cape. The heathens simply had to be stopped before they broke through farther to the west. 'How do you feel about it, Douw? I came to warn you as soon as I could. Man, you can't risk staying up here alone. You must come down to Van der Wath's place. Then we can get on the same patrol. Heh, Douw?'

Up till now Douw had listened eagerly to his long lost companion, but at this point he looked away. His eyes could not even face those of Ouma Katryn.

'I'm sorry,' he said hoarsely at last. 'It's not my war. I cause trouble to nobody, so that nobody should trouble me.'

Tielman was completely flabbergasted.

'But, damn it all, how can you try and stand apart? Heh, Douw, man, don't we all have to stick together against robbers and murderers!'

'I'm not standing apart. I only want peace with everybody.'

'Do you think these swine will leave you in peace . . . ? Douw, man, how can you talk this way? Have you forgotten that day at the cave beyond Keurbooms?'

Douw stuck out his chin and shook his head.

'I'm sorry, I'm staying here on Prinshoop.' He no longer used his friend's name, as if he had now lost the right to call him Tielman. Though his face looked guilty, it also showed a defiant stubbornness, as if he wanted to tell the white-skinned masters that they could go to hell.

'May our Heavenly Father have mercy upon us.' The old woman spoke up for the first time. 'May He save us from bloodshed and violence. May He teach us that our adversary always has some right on his side, too . . .'

'Well, I'm not going to sit still while my people are being murdered. I'll do my duty as a citizen!'

My people.

Choose, his stiff neck said. Not: *For he that is not against us, is with us,* but: *He that is not with me, is against me.*

10

Uncle Speelman had luckily carved two wooden plates, so Sieur Tielman had something to eat off, too. Ruth bustled about between cooking-shed and table, worried about the thin barley soup, carrots and stringy dried meat. She got flustered about the last tallow candle, and went to scrub her face with water and ash

G

before she brought the hot milk and the griddle-cakes to the table, sitting down on the darkest side beyond Ouma Katryn. It was better that nobody should look at her. Now she could watch Lafleur's treacherous face and feel once more her uneasiness whenever Douw answered with that warm, husky voice. She could understand his anger a moment before when she had addressed Tielman as 'Sieur'. But what else could she call a white man? And she did have to ask if he wanted more soup.

Her anxiety was more immediate than all these stories of murders and fighting which she had had to listen to. She had felt it in advance, this throttling silence when Douw said he would not go to fight ... Poor, poor Douw, he was only afraid of tenderness and gentleness ... and afterwards he would feel guilty ... No, no, she had no right to think like this ... not she ... Why did everyone remain silent for so long? She wrung her hands under the table and started when Uncle Speelman abruptly pushed his head forward: 'Sieur Tielman, what do the Dutchmen say down there?' he asked in a shrill, excited voice. His head butted forwards, seeking for more words: 'Do they say there is a hot-bed of vultures up in the mountains? Do they say we're rogues who don't work for the Dutchmen?'

'Not that I know of.'

Old Speelman still butted forward, in the grip of an indignant suspicion that refused to subside. He looked so like a silly old billygoat that Ruth suddenly screamed with laughter. She laughed so much that she no longer saw or heard, wonderfully released from tension. But when she stopped and perceived the silence, she felt even worse than before. Oh, the disgrace! In her anguish about what she should do now, she could only think of her next task. Jumping up, she brought the Bible and put it down before Ouma Katryn.

'Ouma, the Book.'

Later she went out to the lean-to to excuse herself to old Speelman.

'Laughing is better than crying,' the old grey-pate grumbled. He sat close to the fire in his skin cloak and did not even look up.

A Man Apart

Ouma Katryn did not say a word about it. She slept very badly that night and once nearly fell out of the bed when she was feeling around her with outstretched arms, raving in an odd, breathless voice: 'Thomas! Thomas! Look at me!' Ruth was not sure if Ouma Katryn was talking about her son, Thomas, or about one of her two grandsons with that name. She pressed her young body closely to her Ouma; held her and stroked her till her old bony body was once more warm and still. All that time she had lain listening for voices outside, to hear if Douw and Sieur Tielman were still talking to each other. Only when it grew chill, did she realise why a patch of the mattress underneath her cheek had got so wet. ....

Next day the young white man left very early . . . Never before had Ruth seen Douw looking so embarrassed. Only Ouma Katryn was still dignified and friendly when she asked Tielman not to forget to give Mynheer Lindstrom greetings from all of them. And perhaps Douw, and perhaps she, too, would come down for a visit to the fortress farm.

'Thank you, Ouma Katryn. He'll be glad to hear from you.'

The young burgher bent to adjust his saddle-cloth and girth, before he added, for Douw: 'Approach carefully, if you come. The men are trigger-happy. There are so many spies, one can trust nobody.'

Then he swung himself on to Vonk. Douw went with him for a way. Ruth stood, watching how quickly they became smaller, down the valley and across the hill to the pass above. Douw returned quickly, depressed and in a hurry to go and break stones to use in making the oven. The nearest slabs of exposed rock were far from the house for stone was rare in this green mountain country. Lafleur went to herd the cattle and Ouma Katryn and uncle Speelman set off on a search for edible bulbs to augment their meagre food supply. They would have to walk far. Ruth was alone at home. She was aware that, in future, she would have to be even more on her guard where Lafleur was concerned.

After the women's room and the lean-to, she tidied the beds of the two young men in the wagons. She could tell by the smell that Tielman had slept on Douw's little mattress. She hung out the bedding to get sun and air and stood, listening and looking around her. It was quiet; quiet in a way different to other days. Everything seemed peaceful, however, and the lazy farm dog, Waaksaam, lay with his head on his paws, beside the cooking-shed.

The garden was a mere hundred yards away. She opened the hen-coop, in the corner farthest from the seedbeds. 'Come on, Ouma's darlings,' she cooed softly, 'scratch out all the little worms. Peck away all the little insects. Sieur Douw wants healthy vegetables.' She squatted down beside them. When the cock strayed too close to the corner where cabbages and carrots were running to seed for the next sowing, she piled up thorny branches to protect this forbidden food. Twice she stood up to look around the farm and once went to the kraal to collect last night's dung and bring it to the garden. Her long calico dress impeded her so much that she tucked it up above her knees. If Douw were to see her now . . . her legs so milky brown and heavy and soft . . . so different from his lean, muscular legs . . . Once more she squatted down beside the fowls. She and Ouma had saved up eleven eggs by now. Now one of the hens should get broody. Eleven downy little chickens, so round and wonderfully silly. 'Come, come, little darlings . . .' she cooed.

In guilty self-consciousness she sprang up again to peer over the fence. The dog still lay beside the cook-shed. But then her heart pounded from fear. In the patch of forest beyond the house, half hidden, stood Douw's horse, saddled. It was treacherously silent around the farm. The gun! she thought. Lafleur!

Without waiting a moment, she ran through the garden gate towards the wagon. Near the hind wheel she held her breath, moving stealthily. She heard clicking sounds from the wagon-chest and saw Lafleur busy filling a knapsack with Douw's big powderhorn, pockets of lead, flints and money. She ran up and grabbed the thief, screaming as loudly as she could, 'Douw! Douw! Come and help!'

Snarling, Lafleur tried to pull loose, to fling her off him. When she kept calling to Douw he hit her on her mouth, violently shutting her lips, trying to throttle her. She only clung the tighter, pressing her face with all her strength against his chest. As in a desperate love struggle, the two bodies which had become one staggered around till feet caught and they tumbled down. Again she got a chance to yell for Douw, but he strained his body away from hers by brute force. She could no longer stop the terrible blows, could only hold on with her arms so he could not get away with Douw's horse and gun. She felt her feet dragging over the ground. Lightning flashed black and green before her eyes, and now it was Douw she clung to, so that he could never leave her again . . .

Then it was his wrathful voice: 'You rat! Stand, or I shoot!'

He had jerked the gun from Lafleur with such violence that the sling had broken.

Half-way to the horse Lafleur froze.

'Did I treat you badly? Didn't we agree you could go at any time you wanted? Heh?'

The Hottentot only stood glaring at his torn shirt.

'Throw the bag this way.'

Douw shook out the stolen ammunition, counted out notes and coins and left a little pile on the ground.

'Thirty rixdollars. False servant that you are, there are your wages. Take it and get going.'

His eyes furtively and vengefully eyeing the gun muzzle which followed him as he moved, Lafleur came to pick up the money.

'Go along the side of the marsh where I can see you, and then over the crest of the hill. If you ever turn up here again, I'll shoot.'

In passing Lafleur looked over to where Ruth was lying as she had fallen, and growled: 'A hot time's coming for you and your watchdog. Just you wait; if it's not us, the white wolves will finish you off.'

'Shut your trap and get going to your Kaffir friends. Get out, I tell you!'

Some way off the Hottentot shouted: 'You're just as bad as a white man!'

Douw stood a long while with his face turned to the north.

'Like a white man,' he mumbled. Then only did he put the

muzzle-loader down and kneel beside Ruth to wipe the blood from her paindrawn face.

'Thank you, Ruth.'

She saw his hand tremble and became so confused for his sake that she strained to rise to her feet.

'Where does it hurt?'

The paralysing pains were in her chest: he could not look at that.

'It's nothing,' she gasped. 'And, Douw, the fowls are in the garden and the gate is open. Go and see that . . .'

But he pushed his arms underneath her, and picked her up to carry her to the bed in the house. With every step his face shook sternly and attentively above her, with every step a small joy shot through her together with the pain, with every step her hands wanted to fly upwards to fold around his head and shoulders. Then the mattress rustled like rain and he said: 'I'll call Ouma at once.'

At the door he hesitated a moment:

'From now on I'll always carry the gun with me.'

Later Ouma Katryn arrived with herbs and salves and soothing whispers; Ruth had suffered only shock and ugly bruises, by the next day she would be on her legs again.

His servant. His watchdog. Proudly she lay thinking that she had been able to serve him. But during the day in bed, where she was continuously aware of herself, she also felt a stormy shame for her body, so sweaty and warm, which fidgeted whenever he approached, and for her hands, which felt so empty now that she had nothing to do. When nobody was looking she kept them busy combing out her frizzy hair and tying it in a bun high up on her head. Let it hurt.

Next day the skies opened again, with long trails of woman's hair, grey like Ouma's. Ouma kept on nodding her head in an old, wise manner whenever she looked at Douw, who now seemed so much more gentle and confused. 'Don't worry, my child,' she said at table on Tuesday evening. 'It's not so bad to be called a Dutchman. There are good white people, too; sincere, God-fearing Christians. . . .'

'As if they aren't always whites before they're Christians!' he snorted fiercely. 'But it isn't that. It hurts me to see our people so bitterly divided.'

'Who are our people, Douw? As we sit here, the blood of all the nations in our country flows in our veins. For all of us it is our neighbours whom we have to love.'

Her grandson sat watching as her hands, covered with the thick, blue veins of old age, drew the Bible nearer. Then he stood up to go: 'All? Ouma should first go and convince the whites that the Lord was a Bastaard, too.'

Early next morning he packed some gunpowder and lead-bullets in a skin bag and saddled his horse. Ruth came running with food for the road.

'Tell Ouma I'm riding over to Duiwelskop. I want to see if we can get a new herdsboy. I'll be away tonight.'

*　　*　　*　　*　　*

Towards noon the next day there was a volley of gunshots, faint and far in the northern mountains, probably in the passes which gave access to the Longkloof. Old Speelman suggested that the burghers must be ambushing the invaders. By now their commandos ought to be ready for the robbers.

Late that afternoon two more gunshots rang out, loud and near, to the west, where Douw was.

'Oh, my God, they're shooting Douw!'

Everything on the farm came to a standstill; everybody thought that an armed man riding alone over the plain would be a target for both sides. Ruth tried to subdue her dismay. Since Douw had carried her to the bed and his hands had trembled so, she had not once dared speak about him to Ouma Katryn. Old Uncle Speelman went to the hill near the house and, shortly afterwards, came running back with the news that Douw was approaching, safe and sound.

'I shot a buffalo!' Douw shouted, still far away. 'I nearly fell over him. It was a lucky shot! He's lying close by in the second dip.'

Old Speelman and Ruth at once helped round up the oxen and

harness them to the rough sledge with which they hauled wood. But it was dark before the buffalo bull with his enormous horned head lay in front of the lean-to. By the light of a big fire the animal was skinned. The women rejoiced over the fat from which they could make candles and soup, not to mention the mighty heap of meat and the strips of drying flesh which would burden the trees next day. In anticipation old Uncle Speelman ran around with a branch, showing the way to chase off vultures. When the lovely smell of frying liver tickled his nostrils, the old man took up his fiddle to make the strings thank the night sky.

Douw was proud as a peacock, and Ruth smiled and laughed all the time. For the first time the people of Prinshoop knew the relief of joy. Only later did Ouma Katryn remember to ask: 'And the Bushman herdsboy? Is he coming?'

Douw was not sure. The half-caste had accepted the ammunition and had even added that they had too many mouths to feed, but Douw did not trust him. They nearly quarrelled. Douw seemed uneasy, as if he did not want to talk about the boy.

In the morning, however, Tkanna came walking shyly along, with three goats on his heels, his bow and arrow over his shoulder and his stick in his hand. The goats were his wages for one year's service with the Bastaard. Did the Bastaard say he could come? No, he had just helped himself to his goats and followed the spoor of Douw's horse.

Surprised, Ruth stood listening to the new sound in Douw's voice while he spoke to the boy and promised him a wage of one ox per year. When he was big enough to do a man's work, he would get more.

'And you're free to go whenever you want to, do you hear, Tkanna?'

Uncle Speelman clicked and slapped his tongue as he talked Bushman language with Tkanna but Ouma Katryn shook her head. This boy was a little heathen. They would have to teach him Dutch and Christian manners. And she and Ruth had to run up some kind of trousers for him at once, and to remove his lice.

Tkanna listened obediently to everything, but his eyes only

started shining when he asked if he could go and see the cattle
and learn to know each one by name.

'You must never give a Bushman a spade and expect him to
dig.' Douw radiantly recited what the others knew well already.
'Animals are all there are on earth for him.'

That evening Tkanna had to be present at evening prayers.
Then Douw did something which his grandmother had long
prayed for: he took the Bible and read a passage himself, as
befitted the man of the house. He read slowly, with pauses to
spell out each word correctly, yet with dignified emphasis. Why
did he read for the first time tonight? To impress Tkanna? Ruth
sat watching wide-eyed. Her heart beat gladly, but also with the
kind of jealousy she had felt in Tielman's presence.

'Will Ouma pray for us?'

While the old woman prayed, Ruth peered at the little Bushman sitting with wide eyes, staring at these strange doings. She
stretched her hand across the table to close his eyes, gently, as
her fingertips had wanted to touch Douw the other day.

The arrival of Tkanna freed Douw's hands to start work on the
framework of the remaining two rooms of the house; to plant
the wall-poles, finish the worst labour on the roof and put into
place the heavy roof-tree, the trusses and other supports.

Then came a Tuesday eight days after Lafleur's departure.
Douw was about half a mile from the house, on the edge of the
forest, chopping spars; old Speelman at the waterside soaking the
buffalo hide; Tkanna with the livestock by the upper lake; Ouma
Katryn busy with the boy's skin trousers and the soap cauldron;
and Ruth trying to keep the myriads of birds away from the strips
of meat drying in the trees. Ruth became aware of danger when
the vultures at the forest's edge flapped up to settle farther away.
When she listened, she could hear that the doves, which had
formerly been cooing in the trees below the house, were now
silent.

With the memory of Lafleur still haunting her, she ran to the
wagon-chest, picked up the big powderhorn, the pockets of
bullets and flints and hastened to the bedroom. She tore a hole in
the mattress and buried it all amongst the stuffing. There it would

be safer. Douw carried with him the gun and the small powder-horn.

As she left the door, she saw a file of black warriors come running bent low around the marsh. They were driving the horse before them. Kaffirs! Almost simultaneously she heard horses' hooves pounding behind the house.

Her eyes fled over the yellow Hottentot faces, over Ouma Katryn's mouth open to cry out, but all she thought of was to run, run, straight to where Douw's axe was still sounding like a sluggish heart.

Behind her horses were trampling round the house. The murderers were looking for the ammunition! The horse! Douw's gun!

She pulled her dress higher to run faster, although already she knew she was too late. The villains would have heard Douw's axe and would have known that they had to stalk him. When the chopping stopped, her terror flew ahead to the thunderous gunshot about to explode. One only. After that, confused sounds of struggle and then branches beat at her face and she saw black bodies straining to hold Douw; two, three Hottentots on horseback riding round the felled tree, the front one, with red satin waistcoat and a bunch of ostrich feathers on his hat, clearly the leader, reining in his horse before Douw. Arms grabbed her, jerked her to a stop. But he lived, Douw still lived!

At a sign from the leader the Kaffirs stripped Douw of his fire-arms and let him go. Ruth's heart pounded in her throat; he stood so defiantly erect and asked so loudly:

'Why do you trouble me? I'm not fighting for the Dutchmen.'

'It's war,' the leader answered, high and mighty. With much pomp he announced that he was Dawid Stuurman, brother of the great Hottentot captain, Klaas Stuurman, and that he was leading military operations in this part of the country. They were going to exterminate every white man and take back their country. 'Every horse has to gallop, every gun must shoot. Will you fight with us?'

'No. This is not my war.'

'Then we take your horse and your gun.'

Dawid Stuurman's eyes narrowed in his swarthy face.

'But I've heard you got on so badly with the whites?'

'Yes, freedom is only for a white skin. But I swore that I would never do unto another man what was done to me . . .'

'Then you're a spunkless coward!'

At this stage more Hottentots and black warriors came trooping down from the house, Lafleur in the van. The traitor was furious because they could not find Douw's supply of ammunition.

'Where's the ammunition, hey?'

Scornfully Douw looked at his former servant, silent.

'Open your bloody mouth! Captain Stuurman is speaking to you!'

Lafleur came closer and spat in Douw's face: 'You half-caste dog! You didn't think I would get the gun and the horse after all, heh?'

Douw turned to Dawid Stuurman: 'Unfaithful dirt like this is not worth relying on once the bullets start flying.'

A snarling Hottentot raised his gun, priming the cock.

'Where's the ammunition?'

Douw's face turned grey. His jaw worked before he got out:

'I've been hunting a lot. Can't you see all the meat drying in the trees? All the ammunition I have is here.'

'You lie!'

Behind them Ruth stammered: 'It's true! And he gave some away to the deserters at Duiwelskop.'

This made Lafleur swing round, grinning with interest:

'Ah, the faithful watchdog, the little bitch with the closed up legs. Will you open up today for Lafleur?'

When he pawed her so that her dress tore at the neck, the excited Hottentots laughed, but the black men stood watching with disapproval. Suddenly Douw sprang forward and flung the Hottentot to the ground.

The other Hottentots tackled the struggling Douw and mauled him till blood spattered from his nostrils. The black warriors stood like statues; rather sudden death from an assegai than this! Raging, Lafleur tore Ruth's dress even more. But on his mount Dawid Stuurman's crown of ostrich feathers shook impatiently:

he wanted to behave like a dignified leader. 'Enough,' he raised his voice, 'enough of this. We can't waste our time.' And to Douw: 'Then we take one of your oxen as food for the road. And watch out when we come again.'

He swung his horse round with a swagger, before making it rear to stop again, a great general with a sly after-thought: 'One day I would like to talk some more with you.'

A moment later the band of robbers filed from the forest: one of them looked back in mockery. It became silent.

Panting from humiliation and anger Douw stood looking at the ground before him.

'I hid the ammunition,' Ruth whispered, 'in the mattress.'

She clutched the torn dress over her breasts when he raised his head and stared at her. It was as if his wild eyes were seeing her for the first time.

The forest rustled as Uncle Speelman came peering through, but Douw fiercely waved him away: 'We'll come later. Go!'

He did not even look to see old Speelman go, he merely came slowly towards her:

'What would I do without you, Ruth? You're the only one who always stood by my side.'

His voice was hoarse and uncontrolled as if he was not wholly in his right mind. When his hands touched her arm and locked around it, she knew his passion was that of a man with a woman, but a man screaming like a child from the need to wreak his despair on her who was soft and defenceless.

'I ran away from you, Ruth, and never knew it. Now I know that I needed you all the time . . .'

His arms locked so hard around her that it hurt. She wanted to recoil and flee. Did he have to be so unexpectedly brutal and cruel? Was there mockery in his jerking lips: 'I need you, Ruth?' But then she felt the greater terror of his own humiliation smouldering in his eyes and she put her arms soft and pliant around him, knowing that she still had to give before she dared receive.

There, beside a felled tree amidst the countless intertwining arms of the forest, she felt her man come home at last, as she herself won the assurance to whisper joyous words of love: 'Oh, Douw, my Douw . . .'

At dusk they came home to where the others waited anxiously.

'Ouma Katryn,' Douw quietly said, 'tomorrow I'm going down to Van der Wath's farm. I want to get back my horse and gun. I don't know how long I'll be away.' Then he slapped the boy on the shoulder: 'Don't feel bad about the ox, Tkanna. And look after Ruth and Ouma Katryn and Uncle Speelman, heh? I'm counting on you.'

After that he turned to Ruth to ask in front of them all: 'Ruth, will you wait for me?'

'Yes, Douw.'

I I

'In this wide, empty land where, up till now, civilisation has been established only in one small city and four villages, the nearest of these two hundred miles from here, so many people have collected on this farm in the wilderness, that it looks like a young town. The only buildings are Cornelis Van der Wath's farm house and a few rough outbuildings and Hottentot huts, but many tents have been erected around the thirty ox-wagons with their white hoods harbouring nearly two hundred souls: white colonists and their families who have fled from isolated farms, nearly a dozen half-castes, a dozen slaves and half a hundred Hottentots.

'By day there is much social coming and going, so that one can nearly forget the war. But at night it is another matter. Then a wide circle of fires burns in the open around the farmyard and burghers and faithful servants regularly relieve each other as sentinels. Every living creature shelters inside the laager; the great herds of sheep and cattle, which are the frontier farmers' main sustenance, in hurriedly enlarged paddocks called kraals;

the majority of women and younger children in the house within
the fortified wall around the house, a high bank of earth supported
on the inside by a breastwork of logs. At the four corners stand
strong turrets with embrasures on which to rest guns; at the
slightest sign of trouble these can be manned by sharpshooters.
If matters turn desperate during an overwhelming surprise-
attack, every soul can withdraw to within this last fortress.
Opposite the front door is a solid gateway with iron bolts made
from wagon-rims.

'It is now winter and, especially on rainy nights, the colonists
are on the alert. On open terrain in the daylight they only fear the
renegade Hottentots who also possess guns and horses, but on
dark nights, when it is so damp that a gun's powder might not
catch, they have to reckon with the assegais of the Kaffirs. And
there are rumours that Congwa's whole fighting force of a
thousand warriors is somewhere in this neighbourhood in
company with Stuurman's hundred mounted Hottentots. So far
we have had no attack, only a few skirmishes in the forest to the
east; apparently the invaders are still spread out collecting loot.
Yesterday, August 6, 1799, a burgher and one of "our" Hottentots
were wounded in an ambush. Alas, this, up till now invisible siege
is serious enough to hamper my researches considerably. I
accompany the burghers for some distance whenever they ride on
scouting missions, very ill at ease because one rides for hours
through an empty, quiet landscape, then suddenly, according to
the nature of warfare in this country, finds oneself in a mortal
ambush. By now I have learnt how to collect a botanical sample
with one hand while holding my horse's bridle in the other. I'm
afraid my collection is going to contain an unwarranted preponderance of plants from the region of Plettenberg Bay!'

Bengt Lindstrom smiled wryly as he stared through the tent-
flap at where Kassiem stood grumbling while he rummaged in the
half-empty spice-box. Beside the fire Jan Karieka sat laughing at
him—to him meat, the only plentiful food, was all a hungry
stomach needed. 'Just tell me if your peppers and cloves are all
used up, and I'll go and pick much better herbs for you, up in
the mountain.'

'Get out, you raw Hottentot!' the Malay insulted him. 'Good herbs and spices only grow in my country.'

'How do you know? You were born in this country.'

Kassiem swung his kitchen knife. 'Enough of this silly twaddle. Go and look for trouble in Kaffirland!'

By now Jan knew how to plague Kassiem, and so he slyly answered: 'You're talking to a Christian man.'

Lindstrom listened no more and wrote on:

'After the great discord caused by the British Occupation, the colonists are at present all of one mind in the face of the common danger. Wherever Orangists and Patriots meet, the same sincere wish is expressed: that the British Government should at once abandon its hesitant attitude and throw its forces into the struggle against the Kaffirs and the rebellious Hottentots; that the burgher commandos should be properly armed and given full powers to drive the heathen back across the Great Fish River. It should be a concerted, universal attempt by all Christians. I hear many a pious wish that the burghers of the Boland—the older, more settled areas closer to Cape Town—should set out at once to come and help.

'On the other hand the attitude of the colonists has become much more suspicious and intolerant towards the other population groups. I do not think I exaggerate when I say that relations between races here in the Cape of Good Hope are now, as never before, passing through a crisis. Only a few years ago—the colonists say, before the arrival of the British Occupying Forces—this was not the case. Then the Europeans were undeniably the masters because they could enforce their authority, while the Hottentots and the different kinds of coloured people within the Colony accepted it as such. Naturally there had been trouble with the Hottentot nation in its disintegration and ruin, as well as with Bushman poachers in the mountains of the interior, or with deserted slaves, or rebellious half-castes emigrating towards the interior. But the European colonists, Hollanders, Germans and French in origin, and the Christianity they brought, had everywhere been the new, rising sun. In the last generation the clash with the numerous and energetic black nations—Xhosas, Tamboukies and so on, usually called by the Arab appellation of Kaffirs, "Unbelievers"—had begun on the eastern frontier. For the first time the colonists were faced by a mighty opponent who did not want to relinquish his land, his language or his customs but, on the contrary, revealed an urge to conquer, which has turned the eastern frontier during the last twenty years into a battle arena.

'Recently, when the British Occupying Forces crushed the rising of the small French-inspired republics of Swellendam and Graaff-Reinet, the black nations saw their chance. Local inhabitants have assured me that this was the first time that hordes of Kaffirs had burst through so far to the west. Their hatred of the British, who were ignorant of local conditions and unconsciously caused the débâcle, is therefore comprehensible. But it is mainly the reaction of the coloured races within the Colony to this new advent that to me seems so significant.

'In the first place, the humiliation of the colonists was for many an incentive to plead their own, often legitimate grievances, relating mainly to the expropriation of their lands by the Christians and, ultimately, to rebel, first in partnership with the British troops, and then, when the latter wanted to get rid of their troublesome allies, with the invading Kaffirs. They could see clearly now that the colonists were afraid of the warlike Kaffir nations. And when the colonists were subjugated and made powerless by British troops, the most seditious elements amongst the Hottentots, chiefly the wild Gonaquas on the eastern frontier, rose in revolt and made common cause with their former archenemies, the black nations. This course of events is going to have grave results for the whole Colony.

'In accounts of atrocities given by the fleeing colonists, it always strikes one how the black warriors are mainly preoccupied with trying to seize as much cattle and grazing land as possible, whereas their Hottentot allies are guilty of hysterical and extravagant cruelties. The latter's greater violence, surely, can not only be ascribed to their greater knowledge of the "Dutchmen", as they call all white people. It is rather as if they have to gird up their loins so as to be able to fight with hatred against the colonists and the loyal Hottentots, as if, for them, it was a kind of fraternal feud or civil war. Most Hottentots have already accepted the Dutch language in its Cape form as their mother tongue, and adopt the Christians' clothing and other customs as much as they can.

'On the other hand the great majority of Hottentots, black slaves and "freed blacks", as well as the Malays and the Afrikaner half-castes within the Cape of Good Hope, did not take part in the revolt. Many of them fight loyally side by side with the white burghers. For them it can be no easy choice to take part in a war against their brothers. Yet I think it is beginning to appear that the great majority of coloured people within the Colony have already chosen to stand with the Christians against the black heathen. I hear of many cases where Hottentots, who deserted to join the seditious chiefs, soon came back again, sometimes with their stolen guns, to fight once more by the side of their masters. However the war may develop, this need to take sides is a burning reality in the minds of the people.

'For the European colonists, too, there is a grave choice— whether fully to accept the loyal coloureds as their allies and fellow-citizens. I could put it like this: either they must show sincere gratitude, or else for ever after distrust all those who cannot claim pure European descent and suppress them as permanent subordinates. I much fear that they may choose the second course. Yesterday, in conversation with young Thomas Muller, a burgher who fled from the Sundays River Valley, I realised that for him only whites and non-whites existed—the latter term, which I had not heard before, being a collective name for the many kinds of coloured people—and that there would always be separation between the two, just as eternal enmity between Jew and non-Jew had been ordained by the Old Testament. For me these were strange words to come from a young man who looks as if he himself could not be of pure European descent, although he is always dressed, like a prominent citizen, in a satin waistcoat and trousers of the latest cut. Furthermore, he is one of those colonists who never address a Hottentot with a gentle word, but are always intent on asserting themselves as the superiors, as the white men . . .'

Lindstrom sighed, scratched his head, and at last laid down his pen to take up his spyglass and go for a walk through the village of wagons and tents. Everywhere, at open fires, women were busy preparing the lunch of griddle-cake, meat and weak coffee, and old men were standing around hoping for a chat or, perhaps, a fill from a generous tobacco-pouch. As he often did, Lindstrom walked to the raised fortress wall with its wide view. He held the spyglass to his right eye, examining the valley and surrounding mountain slopes. There were several thousands of cattle and sheep which the herdsmen had to drive out every day, though never too far from the laager; and, of course, there were often quarrels about the pasture which was getting scantier every day. On a high isolated hill a Hottentot scout, known for his eagle eyes, sat watching too.

The green winter landscape lay clear in the pale sunlight and he saw nothing suspicious. But to the west, where the wagon-road curved round the slope, a little more than a gunshot away, an unusual scene drew his attention. Two or three horsemen were urging their horses to a gallop so as to catch up with a man on foot and halt threateningly around him. When he trained his spyglass on this pedestrian he thought he recognised the Hottentot half-caste, Douw Prins. He had refused to come with Tielman, why should he be here now? And without his horse or gun? It seemed the horsemen were refusing him entry to the laager; one had even taken his gun into his hands.

Lindstrom lowered the spyglass and hurried in that direction. In front of him the voices became louder, angrier. He started running.

It was Douw Prins, standing erect amongst the horsemen, and the burgher pointing his gun at him was the impetuous Thomas Muller.

'Wait, he's no spy,' Lindstrom panted, 'I know him, he's Douw Prins!'

'I know him too!' young Muller said vehemently. 'He's a cheeky bastard who rode transport for the Hottentot vermin and insulted Fieldcornet Scheepers and me. It won't help him to play the innocent! I say we must shoot him here, on the spot!'

'Bring him before the fieldcornet,' Lindstrom proposed, 'so the matter can be cleared up.'

The other two burghers agreed at once, perhaps ruffled by Muller's unreasonable passion.

In the presence of the fieldcornet the young burgher repeated that Douw could not be trusted, while Douw explained how Dawid Stuurman's gang had robbed him of his gun and horse and how he had come to serve in the commando and win back his property. His neck stiff and his words jerky, he looked the fieldcornet straight in the eyes. Lindstrom saw that the growing number of bystanders disliked Douw's utter lack of apparent fear or submissiveness. As calmly as he could, Lindstrom explained what he knew of Douw, and tried to clinch the matter by declaring that he had full confidence in him and was prepared to lend him his extra horse and gun so that he could bear arms against the enemy.

'Thank you very much, Mynheer Lindstrom. I want to ride with Tielman Roux,' Douw added. It was noticeable that he had not addressed any other man as 'Sieur' or even 'Mynheer'.

'I know about you,' the fieldcornet, a corpulent man, nodded. 'My shepherds tell me you've started farming up near Spitskop.'

'Yes, I call my place Prinshoop. In the spring I'll go to Swellendam to get my letter of tenure.'

The fieldcornet's eyes narrowed like those of the other burghers, but he was more concerned over the fact that Dawid Stuurman's robbers had already crossed the Keurbooms and were overrunning the Outeniqua area. Dawid Stuurman, the perfidious brute who boasted of having murdered a former employer by means of poison. He wondered how many men were with Stuurman; then said aloud: 'We'll have to go and look. You can help us track him down.'

That settled the matter, except for Thomas Muller, who looked with undisguised hatred at the cheeky coloured man. As they turned away and Douw for a moment returned the young burgher's violent gaze, Lindstrom realised with a shock how similar the two young men were. They were both about the same size, slender and sinewy, but it was not so much their build as the watchfulness of their eyes, making them look perpetually on their guard, as if expecting some kind of unpleasant surprise or humiliation. Both seemed afraid of what other people could do to them.

At Lindstrom's wagons Douw thanked his benefactor in a stuttering voice. The rest of the afternoon he stayed morosely to one side, busying himself with cleaning the borrowed gun and fastening a strap to an old powderhorn. Later he walked into the veld to inspect the horse.

In the early evening the burgher patrol returned from guarding the Government Post in Plettenberg Bay and the bank of the Keurbooms River; the fieldcornet had sent a message that he needed more men for next day's patrol against Dawid Stuurman. Tielman Roux was with them.

'Evening, man,' he greeted Douw.

Douw did not know what to do with his smile or his hands.

'I came after all.'

'Man, I'm glad. I'm only sorry you had such a silly reception.'

'I want to ride with you.'

'Of course; how else?'

Then Lindstrom arrived with mugs of wine.

'We meet again and we must celebrate. Come on, Douw, tonight you drink with us. Even if it's only a toast to Tielman who has fallen in love and wants to stay in Plettenberg Bay for ever!'

'Who is she?'

'A widow with seven children,' Lindstrom said teasingly.

It was a cold night and there was only one small fire for everyone; servants and all crowded closer to the warming barrel of wine. Douw explained what had happened to him. When Tielman wanted to know what had occurred between him and Muller at their previous meeting in February near Gouritz, Douw's voice became embarrassed. Then he tried to joke: 'I nearly turned back to join Stuurman.'

The young burgher looked at the ground: 'And why didn't you?'

'I have too much respect for you.'

Douw emptied his mug, and added, with a bitter laugh: 'Lafleur's kind talk of freedom, but to them freedom means lawless violence and bloodshed. Then a man isn't free at all.'

Tielman remained silent, and Lindstrom who knew of his high esteem for the sallow Graaff-Reinet burgher who so much disliked Douw put in:

'When is a man free?'

'When he can count on the respect of his fellow-men.' His eyes said: When you whites do not emasculate a man in your thoughts to a Hottentot or half-caste.

Unexpectedly the thin-lipped Barend Ockers spoke up: 'These days many of our Afrikaners are trekking to the north, towards the Great River, where one can still be one's own boss in the wilderness. I would have trekked, too, if there hadn't been so many crooked souls up there. Men like Jager Afrikaner whose only law is murder and bloodshed. No, that road, too, is full of thorns.'

'Yes,' the Swede nodded sombrely, 'trekking is running away. If you people of the Cape cannot get on with each other, here and now, where will you be able to?'

Now Tielman looked sullen; always this kind of talk had to come between him and Douw. He got up to go with the excuse that he had promised to say good night to a friend. By the time he returned the sentries were being posted and everybody had to be silent.

Before dawn the commando set off up the mountain towards Paardekop. The fieldcornet had ordered the people left at the laager to be on the alert and to keep the trek-oxen at least near the wagons in case of a sudden alarm. But the whole day they heard no gun-fire and nothing happened.

At noon the next day Lindstrom was surprised to hear a wagon come bumping and jolting down the hill with a bunch of cows, calves and goats following behind; Douw's wagon, he saw, with Ouma Katryn, Ruth, old Speelman and a young bewildered Bushman. Ouma Katryn and her people were overjoyed to meet Lindstrom again, but also sad at leaving their house and garden. The members of the commando had sent them down. Since Douw had joined them Stuurman's bloodthirsty henchmen would seek to take revenge on his people.

They were still recounting how, the night before, they had had to find room for the whole commando to bed down under the lean-to, when shouts were heard: 'They're shooting!' Southwards, in the direction of Die Poort on the Cape wagon-road, sporadic volleys of shots resounded. The firing went on for an hour. Old men went around congratulating each other on these sounds of battle: surely the commando had flushed out Stuurman and Congwa's villains and had shot them to pieces?

But when the sun sank to the mountain ridges, the alarm was unexpectedly raised. The cattle kraal outside the laager was going up in flames.

Panic-stricken, the people rushed around, nearly shooting at their own Hottentots. Where could the enemy be? Why hadn't the dogs barked? Meanwhile a troop of Hottentot horsemen came swiftly round the left side of the mountain while a whole impi of Kaffirs rose from the thickets between the laager and the herdsmen. In a wide semi-circle they drove off the more distant cattle.

Every woman and child ran to the fortified house. Greybeards fell flat to fire from between the foremost wagons, while the handful of able-bodied men grabbed the nearest horses and set off in pursuit. Ahead of them the enemy Hottentots dismounted to fire, then flung themselves back into the saddle, repeating this tactic often enough to give the Kaffirs time to drive off their booty. It was soon clear that that was all the attackers wanted, but there were far too few men to pursue them so late in the day. It was getting dark in the mountains and to follow would be an impossibility. Impotent, they had to watch the robbers get away with several hundred cattle. One Hottentot herdsman was stabbed by assegais.

An hour later the commando returned, now realising how cleverly the raid had been planned. At Die Poort the Kaffirs had kept on showing themselves on the fringe of the forest and had led the burghers ever farther to the west, through thickets where horses were of no use, finally disappearing in the green maze. One black warrior had been killed but that was all.

Tired and disheartened Tielman and Douw arrived at the Swede's fire where the two women got ready warm water for washing, coffee and food. Douw sat worrying about Prinshoop, left to the mercy of the barbarians and wild animals, while Tielman's face was sombre for another reason. His gloom was justified for hardly had they sat down before the young burgher from Graaff-Reinet walked over with two other men.

'Mynheer Lindstrom,' Thomas Muller said loudly, 'do you still trust this cheeky scum whom you protect? After today's ambush? Don't you think he's hand in glove with the enemy?'

'The enemy must have seen you coming yesterday,' was Lindstrom's opinion, 'and made their plans accordingly.'

'Well, I think he's a treacherous spy! We must take him behind the kraal wall! At once!'

These brutal words brought a silence round the fire. Douw's mouth crumpled helplessly as if he might break out into uncontrollable anger at this new injustice. Then his head jerked aside, pathetic, like a child's about to cry. But now he faced Ruth, Ruth's eyes bravely and faithfully encouraging him, the eyes of Ruth who once already had said: Your self-respect is also my self-respect.

And before her, from her who did not possess the least racial pride, he won the self-possession to rise and look calmly at Thomas Muller and find the words which a man must say under such circumstances: 'It is true that your war is not my war. But I'm no spy. I'll prove that your accusation is a lie. Listen. The robbers came to raid our cattle. They'll come again. It's stupid to sit here waiting for them to ruin us utterly. We have to go over to the attack. We know they always retreat to their strongholds in the Tzitzikamma mountains where they hide the captured animals. It's dangerous to pursue them there. But it's exactly what they would never expect now they think they have scared the Christians. So I propose that we go there with a commando and take back our cattle. Then you'll see if I'm a spy; if I work for the robbers who robbed me, too.'

The sallow burgher looked taken aback, then scornfully asked: 'So you could lead us into a worse ambush?'

'I've never been in the Tzitzikamma. I'll ride in front if you're too scared.'

The bystanders drew in their breath, not only because the Tzitzikamma was a deadly place. Even Tielman, who had previously stared at the ground rather than at Douw, now looked at Muller. The latter hesitated before he said curtly: 'If enough men want to risk it, I'll risk it too. That doesn't mean that I trust somebody like you. What war are you fighting if you're not fighting our war?'

'I fight to get back my gun and horse.'

'But we fight to clear this country of vermin so we Christians can live in peace!'

Like two furious cocks they faced each other.

At this Tielman came forward uncomfortably and said: 'I'll ride to the Tzitzikamma. What do you say, men?' he continued, to the two burghers, who did not like this quarrel between a half-caste and a white man.

'Don't let's be over-hasty. We'll first have to persuade Jerling to be our guide. He knows all the bush tracks; only last month he and Callender went quite a way into the Tzitzikamma.'

'We must first approach the fieldcornet,' the other added, and stood aside so that young Muller's blonde wife could reach her husband. She had come to call him for supper.

If Douw's and Muller's vehemence towards each other had seemed exaggerated and inexplicable to the other people around the fire, it was apparently less so to Ouma Katryn. A tender smile hovered over her old face when she rose to say reproachfully yet fondly to young Muller: 'Thomas! Thomas, why are you so quick-tempered? Have you forgotten your father and mother already? Have you forgotten your grandfather and grandmother too?'

The bystanders paid little attention to this apparent raving from the old crone with the white hair, but the young man clearly

did. His face turned ashy grey and his eyes stared at Ouma
Katryn as if he were seeing a ghost. Only then did Lindstrom
suspect why Douw and Thomas looked so like each other and
why Ouma Katryn's face radiated such loving joy. She had
traced a member of her family.

Without taking any further part in the discussion about the
proposed patrol, young Thomas put his arm round his young
wife and led her away. His head still defiantly erect, Douw
watched his persecutor go; his eyes saw a white man, not a
cousin.

The next day was entirely occupied by preparations for the
punitive commando. Many burghers opposed the project, and
the fieldcornet decided that participation should be voluntary.
The result was that only four burghers were ready to go, while
the others offered a dozen or so Hottentots and half-castes to go
in their stead. At last Jerling's plea that attack was better than
mouldering in the laager had the desired effect, and more men
offered to go. Of Lindstrom's people, Barend Ockers and Jan
Karieka also volunteered; Karieka because he had already been in
the Tzitzikamma, far beyond Formosa peak. Finally seven
burghers were chosen: Jerling, Kritzinger, Mouton, Ferreira,
young Botha, Tielman Roux and Thomas Muller; and three half-
castes: Douw Prins, Dirk Philander and Barend Ockers; ten
mounted Christians as well as seven Hottentots, all in all seventeen men, each armed with a gun. No more could go: the laager
needed defenders. It was a small commando but suitable for
scouting and swift surprise attacks through the wild Tzitzikamma's forests and gorges. To remain unseen and unheard they
would not hunt and would only light fires after dark inside
thickets. Each man was provided with fifty rounds of shot,
bedding, and food for eight days; the latter could be loaded on
the pack horses. Though an elderly man, Jacob Jerling would be
in command, since he already had had several expeditions in that
area to his credit. They would depart at dawn.

Lindstrom wanted to go too but the fieldcornet sternly refused:
'We're not going to look for plants, Mynheer. We have to be
able to rely utterly on every man. It's my opinion that one can

only count on a man when he fights for his country and his loved ones.'

Though Lindstrom hardly saw them that day, the faces of a few women kept wandering restlessly beneath the surface of his thoughts: Ruth, who knew that Douw was the cause of this dangerous patrol; Ouma Katryn, friendly in a sad kind of way as she stood asking Anna Muller about their hardships on the frontier. Great-grandmother Katryn asked if she could hold the lovely baby for a moment; the young mother's respect for the older woman was shown by her hesitant arms and big, questioning eyes.

12

The sea's eastern rim slowly paled to mother-of-pearl while the line of men and horses hurried past just inside the water's edge along the beach. Between high red rocks and the shell-rich caves they swung left, keeping to the shallow side of the lagoon, where the forest path yawned indigo underneath a fringe of monkey ropes. Two Hottentot scouts went ahead; then followed the men with their horses and the three Hottentots leading the pack horses with the provisions, and lastly two more Hottentots who covered their rear and swept away their tracks. No man spoke, no enemy could have seen or heard how and where the Tzitzikamma forest had swallowed the commando.

For hours on end they weaved their way between trunks, roots and vines, on a path that belonged more to the past and to wandering forest creatures, than to hurried human beings. Sometimes there were deep ravines but mostly the path wound upwards, towards the coastal mountains. Not much farther, Jerling encouraged them, soon they would be on a high shelf, six or seven hundred feet above the sea, where there would be long stretches of open country, easy to ride over. At a stream, where enormous purple dragonflies whirred their wings unhindered, they swallowed cold food and water and took out tinder-boxes and pipes. There was something in the ubiquitous, apparently endless forest that made the men whisper even now.

When the sun started to gleam high up, through the roof of leaves, they unexpectedly came out on a nearly forgotten land-scape; an open grassy sward with, to the left, the green ribs of the mountain on which darker stripes announced the deep, difficult ravines and, to the right, the blue floor of the ocean. The scouts spread out; from now on the commando had to have eyes to all sides. Yet they must advance as fast as possible. Sometimes the forest swallowed them again, so completely that they forgot the colour of blue sky. Because of the confusing game paths they kept moving more or less due east; to deviate towards mountain or sea would not have helped much because there it was steeper and denser still.

Wherever there was no path, the forest became a torture; a merciless refrain of trees fallen down in the most impossible places, rotten wood that unexpectedly gave way beneath their feet, sharp sticks tormenting their legs, branches tearing their clothes or catching on gun straps, and often pockets of mud where their feet stuck fast and the horses balked. Grumbling and cursing did not help. Jerling and Ferreira insisted that speed and surprise was their only hope of success. That way they could also stay ahead of any pursuers.

The first sign of human existence which they met came when the scout on the mountain side stopped short and pointed to the flattened earth. Here a big herd of cattle had passed, towards the east. No earlier than yesterday, the trackers agreed. They also found bare-footed spoor. Kaffirs. Would it be their own cattle, driven in a great curve higher up across the Keurbooms? And would there once more be a path to follow?

However much they might be hurrying to surprise the enemy they, and especially their animals, had to have time to rest and remain fresh. The sun was still high when they put the horses to graze. In a clearing away from the path, hidden behind trees, they held a council of war. Jerling and Karieka told all they knew of the country ahead, and then everyone else was free to speak. They had to stay close together and take care that nobody saw them on the journey back—about that all were agreed.

'And if we come to blows with groups of the enemy,' Ferreira added grimly, 'we have to see that nobody lives to tell the tale.' He was an intrepid, cold-blooded man in his prime who had served in several fighting commandos in the Suurveld, so the younger ones were not affronted when he added slightingly: 'Why do you pull such faces? You raw cubs, blood is going to flow. And the trip back will be the toughest of all! You're going to learn what standing together means!'

It was true that the men were still unsure of each other and of each other's courage. Around the camp-fire, which they only lit when it was dark and the smoke could not be seen, they sat in a close, dour circle trying to warm body and spirit. The seven white burghers got the best seats and the first coffee. The young Graaff-Reineter had acted the whole day as if Douw did not exist, while Tielman looked depressed, and had nothing to say to Douw in the presence of the others. Douw sat, with proud eyes, watching the embers in the fire.

It was still night when they started the morning stage. Again there was no path and a cold west wind blew showers of rain against their backs. The worst part was the wet grass and branches, dispensing icy baths, especially to the Hottentots in front. The clouds thinned later, though, and the landscape opened so they could progress more swiftly. After another of the eternal, abysmal valleys, they got a view of mighty Formosa peak to their left. The burghers were amazed that this lovely, well-watered region did not have a single inhabitant. The Tzitzikamma was clearly a wilderness inaccessible to ox-wagons, but just think what a man with enterprise could start around here? Jan Karieka told them about Damon, a run-away Negro slave who, according to reports, had been living for years all on his own in the forest on this side of Storms River.

Towards noon, when they reached the edge of a strip of forest, the foremost scout stopped with raised hand. Ahead, in a clearing, a man was busy dragging poles to a half-completed fence around a garden. He was coal-black, in clothes of skin, no lazy barbarian, for his wooden hut was trim and big and a water-furrow ran across the large patch of land which he had deforested and planted with fruit trees, vegetables, tobacco and wheat. Quite alone!

The men did not move as they stared at this strange Damon. How could a man, a black slave at that, so far from the country of his birth, live all alone with such diligence and courage? Did he love his freedom that much? Though it was only a strange, black man, the sight moved Douw profoundly, like a vision of his own Prinshoop, his own paradise where he wanted to flee the whole world. In such loneliness?

Ferreira turned to Jerling. Slowly the latter shook his head; this Damon was no barbarian canaille.

The commando rode from the forest, surrounding the slave who stood rooted to the spot.

'Can you keep your mouth shut?'

There was only fear in the hermit's eyes, but he nodded.

'Then you can live. But you haven't seen us, you know nothing about us. Do you understand?'

The black man nodded once more, bursting out in a mixture of broken Malay-Portuguese and Dutch to prove that he had understood. His voice was hoarse, and stumbled as if he had not spoken for a long time.

'How many? Kaffirs? Hottentots? How long ago?'

Jerling pointed to the cattle tracks still visible against the forest's edge, even after the rain.

Damon gestured to show how far the sun had moved on—three or four hours—and counted the number of Kaffirs on his fingers: fourteen or fifteen.

'Get a branch and wipe out our tracks.'

When the commando rode slowly away, the lonely Damon showed such gratitude, such a sense of servile obligation, that he actually ran to get the branch with which to wipe away their tracks. Fear had made him a slave once more. Douw turned his eyes away, spurring on his horse.

'Did you see he had even made his own earthenware pots?' he

heard Tielman ask beside him, but he could only answer with a smile: it was as if words would have said something too poignantly ineffable about himself.

About two hours later they saw the raiders and the cattle for the first time, milling upwards against the steep opposite bank of the Storms River. It would take the commando a full half-hour to cross the rough ravine and the afternoon shadows were already lengthening. Early next day would be a better time to attack.

'Don't show yourselves,' someone hissed.

Quickly they deliberated. The Kaffirs were most likely driving the cattle to some safe place where Stuurman and Congwa's robbers retreated after their raids. A strong force of mounted rebels might even be in the neighbourhood. Ferreira, however, insisted that they should overtake the Kaffirs and surprise them from the front. Excited and anxious about the fighting which awaited them, the young men did not say much. That evening Tielman unrolled his blanket close to Douw's.

He did it from loyalty, for he had not liked the way in which the young Graaff-Reineter had spoken to him about Douw. Thomas Muller had looked for some time as if he had wanted to say something, and finally had approached him as he stood sentinel in the twilight hour.

'This . . . Hottentot of yours,' he wanted to know, 'is that old girl with the grey hair his grandmother?'

'Yes, he calls her Ouma Katryn.'

'Ouma Katryn what?'

'Her surname? I'm not sure. I think I heard Arendse.'

'Arendse?'

'Yes.'

'Where do they come from?'

'From the Koo area. From a farm called Sandfontein. The farmer is called Meyer, I think . . .'

After this Thomas kept looking at the ground as if he already knew all he wanted.

'And the black girl with them?' he asked, with a new vehemence.

'She's Ruth. She's the abandoned child of a black slave by

126

a maid-servant apparently half Hottentot and half Javanese. Ouma Katryn reared her as her adopted daughter. Why do you ask?'

'Just curious. I'm wondering how you could be so intimate with a pack of Hottentots.'

'Hottentots? They're no Hottentots!' Tielman became annoyed. 'Why do you call Douw a Hottentot? He's much more of a half-white.'

The word half-white made young Muller sneer: 'It's not fitting for a white man to be so friendly with a cheeky Bastaard! One can't trust a single one of them.'

Dismayed, Tielman began to stutter: 'But . . . but . . . Douw's an honest man. I know him well!'

'Well? You soft Bolanders still have to learn that if you let go one finger's width, you've already lost the whole hand.'

'Damn it, man, are you preaching at me?'

At this young Muller shrugged his shoulders and walked off. Tielman was the more upset because he had considered Thomas to be a hero ever since the time he had raced through the British lines at Mossel Bay.

The next day there followed more murderous patches of forest and precipitous gorges which they had to pass so as to get around and ahead of the Kaffirs. They and their exhausted horses were allowed only a short half-hour of rest. Ferreira and Kritzinger's opinion won the day: they must press ahead to the robbers' hideout; they should not only bring back the stolen cattle, but hurt the vermin as seriously as possible.

Unasked Douw gave his opinion: yes, they must surround the hide-out, and surprise the ruffians so as to avoid unnecessary bloodshed.

'There will be fighting in any case,' Jerling curtly silenced him.

'He's shivering in his pants,' Muller remarked, with a loud laugh.

The narrow plateau between the Tzitzikamma mountains and the sea opened up, with sour grass and heathy scrub where the horses could advance much faster. Yet continually they had to seek cover, which amounted to choosing the worst and densest terrain. The men grumbled, but with the enemy both in front and behind them, such precautions were necessary.

The morning stage brought them to a little river where they could rest for lunch. The men were lying tired and sullen in the shade beside the water when the Hottentots, scouting ahead to the next ridge, came back in a hurry. The hideout of the robbers was just ahead of them, in the next valley.

The men quickly took a bite, lay back for a moment, and then cautiously mounted the opposite slope. In the fold of the earth, below a rocky hill, lay a Hottentot kraal. The enclosures for the livestock were big and, in the meadows and on the surrounding slopes, grazed mighty herds of horned cattle and flocks of sheep. Sharp eyes took in all the particulars: the dozen or more reed huts, the horses behind the paddock, the shepherds, young boys, farther away with the flocks, the few women and children still stirring around the huts. It was the warm, lazy midday hour— the best hour to surprise these indolent people. Would there be men sleeping inside the huts or were there only women and children? Were all the men still away raiding the Longkloof at their leisure, or with Stuurman's troops around the Keurbooms valley?

'Look, they've got imported Dutch cattle, too,' a burgher whispered, 'they must be stolen.' Karieka even claimed that he could see where tails and ears had been cut short so as to wipe out the brands of former owners.

Jerling and Ferreira took quick decisions. Even though the Kaffirs behind them might hear, they would attack at once. Two Hottentots were to stay with the led horses, while seven men stole round the back of the hill. As soon as they were in position, the remaining horsemen would charge along the valley. Everybody had to stay out of sight behind the crest of the rise until Karieka, with the seven sharpshooters, gave the call of a pheasant. Then the attack would be swift.

As the men disappeared behind rocks or bushes, the eight horsemen sat, their guns on their right thighs, checking that their bullet bags were ready and their powder-horns hung right. Licking his continually drying lips, Tielman peeped at the veterans, Ferreira, Kritzinger and Philander, with their hard falcon eyes, at Douw sitting so erect in his saddle, at Muller bending forward as if he were already charging. His heart was beating so loud that he never heard the pheasant, only Jerling's hoarse:

'Now!'

Then Vonk jerked forward with the other horses, swerving over the uneven ground, their hooves one thunderous drumming once they were down the slope and charging across the black turf of the valley. Ahead the circle of huts loomed ever bigger. Women and children swarmed out of them, like ants from brown ant-heaps. One could not hear their screams above the thunder of the hooves. Suddenly white smoke puffed from the door of a hut, making Botha's horse wildly twitch up its head. Above, on the rocky hillside, another white puff showed. Without anybody having given the order, the horsemen, too, fired from their saddles, in an instant clearing the street between the huts. When they reined in their ploughing horses, trying to see where the sharpshooters could be, dust clouds billowed over two or three bodies on the smooth, trodden earth. There was a smell of dust, gunpowder and sour, anxious sweat. Men dismounted, pushed gun-muzzles into huts. Another shot resounded.

'There!' Tielman yelled. An armed Hottentot burst from the back of a hut, racing down behind a fence to where horses milled in a bunch, towards a stallion whose roan colour proclaimed that its dam or sire had been one of the recently imported Arabs. Douw had already seen him, perhaps had been looking for just such a chance, and was pounding after him. Tielman spurred on Vonk, racing to help. By now the Hottentot was among the horses, trying to get the roan. To Tielman it seemed as if Douw fell off his horse on top of the Hottentot, gasping for air with protruding teeth as he tried to switch round his gun. Tielman did not know where to fire. The next moment the Hottentot rolled like a bunched-up ant-eater, shot out arms and legs as he landed in the thicket below and ran into the bushy valley. Tielman aimed at him but got no chance to shoot: perhaps part of his stomach was fleeing together with the man. Then he turned to

Douw who had had a hard fall but was now succeeding in calming the roan stallion. Panting, Douw held the gun high for Tielman to see and triumphantly patted the roan's neck. They were now his.

'Why did you let the snake get away?' Kritzinger bellowed, as he came storming along.

It was a dangerous moment needing a soothing answer, but Douw hardly hesitated before he replied: 'I only wanted these.'

'You scoundrel, you can't think only of yourself! You have to think of the safety of the whole commando!'

'There was no time to shoot,' Tielman said.

Behind them somebody screamed horribly. Another Hottentot had been dragged from a hut. As they ran over, they saw how one of the commando's Hottentots, Witbooi, raised his gun on Ferreira's command and summarily shot the yellow man. They could not dream of taking prisoners yet Witbooi was overcome by sickness as he was reloading his gun and fell on his knees to vomit. Even Ferreira turned away.

The men piled all the muzzle-loaders, saddles and ammunition which they had found in the open clearing between the huts. It was quite an arsenal, proving the kraal's guilt, and suggesting strongly that the absent Hottentot men were away on another murderous raid. In one of the huts they also came upon an elderly white man who had slept through the din; dirty and slovenly, but clearly a white man with sea-blue eyes.

'What are you doing amongst the heathens?' Ferreira angrily asked this feckless character.

Reluctantly the white man told him that he had long ago deserted from the Dutch army, in the days of Governor Van de Graaf, and had been living here ever since in peace and quiet. It was many years since he had had a gun in his hands. He looked the part; a grey wreck of a man whose only love was sleep.

'Have you no longer any respect for your white skin?'

No, that did not interest him.

'Sies! I hope you don't consider yourself a Christian any more!' Ferreira scornfully flung at him. No one took any further notice of this down-and-out; they had to hurry, and had more than enough to do with the women and the livestock. While the majority of the men rounded up the horses and selected the best and youngest heifers, cows and oxen, the strongest animals who would not get footsore and lag behind along the road, Ferreira, Jerling and some others stood guard beside the guns and saddles. They had to put up with the moaning and wailing of the women. Not only had two of their men been killed; overwhelmed with grief one woman held up her dead child before the white men.

'Are you fighting women and children, too?' her voice shrilled over and over again.

Ferreira ignored her at first. Then he wrathfully pointed at the silk dresses and elegant shawls and bonnets which she and the other women were wearing. 'Those come from the burnt-down farms where your men have murdered Christian people. We're fighting robbers and murderers!'

'You are robbers and murderers, too! You are robbers and murderers, too!'

Beside himself, Ferreira raised his gun.

'If you don't shut up, we'll burn down every hut and shoot till you're silent!'

Jan Karieka cracked his long whip with an echoing boom that enforced respect.

But, at the two most distant huts, silence could not be enforced. They were rough, temporary huts of branches and unbleached matting, looking as if they had been erected recently. There, a number of more or less naked Kaffir women still wailed with shrill, drawn-out cries; undoubtedly the women of the raiders who were about to arrive with the stolen livestock.

However much Jerling and the others tried, these black women did not understand either reason or Dutch and continued to gargle long howling yells, as strange as the wild, sweetish smell of their deep bronze-brown skins, as strange as their speech and clothing.

'You don't belong here! Get out! Go back to Kaffirland!' Ferreira yelled in their language; and then in Dutch: 'Burn down the two huts and chase them away!'

When the women clutched their bundles but refused to go,

the hot-headed Thomas Muller swung a sjambok to hurry them along. Jerling stayed his hand: 'Man, they're women after all!'

Amid clouds of dust and suffocating swirls of smoke the commando got the lead and pack horses coupled and started driving the herd of cattle to the west, as quickly as possible back to Keurbooms. Cattle that dropped out would have to stay behind. They did not even think of taking the slow-moving sheep along but merely slaughtered two as fresh meat. Long before dark they would have to tackle the Kaffirs. They had to get far away before a superior force of Hottentot horsemen came through the pass and overpowered them in their turn.

Only then did Tielman feel how his hands trembled, how tense he had been. He laughed exaggeratedly when Jerling made a joke:

'Hey, men, won't this later be called the Battle of the Women?'

Other men laughed, too; after their baptism of fire the commando, for the first time, felt the unity of a group which could count on every member, a comradeliness born from violence and blood. But nobody spoke to Douw as he rode on his new horse with his new gun over his pommel. Tielman could see that Douw was painfully aware of the disapproval of the others, including the other two half-castes. He felt very worried when he saw the glance of hate which Thomas Muller shot at Douw and remembered how the merciless Thomas had made a young herd-boy grovel before he consented to spare his life. And that had only been a child! What made Thomas be so harsh towards everyone with a brown skin? But then why was Douw, too, so difficult and so fanatical about his dignity when other people were around?

Tielman saw again how Witbooi had thrown down his gun and fallen to his knees, his mouth jerking, and how, when his own eyes shied away, he had noticed Thomas Muller looking down at the Hottentot with the tiny round hole in his forehead, looking down as if he were shuddering and yet wanted to store up in his memory every spasm of the dying man.

Tielman felt such aversion that he spurred Vonk into a crazy race towards Douw, pretending to attack his friend: 'Give it back! It's my horse and my gun! Mine!' With pleasure he saw that Douw defended himself with the same hysterical fun and that some of the other men were laughing too.

'Quiet! You know we're riding down-wind.'

Now that the ardour of the fray was past, Jerling had once more become the commander. He sent two Hottentot scouts ahead to see how far the Kaffirs had advanced. The horsemen pressed the cattle forward, rarely giving them a chance to get a mouthful by the way; the animals were fat and over-fed as it was. But nobody raised his voice to drive the animals on; they had become silent in anticipation of the new battle.

When the Hottentots came racing back, the whole commando halted. Jan Karieka hurriedly reported that the Kaffirs were approaching hardly a mile ahead. They had smelled trouble, for they kept to the edge of the forest and close to the precipices on the seaward side.

'A Kaffir is always scared of the open plain,' Ferreira nodded. Jerling told the four Hottentots, who were the best herdsmen, to follow slowly with the cattle and the pack horses. 'Stay in the open.' Then the rest of the commando spurred on their steeds.

'Left. Keep left, along the edge of the bush.'

Ahead of them, across a shallow dip filled by protea scrub, horns and shoulders showed a moment against the sky before milling sharply to the left, driven along by figures running like erect, black ants, shrilling and yelling, beating and stabbing with their assegais to goad the animals still faster. Hooves thundered once more, hearts raced.

'Head them off! That bush is too dense for our horses!'

The foremost men fired a few random shots to frighten the cattle away from the forest side but, when they reached the first trees, the great mass of the herd burst through them, bellowing with pain with two rows of Kaffirs bent low, running alongside. Ferreira, who had experience of such matters, intercepted the hindmost cattle to drive them away from the forest edge and then swiftly dismounted to throw his horse's rein over a broken branch and follow at a run.

'Keep behind me! Stay together! And don't shoot blindly, every time a man has to reload, he's in mortal danger!'

There was no time to shrink back. The underbrush between the trees did not look too dense, though, and they could see for many yards between the trunks. This was the country the Kaffirs preferred to fight in, but weren't they on the run already? And not one man in the commando wanted to lose a chance to re-capture so many fine cattle. The men ran as a group, watching on all sides, their guns at the ready. To their right there were cracks and thuds where cattle burst through, or rushed back past them. Suddenly Ferreira's gun bellowed. Ahead of them, a black figure bounded from a curtain of leaves and tumbled down. More shots rang out. Nervously the men aimed all around them, or blindly fired at anything which moved. Ahead of them the ground began to slope steeply down into one of those dangerous ravines where one had to keep one's eyes on one's feet, and an enemy could surprise one with a swift stab of his assegai, an enemy as dark as the shadows of the forest itself.

'You fools, save your ammunition!' Ferreira shouted.

'The animals are going to break their legs down this cliff,' a man panted, when an assegai whistled from a patch of bush and cleaved the right arm of one of the burghers, Mouton.

'Stop here!' Ferreira bellowed. 'Sharply to the right, now. Turn aside as many cattle as you can and drive them back.'

Suddenly, without apparent reason, the men felt they were in danger. They rushed at the spate of animals, yelling and waving their arms, so that the stampeding, horn-clashing beasts would turn back. Tielman glanced over his shoulder, fearful because the men no longer formed a compact group. He noticed Thomas Muller running behind Douw and raced to keep up with them.

Then there were no more cattle, and they could relax. Barend and the wounded Mouton went after the cattle, while the rest of the commando covered the rear, spreading out to collect stray animals. Tielman felt that he was proving his calibre as a warrior by covering Douw's and Muller's rear. But why were they so careless? Were they competing with each other to see who would venture farther into danger, far away from the rest of the commando? Were they crazy? He was extremely nervous when he stumbled over a dead branch on to a bundle of scattered assegais. His eyes darted around him. The other men were completely out of sight, far to the right. Abruptly a single shot thundered ahead of him. Where Douw and Thomas were!

When he rushed forward, around a fallen tree, he saw Douw crouching down to look at a Kaffir with a gaping wound in his chest from which blood welled with every gasping breath. His gun muzzle was still smoking. But what brought Tielman to a paralysed stop was the sight of Thomas Muller running up from one side, an assegai in his hand. He raised the weapon ever higher, its sharp tip aimed at Douw. Not at the twitching Kaffir, at Douw.

Tielman shuddered. It was as if he had to battle with himself before he could leap forward and call Douw's name. Then Douw looked up, seeing Thomas with the assegai. And while Douw came erect, Thomas's arm slowly trembled lower, till the assegai slipped from his fingers to bury itself in the ground between the black body and Douw. Thomas's face was distorted, like that of a man weeping, as he mumbled: 'How does one keep this away from you?'

Grey in the face, Douw could only look.

Rage took hold of Tielman, making him yell: 'Dammit, why do you stand like that! We're alone here in the bush! Come on, let's get out!'

After the skirmish in the forest, the commando was richer by a hundred and seventy cattle and, together with the three hundred from the Hottentot hideout, they drove back a big herd to Keurbooms. More than two hundred to make good the losses of the people at the laager and twelve for each member of the commando's seventeen men, as well as a share in the horses, guns and saddles. Because Douw had claimed the desirable roan stallion, he got the fewest and weakest cattle.

'Let's press on,' Jerling ordered, 'the sooner we're out of the Tzitzikamma, the better for our health.'

That night the commando's circle of watchfires burnt near the hairy gash in the earth made by Storms River and the evening after that on the coastal plateau past Bloukrans. Only one more day and they would taste the triumph of letting the exhausted animals swim the Keurbooms. A heavy shower of rain aided them by washing out their tracks and making pursuit extremely difficult.

The men were too occupied with the animals to have much time for talk, yet Tielman noticed how deliberately Thomas Muller now avoided him and Douw. During the long hours in the saddle or while he led Vonk along the forest paths, he relived the brutal experiences of the past days: the wailing women, Witbooi hunched beside the Hottentot's corpse, even more, the assegai in Thomas's hand, his strange, screwed-up face, and the words that had sounded so irrelevant: 'How does one keep this away from you?' Keep what away? The assegai? But why did he want to stab Douw with it? So that others could believe it had been done by a Kaffir?

Tielman was scared when he thought of Thomas. It was not normal to hate like that. Or had he only imagined the scene over the warrior's body, or understood it wrongly? It worried him so much that he felt after a time that he must go and discuss it like a man, not only brood over it like a child; discuss it not with Douw but with Thomas.

The evening at Bloukrans he went to where Thomas was taking his turn at sentry duty. 'Have you still got something against Douw?' he asked, straight out. 'Are you still convinced he is a spy?'

By the light of a nearby fire Tielman could see clearly what he had only vaguely sensed before; more than anything else, Thomas's rancour was fear. Fear of what? His sun-bronzed head was motionless while his eyes kept darting around Tielman.

'Did he talk to you about me?' he asked, his voice hoarse.

'Not a word. I don't discuss you with each other . . .' Tielman's voice died away as he suddenly realised that he had not mentioned the matter to Douw, because he had not wanted to discuss a white man with a half-caste.

'Well, why are you making a mountain out of a mole-hill, then?' Muller's voice rose harsh and fierce. 'I just don't trust any brown-skin, that's all!'

'Even if they're our loyal allies . . . ?'

'Only as long as we are their masters. And show it.'

'By always abusing and shouting at them?'

'Look, Tielman, I know you come from the sleepy valleys of the Boland. You people still have to learn what we frontiersmen already know, that you dare not relax one moment before the black peril. But if you don't want to realise that we have a sacred duty towards our people, that we have a sacred calling to subjugate the barbarians within our frontiers, if you forget that you're a white man, then I say, shame on you! The blood of our women and children will be on your head, despicable white man that you are! Shame on you, who puts a Child of Ham like Douw above your fellow-Christians!'

'But Douw has white blood, too, and he's Christian, too.'

'Don't talk to me about half-caste dogs. They're all abominable traitors ready to stab one in the back!'

Trembling with dismay, Tielman stood before the young Graaff-Reinet burgher who looked as if he wanted to hit out at him. Was the man possessed? Had all this violence left only madness and hatred in him? His own self-respect and manliness forced hard, cold words into his throat: I have more respect for Douw than for you. But instead of that his trembling lips pronounced: 'A white man does not steal up from behind like a Kaffir with an assegai!'

Thomas's face became waxen and rigid.

'I don't know what you're insinuating,' he mumbled huskily, at last, 'and I never want to know.'

When Tielman fiercely swung on his heel, he knew that he had made an enemy of this man. Later, sleepless, with his head on his saddle, he helplessly surmised that he had lost Douw, too. A faithful, honest man betrayed by the treachery of words; Douw, his friend, who was continually being stabbed in the back by a half-caste.

13

From long before the first paling of the eastern sky, the old woman sat leaning against the shelter, watching the new day being born. While the crests of mountains and trees were etched ever more sharply by the limpid light, slowly spreading across the whole vault of the sky and filling the valley with the shapes of wagons and tents and patches of forest and the silky folds of mountain slopes imperceptibly assuming their daylight colours, her own countenance, too, became revealed in the holy peace of the re-born dawn; the old yellowish skin wrinkled over the forehead and the broad cheek-bones and deeply folded around the slightly flattened nose and the slack mouth. It was a stern, worn-out face without expectation of new joy, haloed by long, slightly curly hair which, grey-white from age, belonged less to the morning than to the colourlessness of the receding darkness.

The light expanded above her head across the sky, a pearly and crystalline flood slowly deepening to a golden down over an awakening blue, while all objects on the earth below solidified ever more into their own colours and shapes: brown, green, black, clearly delineated and apart. Everywhere around her life awoke with the light, birds began to sing, cocks to crow, lambs and calves to call for their mother's milk, as well as the first sounds made by the humans as they threw wood on the morning fires, licking with red tongues at pillars of smoke. Ouma Katryn saw and heard the new day, but her face kept an absent calm because she really only existed in the timeless country of her memories.

It was a country filled with dear human faces and human names, and with a sluggish, patient sorrow that kept on demand-ing more of her motherly attention than she could spare to praise her Creator's morning glory. Her hands lay slack in her lap, on the rag doll she had filled with sawdust, last night by the firelight, the rag doll she had made for Anna Muller's infant, the comic round-bodied granny doll that she would probably now never give to her great-grandchild; little Hennie, with his blond curly hair who would never be taken for anything but a white child. Yesterday, after the return of the commando with blood and mud on their clothes, when she visited the Mullers' wagon once more, Anna had hurriedly blocked her way. The blonde young mother was very embarrassed as she told Ouma Katryn that her husband had said she should never again set foot there. Ouma Katryn had understood that this was because of Douw; she had also understood that Anna Muller did not know that she was Thomas's grandmother. If Thomas wanted to deny his family now that he had become a white man, she, Ouma Katryn, would not betray him. No, Anna did not need to know. Ouma Katryn was sorry for her: if Thomas had married her, with her blonde hair and rosy-white skin, so that his children would have less chance of showing their half-caste ancestry, then who could be sure that he really loved her? Ouma Katryn had just returned sadly to her wagon, and gone on finishing the granny doll with sawdust and rags.

Now the eastern edge of the ocean was growing brilliant; the sun was about to rise, radiant, blinding to a human eye. Behind the old woman's eyelids wandered the shades and figures of her family. Her husband, Hermanus Arendse, killed thirty years before by a poisoned arrow one night during a Bushman raid. The five children who had died, and the two who were still alive: Lea and Thomas. Lea, born dark of skin so that she had only married a half-civilised Hottentot, Samuel, and all their children had been olive-yellow: Hermaans, Douw, Katrien, Sampie, Mietjie and little Lea. Thomas, on the other hand, so light-coloured that he was able to marry Maria Jacobs, the lightest Bastaard girl of the whole district, and get by her children even lighter of skin than he was himself. And when their children, her grandchildren, were born—children so white that only local people would know their parents had been half-castes—they took the surname Muller from their white great-grandfather, her own father, and trekked away to the wild frontier districts where no one could point a finger at them. There, near Graaff-Reinet, one of these grandchildren, Thomas Muller, had lived for a considerable time as a white man, first acting as a hunter and then settling down as a farmer. Had he denied his own parents, too? With their consent? And his brothers and sisters? Where were they scattered in the wide, cruel world?

Ouma Katryn passed no judgement, she only searched for the links of her family's broken chain, full of yearning and compassion especially for the branch of her family which strove so hard to advance in life by becoming whiter. She did not blame them for the estrangement and division of her family, because she understood; she did not even blame the Dutchmen for the selfishness that made other people strive, in such a desiccating, loveless way, to win for themselves equal human dignity. Yes, she, whose blood flowed in the veins of dozens, she understood the thorny path before a half-caste could reach full human worth; she understood young Thomas's fierce behaviour to those whose skin was browner than his own—for then he tortured himself, then he flogged his own shame.

While the first sunlight shone over the folds in her old, worn-out face, Ouma Katryn's heart bled at the cruelty of all desire to be and to become. But she was resigned, for such was God's will.

But what of Douw? The thought brought unease for the first time. Yes, what of Douw, the rebellious one whose family had slid back to a darker skin? Douw, who now strove to attain his self-respect? And what of Ruth?

The old woman shifted stiffly so that the soft sheepskin blanket slid from her shoulders. She looked inside the shelter where the girl still lay sleeping. Over the silky soft skin a honey-blush now glowed, on her full lips a smile hovered. For her every day brought more promise of Douw. Ouma Katryn had known it since the day Ruth had stopped sharing her longings and secrets with her grandmother and since Douw's eyes no longer fled in the presence of Ruth. It was good so. If only Ruth did not worry too much about her frizzy hair and dark skin which Douw had so pointedly referred to in the past. Her heart would have to grow free from the humiliation of the past; she would need to be free to be able to give whatever a woman was capable of to a man as difficult as Douw.

Douw: proud of his new gun and his saddle-horse he had come riding back to the fortress farm. But also he had been violently upset. At first he had not wanted to speak and had gone out to the plains, to the little Bushman, Tkanna. Tkanna, the boy whom he had never been. At his return he sat apart from the others, cleaning his gun over and over again. When at last he noticed his own people, he said that he was not going to stay one day longer in the laager than was necessary and that, in two days at the longest, he would ride over to the Government Post to stake his claim to his new farm at Prinshoop. Was this because of the black man whom he had had to kill? While she meditated, Ouma Katryn watched how the valley's last shadowy corners filled with light and golden sunshine. No. A man's honour was more than another's death. Something had not yet been revealed. Something that concerned a man's pride and, therefore, in Douw's case, involved a white man. She sensed the same thing in Douw's young hunting companion. And yesterday Thomas had forbidden her to visit his wagon. Thomas? Douw would not tell her anything. But young Tielman was softer, more indulgent; he would not keep silent if she asked him.

Now there were many more morning sounds in the town of wagons and tents. Only here and there were morning prayers being said, for not every household was strict in honouring the Lord. It was the one fault in a good man like Mynheer Lindstrom; she still remembered the day she had called him a heathen and he had nodded and answered: 'Yes, Ouma Katryn, yet I am not without faith.' What kind of faith could that be . . .?

She heard the rustling as Ruth pulled her dress over her head, and felt the warm arms and the still warmer lips as the girl kissed her.

'Morning, my little old granny.'

'May the Lord bless today, my child,' the old woman sighed, when the girl was already whisking away to the river to wash. For her the day only began after she had praised her Creator and

so she sat motionless until Ruth had returned and sat down beside
her. Then she falteringly struck up one of her favourite evan-
gelical songs:

> 'Op bergen en in dalen,
> En overal is God!
> Waar wij ook immer dwalen . . .'

When her lips at last fell silent, her hands folded around the
rag doll and lifted it slowly to Ruth's lap: 'Take it, my child,
keep it for your first-born.'

The girl's face rushed dark with blood and only after several
moments could she whisper her thanks.

'Of course it'll only be after God's minister has properly united
you two in wedlock.'

Ruth's hands stopped trembling.

'No, Ouma Katryn,' she said, unexpectedly firm, 'it's two weeks'
riding to the Cape from here. If Douw wants me, I won't wait.'

The old woman turned her head and saw that the girl was
blushing again but resolutely answering her gaze. In the thoughts
of both an ox-wagon rumbled on endless stages to the west where
the sun kept on setting ahead of them, night after night, ever
farther towards the far Town of the Cape where alone all marriages
could be effected. Slowly Ouma Katryn's face creased into a kind
of grin and she dryly remarked: 'Ruth, you're hardly more than
a child, but you, too, will get older. You'll learn that if a woman
can't hold her man any longer, Christian bonds are a great help.'

Her old face became quiet once more and closed to passions,
as it had been throughout the morning's birth. 'I'll talk to Douw.'

'No, please not, Ouma Katryn. He . . . he . . .'

The old woman did not reply. Douw would soon go over to
Plettenberg Bay. First she had to talk to Tielman.

It was not easy to get Tielman alone. That morning there was
much talk about matters of war; that is to say, talk in which men
could sway on their heels, beat wagon-rails with their fists and
puff stifling clouds of smoke from their pipes, while they discussed brave doings which a woman was not supposed to understand. It was said that a commando of burghers had been called
up in Stellenbosch to come and help their compatriots hereabouts,

and that General Dundas himself was advancing overland with a big force of soldiers. The most concrete proof that matters were improving was that a first load of ammunition with an escort of armed burghers from Swellendam had reached Ganzekraal yesterday. This ammunition was being handed out to the commandos of Olifants River and the Longkloof, and Commandant Botha surely would not forget the need of those in Plettenberg Bay. Dawid Stuurman and his evil minions would soon have to give way. These brave expectations were somewhat dampened by the rumour that that misguided poltroon, Honoratius Maynier, was travelling with General Dundas, supposedly to act as mediator in his capacity as expert on frontier matters; but by this time several burghers had opened their casks of peach brandy to drink to Victory! Every Hottentot in the place was clustering around to beg a drink. And this in broad daylight, with the enemy all round! Ouma Katryn had to withdraw, quite indignant.

She only cornered Tielman towards noon when he had put on a clean linen shirt and was borrowing a mirror in Mynheer Lindstrom's tent; clearly preparations for a gallant visit to Sannie Botha. When the old woman approached the tent, the young man courteously took his pipe from his mouth, while Lindstrom looked up from his folio of plant drawings and pointed to a camp stool. She hesitated, but then sat stiffly down.

'Tielman,' she asked, in an old person's direct manner, 'tell me what happened to Douw during the patrol? Between him and Thomas?'

The young man became very embarrassed, glancing at the Swede.

'You may speak before Mynheer Lindstrom. He's no teller of tales.'

Visibly reluctant, Tielman told of Thomas and the assegai. 'I can't understand such a thing. Perhaps I only imagined it.'

Bowed over and sitting very quiet, Ouma Katryn said: 'Ach, child, Thomas has had a hard time. He lost his father and mother and his whole family. He is so alone in the world that he's not always in his right senses.'

The young man from Stellenbosch was in a hurry to go and

shave. He explained that he wanted to ride back to his parents on their Berg River farm as soon as conditions allowed. That was why he was courting Sannie so hastily, so as to be ahead of other young men. War-time was a blessing to lovers, because it threw people so closely together. But he would return from his parents soon and join the Stellenbosch commando.

When he had gone the two old people sat silent beside each other. Then Lindstrom remarked sympathetically: 'Ouma Katryn, it looks as if you have a lot of trouble with your family.'

The old woman looked sharply at him: 'For a man you're quite observant. Tielman doesn't know. Nor does Douw know that Thomas is his cousin. I still don't know if it's the Lord's wish that I should tell him.'

'But surely Ruth knows?' By that Lindstrom wanted to imply that she should perhaps leave it to the younger generation themselves.

Ouma Katryn nodded, as if to emphasise her own words: 'One's tears may dry up later on, but never one's loving . . .'

Abruptly she looked at the Swede and asked:

'Mynheer, in your country, are there as many people of different nations and languages as here?'

'No, Ouma Katryn, in my country people's eyes and hair may be a little longer or darker but they are all one nation with one language and belief. All white people.'

'All Christians?'

He hesitated before nodding. With a sigh she ruminated: 'And you, Mynheer, who are a learned man and have come to our country to sort out all our many kinds of plants and make pictures of them, what do you think when you look at mankind?'

'That they're very much like plants,' he laughed, 'and want to take each other's places.'

'No, that's not what I mean.'

'Ach, Ouma Katryn, how shall I put it? To me mankind is a child which still has to learn everything, still has to discover everything in creation. I, too.' Now he also was serious, and when he saw she was waiting, he went on: 'My belief is that ignorance is mankind's greatest sin, that all our hatred and faults come from ignorance and that man can only change through new knowledge. As a scientist I know that all people are one great family belonging together. But at the same time I believe that the unity of love between all people will only come about if we work for it. If we do not search and build ourselves, we'll remain in eternal hatred and bloodshed. Praying and believing are not enough by themselves.'

Sorrowfully the old woman shook her head: 'I suppose a man is always a bit more of a heathen than a woman. You always want to do things that amount only to more discord and bloodshed. Mynheer Lindstrom, here in my heart I know that only praying and believing are important and that mankind is nothing without being humble.'

Somewhat stiffly the savant answered: 'I, too, am humble, Ouma Katryn, in my way . . .'

Supported by Ruth's arm, she afterwards walked around the laager, talking to people along the way. Ouma Katryn, with her friendly and impeccable dignity, had many friends among the burghers' wives, who would not have allowed the slightest familiarity from any other coloured woman except their own, faithful servants. Today an easy indignation about the men's conduct was a communal bond; the latter were being much too liberal with their supplies of peach brandy. Victory or no victory, the young men were going too far, boasting and tomfooling on their horses like that, and playing ridiculous jokes on each other. Tielman and Thomas were taking part in the hysterical fun and some of the young girls were joining in too, so boldly that one could even see their uvulas wagging!

Ouma Katryn and Ruth joined the group around the corpulent Mrs. Van der Wath in her vegetable garden behind the fortified house. It was a bright sunny day promising spring, and all the women wore bonnets, nodding like prim white flowerheads at each other with each: 'Ach, Lordie, yes . . .' or 'Goodness me, a man is but a child.' Their voices rose and sank, concealing their secret pride that their men could carouse so high-spiritedly.

Mrs. Van der Wath's vegetable garden was the great attraction for the women. They looked covetously at the beds where young green sprouts were budding above the fertile black earth. All of them were far from their own farms, so that their cookery now had to rely on meat, dry pulse, flour and milk. Many of them openly begged a carrot or two, a head of cabbage or a sprig of parsley—anything, so long as it was green. 'Aunt Malie, you know yourself, a young child has to grow . . .' Or: 'For my old man who grumbles so much . . .' Quite a number of the women were pregnant, and while they paraded through the garden, stately in their long printed calico dresses which covered their generous bodies to their ankles, a gentle herd grazing with poise and self-assurance, they, former fugitives from the face of death, affirmed man's connection with growth and re-awakening.

When Mrs. Van der Wath could pay attention to Ouma Katryn, the latter took some dried buffalo meat from a piece of cloth. 'Mrs. Van der Wath, the winter's damp has got into my people, and now I'm looking for some kind of medicine. If you could exchange this for a sprig of wild wormwood, I'd be very glad.'

Then it was Ruth's turn; she had been looking longingly at the rows of fruit trees and rose shrubs on which the first buds were showing. 'Mistress, if Mistress wouldn't mind giving me a few cuttings?' she asked shyly of the voluminous white woman showing bulges of fat as other people would show wrinkles.

Ouma Katryn looked at the dark girl, as if she had suddenly thought of something, beyond the knowledge that Douw would not like Ruth's humility before white people, to the fact that the gulf between Douw and Thomas would be deepened by their women. And their children . . .

Gradually the old woman's brooding thoughts were penetrated by a new silence around her. Mistress Van der Wath and Ruth stood half turned, like Lot's wife, to listen. The men's racket had also stopped. The only sound in the golden afternoon was a soft, far palpitation, as if the beating of the earth's heart had become audible. Somewhere to the north it boomed in the mountains, an irregular sound that went on and on.

For long moments the whole laager listened. Suddenly the men left everything else and rushed to their horses and guns. That must be the men of Longkloof! Up there Botha's commando was coming to blows with the enemy. Stuurman's snakes were probably trying to get away through the mountain passes. They had to go and help at once.

The fieldcornet shouted himself hoarse before he could get sense out of them. Only half the men could go. Their foremost obligation was to protect the women and children, as well as their herds and flocks, without which all of them would be plunged into even greater misery and poverty. The enemy was sly, they should always stay on the alert. And should a proper commando, capable of fighting for days, not be provided with a wagon with supplies, two teams of oxen and some meat on the hoof? Hurry, but slowly.

'Goliat, go and tell all the herdsmen to bring their animals closer to the laager. Let them kraal the animals earlier tonight.'

Now the women's attention shifted to the preparations being made down by the patch of wild olives where the road left the farmyard. Ouma Katryn grasped Ruth's arm when the girl wanted to run down to where Tielman stood talking with Douw. They watched blonde Anna Muller fall weeping round her husband's neck and then run to pour out her troubles to the fieldcornet. Might she have guessed something from her husband's vehemence towards Douw? The end of the matter was that the sober fieldcornet decided that men with young children should stay in the laager. Thomas had to stay.

'Just look how Pronk trots!' Ruth ecstatically exclaimed, able at once to forget Thomas and rejoice in the present: Douw, so proud on his new roan stallion, envied by every burgher. 'Such a lovely horse, heh, Ouma, and he's showing off because he knows he's lovely, heh, Ouma?'

Hours later the old woman got a chance to meet Thomas apart from the others, without attracting anyone's attention. At sundown, when her grandson went to water his horse, she followed him down to the ford and said: 'Thomas, you forbid me to enter your wagon and I, too, prefer to talk to you when nobody else is around. Don't be upset, my child, I only want to ask you something.'

His hand dragged so convulsively on the halter that the horse had to stop drinking. But there was no chance of escape, he could not avoid her for ever. First he knee-haltered his horse and then waded through the reeds to where she sat waiting for him on a log. His grandmother saw how fiercely he tensed himself so as not to surrender to weakness.

'I recognised you at once,' she softly said, 'you're the image of your grandfather Hermanus. Just like your cousin Douw.'

Too late the old woman realised she should not have said how visible she found his resemblance to Douw. He spoke no word, standing rigid and cold before her with his face bluish from the first evening shadows. Blood of her blood! Her own grandchild for the first time in his life consciously standing before his grandmother! Ouma Katryn's head sank before she asked, more softly still:

'Thomas, I only want to know a few things. I give my word of honour that what you tell me will remain between us, a family affair. Tell me, where are your parents now? I heard they had trekked off to a far-off place behind the Zwarteberg mountains and that their farm is called Kromdraai?'

He nodded vehemently, but still did not speak.

'I could say good-bye to all the other children. I want to look up your parents before I die. But your father . . . Tell me, Thomas, where is Kromdraai? How does one get there?'

His eyes flashed down to her calm face: it seemed as if anger and suspicion enveloped him as soon as anyone came too close. Then he mumbled: 'In the Olifants River district. You keep to the left of the mountain, following the slope. It's rough country, four or five stages by wagon. Then you'll pass right across Kromdraai.'

He had to repeat it. Then she asked: 'Are your two elder brothers, too . . . out in the world?'

'Yes. Karel lives near Bruintjieshoogte, and Petrus fled from the accursed English into Kaffirland, under the protection of Gaika. Now they daren't return.'

'And your sisters?'

'Lena and Hettie are still at home. That's all I know about them . . . I've been away so long . . .'

His voice sank into morose dejection. For girls it would be much more difficult to go out into the world by themselves. Were they, perhaps, too brown-skinned to marry Dutchmen? Did they, because of their white brothers, have to stay at home and become proud old maids, withering bitter as gall? Ouma Katryn sat quietly looking at Thomas as if she wanted to read the sad, hidden truth on his face. Without waiting to be asked, the young man spoke again, his voice now gushing by fits and starts: 'It's a stone house on a grassy slope. A crooked karee tree stands in front of the stone veranda. And just behind the house there's a stone and thorn-tree kraal . . . on the red-baked hill which runs in a wide circle around the valley . . . the only place in that godforsaken desert where there are trees and shade and some water . . . and a waterfall once a year . . . a jet of water where we children could play.'

Surprised by his sudden change and full of her own tenderness, the old woman saw Kromdraai through his eyes, once more become those of a child. She hardly realised how he was being exposed to the betrayal of weakness; she had returned completely to the pride of twenty years ago: 'Yes, my child, my child . . . I last saw you as a little boy before your people trekked away to Kromdraai. You were such a lovely white child . . .'

He sank down on the log beside her, his body quivering, his hands wrestling over his face.

'Oh, Ouma, the Lord hears me, life is cruel . . . Sometimes I hate myself so much that I feel like dying. It's years since I've seen my own mother. And it's best if I never see her again . . . never again . . .'

The old woman knew that this was the first time he had had a chance to lighten his heart of its load of pent-up pity and scorn for himself. Now she, too, no longer had control over her own emotions. She raised her hand and stroked his hair as she would have stroked a small child. Her hand brought compassion but her voice blamed him: 'I understand, my child, I understand . . . But did you have to raise your hand against your own cousin?'

Fiercely he bounded to his feet, no trace left of his momentary weakening. 'Anything that reminds me of the past, I'll stamp out root and branch! A tepid person, a half-hearted person doesn't get anywhere in life!'

'My child, Douw knows nothing about your past. You lifted your hand only against yourself . . .'

'Enough!' he snarled, even more embittered than before. 'If I want to be a white man, I must become like a white man!'

'My child, my child, this is blasphemy! How can white people be children of the Evil One?'

'I don't know!' His head stabbed forwards, madness in his eyes. 'I only know the world belongs to them.'

Then he swung round, stamping away through the reeds, rustling, full of new darkness.

'What shall it profit a man, if he shall gain the whole world, and lose his own soul?' The old woman murmured the admonition that ended on silence.

She remained sitting on the log while the vehemence drained away in the darkening eve. Where the birth of light had started the day with crystal clarity, the birth of darkness brought more passionate, glowing colours, orange, and red and purple-blue, slowly, like remorse, fading from the sky and the horizon into the oblivion of the night. Ouma Katryn was not afraid of lurking enemies or beasts of prey; she remained sitting upright in her black dress, an image of sorrow, barely aware of the increasing cold gnawing her old, rheumaticky legs.

When silver sparks appeared on the black firmament, she pulled the black shawl over the pale stain of her hair and rose to walk back, erect, a moving figure of darkness.

Part Three

Part Two

14

Up the last, steepest slope the rear oxen stumbled, causing the front wheels to swivel across some ugly rocks. The wagon slanted sharply and fell over, nearly flinging the rear oxen down the precipice. Every man present came to grab the straps at the side, dig in their heels and hang on till the oxen had calmed down and the wagon could be righted. The cost was a broken front axle, a warped wagon-tent, and, of course, the men's bad humour. Douw, Tielman, and Mynheer Lindstrom's servant set to at once to get an emergency axle fastened to the broken one. Old Speelman took over the team of fourteen oxen, and Tkanna, who felt guilty because he was still so inexperienced as a team-leader, went ahead with the cows and his five goats.

When Ruth saw she was no longer needed, she eagerly put her arm around Ouma Katryn: 'Come, Ouma, let's go and look. It isn't far any more, just beyond the pass.'

She felt dizzy from the lovely blue day and the excitement of seeing what had become of Prinshoop. Everywhere there were spring flowers between the tufts of grass and reeds and, if it had not been for Ouma, she would have run singing to the top.

Slowly, so slowly, the well-known valley under its long hill opened in front of them and lay green before their feet. Over there, against the fringe of the forest, their house stood as always. Their house . . .

'Look, Ouma, look! Our house has not been burnt down!'

And over there ran the footpaths which their feet had trodden, scarring the hill, across and down to the gorge in the forest with its lacework of ferns around the pool of honey-brown water.

She focused her eyes to see what had happened to the garden

and the kraal. She wished she had the wings of the black crow which was soaring over the lake; big, soft wings able to stroke the whole farmyard with their shadow.

'Does Ouma want to wait for the wagon and ride?'

'No, my child, I'll walk with you to the house.'

'To our house, Ouma Katryn.'

The old woman's face crinkled full of deeper wrinkles of laughter: 'Then Douw will have to build on more rooms.'

'But he will, he will!'

Behind them Douw called Tkanna to come and take the lead once more. Douw did not sound angry, he was never angry with this shy child of the plains. Ruth and the old woman were not far away when a whip smacked behind them and a man's voice sang out strongly: 'Hartland . . . ! Blomland . . . ! Blokberg . . . ! Togetherrr nowwww!'

Where Douw had cut a ford through the marshy land near the stream, Ruth took off her shoes to greet the black turf with her bare feet. Lower down the tiny stream babbled happily past the flat washing-stone which she herself had rolled into place. The old woman stopped:

'Wait, Ruth. Let Douw go first. Prinshoop is his.'

Behind them Douw urged on the oxen. Near the homestead he sprang bareback on to Pronk, urging the roan to a gallop. They watched as he sprang down at the open door, looked inside, walked around the house, then went on to the hard-pear tree where he had hidden his wagon-timbers, axles and yokes under a pile of leaves. Only then did he notice that the women were standing waiting and waved to them with both arms: 'The house looks like a pigsty. People have been in it, but they didn't take anything. Come on, let's move in!'

He tramped around, too reserved by nature to know how to express his joy.

'Aie, but I'm glad to be away from that suffocating ant's nest full of people. Here one can breathe again.' His eyes singled out Ruth: 'Girlie, it'll need a lot of cleaning.'

Ruth did not trust the glow in her own eyes and only nodded quickly and laughed as she ran past him. No elephant had flattened the fence and, inside, the young fig shoots were actually budding, the barley was stretching its arms in lush ranks to the sun and even the vegetable beds did not seem to have been plundered. Ruth knelt down to press her face into a hot pumpkin blossom. 'Thank you, thank you,' she whispered, but shying away from her own passion, quickly added: 'Our Heavenly Father'. Life could go on as if they had never been away, as if there had never been an abyss of embittered estrangement and humiliation between him and her, as if there were no bad Dutchmen in the outside world.

Soon there was a great to-do around the farm. Tielman and Esau helped to unpack and to chop new branches for the kraal fences. Tomorrow Esau would return to Mynheer Lindstrom while Tielman would leave for Stellenbosch, but first he and Douw would scout around to see if there were still any robbers in the area. At the same time they were going to hunt, their last hunting trip together as bachelors.

When Douw closed the kraal gate on his lifestock—already grown to fourteen oxen, seven cows and five calves, without counting Tkanna's five goats and Ouma Katryn's two pack-oxen and fowls—Tielman laughed in a hesitant way.

'Man, I think Stellenbosch is going to be much too quiet for me now. I think I'll come back to start a farm round here too.'

'Where? All the land round here has already got an owner.'

'Do you remember how lovely and empty it was near the Tzitzikamma . . . ?'

'That's right . . . Where that . . . Damon lives . . .'

There was such a strange note in Douw's voice that Ruth looked up. She wanted to hear more about this Damon but Douw went on, curt and matter-of-fact: 'But who knows if the war is really over? Who knows if one can risk it in out-of-the-way places?'

In the morning it was time to wish 'Happy Journey' to the young man from the Boland, who was to go straight on after the hunting trip, back to his father's wine-farm or, at least, to Swellendam, where the Stellenbosch commando was supposed to collect. Tielman, the only Dutchman Ruth managed to address without the customary 'Sieur'; every time she had to watch her tongue so as not to anger Douw.

Douw was away for fully five days. Ruth was busy cleaning the house, planting cuttings, gardening, or simply looking for more work to do, but all the time she became more and more uneasy. The great green forest to the seaward side had swallowed him without a trace. Her love need no longer be a secret shame but she still tried to hide her anxiety from the others. When nobody saw her, she went to sit on the high peak from where one could look southwards over the Knysna forest to the far, blue sea. From there the forest looked like an enormous animal's body bulging black-green and hairy in all directions below her. Who could say if the murderers were not still hiding in its depths? Of course the commandos had succeeded in driving Stuurman's main force back into the Couga mountains, far to the east, but still the field-cornet had warned people not to be in too much of a hurry to return to their farms. But Douw would not listen. Why did he always expose himself and his people to danger? Oh, a man thought only of his own pleasure!

And then, the second Thursday in September, just as she returned from an anxious vigil on the look-out hill, lo and behold an elephant's tusk leaning against the door, a mighty tusk nearly as tall as a man, ivory-white and smooth except for the still bloodyish base. And near the fence Douw's horse was rolling, feet in the air. But the owner wasn't anywhere in sight, he had left at once with Speelman to round up the oxen. Of course, for him, hauling loads of elephant flesh would be more important than greeting her.

An unreasonable anger at Douw took hold of her. She knew she was unreasonable; good ivory was as costly as pepper and they needed every stiver they could earn, especially if they had to journey to the Cape for the marriage. But for that very reason she was angry.

It was dark before the men came back with a mountain of meat and a second tusk, tired out from the struggle with the oxen which had absolutely refused to approach the elephant. Ruth brought a tub of water for the man of the house but she did not utter a word. She put the Bible before him, still without a tongue. Douw was the last to notice; he, who was normally so silent, had much to tell.

From his talkativeness she knew how much he had enjoyed himself, what great friends he and Tielman had been once more. It made her remember bitterly how this same Tielman had been shy of befriending Douw when other whites had been present. But trees and elephants had been welcome to see his friendship! She forgot how Douw, too, closed up before other people. In the past, she had always been grateful for Tielman's friendship, now she listened, hostile, as Douw recounted how Tielman had wanted to take back some kind of souvenir to the Boland and how they had wandered for days through the forest before they could get close enough to a herd of elephants to shoot a bull. Not to mention their joy when they also came upon a skeleton with two yellowed, but still valuable tusks. Of course! Young bachelors had to enjoy their last freedom before their wives-to-be could clap them into jail!

That whole evening and following morning Ruth was dumb whenever Douw was near. They were often beside each other while they dressed the meat, salted it and cut it up to dry or for making soap. He clearly looked for chances to be near her, to talk to her. Her attitude bewildered poor Douw, who was unskilled in matters of the heart. Ouma Katryn began to look askance at her; since when had Ruth been one for moodiness? Of course! Ruth was made of honey and sunshine and stone; Ruth could never be angry!

She felt so miserable that she finally stayed near the laden trees to keep birds away from the drying meat. No, she did not want to eat, she called back to Ouma Katryn. Who could eat with so much bloody meat around her? Her unreasonableness was a misery she could no longer understand or stop. She stood with her back to the house, but she heard when the old woman spoke with Douw and recognised the footsteps approaching the tree where she stood chasing away the black crows.

When he came up to her, she retreated, deeper into the forest.

He had to quicken his step. Then she ran, blindly, through shrubs and branches.

'Ruth! What's the matter?'

Behind her he started running, too, and bounded ahead to grab her arm. Panting, she strained away, face averted. When he took her other arm as well, and turned her towards him, she burst out moaning: 'Oh, Douw, Douw, you should not have stayed away so long!' She shook with desperate sobs.

'But Ruth, listen, you know Tielman wanted to . . .' he began. She interrupted him, still more passionately: 'I thought you were dead!' Her wild eyes and trembling body said more than her words; said: Douw, Douw, wipe out the humiliation, wipe out the shame of the others; said: Douw, think of me, too, Douw, save me from despair, Douw, break down your walls, Douw, and save me with your love that will wipe out everything, everything . . .

Douw's hands trembled on her shoulders; he had possessed her one afternoon in passion, and said before others: 'Will you wait for me, Ruth?' but he had not yet told her: I love you. She struggled and strained away from his hands, in fear; fear of him, fear for her right to love him.

'Ruth,' he stammered, 'Ruth, can you forgive me? I was too proud, Ruth, I thought only of myself. I wanted to . . . alone . . . only . . . Listen, Ruth, I want to tell you . . .'

He had to force her to sit down beside him and turn her face to him while he told her of the run-away slave, Damon, living so utterly alone in the Tzitzikamma forest; of the love of liberty that could drive even a black heathen to such a flight. How deeply this had moved him, but more still the further realisation that man was not created to be alone, that pride and honour became a mockery if one could not achieve them together with others. She, Ruth, was the only person with whom he wanted to share his life . . .

After all the harsh and lonely years his voice struggled to find the words to speak to a loved one. Then, to his total dismay, Ruth once more shook with sobs.

'Ruth, I'm asking you to be my wife! We can marry as soon as you . . .'

'No, no,' she moaned, 'how can you ever forgive me for young Sieur Piet and Salomon! But, oh, Douw, it wasn't you, it wasn't you . . . !'

'Quiet, it was my fault, I drove you away!' He vehemently closed her lips, kissing her mouth and folding his arms around her until she stopped trembling.

'I love you, Ruth.'

Behind them, behind the green wall of foliage, birds of prey flapped their wings, settling on branches loaded with bloody strips of meat, flying away reluctantly when old Speelman shouted and threw stones.

'We must help,' Douw whispered, 'tonight we can be together again.'

He stood up and helped her rise. But when she found her feet, her ankle gave way under her, so that she clung to him with an exclamation of pain, and they both fell back again. He wanted to help her rise once more, but she lay slack and heavy, with closed eyes.

'We'll have to wait till we're married, Ruth . . .'

The girl still clung to him, and now her arms around his shoulders said that only the desire in their young bodies should exist in the whole world.

'Douw, Douw, I loved you since I was a little girl. I waited so long to be yours . . . so long . . .'

Behind them, on the edge of the forest, the old Bushman no longer shouted at the vultures and crows which were still trying to tear off lappets of red meat; hoarse from shouting, he now struck notes from his fiddle, impetuous and warning, then again lingering and dreamily filled with peace.

That evening after prayers, Ouma Katryn said: 'Douw, to-morrow you will have to play the cooper and make a barrel for us to boil the soap. Speelman and I are going to collect honey, it is springtime and every bee is finding a flower. Then when you ride to Swellendam, you can take honey and soap with you.'

'Yes, and the elephant tusks to bring in some money too. And of course the wagon timbers which I haven't made yet,' her grand-son agreed.

'It'll have to be soon,' the old woman tranquilly went on. 'I want to go to Towerwaterpoort before the worst heat of the summer. Especially if you and Ruth intend to go on from Swellen-dam. What are your plans? To make it one trip and go on to the Town of the Cape?'

'Goodness me, there's so much still to be done! The house has to be finished, the road down the mountain improved, the wagon, the . . .' Douw fell silent, and looked at Ruth who answered his gaze with soft, glowing eyes. She agreed with everything he decided, in advance.

'Yes, Ouma, we'll want to go to the Town as soon as possible.'

'Then we have to leave in two weeks at the latest.'

'We? Who else is going with us?'

'I'm going with you,' the old woman said firmly.

'And who'll look after the farm?'

'I've already spoken to Speelman. He and Tkanna will.'

'And the wagon? Who'll lead the team? I'll have to go and hire somebody first. It's a whole month on the road.'

'I'll take the rope,' Ruth said.

'Heaven forbid!' Douw wanted to say more, but the two women were taking over the conversation.

'Oh, Ouma Katryn, I've nothing decent to wear!'

'Don't worry, my child, we'll make you a frock from the piece of cambric that's left over. And we'll cut my petticoat with the hoops to . . .'

Douw stared at the two women, hit the table with his fist, and then turned to the little Bushman:

'Heh, Tkanna, could you watch the cattle all by yourself, while we're away?'

'Yes, Baas Douw!' the boy eagerly nodded. 'Tkanna watch good. Tkanna make bow and arrow. Tkanna hit spotted cat with arrow. Hit robber in ugly face. Run away. So.' And he bounded to his feet to demonstrate how the robber would clutch the arrow wound and run away stumbling till he fell down, dead.

When the laughter abated, old Speelman nodded. 'It's all right,

Douw. Tkanna and I will manage everything. We've got the assegai you brought along, and I have my bow and arrow. It's you who'll have trouble with the oxen going over Attaquaskloof.'

'We'll manage . . . we'll have to.'

Douw was a hasty man, and he at once began thinking of the preparations and what Speelman and Tkanna would have to do. One never knew. The peace on the eastern frontier was not yet final. He caught fire with sudden energy, threatening to tackle some things on the spot. At this old Speelman left, groaning about his rheumatism and calling to Tkanna to help put more wood on the watch-fires. Ruth made fresh coffee. As soon as they were alone, Ouma Katryn rose and made the two young people come closer so that she could press them to her heart.

'Oh, my children, I'm so glad you found each other. Be good to her, Douw, because of all the girls I know in this cruel world, she is the most faithful. Take her, Douw, I taught her everything I could, needlework, cooking, what it means to be a Christian, how to honour a man . . . Be good to him, Ruth, for he has been hurt, too . . .'

She was so affected that her voice faltered, but when she spoke once more it sounded as if she were reproving them: 'It is right and proper that you should not act like heathens, but be married in the proper Christian way.'

Soon after Douw had gone outside, Ruth slipped out, too, into the starry night, to where he stood waiting beside the kraal with the assurance of his arms, with the greedy possessiveness of his mouth, with the passion capable of discovering peace in a young body.

'I'm a heathen,' she whispered.

'You're a Christian, too, Ruth,' he laughed at her ear, 'it's you who brings the Bible to me every night.'

In the dark night which made everything so much more part of the odorous earth they laughed like children, shyly meeting each other before they would be allowed to play together.

15

In the early summer of the last year of that century three treks crawled in separate directions through the vast Southern land where sunlight so far dominated that everything standing or walking upright, threw a darker, lonelier shadow. Douw Prins's wagon was on its way to the Town of the Cape, the only city in the country, always keeping close to the well-watered coastal mountains. Weeks later an old woman and an old man with two pack-oxen trekked northwards to where the Zwarteberg mountains' farthest, most arid slopes ended in the burning plains of the Karroo. The Swedish botanist, Bengt Lindstrom, in the company of four burgher hunters, advanced much farther northeast up to the mighty Gariep or Great River where there was once again the relief of water and shady trees, and hippopotami and elephants and endless herds of game in an uninhabited country.

At times, tired of sitting, a traveller might rely on his own legs, or make his horse race across the trackless plain in pursuit of game. But, throughout, the progress of travellers was determined by the pace of their oxen; the slow, patient oxen capable of covering two or three stages totalling some ten hours a day, at so uniform a pace that all sense of motion was lost.

Though his wagon was not loaded heavily and they advanced as fast as they could, Douw remained impatient. On the heights behind Attaquaskloof, they had wasted nearly a day tracking down a certain colonist so as to sell some of the wagon timbers. Now they would need all of eight days to reach Swellendam.

At this village his visit to the Landdrost caused more delay. The secretary in the Drostdy office read the recommendations of Mynheer Lindstrom and Tielman Roux and got as far as recording Douw's application for a loan-farm and accepting the twenty-four rixdollars quit-rent money for one year, but he then declared that Prinshoop would only officially come into existence after Douw's local fieldcornet had measured it out and affirmed it. Meanwhile Douw had to be content with a provisional letter of occupancy. After that he had to wait another hour before the secretary deigned to write out a paper to the Lords Commissioners of Marriages in the Cape, in which he declared that the Landdrost office knew of no legal cause why the Hottentot half-caste, Douw Prins, could not be bound in wedlock with the young free-black spinster, Ruth Arendse.

From Swellendam to the approaches to the Cape, was six more days. According to the regulations they would have to wait four weeks in the Town of the Cape so that their banns could be read on three consecutive Sundays. That meant they would be away from home for two whole months; not to mention the expense! The reverend minister alone had to get five rixdollars, and the beadle was sure to demand his cut as well. In her indignation Ruth said it was a shame that the authorities should make it so hard to get married. Ouma Katryn sternly silenced her: she would see to all the details and herself speak to the venerable Dominee Serrurier. As for the expense: her barrel of honey would surely be enough to pay for all their food?

Usually she and Ruth sat on the wagon-chest, passing the time catechising Ruth thoroughly in Christian dogma and history. Whenever Douw was near, he, too, had to answer questions which the church authorities were likely to pose a prospective bridegroom. It heightened their growing expectations about the city they were nearing and which none of them had seen before: the Town of the Cape, swarming with people of all colours and odours; an ant's nest of Godless and Christians, poor and rich; certain to astound simple children of the country seeing it for the first time.

From Gantouw Pass Ruth took the lead-rope. Her eyes grew wide as she stared at the many lovely farms so close to each other, covered with vineyards and orchards. To the left was the apple-green half-moon of the sea, while straight ahead shone the bright face of another ocean. In between a wild stretch of dunes pushed up to the horizon where the long, blue wall of the mountains ended in the mighty mass of the Table itself. Table Mountain, with, small and distant at its foot, the Castle, two church towers and the houses of the city. And out on Table Bay, tiny like toys, a whole array of ships with their gossamer masts and rigging. That evening Douw pressed on to the public camping-ground, one stage this side of the city. Table Mountain towered high and majestic against the night sky, really a table—'like the Creator's communion table,' the old woman in her emotion whispered to the girl who had come to hold on to her, for the last time, like a baby daughter.

The camping-ground swarmed with wagons and oxen, coaches and horses, with no green leaf in sight for the hungry animals. But hay was to be had, at flagrant prices from merciless money-grabbers; the first representatives of the city whom innocent countrymen were to meet. Douw bickered and grumbled, while the two women mysteriously busied themselves inside the wagon by lantern-light.

At dawn, when they left, Ruth was unrecognisably arrayed in a stately dark blue dress, matching bonnet with ribbons, and shoes she had obtained goodness knows where.

'No, Ruth,' Douw proudly stopped her, 'today you don't take the lead. My future wife is not going to make a laughing-stock of herself before the conceited city people. I can manage the oxen by myself on this flat ground. No, Ruth, you ride.' And he smacked his whip thunderously so as not to hear her protests.

The sun had risen high above the heavy sand and brackish waters of Salt River when they reached the outskirts of the town. Here there were ramparts and a few windmills turning their sails; on the seaward side, some brown boys played by the wreck of a boat. Douw stopped, and went over to stroke Pronk, who had had to follow so patiently behind in the wagon's dust, and then walked over to the boys. As he approached them he shook some coins into his hand. A minute later he returned with a boy who took the lead-rope as if he had been born to it. His name was Kiepie, originally Cupido, and his sallow countenance bore witness to much love between many kinds of ancestors.

'I hired him to help us as far as the camping site.'

Ruth worried about the extra expense but Ouma Katryn silenced her, with a smile:

'A man always has his pride . . .'

And it was true: Douw did not know the city, and if he had had to keep on asking and getting in the way of others . . .

Slowly they approached the squat mass of the Castle and the stretch of houses and gardens bordering the road on the mountain side. The immense grey-blue table of the mountain towered ever more steeply above them. Then there was a long, white-washed building, the Barracks and Infirmary, and still longer rows of trees around an enormous open square on which lines of soldiers were marching up and down.

'That's the Parade!' Kiepie called out the information to these country visitors who were looking at everything with such wide eyes. The square bordered a street with a double row of oaks and pines alongside a dirty canal. On this side of the Parade there were ox-wagons and vendors' stalls under umbrellas. People were everywhere: barefoot slaves in blue jackets and wide trousers; Malays with steep *toering* hats on their heads and wooden *kaparrings* on their feet; soldiers and sailors in the company of extravagantly dolled-up girls of any race on earth; dignified ladies and gentlemen ambling along under umbrellas held over them by slaves; salesmen and pedlars rushing around to proffer every imaginable kind of merchandise as loudly as possible. It was not only noisy, the din was also a Babylonian confusion of languages. Wherever the three visitors looked were different streets and imposing flat-roofed, snow-white houses with curled gables, two or three stories high. Without Kiepie they would really have felt lost.

Deftly the boy threaded his way past the other vehicles, and at last brought them safely to the Boereplein or farmer's square. With a sigh of relief Douw came to a stop beside a row of shady pines alongside the canal. The worst was past.

'Come again tomorrow to see if we need you,' Douw dismissed the boy.

But the worldly-wise Kiepie knew how to earn another stiver.

The Sieur could stay with his wagon, while he would go and tell the best trader in the capital that a wagon had arrived with ivory to sell. The little rascal had already identified the load!

The 'Sieur' touched Douw's heart so much that he gave the boy two stivers, adding that he also had wagoner's timber, soap, honey and a buffalo skin to sell.

'No, Kiepie,' Ouma Katryn firmly decided otherwise, 'first you show us where old Dominee Serrurier's parsonage is. Come, Ruth, take my arm, you're coming with me. Boy, lead the way.'

Ouma Katryn was right: the more the marriage ceremony could be speeded up, the better. Meanwhile Douw had much to do, watering his horse and the oxen, spreading the bale of hay before them and keeping a sharp eye on his wagon. City people would have quick hands as well as eyes.

Kiepie must have hurried and earned stivers at more than one address, for it was not long before several well-fed gentlemen with watch chains and clay pipes arrived. Merchant this and merchant that; they spoke a stiff High Dutch which Douw had not heard for a long time, and one of them even a determined English which he refused to betray by using any other kind of speech. Douw's choice fell on the one who looked the friendliest and spoke an easy-going Cape-Dutch like himself. Douw named his prices, much higher than was current with travelling traders in the Outeniqua area: nine schellings the pound for the elephant tusks, two rixdollars for each ironwood axle, seven rixdollars for a hundred spokes of assegai wood, and one rixdollar for two felloes of genuine stinkwood. Everything in cash, real minted coins and not the new paper money.

The merchant argued the price of every item but Douw stood fast, determined not to be cheated; after all, he knew that the disturbances on the frontier meant meagre times for the Cape merchants. Competition from the others made the merchant come to a quick decision. Was there, he asked, any merchandise Douw would like in exchange? Yes: Douw named his needs. Above all grain, so hard to get; barley, wheat and a barrel of flour as well as a barrel of gunpowder and sixty pounds of lead; a few rolls of blue bafta material and printed calico for clothes; coffee, sugar, a bag of salt; tar; a flask of brandy for medicine; nails; iron for wagon-wheels and work in the smithy; and a large bottle of snuff.

Somewhat later they reached agreement and the transaction was sealed with a glass of sweet Constantia wine emptied then and there. Douw would get only part of the ammunition, more wares than he really needed, and half the remainder of his money in solid coin: it still amounted to the respectable sum of more than one hundred rixdollars. At the last moment he also bought two good locks to put on his wagon-chest. Proud as a peacock he wandered around his wagon, unable to sit down and wait for the womenfolk's return.

When he saw them at last approaching across the square, he dragged a bundle of notes from his jacket pocket and held it out before they could speak: 'Here you are, go and buy everything you women need!' With the other hand he pulled Ruth towards the wagon: 'Just look what's inside!'

The girl's eyes shone as she looked at all the wealth, above all because Douw was so content. Only the old woman seemed unmoved, even when Douw pressed the large bottle of snuff into her hands:

'Thank you. I'm glad, my boy. But the Lord's matters come first. Get on to your wagon, close the tent flap, and put on your clean clothes. Old Dominee Serrurier said you two had to be at his presbytery within half an hour.'

'But I can't leave the wagon! Not now! Everything'll get stolen!'

'Aren't you in the Cape to get married?' the old woman indignantly wanted to know.

At this Douw's eyes flashed, too. Without a word he went and asked a Hottentot driver and a Madagascar slave from the two nearest wagons to keep an eye on his possessions during his absence. On his return he would thank them with a tot of wine and a plug of tobacco. If only he could trust them!

The clock in the Groote Kerk's tower sounded a solemn half-hour as they reached the presbytery. Half past eleven. There

was a gate, then a side door where a black-clad beadle led them
into an impressive room. Everybody had to sit down on bright
leather-covered chairs in front of a grey, corpulent man. His
serious dignity announced that he was Dominee Serrurier. He
started by addressing a few words to Ouma Katryn before he
opened a big book, dipped a quill in an ink-well and began a
series of questions concerning Douw and Ruth. Their names?
Ages? Birthplaces? Were they baptised? Was this their first
marriage? Were they blood-relations? Could the bridegroom
show an official document allowing their marriage before God
and man?

The Reverend Serrurier hesitated when he asked the dark
Ruth if Ouma Katryn was indeed her guardian, and if she were
or had been somebody's bondswoman.

Dumbly Ruth nodded and shook her head. It was Douw
who answered: 'No, Reverend, you may write her down as free-
black.'

The old minister looked surprised at the young coloured man's
tone of voice, eloquent of embittered experience.

'My son,' he said emphatically, 'before God there is no difference between people, and before His Church on earth there
are only Christians and heathens, all of them born in sin. May our
Heavenly Father grant you the grace to put Christian living
higher than the worldly laws and customs with which we all
have to make our peace.'

After that he told them that the banns must be read on three
separate occasions. To oblige them, however, it could be done
during three consecutive evening services; this evening for the
first time. Thus he would be able to solemnise their marriage on
Sunday, just after the morning service, only three days from now.
Deo volente.

'Only three days!' Ruth rejoiced as they left. 'You see, Douw,
you need not have worried. It's Ouma Katryn. She managed it.'

Douw smiled, too, and squeezed his grandmother to thank her.
Ruth wanted so much to take Douw's arm but still felt too shy,
especially before these Cape women who sat so shamelessly
looking at one from their high verandas. And so terribly elegant

at that! By now it was midday, though, and the streets were becoming quiet. In many places Malay and black slaves, of whom there were many in the city, had simply sat down beside a shady wall, nodding their heads in a carefree nap.

When they arrived at the farmer's square, the flask of brandy was missing from the stuff on the wagon. The two neighbours assured Douw, with unsteady voices, that they had not seen a thing.

After they had bought fruit and a fish-pie from a hawker with two baskets dangling from a pole across his shoulders, Douw saddled Pronk.

'I'm going to look for another place to camp,' he announced. 'You two stay with the wagon.'

He stayed away for hours; which did not seem too long to the two women, there was so much to stare at. After three o'clock the city awoke from its afternoon sleep. Coaches and promenaders came past along the avenue. Slaves trotted with slapping feet across the square carrying sedan chairs containing well-dressed ladies or gentlemen with powdered wigs. Their fellows carried water from the cascading fountain on the square, refuse to the sea below Rogge Bay, or baskets of vegetables, fish, and loads of wood, while others walked on their masters' heels holding colourful umbrellas over their heads, even when clouds shifted over the rim of Table Mountain to cover the sun. A city boasting its wealth. A city of slaves.

With beating heart Ruth sat taking it all in. She saw how the burghers turned away annoyed whenever English officers passed: stiff-legged conquerors in red and blue uniforms embellished with gold cord and other fineries. But she saw, too, how the young beauties on the open, raised verandas of their white houses whispered and giggled to attract the officers' attention. She heard how the Dutchmen's High Dutch became higher the more elegantly they were dressed; she heard many strange tongues, from which she often recognised a Malay or Portuguese word and now and again an English one but mainly Cape-Dutch, which all the coloured people spoke with an accent only slightly different from her own. Then she saw a spectacle surpassing everything else in strangeness, making her ask Ouma Katryn in a whisper what it could mean.

It was a funeral procession coming along the avenue on its way to the cemetery. Behind followed the sorrowing family and friends, but in the procession were many other people uncontrollably weeping and lamenting.

'Was it such a big family, heh, Ouma?'

The old woman explained that these people were hired mourners. She had heard that it was the custom in the Cape to augment the importance of a funeral with professional weepers. The extravagant ones at the back of the procession had been hired to make the train look longer. Ruth had been wondering why there was such a long tail to the procession, men who kept on changing their places in an unedifying way, as if they were scared of being the last. Now she heard that the two walking at the end were supposed to be the next to die so anyone near that position kept on changing places. Her eyes widened even more: one of the mourners was keeping his sleeves before his face in a funny way as if to wipe away tears. She suddenly understood what the flat flasks were which bulged from the pockets of some of the mourners. A drunken man could weep more easily!

'Ouma, this is wrong!' she whispered, so upset that she did not want to look any longer. 'Why, Ouma? Only to show how rich the dead man was?'

The old woman put her arms round the girl, and answered after a while: 'Man is born in sin, my child. I still remember my first head-cloth, a blue one with yellow flowers. How I thought my head-cloth made me better than all the other girls. . . .'

Shortly afterwards Douw returned from the direction in which the procession had disappeared. He had found a good place for camping, to the west, past the cemetery and the broken jetty, at Green Point, outside the town, where there was grazing and a big lake with fresh water. It was common ground which all might use, on condition that, by night, fires were screened on the seaward side so that ships did not take them for signal lights.

But Ouma refused to move at once. Tomorrow only; the animals could wait till then, they still had enough hay. She wanted at least to attend tonight's service, and assure herself that the first banns were read. Douw had to give in. Ruth made peace by proposing coffee. But before they could make a fire, Douw had to buy wood, at a shocking price. He summed up his opinion of the city with a disapproving:

'Their dogs are as fat as they are.'

That evening Ruth sat pressed close to Ouma Katryn on a back bench in the big church with its high vault and enormous, round pillars, hearing the first banns of the bachelor, Douw Prins, and the spinster, Ruth Arendse, of the parish of Swellendam. The holy solemnity of the occasion largely passed her by, so impressed was she by the size of the House of God, by the organ music, by the rich women actually quarrelling as they pushed their chairs past each other to be closer to the front, and by the to-do at the end of the service. Then there was a great bustle in front as the slaves of notable citizens jostled each other to hold up lanterns and umbrellas and conduct their masters homewards. For her Cape Town was a wonderful and atrocious place.

That night, under the wagon-tent on the square, she could not sleep for long. She was scared, too, after a drunken brawl had started lower down the square between cursing men and screaming women. The guard had to come and put matters right by the light of lanterns. Afterwards two of these guards regularly made the rounds across the square, guns over their shoulders and a rattle and lantern in each hand. Like slow fireflies people kept moving till late across the dark, uneven streets. The only passers-by without lights were servants who came furtively to the evil-smelling canal to empty their slop pails. She heard the guards swing their rattles as they loudly sang out: 'Eleven o'clock! All's well!' And later still: 'Midnight . . . !'

Early next morning she helped Douw harness the oxen and they rode over to Green Point. A team-leader was not needed, for where the canal ended, the city ended too. They moved past a line of ramparts and along a dirt road without traffic. Down by the sea, to the left of the luxury homes and the more distant fishermen's huts, were a last few buildings.

'Thank the Lord, now one can breathe again,' Douw said.

'Douw, is the Cape not like . . . not like you expected it to be?' Ruth softly wanted to know, trying to hide her own excitement.

'This Cape?' Douw looked at the girl sitting beside his grandmother on the wagon-chest, the old bitterness back in his face. 'No, I had heard that there were white men here too rich to work; but I hadn't known how many slaves there were. I hadn't known how many slaves there were in the world.'

The girl looked away. 'Do you always . . . have . . .' she began, when the old woman pushed her black shawl from her hair and broke her long silence, speaking so loudly that Ruth started: 'Yes, Douw, do you always have to tread on this one thorn? Do you everywhere have to stumble over your pride?'

'My pride?' Douw's jaws clenched whiter, his face alienated in a far, fierce land of loneliness: 'Is it wrong when I thank God I'm not a miserable slave?'

When his bride-to-be turned her head, she first saw the old woman's silver hair gleaming like a halo against the rising sun, and then, past it, while Douw's fierce face still filled her damp eyes, something else that made her whisper anxiously: 'Douw! Look over there! What's that?'

To the right of the road, behind a whitewashed stone wall, stretched the cemetery. But obliquely ahead, on a little knoll visible above the highest tombstones, a dark horror reached against the sky, two high black posts with a crossbeam on which hung a man, or rather, something plundered by birds and no longer a man.

Douw did not look, he had seen it yesterday. He only said: 'The gallows,' and cracked his whip, walking beside his team. He did not want to look.

Ruth did not know what superstition or premonition it might be, but she felt cold fear folding closer round her heart. She was so paralysed that she could only avert her eyes from the horror when Ouma Katryn pulled her shawl back over her head. She, too, no longer wished to see.

The camping-ground was a pleasant place with green reeds and grass and even a patch of bush above the rocky coast where they could pick berries. They collected driftwood for an evening fire. Kiepie traced them there and sold them a brace of fresh fish. It was a place where they could really take a breather. But Ruth's terror of Gallows Hill never completely disappeared. She never completely forgot that she had only to lift her eyes to see the spectre of death, hanging stark and black before the white city in the arms of the mountain.

And this feeling, even though displaced by the hurry and the excitement of their last hours in the capital, and the joy of at last becoming Douw's wife, this nameless fear stayed part of her beating heart, even when, after the Sunday morning service, they stood before the pulpit in the church in front of the sea of white and brown faces and the minister of God finally raised his arms to bless them ere they departed. Two who would henceforth be one.

*   *   *   *   *

It had become early summer when an old woman and an old man set off towards the north from the Outeniqua mountains. She rode on an ox, her bonnet drawn low over her face to protect her from the glare of the sky, while he led a second ox on which had been packed their meagre travelling necessities: a few mats, blankets, a kettle, some food and the life-sustaining skin-bags filled with water. Northwards, across the upper reaches of the Olifants River, the dry, stony earth here and there showed harsh, red cracks in which traces of water and green plants were sometimes to be seen. They travelled in the cooler morning and evening hours, for this year it was clearly warming up to be a terrible summer. Where there were roads to follow, they were mere wagon-trails across the bumpy earth. Where they met people, and not merely burnt-down or abandoned farms, respect was shown to their grey hairs: in that harsh landscape, an old person was no dangerous competitor. It was not too far nor too long a journey, though the fantastic red fissure of the Towerwater Pass was so narrow and rocky that it demanded an endless, scrambling struggle. Beyond it, they turned to the west, along the Zwarteberg mountains' bare northern slopes, till they reached a stone house beside a dry river-bed. Kromdraai, where family hearts were beating, where the pain and longing of a harsh, dividing land dwelled together in one house. Ouma Katryn once more saw her son and daughter-in-law after so many years of separation; she saw with her own eyes how their two daughters, the one milk-white and the other olive-dark, were becoming withered spinsters; she saw no end to her mission of love.

* * * * *

Hundreds of miles to the north-east the landscape was empty, inhabited only by enormous herds of game trekking across the plains in their search for water in dust clouds of an hour's duration, and by tiny bands of little yellow people living in caves in the hills. Many of these 'Chinese' Bushmen had only in recent years become aware of those rare travellers or hunters who penetrated so far with their horses and their houses on wheels.

It was a world with a vegetation totally different from that of the winter rainfall area of the south, with many thorn-trees and, above all, grass that after good thunderstorms grew so high that it would stroke a horseman's knees.

But this year was a strange one. Bulging clouds were borne daily across the heat-pale sky, while dust-clouds and whirlwinds raced over the tortured plain, dragging no more than a dust-wetting shower with them across the horizon. And to crown it all the sky was twice darkened by mighty swarms of locusts drifting out of the north, out of the wild heart of Africa, to devour the grass and to frighten the milling herds of game. The little group of hunters led by Eben Schutte shook their heads and kept straight on past the water-holes to the Great River where there would still be hippopotami at least.

When Lindstrom met Eben Schutte at Graaff-Reinet, he had grasped with both hands the chance of being able to travel far north with so strong an escort. True, Maynier had concluded some kind of peace with the Kaffirs and the rebel Hottentots, but the frontier districts were still dangerous for a lonely traveller. Furthermore, Lindstrom was overjoyed to be in Schutte's company: a robust, friendly man with level blue eyes, intrepid and a deadly shot, only hasty when he had to be, and only at home in the wide hat, coarse blue jacket, leather trousers and veldschoen of the self-supporting, pioneer stock-farmer and hunter who had tamed the southern corner of Africa in a single century. He had settled his family on a Swellendam wheat farm until the disturbances were over, and had now brought his fourteen-year-old son along on his first hunting trip. With him had come three other colonists, each with a wagon and two or three servants.

One evening, round the camp fire, on the farthest border of the colony, they found themselves talking about the country and its future.

One of the hunters nodded significantly: 'Ach, just look what we're getting these days. Bad weather, locusts, English, and Hottentots becoming treacherous turncoats. Not to mention that clever idiot called Maynier!'

'Don't forget the betrayal of our own blood,' another added. 'The Orangist lickspittles stabbing our people in the back to curry favour with the foreign tyrant.'

They puffed faster at their pipes as a sign of fierce unity; all these colonists were nationalist Patriots.

'But are you really a people, a nation?' Lindstrom dared ask. 'You're only a handful of colonists in this huge country. Until recently you were a Dutch colony, and now one small British army has been enough to subjugate you. You are not even the only inhabitants. What about the yellow peoples who possessed it first? What about all the different kinds of half-castes? Or the black nations advancing from the east?' He had lowered his voice so that the servants at the other camp fire should not hear. 'We are five white men and one boy, but with us there are three half-castes, two Bushmen, half a dozen Hottentots, a black slave and a Malay. What about them? And how are you ever going to manage without their labour?'

Swift to suspect criticism, the burghers now looked sullen.

'It is our country,' one grumbled.

After a silence, another said: 'How can we consider these

backward, dirty heathen as our fellow-citizens? It's not possible! Not ever!'

'That's right! How could a jackal and a springbok ever be one!'

More than one head turned to look beyond the servants' fire to a smaller fire on the outskirts of the camp. There sat a circle of more or less naked yellow dwarfs come down from the Lord knew which mountain to guzzle fat hippo meat. These Bushmen no longer squatted or danced, but had sagged down flat on to their buttocks so that their out-stretched legs could prop up their bulging stomachs. They would continue choking down half-raw strips of meat, even though later they would have to lie flat so as to push more down their throats with their fists.

Lindstrom looked at Eben Schutte who had remained silent. The latter pushed the coffee-pot back on to the embers, before he spoke his mind: 'Cousin Bengt, we feel ourselves to be one, one nation. That is the most important thing. We are no longer people from the old Fatherland, from Holland, we are African farmers. And since those Bushmen of the sea, the English, took the Cape, we are feeling more and more like a nation of our own, wanting a government of our own. I don't know when, but one day we'll get it. But you must understand me: in this country there are not only Christians and heathens; there are also our people and the others. I'm not even speaking about the Kaffirs. That nation is much too foreign to us. Like water and oil we'll never get on with each other. Never!'

'But what about the others? Yes, what about the Bastaards with your blood and your language and your way of life, who are like Ruth, wanting to be what you are? Who fought loyally at your side against the enemy? What about them? Some day in the future?'

The men could not reply that it was the Lord's will to create separate nations: a half-caste had clearly been made by man. Nobody gave any answer except a reluctant grumble.

'Please understand me,' Lindstrom hastened to add, 'I ask as your friend and as someone who has fallen in love with this lovely land. But I'm worried when I think of the future.' He told

them about the two cousins—Douw Prins and Thomas Muller—
though he mentioned no names.

Schutte took refuge in his umpteenth cup of coffee. Pipes were
once more filled.

'No, cousin, tomorrow will have to look after itself. It does
not pay to look for trouble across the hill.' Eben Schutte gave a
wry grin: 'Even yesterday's troubles often have to look after
themselves. We don't always want to be reminded of the origin
of the half-caste Afrikaners. But it's my opinion that a son has no
right to put on airs before his father, even if he's an unwanted
stepchild.'

It was meant as a joke, and it did make the men laugh.

Lindstrom did not try any more, nor did he know what more
to ask. Later, somewhat depressed, he walked to the river-bank
to stare up at the night sky with its stars shining so brilliantly in
this southern land. In front of him the big river murmured.
Around in the night were vague animal sounds, a peewit's hoarse
cry of fright, jackals and hyenas snarling and howling around a
hippo carcass, and something which sounded like a grunting pig,
only deeper. Then he heard steps behind him. It was Schutte,
gun in hand.

'Cousin,' he warned Lindstrom in a muffled voice, 'you must
never walk far in the dark. Here an unarmed man does not live
long. Listen, that is a lion out there.'

Lindstrom listened to the deep-chested grunt. He felt urged to
whisper too: 'In another hundred years there will be no more lions
in this place.'

'That's only too true, cousin,' Schutte's tranquil bass came in
answer. 'Yes, then we'll really have troubles. Up till now there
has been enough space to stay a free man and get away from
people. Then? I suppose then it'll no longer be possible.'

At that moment Lindstrom realised that this man, like so many
of his countrymen, had become a new kind of nomad, in love
with the freedom of loneliness; and that it was exactly that which
he himself had come to seek in Africa. Loneliness in which there
would be a place for him.

Was he, too, a kind of nomad trying to avoid the responsibilities of laws, of bastard children or any other frustrating local problem, by continuing to trek away from them all? Would he feel like a prisoner on his return to Sweden?

The pioneer at his side now pointed northwards, across the river: 'But cousin, over there a whole unknown world is awaiting us. Wild and empty. When my sons are bigger, my wagon trails are going to lead that way.'

Now his voice sounded younger, in love.

16

For her it was a summer like none before. At moments she was filled with wonder that she dared to be so happy. But mainly her life had become a matter of course, as simple as the sun filling the days with light and warmth. Here, on the flank of the mountain beside the forest, the earth did not wither as she had been used to seeing. Here everything swelled and grew, a green and gold fulfilment of the light. Was she not already carrying Douw's child, was the warm honey of her skin not glowing as if itself radiating sunlight?

Whenever she saw Douw approach, she wanted to put her arms around him and enfold him with the warm softness which brimmed from her whole being. But always she stopped herself with the tender knowledge of his clumsiness when confronted with her surrender, the timidity which made him still stand aloof until he could come to her abruptly and roughly. She knew, too, that this was because there was still a corner of loneliness in him where he would allow nobody, although he had learnt to talk to her about many things other than mere work. But she accepted it proudly, for so her man had to be, so she could feel every evening when he was not too tired for love, that she was receiving his child all over again.

Her work was so much lighter than his that she never tired.

Every hour of the day was blissfully filled with all she had to do in and around her house. Yes, her house.

She missed Ouma Katryn a lot and old uncle Speelman, too, especially now that her only company came from those two bashful ones, Douw and Tkanna. Everything Ouma Katryn had ever said or taught her was still around the house, but now it was she, Ruth, who knew what should be done. 'Ouma Katryn is like a white person,' she whispered once to herself, 'Ouma Katryn talks with her head, with her head.' Oh, she knew she was a bad Christian. She was glad that Douw read nightly from the Bible and followed it up with a short prayer; but glad for the wrong reason: she was only happy that he had found more peace for his soul since he had seen how white and brown worshipped together in the church. Even though the Heavenly Father and Ouma Katryn might shake their heads, how could being happy be a sin? In these days Ruth learnt to sing, any old tune that hardly needed words to let the hours speed past as light as little birds.

The last purple chalices of the wild sweet-pea tree fell into the washing-pool which became more shallow and tepid every day. Now cicadas shrilled their ecstasy the whole day long and doves cooed more lazily. Lovely and warm, sometimes almost unbearably warm, the summer days passed over Prinshoop. There was so much that had to be built up from nothing that Douw had no time to spare. Progress there was, for sure. The big water furrow was finished so that the late vegetables in the garden could be revived in time. And then there was the house. Before Douw started the living-room, the hearth with its chimney and oven was built of stone, and two walls as well as the roof of the kitchen were covered and clayed over. Then the house had two finished rooms: the bedroom's private sanctuary for her and Douw, as well as the kitchen where, if the nights were cool enough, one could sit late at night to enjoy the fire. Here the young Bushman slept, ready to grab a firebrand as soon as he heard a sound outside near the kraal.

Tkanna was becoming quite a big boy, nearly as strong as a man, and, whenever he could leave the animals, he came to help with the sawing and carrying. Often Ruth became jealous when she heard how these two, so timid with her, could babble away together. Like two boys. But how could she really be jealous of Douw and the boy? She was too grateful that Douw had changed so much that he could laugh; she would do nothing, nothing to burden the light passing of the days. She would not even tell Douw about the child. A man is so silly, she sometimes thought, smiling, he ought to realise by now that she no longer had periods. No, she would not tell him. He had to see for himself, later. In the most natural way. He who formerly could only look directly at a person, above all a white man, when he was angry from pride, and looked sideways at all others, could now face her simply and without defences.

She would always remember that moonlight evening when they had stood by the kraal fence and he had held her and whispered: 'My Ruth, with you I can be a human being.' Remember it, whatever happened.

Only when Douw went down the mountain, to see the field-cornet or for a timber permit, did she become restless. Three times he had been away like that, and three times he returned as he had used to be and for days remained turned back upon himself.

It was not only that Douw had been hurt once more by the arrogance of the Dutchmen towards all who were not whites like themselves; it really seemed as if the outside world contained only bad news.

Real peace refused to come on the eastern frontier, especially since Maynier had been appointed Commissioner. The colonists were furious because Maynier had not punished the Hottentots who had stolen and murdered so terribly but, on the contrary, had rewarded them. How could such injustice promote law and order in the country? And now they were angry with the new governor, too. Not only had he threatened to forbid the felling of trees anywhere in the Colony, but had also announced that in future an expensive licence would be needed before a colonist would have the right to hunt. To hunt! And any tell-tale inform-ing on his neighbour would get half the penalty. Regulation after regulation rained down on their heads from the Castle in Cape

Town. Even a wagon or cart was no longer supposed to appear
on a public road without the owner's name-plate on it . . . Might
old Lord Macartney's gout really give him hell!

The day Douw returned from visiting the Englishman, Peters,
who had been appointed to mark every single tree before they
could be chopped down—at six stivers for each marking—he
went to dig a hiding-place some way from his house in the forest:
a deep trench which he lined with slats to prevent the wood from
rotting. He made a rough lid as well, to be hidden in its turn by
swept-up leaves. In this hiding-place all the felled and fashioned
beams and timbers were stored away.

On the way home Douw stopped in his tracks.

'Listen.'

The light breeze was from the south-east, and from the direction
of Plettenberg Bay they could hear lumbermen's axes in more
than one place, far and near.

'Listen, one can hear an axe a long way off, heh? The others
are felling trees as much as before. Don't tell me all that timber is
for the English ships and cannons.'

'Our building is nearly finished,' Ruth said. 'You won't have
to chop much more.'

'Yes, but how do we make money if I'm not allowed to sell
wagon timbers any more? This man Peters says they're going to
be stern with the parasites who are destroying the forests. I'm no
parasite. The Dutchmen take all the land for themselves, they get
all the permits. Where else could I try to make a living, except in a
place like Prinshoop which is too out of the way for them? And
those hordes of woodsmen down there in the forest don't even
try to farm the land. They merely chop dozens of loads and waste
the young trees. Why doesn't he tackle them first?'

'We'll manage, Douw. We will . . .'

'They want me away from here, that's what it is,' he continued,
still more vehemently. 'The Government's forest land is down
there, not up here on the bare mountain top. I know, too, why
the fieldcornet can't find the time to come and measure off my
farm. He doesn't want to.'

She hooked her elbow round his and stroked his arm till he

quietened. But even though he seemed afterwards to have forgotten, the outside world was something which she had to isolate
with her love and render harmless. Let them stay on top of the
mountain for ever. Let them lack many things, so long as Douw
could be happy. It was a good thing that he loved curdled milk
more than coffee.

Every meal was like an offering to his appetite. She remembered
every recipe Ouma Katryn had taught her, but, aie, how could
she prepare the eternal dried meat and griddle-cake and driblets
of vegetables so as to make them taste different? It was she who
went regularly to the snares and traps to see if there was going to
be fresh meat. 'Grow, men, grow,' she encouraged the young
fruit trees. If only uncle Speelman had been there to smoke out
some nice honey. She herself was too scared of bees; she had
heard of people chopping down trees to get at the honey in a
hollow trunk, but that was a sinful waste.

The evening she heard Tkanna speak of a honey-bird and a
hollow tree with bees; she got him alone and begged him to drive
the livestock in that direction as soon as possible. She gave him a
piece of rag and an old tinder-box. 'It's yours, keep it. But then
you have to bring lots of honey, heh, Tkanna?' She was rather
put out when the boy eagerly suggested they should make honeybeer, but merely nodded. Though the Lord might punish her for
neglecting Tkanna's education!

Sometimes she thought she was so happy because she did not
get scared about nothing; she was simply a thing of summer
ripening in all simplicity. Then she was thankful for Tkanna, so
much a child of the veld that tomorrow did not exist for him
beyond the mighty marrow-bone of the moment that was. But
mainly there was only the pleasure of the work which she and
Douw and Tkanna did, so often together. The warm smell and
rough feeling of a freshly cleaned pole, the grunt of contentment
with which Douw let a cured thong slip for the last time through
his hand, the satisfaction when a new fire licked upwards, red and
yellow around the black-bellied pot on the hook, the warmth
around her heart when she went to touch the young fig and peach

trees in the garden to see how they were growing or when she pressed a swollen pumpkin, their own, first pumpkin, against her breast. The goodness of something that belonged to them because they had made or planted it, the simplicity and the wonder of their child, who slowly, through the summer days, started to throb and swell and even extravagantly to kick within her womb.

*   *   *   *   *

The first quarrel since their marriage rudely surprised her. Formerly Douw had shaved regularly, but in the past months he had not touched his razor. It was not exactly a full beard, his growth was too woolly and sparse, like uncle Speelman's little tufts, but Douw vainly cosseted it; he was convinced it made him look like a real pioneering stockfarmer. It was this that made Ruth say one evening, while she was stroking it: 'Douw, do you think your beard is nice like this? Wouldn't it be better to shave your cheeks and only keep the goatee?'

He rose so vehemently from his camp stool that it fell against the hearth.

'It's my beard! You have nothing to do with it! Stop scratching at me, do you hear!'

His hands gestured wildly as if he wanted to push her away. Amazed, she recoiled:

'But Douw, I'm only asking.'

This only made him more furious still, blindly unreasonable:

'Don't act as if I was a child! Rather look at your own appearance! Look and see what you look like yourself!'

Only when he had walked away into the night and tears blinded her eyes, only after a long session of fretting, did she understand why she did not like his beard and why he had reacted so fiercely: in the untouchable sanctuary of his loneliness he was still choking down his shame, tied to a wagon wheel before a big Dutchman with a luxurious full beard and a sjambok. It was of no avail to think how childish it was—did he not say himself he was no child?—to try to associate his pride with his own beard, for had he not also said: Look at your own appearance! and did that not mean that he was still looking down on her dark skin through a white man's eyes? Still? Or was she herself now exaggerating, she hysterically wondered. No, no, it was so.

Paralysed she remained standing there while the frightened Tkanna rolled himself into his blanket, head and all. From sheer force of habit her hands found the strength to wash the plates and mugs, to throw the tub of washing water outside and light a second candle to take to the bedroom. Passionately she planned how this breach between them could be mended. She neglected herself, it was true; she walked barefoot all day in her oldest, most slovenly dress; she must wear her pretty, flowered apron more often, and iron it, too. Yes, she had to dress better. Even if it was hard on her best dresses, she had to. And she would, from next morning; and never go bareheaded, so that her frizzy hair would not show. Her dark skin? The Lord had given it to her. What could she do about that, other than hope that their child would be light like Douw and not dusky as she was? To hope more passionately than ever? Oh, she had to learn to obey her husband in all respects and not to nag at him or try to change him. She had been too happy, she had begun to forget that life was a struggle. A woman's duty was to give all the love she could. Only to give.

Aware of a crying injustice she forced her thoughts to silence.

Later she no longer sat beside the bed waiting for him, but got in, a small towel in her hand so that the pillow did not get wet. She was no longer upset for herself, only scared of when he would return. Afraid, too, because he was now most likely striding without his gun far away in the darkness. Through the window with its oiled paper pane, she could vaguely see one star above the dark mass of a tree. 'Dear Lord Jesus,' she prayed, 'help me to think only of Douw and not of myself.'

After her prayer, she took off her nightdress.

Motionless, she lay on her back to listen. For a long while the only sounds came from crickets and the frogs in the marsh. When she heard his footsteps, she clenched her eyes so as to spare him more embarrassment. Didn't she know his movements by heart? Then the sweet smell of the extinguished candle drugged her nostrils and the mattress rustled under the weight of his dear

body. He lay rigid and still. Through the thick dark she could feel
how sorry he was, how he longed to end their disagreement, but
how impossible it was for his pride. Her obstinate Douw. It was
she who had to conquer her own rebellion and roll with anxious
humility closer to him and ask his forgiveness, first with her
lips on his motionless shoulders and then with her entreating
fingertips. And when he still remained motionless, to find, in her
despair, words she had not looked for:

'Douw, Douw, your son will be born free.'

Slowly he turned to her and took her in his arms, in growing
surrender perhaps born from the realisation of how well she
understood him, but without words, with the passion of a man
who had to possess before he could acknowledge tenderness.
Even when she moaned with lust, her eyes were still wet, though
she was worlds away from tears. She herself did not know why
but, when their loins parted again, she took his hand and led it
over her swelling breasts to the rounded curve of her belly, and
whispered:

'What shall we call your son?'

'Samuel, after my father,' he answered after a while, and then
louder, more firmly: 'Samuel, as it should be.'

His hand stayed on the living bulge.

'When?'

'In the winter. July.'

So she told him herself, at the moment when they both needed
to hear it.

Days later, after Sunday morning's great wash, he surprised
her beneath the wild sweet pea tree, where she sat trying to comb
her frizzy hair straighter over the mirror of the pool.

'Ruth,' he stayed her hand, embarrassed, 'it's not necessary
at all.'

That afternoon he shaved off his tufty beard. He told her he
had found a grey hair and it had made him feel old. Tenderly
Ruth laughed at the mole on his cheekbone that now sat bare as a
little tortoise on a wide plain.

Laughing breathlessly, she later showed him the two geckos
who had moved in under the roof.

'Look! For them too it is now a house!'

'Aren't you scared a gecko might bite you and make you laugh non-stop till you die of laughing?' he teased her.

'But I'd laugh first, and laughing is nice!'

Golden days with the odour of earth and sun. Mild evenings with the smell of smoke and food, and then of a beloved's body.

17

In April, when the days were still tepid but the nights began to grow chill, Douw completed the last room, the sitting-room, the proud centre of the house that would be Ouma Katryn's as soon as she returned in the autumn.

He was sitting on the roof, busy applying tar to the seams, when he saw visitors arriving across the heights to the west: two men on foot, followed by a trail of women with children on their backs, as well as a bunch of livestock. He frowned. Hottentot women. But the men? Might the half-caste from Duiwelskop, Tkanna's former master, be one of them? No, their beards were too long and luxuriant. They were two English deserters, with ragged clothes and pistols in their belts. Douw descended, got his own gun, and stood considering the matter. It would only cause trouble if this caboodle tried to make themselves at home on Prinshoop.

From the corner of his eye he saw that the young Bushman had noticed them too, and was making his animals graze closer along the valley. Tkanna always carried his stick and his bow and arrows.

'Ruth,' he called towards the cooking shed, 'take the axe with you, close the front door, and stay in the kitchen. One never knows.' He put down his loaded gun just inside the bottom half of the door.

It did not seem that there was anything to be scared of. This

trek looked much too miserable and battered. When they reached
the big yellow-wood beyond the kraal, the women sat down and
the few sheep, goats and thin cows also sought the patch of shade.
Only the two men came closer, not arrogant like robbers, like
two meagre crows coming to beg.

The bigger of the two deserters started his story in his bad
Dutch, now and again helped by his lean, bitter-faced companion,
and later by one of the women who ranted about the nastiness of
the world rather than added information. Their story was confusing but it amounted to this: they had been keeping along the
coastal mountains during the summer, wherever shelter and
grazing were to be had, and had at last arrived at one of the few,
remaining Hottentot kraals. Here Spyker, the half-caste who had
been their leader, heard that the English were paying forty
schellings for every deserter handed over to the authorities. He
and the local Hottentots had made plans to exchange Edward
Murphy and Alex Frazer, the two run-away sailors, for two barrels
of wine. But the women, who were proud of their white
lovers, heard of it, and so they fled with all their possessions
during the night, fled back to the east, for their ultimate destination was the Tzitzikamma. They had heard it was the best place
for people who wanted to be left alone.

Or who want to live off others, Douw thought soberly.

For from what could they make a living? The two vagabonds
looked incapable even of stalking buck with their two pistols.

'You are tired,' Douw merely said. 'Stay here tonight and rest.
We'll give you food.' He pointed to where his wagon stood in the
rough shed. 'The children may sleep on the wagon.'

To Ruth, he said: 'Don't allow them into the house.'

Douw saw to it that their evening fire was lit under the yellow-
wood tree. They were given flour for ash-scones, dried elephant's
meat, two heads of cabbage and curdled milk. Hospitality demanded that he spend some time at their fire and hear how
Murphy and Frazer had been forcibly dragged from their homes
and thrown on a ship of his British Majesty, how they had
deserted as soon as they had set foot at Algoa Bay, and how slave
chains, a military trial and most likely the gallows awaited them

if they were caught. His sympathy dwindled the more they refused to believe that he kept no strong drink at his home, and the more he summed up the character of these war-wearied heroes: Frazer, a thin, bitter-mouthed man carrying a grudge against all of life; Murphy, a big, lazy weakling who was only interested in lying with the women.

Next day they did not start moving towards the Tzitzikamma. No, first they wanted to have a proper rest. Worried, Ruth came to complain about the way the women were begging everything in the house. They had noticed that she was expectant, and were softening her heart with their own white and yellow children. That evening Douw spoke firmly to the unwelcome guests: he and Ruth were not only poor but their position was being endangered as far as the white farmers of Keurbooms valley were concerned. The latter would say that Prinshoop was no farm but a hot-bed for loafers and robbers. What was more, he could be fined if it leaked out that he was harbouring deserters. In three nights it would be new moon, and dark enough. Then their trek would easily pass the Government Post at Plettenberg Bay. He would not allow them to stay a day longer.

In the morning he called Murphy and Frazer: 'Who will eat, must work.'

With spade, pick and crowbar the three men walked to the mountain slope where he wanted to level a few nasty bumps in the road. Douw worked with a diligence that was all the greater because he could set an example to white men and order them around. Murphy was slack and moody; Frazer not up to the job.

At noon, after Ruth had brought them their food, Murphy remained lying in the shade. Only much later did he come to help and then he quickly struck the spade, Douw's only one, so petulantly against an outcrop of rock, that the blade bent. Douw lost his temper: 'Damn it, are you a stupid child!'

At this Murphy pulled his ragged pants up higher and pushed his fist under Douw's nose, cursing: 'You damned Hottentot! Who are you to shout at a white man? I'll break your neck!'

He ranted on about the noble family across the water from which he was descended, and how he deserved much more respect from people.

Bolt upright from anger Douw looked him in the eyes till he got a chance to ask: 'Tell me, do you know of any white man, however despicable he may be, who does not think his white skin makes him better than other people?'

Without waiting for a reply, he grabbed the tools and walked back home. He heard Murphy puffing and egging on his companion, but his neck was too stiff to let him look round to see if danger threatened from behind. Back at his house he took his gun, saddled his horse and told the women to pack their belongings. When the two deserters came sauntering along, he had already driven their animals past the house.

'Get off,' he ordered, 'or I shoot. Your animals first.'

It was another half-hour before the trek got under way, and after their departure he and Ruth had to delouse the wagon.

*   *   *   *   *

It seemed as if the approach of autumn was making human beings migratory like the swallows, for within a week of the deserters, Tielman Roux, as well as Ouma Katryn and old Speelman made their appearance.

Tielman visited Prinshoop for only a short while, to greet his old friend and tell him that his own banns were now being called in the Cape and his wagon coming along the coastal road to fetch his fiancée. Within three weeks he and Sannie Botha would marry and would spend the winter on his father's farm in the Boland. But next year they would return to Keurbooms, and then big things would happen. He and another man had plans for a sawmill at the mouth of the Keurbooms River. Douw must come down one day to look, he would be surprised. Douw was delighted that his old hunting companion had come so roundabout a way just to greet him, but Tielman could not stay long. From his pommel he unfastened a small barrel, a gift of red Pontacq wine which he himself had pressed. With this Douw was to drink a toast to him on his wedding day, the last Sunday in

May. And, far away in the Boland, he would raise another glass to Douw and Ruth's marriage. Laughing they tasted the wine at once. Then Douw ran to catch Pronk and ride some of the way down the mountain with Tielman.

Two days later, just before dusk, the dogs started barking. Across the north-western slope more people came; an old man leading a pack-ox, and two women on riding-oxen. Ruth came running to where Douw had just finished milking the cows, calling: 'Douw, it's Ouma Katryn!'

They both stood staring when they saw that Ouma Katryn had brought an unknown woman with her, a big, yellow, youngish woman with a square, broad-boned body, a hungry mouth and furtive, moody eyes.

When Douw lifted his grandmother from the ox, she gave him a smacking kiss, then turned to embrace Ruth and look her piercingly up and down. Ruth wept, and the old woman was deeply moved.

'I'm glad, my child. I see I come in time.'

Then only did she introduce the young woman: 'Douw, this is your cousin Lena. Your Uncle Thomas's elder daughter. Ruth and Lena, you two are cousins by marriage.'

Hesitant kisses were exchanged. Ruth and Douw looked furtively at each other, but hurried to help with the unpacking and prepare the front room for the two women. Ouma Katryn admired the finished house and continually stopped to put her arms around Ruth. The successful brood of chickens also had to be admired at once. Cousin Lena with her pouting mouth spoke little. Old Speelman was glad to be back, but he could not rest until he had gone to the kraal to look at the fat-tailed sheep and the young calves.

'Haitsa, how their bellies shine, heh! Up here in the green mountain the Child of the Bull can slobber away to its heart's content.' He peered round at the house and quickly whispered to Douw: 'Lena has to look for a man. No heifer grazes near her own kraal.'

Douw raised his arms to the sky but said nothing.

That evening the conversation in the kitchen was not so much about the people of Kromdraai as the terrible drought in the interior and the suffering which awaited man and animal now that an Egyptian darkness of locusts had devoured so much of the remaining pasturage. Ouma Katryn was weak from the long journey and went to lie down early. For a while Douw and Ruth kept up the conversation with the strange girl, who only had eyes for the dung-smeared floor.

In the morning there was much animation among the women as they compared clothes and exchanged gifts. Lena got quite lively, too, as she displayed her treasures, among others her embroidery with threads of seven different colours and a lovely bonnet of lace and cambric. Her pride was an enormous pin-cushion of red satin. She had an irritating habit of playing with it by viciously sticking pins into its red hillock: it was as if she aimed her pricks at other people.

Only towards noon when the irons were warming on the fire and Ruth and Lena were away at the pool, could Douw get his grandmother alone, where she sat with hanging arms against the wall.

'Why did Ouma bring her along?'

The old woman sighed: 'Ach, my child, I was so sorry for her and Hettie. They get on so badly, they more or less hate each other. It's better that they should get away from each other. Do you know, Douw, she is twenty-six years old, and she and Hettie can't marry so long as they stay together in one house. It's enough to make one weep. I talked your aunt Maria round into sending poor Hettie away for a time, too, to her brother's home. He had said he would take her when I went over to talk to him. Aie, that was a bad journey. Anyway, let's hope Hettie will now be able . . . to start a new life. She's light enough.'

'And Lena is dark enough to come to us!' Douw became angry as he spoke. 'Here in the mountains where there are only baboons to marry! Damn it all, how you women succeed in messing up a man's life!'

The old woman remained calm: 'Don't worry, time will bring counsel. It could not be otherwise . . .'

'And this family of ours which runs after whites and doesn't know what to do with itself,' Douw raged on. 'Who's this Thomas of whom she spoke this morning? Her father?'

'No, it's one of her brothers.'

'Is he Muller, too? Or has he changed his surname?'

'None of her brothers have changed their names. They're all Muller: Karel, and Thomas and Petrus ... Hush, there they come,' she ended the conversation though Ruth and Lena were still far away. Douw got the impression that the tribe of women were hiding things from him. But his grandmother looked so tired and depressed by her experiences that he did not press the point and stalked off to chop wood, so fiercely that he broke his axe's handle.

That evening in bed Ruth whispered: 'I don't like Lena.'

'Give her work to do,' he mumbled.

Their love-making was furtive so that the two women in the adjoining room should not hear, especially not ugly Lena who would certainly be lying awake just for that.

During the following days Douw noticed that his cousin was strong and could work well. He staked off a new plot alongside the fenced garden and gave her the pick and spade.

'You know yourself that this drought is going to make grain unobtainable, and our mouths are increasing. The rainy season is approaching, and here on the mountain it will rain. You can start by digging up the old plot within the fence. Speelman and I are going to see if we can knock a wooden plough together, to plough up more land.'

Lena dug like a man, morose as ever. Of work there was more than enough. Thongs and smaller straps and leather for shoes had to be tanned and cured, the wagon-shed had to be completed, and wood chopped before the winter was upon them. Ouma Katryn saw to it that the lambskins her daughter Maria had sent along for Ruth's baby were beautifully soft when cured. Ruth now almost always wore a smile as heavy and ripe as her body, and could no longer do hard labour.

Whenever Douw was tired, he whistled to his roan stallion who responded faithfully to his master's love. Formerly Ruth had been jealous when Douw stood stroking his horse, but now no longer. Sometimes Douw saddled Pronk to try to get a buck or a fat zebra. Tkanna was as diligent a hunter, often with more success. One afternoon he left his charges alone in the plain, to return home with an enormous bird speckled grey and brown, standing as high as his own shoulders, food for many days. Tkanna laughed so proudly that his flat face stretched broader still. Douw and old Speelman were astounded to see a giant kori bustard up here in mountain country. It was an unheard-of thing. How had this bird of the plains come to the mountain?

Not much later the young Bushman came trotting homewards, very excited. Baas Douw had to saddle Pronk and bring his small bullets, there were springbok in the dip beyond the pass. Douw and Speelman at first refused to believe him. Springbok were children of the inland plains, since when were they to be found among mountain rocks and bush? But they had to admit it, an hour later, when they were busy snapping the feet of three springbok and pushing them through the tendons to make them easier to carry. Instinctively inspired once again by the old laws of their wild people, the two Bushmen trampled the hunter's triumphant dance around the dead buck.

Crossing the low pass on the way back, they stood staring inland, shaking their heads. It was not for nothing that swarms of locusts had strayed so far south, followed by locust-birds and storks who seemed to have lost their way as well. Although this was May, the sun still burned down on the mountain. From the hazy, smoke-blue distances inland, came a glow as from an oven. The red sand was burning foot and claw like coals of fire. Only now did they realise what a terrible drought it must be.

'The animals know the drought is going to last,' old Speelman thought aloud. 'Oh, yes, this winter is going to be dry. And the summer after will be dry, too. Very dry.'

On the way back Douw rode to the small rivulet running into the marsh, their home supply of water, and then down to the big forest gorge with its bigger stream. He wanted to see how strongly the water still flowed; Prinshoop's water.

But Douw's relationship with the outside world, that is with his Dutchmen neighbours, was his biggest worry. For that reason he was very glad when a shepherd of Cornelis Botha arrived one day and said that Sieur Botha had asked if he could borrow the roan stallion to serve a mare. All the farmers were eager to let their saddle-horses get Arabian blood. Douw agreed at once and let Speelman go down-hill with the man. In exchange he wanted to drive his cows and young heifers with Botha's imported bull; its calves gave so much more milk as well as butter they could sell. Douw was even more glad because Cornelis Botha was Sannie's father, so Tielman must have had some hand in this friendly advance.

When Speelman returned with Pronk, he brought bad news. The valley people had heard that Douw Prins kept a kraal full of thieves and vagrants up on his mountain. The two English deserters had been caught at Plettenberg Bay and their Hottentot females, now settled on Van Rooyen's farm, said that their hide-out had been up there on the half-caste's farm. Old Speelman had of course denied this lie but the damage had been done.

Then came the last Sunday in May, the day of Tielman's marriage. Some of the young fowls, Prinshoop's first brood, nearly fell victims to this celebration, but Ouma Katryn resolutely defended their lives, so it had to be a leg of springbok roast with the traditional raisins and yellow rice and some of their sweet-potatoes six months old. And, of course, Tielman's Pontacq wine, in mugs of tin or wood, as serviceable as the finest glass.

Since Douw had become his own boss, he no longer shied away from drink, and he took a deep sip in a toast to 'Old Tielman, my only friend. Ruth, what do you say, shall we ask him to be godfather to little Samuel?' A plug of tobacco lodged deliciously in his mouth, old uncle Speelman started playing on his violin, first a holy tune and the lovely song about the little prince, followed with a gay twinkle of a polka, a cotillon, and other peasant dances he had learnt to play on festive days in the Boland.

'Good gracious me, on holy Sunday, too!' Ouma Katryn sighed.

'We haven't got an organ like the big church in the Cape,' Ruth smiled, a blush on her cheeks, her eyes radiant because

A Man Apart

Douw was so relaxed that he and Tkanna started hopping around the table. When Douw turned smiling to face her, she stood up at once, somewhat heavy of the leg but yet more knowledgeable than he was. Ever faster the tune raced on. Lena, who had sat chewing her fingers, suddenly jumped up, as sprightly as could be. 'Cousin Douw, let me show you!' Now Douw's clumsy feet had to do their utmost to keep up with hers.

Ouma Katryn put her hands before her eyes so as not to see the great sin, but she did not stop the dancing. It was only from innocent relief that they were doing this, the first time they were together with such gaiety after all the hardships they had had to face. The jollity only quietened down when Lena became too fierce, and spun on and on with wild eyes and swirling dress. Douw sheepishly fell out. If the fun had been an easing of the soul for others, it had awakened a sleeping devil in the big, yellow girl.

'No, Lena, that's enough,' the old woman stopped her, 'it's not seemly for a girl to be the foremost.'

Lena darted outside on her strong legs. As headstrong and wilful as all Ouma's family, Ruth thought.

It was soon clear that the two young women did not like each other. Lena always needed to show how well she could handle a household, Ruth's household. But the real reason was that Lena was jealous of Ruth, so much younger than she herself and already dreamily possessed of her expectations of motherhood. She hid her jealousy behind a condescending attitude about Ruth's darker skin.

When the first clouds of autumn blew up from the sea, Ouma Katryn and old Speelman went down to the valley to take Lena to the farm of Cornelis Van der Wath. Mrs. Van der Wath needed a temporary help, her daughter-in-law had borrowed her trusty maid servant, and when she heard Ouma Katryn had a grand-daughter who had had a decent upbringing, they had arranged it that way. Maria had taught her daughter how to cook and care for a house; Lena could work. Now she would be in a position to meet other people, too. If only she would not cause trouble.

A Man Apart

As they said good-bye, Ruth begged: 'Lena, see if you can't get a young kitten for us. A house is no house without a cat.'

*   *   *   *   *

The year turned cold. The westerly winds forced clouds against the mountain peaks, but inland the sky remained stubbornly clear. As they peered continually up at the sky, it struck them how many vultures were turning high up, like flakes of ash against the blue. It stayed dry. Sometimes the clouds bellied out, accompanied by gusty winds, but it never got as far as a downpour. They had only one good shower, shortly before Ruth's baby was born at the end of July. Old Speelman regularly saw portents of a great drought and Douw kept on watching his field of barley and wheat. In the summer it would be impossible to buy wheat for bread but, if luck stayed with them, he would harvest ten or twelve bags himself, ample for their own needs.

Little Samuel's arrival had made him more level-headed, as if he now had to think twice before taking any decision. He had looked extremely embarrassed the night Ouma Katryn pressed a kicking and screaming bundle of not-yet-human-being into his arms. 'He's ugly,' was all he could say, and pretended to scowl when his grandmother said: 'Hmph, it's because he looks like his father.' His pride in this little tyrant could not, like Ruth's, radiate into the whole world, but only open up slowly, carefully, the way a scout moves in new, perhaps dangerous territory. At the same time he became more considerate towards his wife and towards Ouma Katryn, whose health had deteriorated so much that winter that she often did not leave her bed. The wonder child had to be brought continually to her bedside; if they laughed at her, she scolded them: 'Go on, you don't know what it's like to be a great-grandmother.'

They were not quite without news from the outside world. Cattle herdsmen, who drove their herds higher up the mountain slopes that year, told of the drought, of the regiment of English soldiers marching past, of the fire which malicious lumbermen had started in the state forest close to Plettenberg Bay because they were no longer allowed to enter it. From their eyrie Douw and his people saw the mighty clouds of smoke darkening the eastern sky for days. At night it was a string of blood-red stars winking and conjuring a yellow-purple glow against the sky. They were not over-worried about Prinshoop's safety, the wind luckily was not from that direction. But from then on Douw saw to it that he only felled wood on days when the wind was from the east and Mister Peters would not be able to hear him.

The news of the trial of the Patriot rebels, Douw heard himself. It was after the spring had returned, much too early, when the hard-pear behind the house started flowering and the mountain slopes were a silky green while the ranges to the interior lay parched to violet-brown deserts. He had ridden down to Plettenberg Bay to buy two new sickles and an iron plough-share at the Government Post, and to drive two of his heifers into Botha's bull-run. On his way back, he stopped off at Van der Wath's farm to see how Lena was getting on.

He rode past the stoep where the fieldcornet and two other bearded men sat drinking coffee, so engrossed in their conversation that they did not notice him raise his hat, hook Pronk's bridle to a fencepost and walk round to the back door. Only a white man knocked at a front door.

A small servant girl peered over the bottom half of the door and said Lena would come as soon as she had finished ironing a sheet. Soon she appeared, neat with a red kerchief and a white apron over her dress. She looked hardly interested as they exchanged what news they had. She and her mistress got on well together, but she did not believe she would stay there for long.

'Do you want to go back to Kromdraai?' Douw asked, not keen on seeing her back on Prinshoop, 'to your mother?'

'My mother?' The big girl's lips pressed thinly together. 'What for? She only taught me to be respectable, not to love her.'

Douw did not like the scornful emphasis with which she had pronounced 'respectable'; obstinately he insisted: 'She's probably missing you very much by now. And your father too.'

'My father's lovey-dovey was Hettie. Not I.'

Her laugh was curt, cut off in her throat: 'I only agreed to come with Ouma because then Hettie, too, would leave the house, to go and visit our extra-special brothers.'

Her cousin took off his hat and dusted the wide brim vehemently before he tried again: 'Well, where do you want to go then? We are your closest relatives now, Lena, we have your interest at heart.'

'I'm twenty-six,' she answered defiantly, 'I save every stiver of my wages. I can look after myself.'

When he stood looking irritably at her, her vehement shoulders wilted and she looked straight at him for the first time:

'Ach, just to go away somewhere. We Bastaards don't fit in anywhere.'

Now Douw had even less to say. He could only promise that somebody from the farm would visit her regularly, and then kissed her cheek, smelling dryly of soap and smoke.

When he came round the house, the three white men were standing looking at his roan stallion. Immediately his pity for Lena in her embittered lovelessness turned into realisation that the white men bore the guilt; yes, they with the high price that they put on a man's colour. What was more, Lena had told him the farmers were furiously upset by the trial of Adriaan van Jaarsveld and the other Patriot rebels from Graaff-Reinet, and that the farm servants had better stay far away today. He did not feel at all like talking to them at that moment. He walked erect, but his shoulders cut as narrowly as possible through the sunlight. As he passed, he doffed his hat and mumbled a vague greeting.

Van der Wath returned his greeting, but he did not introduce Douw to the others. Pipes between their teeth, they looked at the lovely stallion. Douw glanced at them, shifted the bundle of sickles and the plough-share more securely on to the pommel, and unhooked the bridle.

'But this is an English horse,' one of them said, causing Douw to stay his hand. The burgher's remark was hostile, as if by that phrase he was implying some dark accusation or other. It was usually so where whites met a half-caste: if Douw had been a humble Hottentot they would have been much more friendly, but where could a proud half-caste fit in? Douw's voice was

much too loud when he answered: 'Tielman Roux told me that
Boland farmers have imported a lot of Arab horses. These days
one gets quite a lot of roans and bays like this.' He did not say
where and how he had obtained Pronk; Van der Wath would
have told them. When the burgher once more took his pipe
from his mouth to make some kind of remark, Douw cut in:
'Fieldcornet, Lena tells me fieldcornet has news about the trial
in the Cape. May I ask what has happened?'

He had said 'fieldcornet', and not Sieur or Baas Cornelis. Van
der Wath's eyes narrowed like the others', but he had to act as
representative of the Government. Nor had he any right to be too
partisan in his account, so he stuck to the bare facts. After the
nineteen prisoners had lain in the Castle prison for one and a
half years and old Commandant Adriaan van Jaarsveld was almost
at death's door from his privations, he and Marthinus Prinsloo
had been condemned to death and eleven other men had been
banished for life, while two more were to be banished for ten
years. Two others got lighter sentences, and two got off scot-
free.

Douw was sincere when he said he thought it bitterly unfair.
But the third burgher turned his eyes on Douw and remarked
rancorously: 'Yes, our people had not fired a single shot, yet
this is the way they are humiliated and ruined. But your people,
who shed the blood of dozens of innocent people and emptied
the country with their robberies, are rewarded with gifts.'

Your people.

The men knew that he had fought with the commando against
Stuurman's villains, their guilty shoulders testified to that. Yet
their eyes glowered at him, as if in future they could not help
looking for a scapegoat where there was the slightest deviation
from their own facial pigmentation—as if some devil drove them
to burden their troubled consciences even more.

'Steady now,' the corpulent fieldcornet intervened, 'Douw
fought with our men.'

But his eyes too smouldered with the cold sentence of exile:
You're a half-caste.

'He only fought for himself,' the other man joined in, 'a

Bastaard only fights for himself.' They watched how the olive-
skinned half-caste tried to control himself, trembling, because
they were deliberately humiliating him. Why? Because he no
longer panted, tied to a wagon wheel, but dared stand before
them as a free man, gun on his back and an enviable horse in his
hand? Because he too claimed the right to be a free burgher with
his own farm? Why, why? Because the cup of fear had been at
their lips too many times? Because they wanted to take out on
him their humiliation at the hands of the English; on any easy
scapegoat, on any coloured man?

Fearing that his anger might be too much for him Douw leapt
into the saddle, grabbed the bridle and spurred Pronk away.
Half over his shoulder, half at the faceless sky, he called: 'God
hears you!'

When Pronk slowed down up the first slope, he tasted salt
blood on his lips, and another salt-bitterness seeping across his
cheeks. In the blind turmoil of his thoughts everything was continually being broken down, everything passionately destroyed
over and over again. Why? Yes, why, why? Later he would
remember only the poor Hottentot shepherd with his flock
beside the road and what had then flashed through him, sublime
and annihilating like lightning: the knowledge that no man could
really be free so long as others had to live like slaves. Later he
would recall it as a vague moment of unease in the midst of
contentment, as a whispered reminder that a man is punished
when he grows too happy and forgets.

*   *   *   *   *

Slowly the spring days filled with light and heat reflected from
violet clusters of chestnut blossoms. It became early summer.

That first summer of the new century the heavens blazed with
a super-abundance of scorching light such as the country had not
known in human memory. From Table Mountain, towards the
sunrise, as far as the countries of the black peoples, from the
southernmost point of this southern land up to its farthest, most
northerly limits where only yellow dwarfs and yellow animals
wandered over the sandy plains, everywhere across the breadth

and the length of the land, the sun ruled in majesty, withering the earth to sand and eddies of burning dust. For nearly two years the frightful drought lasted.

People trekked away or clung to the valleys and wells. Battles on the frontiers came to a stop. Animals died in their countless multitudes, stampeding towards the Great River's sluggish snake of water or towards the coastal mountains where there was still vegetation and water. Springbok, wildebeest, kudus, zebras, quaggas and even the heavier birds of the veld, as well as their ubiquitous followers, the predators of every kind, moved south, for once unafraid of man. High above in the sky followed the most hideous of all birds of prey, the vultures, endlessly born from the sun.

It was above all the half-castes who took to the road in this year bleached so mercilessly by the heavens. Some trekked towards the Great River, some to join Jager Afrikaner's free bands or to try and maintain themselves as a new Griqua nation somewhere else. Or like Lena Muller, blindly to follow the first man who wanted her, a butcher's agent with his wagon and herds of slaughter-animals on his way back to Cape Town.

Only in the autumn of 1801 did the rain come, in over-abundance, with violence, as was so often the law in the southern land. Through the winter and the spring the rains spread northwards across the parched plains of the interior, filling the heavens with towering, milk-white clouds soon straining blue and black under their loads of lightning and hail and thundering water. The brown teeth of water gnawed away the earth, river-beds and ploughed lands washed away, the clay walls of pioneer homes sagged down. But the earth revived once more, lush and green, great joy to animal and man. For hundreds of miles, without a break, the grass grew so luxuriant that older men shook their heads, starting to think of the danger of fire next summer. But rarely had the Colony experienced such a harvest as in that year. The barns and bins were filled, and the warriors once more started grumbling and checking their weapons.

18

For two years Thomas and Anna Muller toiled to build up their devastated farm, to get a roof on to the fire-blackened walls, to plant new fruit trees beside those that had been chopped down, once more to start a kraal and a vegetable garden. It was in vain. Even the rain came too late for them.

In the spring of 1799 they had been among the few families who had dared to return as far south as the Sundays River. The countryside was wild and empty, no mortal in sight, only now and again the charred skeleton of a house where once had been a farm. To seek to create new life on Welgevonden was to invite heartbreak, especially with untrustworthy labourers who ran away so often that Thomas had to make do with only a lame Hottentot and an indentured Bushman herdboy. They would never have been able to survive the drought if Welgevonden had not been near Sundays River. Their only wealth, their livestock, at least could not die from thirst, only be thinned out by the lions and hyenas multiplying rapidly in the wilderness which was once more their dominion. But the regular driving of the weak sheep and horned stock to the river through the thorny thickets in the murderous sun, was a misery liable to break any farmer's courage.

Then once again, as in the spring of '99, good-for-nothings began to arrive at Welgevonden. Thomas was so desperately short of hands that he hired an unattached Kaffir and allowed him to build a hut. It did not take long before Seko's wife and children arrived, too. For some months all was innocence, then more members of Seko's family made their appearance, herds and all. Thomas wanted to chase them away, but Seko explained ingratiatingly that these people were fleeing the drought and that their animals were too weak to reach the Fish River and Kaffirland at once; they would only rest here until the new moon.

A Man Apart

With the new moon only one thing happened: more Kaffirs arrived, apparently friendly, but in such great numbers that Thomas was powerless. Though they all possessed huge herds, all kept on begging for a tip and wanted gifts. Their animals devoured his meagre pasturage and their herdsmen beat his little Bushman when he drove their herds away. His sheep and cattle began to disappear into the stomachs of these sly snakes, while they cheerfully pretended to be completely in the dark. In this way they would simply push him off his ground, for they well knew that Maynier would ignore complaints about blacks. No, that Beelzebub would not stir a finger to promote justice. One day he might perhaps send half a dozen Hottentot soldiers, who would look around stupidly and ask: 'Where are the stolen cattle?'

Thomas did not dare take the law into his own hands and shoot, for their overwhelming numbers would mean the death of himself, his wife and two small children. He simply had to control his anger and hope for later deliverance. But if he could have murdered, he would have started on the glib Seko, whom he had dismissed long ago but who stayed on, claiming to be the interpreter for his people who did not understand Dutch and, even in their own language, seemed only concerned with begging alms.

On a few occasions he had made Anna bolt herself in the kitchen and ridden over to his only neighbour, Bezuidenhout, half an hour up-stream. Here the same cat-and-mouse game was taking place. He and Bezuidenhout bitterly considered what should be done. Just hang on. Just wait. But how long would they have to wait for the rumours about the Batavian Republic to become true: that the Cape was going to be Dutch as before, that the damned English would leave and the Patriots would then see to it that they got a government which really cared for the burghers' interests? Meanwhile they had to go on living with the daily despair of being bit by bit softened up by black scum who only wanted to push the white men off land which had never belonged to them and which they themselves did not want.

Seko, apparently some kind of chief, now became more brutal. A young fruit tree was chopped down in Thomas's absence, to serve as fire-wood! His best milk-cow was supposed to have been mangled by a lion, after which the black vultures slaughtered it for themselves. They could not show him the lion spoor. Then his two dogs died in one day—from snakebite, they said. Finally the evening came that the little Bushman did not return with the cattle. Only next morning did Thomas find his corpse in the plain, his head beaten in with clubs. He had been the only faithful help left on the farm, for that same day the Hottentot took to his heels. When he interrogated Seko, the latter laughed and said that old Freek had run away because the baas was so fond of using the sjambok.

That was far from the whole truth, for that same afternoon a whole gang of mounted Hottentots came riding through the plain where Thomas was rounding up his stock. Ostrich-feathers nodding above his hat, gun in hand, their cheeky spokesman announced that a few of their oxen had drowned in a mud-hole and that they had come to borrow draught-animals from him. Just like that. His men had not even waited before they started driving off Thomas's best oxen.

'Who gave you the right?' the young burgher furiously tried to stop them, though he knew the oxen were already lost. Two Hottentots spurred their horses to both sides of his, gun-muzzles over their saddles pointing at him.

'Maynier gave us the right. Maynier gave us these guns.'

'You dirty skunks, you have no right to do what you please on my land!'

'Your land? This is our country. May we not even borrow our own property?'

Grinning, the spokesman looked at the burgher with his olive-coloured face darkened with blood. He held up four fingers: 'Take four oxen.'

If Thomas were to resist longer, it would be six. Powerless he had to look on.

'The Kaffirs, too, say this is their country!' he yelled after them. 'Liars! Go and tell it to them!'

When he drove the cattle and sheep into the kraal, Anna came rushing up, pale and upset, a crying child on each arm. Disjointedly she told him that she had been on the bank of the dry stream looking for the nest of a wandering hen. When she looked up, she saw Seko and some Kaffirs coming her way. They came so close to the blonde woman that she scented their wild smell. They pretended to be very friendly, but they looked her up and down as buyers would a young heifer or a horse. She would have died rather than talk to them and, scared as she was, tried to push past them. But they stopped her, laughing, till the brutal Seko said: 'All right, you can go this time. This year you can still have white children on your lap. But next year we take the whole country, and we kill all the white men. Then you'll have to have black children.'

She had managed not to run in sight of them. But when she got home, the children had started crying.

Only now, now that she could creep into his arms, did she cry:

'Oh, Tom, it's no longer a life in this place! Let's go away!'

While her yellow hair rustled against his chest, smelling like long grass after blessed rains, he stared with nearly sightless eyes at the Kaffir huts beyond the stream.

'Yes,' he choked out at last, 'yes, Anna, let's go to the laager at Winterhoek until these children of Satan have been put in their place.'

He loosened her arms furiously. 'But God is my witness, I won't leave one hoof for them. Go and pack at once and stay in the house. We'll trek this very night, in the dark while they sleep.'

Through the darkness they worked as quietly as possible to get the wagon loaded with their few possessions, to lengthen the trek-rope so as to harness every possible ox, all twenty-four of them. When everything was ready, he took some old black tar and painted in clumsy letters on the door: GOD IS DEAD.

A little before dawn Anna started to drive the cows and sheep, while he got the oxen quietly under way. He walked with his gun over his shoulder, and his second muzzle-loader on the wagon, loaded too. But there was no pursuit.

'I'm coming back,' he panted, 'do you hear!'

Near Bezuidenhout's farm, he let Anna sit on the wagon-chest with the second gun, while he hurriedly rode over to tell his neighbour that he was leaving but would return in eight days' time with as many burghers as he could talk into coming.

Four days to Nouaga's ford under the highest peak of the mountains, under the blue cloud of Koemoemqua, the Mountain of Mist-clouds. Two days in the Winterhoek laager to talk the fiery young men into ignoring Maynier's ban on punitive commandos. Two days back to the Sundays River where no Kaffir and no hut was to be found at Welgevonden, and where they drove away the Kaffirs on Bezuidenhout's farm by force, without their livestock, and without two young boys whom they illegally claimed as indentured labour. Then they helped Bezuidenhout's trek, too, to reach the laager. Along the way the landscape was barren and empty; all the farms were abandoned or ruins with charred roof-beams.

*   *   *   *   *

That winter and spring strange rumours went through the land. Scared or criminal Hottentots, who did not belong to the kraals of the rebel Hottentot chiefs, swarmed together in their hundreds at Graaff-Reinet, around their protector, Commissioner of Public Affairs, the Honourable Mister Honoratius Maynier. Even the frontier farmers felt so unsafe that when new, intimidating rumours circulated, they trekked away to greater safety. They became nomadic swarms; longing for rain, longing for the presence of great numbers of embittered, lamenting companions, somewhere else, somewhere farther away. People from Winterhoek, including the Mullers, moved to Zwagershoek where the people had temporarily gathered with wagons and tents and enclosures for the livestock; then another hundred miles to the north to an even bigger laager and later, outside the borders of the Colony, to the bare mountains where they no longer stood under English jurisdiction. Later still Thomas Muller's trek would return to Winterhoek, with a punitive commando; another crawling column of dust across an endless brown floor where the horizons receded and melted in shuddering tremors of heat.

A Man Apart

The rumour that the godless English wanted to catch all male colonists and carry them off to serve as soldiers or sailors outside the country, made the harassed fugitives turn once more to revolt.

In July, during the yearly census, a force of armed burghers surrounded the town-hall in the sun-brown village of Graaff-Reinet and demanded that the Beelzebub of a Maynier should be relieved of his post and that Hottentot soldiers should no longer desecrate the church by using it as a barracks. Promises of more ammunition made them hesitate to turn to open violence. In October, however, when vagrant Hottentots murdered their representative and his wife, just outside Graaff-Reinet, afterwards fleeing to the town, to Maynier, for protection, the local inhabitants could stand it no more. This time they encircled and beleaguered the town, clashing with the English garrison. It was like a fierce thunder-storm without much rain; a few houses were burnt down and a few men wounded.

A month later a big force of soldiers commanded by Major Sherlock came charging along from Algoa Bay. But, in place of a humiliating withdrawal, the burghers heard the glad news that Maynier was to be relieved of his post and that Sherlock agreed that action should be taken against the murderers and violators of the law. On the first day of the new year the British commander attended a great meeting of burghers at Graaff-Reinet, in the course of which the experienced Commandant Van der Walt was appointed to lead a commando to the lower Sundays River. At last the robbers' nests would be smoked out!

Meanwhile mighty columns of clouds had started piling up in the skies and the long-awaited rains came at last to break the drought. Every dry stream or river-bed bellowed fiercely for days, a heavenly music for all who had ears to hear. But when the first green greedily pushed through the wet, brown earth, the horses started sickening and dying. Now the burghers were even more defenceless than before. Thomas Muller's horse died, too, and he had to search everywhere and pay dearly with draught-oxen before he could obtain a new saddle-horse, a brown mare by the name of Meisie.

By this time Thomas was tired of unobtrusively avoiding his brothers, especially since he had heard that his sister Hettie was now with Karel, upsetting news to him in his firm resolve never again to have anything to do with his family. He was fed up and tired of sitting cooped up in laagers and when volunteers were asked to go in secret and keep an eye on the Reverend Van der Kemp's Hottentot trek, he volunteered at once. The other three scouts were Bart Greyling, young Delport, and Seer Du Pisani. Whereas his companions wore old clothes, Thomas was dressed in his best, from his saddle-cloth to the corduroy band round his hat.

It was a trek such as that frontier world had never yet seen. Major Sherlock was truly the first Englishman to act as a wise ruler: he let the Reverend Van der Kemp trek down to Swartkops, with a whole hornet's nest of vagrant Hottentots, nearly a thousand strong. There, down by the sea beside Algoa Bay, Van der Kemp could start a mission station and see if he could turn these rotten eggs into Christians. With that in view, Major Sherlock had given them tobacco, brandy, rice, ammunition, seed grain and tools to take along.

The four scouts sat openly on their horses when this extraordinary trek started on the road south.

In the van rode a British officer with some dragoons and Pandour soldiers, followed by the swankiest Hottentots also possessing guns and horses. Then came a number of wagons and carts with provisions and the smaller children, followed by a disorderly procession of straggling people, women carrying children on their backs, small flocks and herds, and even a tame baboon on a rope.

In the middle of this Babel, the long, thin man of God, Van der Kemp, walked with his fiery eyes continuously recognising Christian souls in the rowdy rabble around him, solemn and stately like a secretary-bird with his black coat-tails flapping round his long legs. To show his humility towards his less-favoured brothers and sisters, he wore no shirt under his black waistcoat, only Hottentot sandals on his feet, and no hat on his bald head baking to a flaming red in the summer sun. For that reason, too, he walked the whole way on foot, while his helper, the Reverend Read, with his stupid friendly face, often took refuge on the front seat of a wagon.

To the four burghers this was no comic spectacle. They had to stay a few miles behind the great trek, unseen, for no less than ten days. Their mixed feelings of irritation and relief that this nest of sinners was now being removed under supervision, although the supervisor was this fanatical missionary, changed to worry when they noticed how the Hottentot men started to desert after three or four days. At first they had laughed: 'Van der Kemp's tobacco and brandy is running out.' But later they began to realise that the poor missionary would arrive at Swart-kops with only a train of women, children and old men, whereas all these deserters who could not see their way to leading a Christian life would most decidedly join Klaas Stuurman's bands of robbers, confident that their families would be taken care of.

Where the Sundays River made its great loop opposite the Winterhoek mountains, the scouts left the trek to join up with Commandant Van der Walt. It was just after the morning stage that Seer Du Pisani saw another bunch of tired Christians take to their heels, behind a clump of thorn-trees.

'Let's ride round that way,' Greyling grimly proposed. 'My hands have been itching for quite a while.'

In no longer than the time it takes to smoke a pipe of tobacco, they caught up with the deserters, cornering them against a bank of earth. There were six of them, one a half-caste with a greyish face and defiant eyes.

The four burghers sat on their horses, their guns ready.

'On your way to Stuurman, heh?' Thomas snarled.

The anxious Hottentots protested loudly that they were on their way back to their masters; only the half-caste stood looking at Thomas, his mouth shut.

'You're lying, underhand turncoats that you are!'

The half-caste gave a twisted, hateful smile while he still only looked at Thomas. 'Listen who's speaking,' he smirked.

If a half-caste looked more than once at him, Thomas became

furious, but Seer pushed his horse in between: 'Wait, let me talk. I want to know something.' His voice was tranquil, as if he first wanted to gain their confidence: 'Tell me, the Kaffirs were once your arch-enemies. Why do you turn against *us* now?'

The Hottentots only stared, sullen and stupid.

'If you answer, if you give an honest answer, we'll let you go, unmolested. I give you my word of honour.'

Du Pisani waited, and one of the Hottentots thrust up his chin to blurt out defiantly: 'The Kaffirs take only our country. You baboon-haired creatures take our country and the marrow of our men as well. You turn us into dogs.'

His comrades glared through slit eyes, nodding in agreement. The half-caste, whose own hair was straight, seemed somewhat embarrassed, but made another sullen remark: 'Rather an enemy than a baas.'

For some moments it was quiet, until Greyling said mockingly: 'Yes, with our horses and guns you can act big with the Kaffirs, heh? But for how long? How long before they swallow you?'

Then Seer said: 'Get going! Go and tell Stuurman we're coming with a big commando. We'll let him know where he stands. We're coming to end his war. Away with you!'

Greyling and Muller made their horses trample forward to hurry the deserters on their way.

The half-caste stopped in his tracks and stared Thomas straight in the eyes, scared and yet sneering: 'Your kind always has to show that they're white.'

While Thomas, stupefied, sat dragging at his horse's curb, Greyling made his steed bound forward so that the impudent half-caste fell over on his back: 'You son of a bitch! Didn't we say run!'

But again Seer intervened: 'No, wait, we promised to let them go.'

'Are you one of Maynier's agents?' Greyling asked him in disgust.

'No.' Du Pisani shook his head. 'But Maynier was right when he said we'll only have peace when we make the Hottentots our friends. They're fierce now, fierce as a cornered ox. They're trapped between us and the Kaffirs, and may swing their horns to any side, blind with anger.'

'Damn it, man, they're only hitting at us!'

'Perhaps they don't trust us. And as long as we don't trust each other, we'll stay enemies.'

Thomas Muller still sat with lowered head, his eyes dark and smouldering. But now he burst out furiously: 'Let them stay our enemies for ever! I trust nobody if he's not a white man like myself!' And he spurred on his horse, determined to ride well away from Seer in future.

Yet Seer Du Pisani was no coward. When the commando left Winterhoek with a mere sixty-six able-bodied burghers in the saddle, he was not one of the great majority of heroes who stayed at home with some excuse or other.

If it had not been for their experienced and universally respected leader, Commandant Van der Walt, the commando would have been faint-hearted. It was February when they moved into the dangerous thickets of the Sundays River. After some smaller skirmishes they clashed with Klaas Stuurman's main force near Roodewal. Now it was a matter of firing, this way and that, over rough country and through clumps of thorn-trees, always in the face of superior numbers, including Kaffirs and even despicable white deserters. A heavy thunder shower burst too, so that every man in the savage mêlée had to watch over his gunpowder like a child. In a thicket the Commandant's son got a mortal wound. After he had taken time off to mourn, Van der Walt got back on his horse, and let the battle continue relentlessly till victory had been obtained.

When they reached the Sundays River with their booty of horses, cattle and guns, they found it a thunderous race of mud-yellow water, impossible to ford. Perhaps they would even be forced to wait a long time, for the night before lightning had been flashing all along the northern horizon.

While the horsemen gathered on the narrow strip of riverbank, the enemy once more swarmed from the fringes of the woods and the heights behind them. An almighty multitude of yellow men, who a short time before had been running for their lives, now mocked the cornered baboon-hairs, crawling closer from all sides. Bullets whined, horses snorted, men shouted that they were trapped. It was impossible to charge. The Commandant and two of his fieldcornets had to use their sjamboks to bring the men to their senses, to get them to fall flat and crawl forward behind their saddles and other shelter, so as to shoot open and hold a wider space on the river-bank.

All eyes watched the mad spate of water. But night fell and the river refused to go down. They did not dare light fires. The new, bitter day crept past as they exhaustedly crouched or lay. Once the Hottentots tried to rush them; they failed and three of them remained, lying like rotten skins. The men cursed their comrades who had stayed at home.

When Klaas Stuurman came to stand on the edge of the bush in some kind of uniform, waving his arms and calling that he wanted to offer peace, the Commandant got up and went closer. Give back all the booty, Stuurman proposed, then you may go in peace. Well aware of his men's bad morale and their hazardous position, Van der Walt agreed. The booty was surrendered, the enemy withdrew, and it became quiet on the heights above the commando. But with the light of day, when the burghers saw that the river had gone down enough to cross, the enemy once more treacherously opened fire. Now it was every man for himself, to get as quickly as possible across the unprotected width of the river, a hundred yards or more. On the opposite side the first to cross could dig in their heels, and force the Hottentots to stay at a respectful distance, but a few burghers, among them Thomas Muller, were wounded, one with a chest wound he would not survive for long.

'Faithless jackals!' the burghers yelled across the dividing river. 'Promise-breakers! Dirty traitors!'

The Hottentots did not dare cross the river and face them in the open country, but Commandant Van der Walt made his men press on to Winterhoek. When the wounded burgher died, they stopped and, there and then, dug a grave with knives and sticks in the stony earth. Dismayed the men stood around the grave: if they had marched out with three or four hundred men Stuurman's vultures would have been something of the past, but as it was it amounted to a defeat. Now every murderous robber would take heart and crawl from his lair to attack the Christians. It would become a bloodbath. Might the Lord help them if the Pandours, too, deserted from the British army and joined the Hottentots of Stuurman, in their howling hundreds. Only the presence of the level-headed Commandant, with the marks of his own painful loss still fresh on his face, prevented them from starting a panicky flight back to their helpless women and children.

In the laager it was soon clear that the commando would be disbanded; men's hearts had become like water. The wildest rumours sped around. The whole Kaffir nation was swarming across the Fish River, a mighty horde of locusts to devour the Colony. The only hope for the Christians was to gather together in a big laager, to stand fast where they were, and to hold out till better days were at hand. Might the Heavenly Father guide the black hordes to attack the English forces fattening their bellies at Algoa Bay and Graaff-Reinet, refusing to stir a finger except when they felt like persecuting their white fellow-Christians. Yes, let the Bushmen of the sea bear the brunt for a change. In any case, in the coming year they would have to hand the Colony back to the lawful Dutch authorities, patriots who would know how to maintain law and order. Many families decided to fall back at once to the quieter Swellendam district and there await the end of the terror. This was Thomas Muller's intention.

The evening before Thomas's departure for the west, Seer Du Pisani arrived at his wagon. Anna was busy washing the flesh-wound in her husband's upper arm, and putting an inflammation poultice over the yellow-purplish hole.

Seer had come to say good-bye. He bemoaned the difficult times.

'Yes, this is more than flesh and blood can bear!' Thomas raged. 'Don't give me more soft talk about the Children of Ham. As far as I'm concerned, everyone who is not a white man, is a false barbarian, and that's that! Bastaards and half-civilised Hottentots who know our ways are the worst when it comes to stabbing us in the back. We whites have to stay boss, and that's that!'

'We Christians . . .' Seer began.

Thomas's mouth twisted with hate: 'Every rebellious devil who does not want to obey must be shot on the spot!'

Seer Du Pisani stroked his beard with a languid hand. He did not look as if he was on guard against his hot blood but rather as if he constantly had to learn a grief-ridden patience, an aloneness emanating from the stubborn intractability of things and people. He looked at Thomas, his own olive-brown face embarrassed, as if searching for what to say: 'Yes, Tom, this is a hard country.'

'Exactly. I tell you one can't afford to be soft, one has to be hard if one wants to live.'

In a whisper Anna asked him not to tense his muscles so, the wound might start bleeding afresh.

Seer filled his pipe and offered to fill Thomas's too. Through puffs as blue as the first evening dusk gathering on the distant Winterhoek peaks, he said: 'No, Tom, not hard, just tough. That I learnt in my barren Karroo country. But you know, even there in that desert, even the toughest plant lives for the moment when the rain returns, when the sap streams through it and it puts out green leaves and blossoms as soft and pretty as can be.'

The dark young man looked with a frown at this fellow who talked like a parson. His blonde wife bent over him to push down the dressing with gently caressing fingertips; there were tiny tracks of pain around her mouth, the mouth that never spoke while her husband held the floor.

'As if clever talk gets one anywhere,' Thomas snorted as he rose, and put on his waistcoat of flowered satin. 'Let's stop this. I still have to get my oxen tied to their yokes. We leave before dawn.'

Just as he was going to shake hands, little Hennie came running past with a toy whip which he could already crack quite cleverly. Mollified, Thomas picked up his little boy, his voice hoarse and sentimental: 'Heh, big man, you're going to become a true farmer's son and a shot in a thousand.'

He stroked the child's hair, and came forward to stretch out his hand, as if he really wanted to say good-bye like that; with the rosy cheeks pressed to his own dark face.

'Cousin Seer, how can one be anything but hard, when one has to help such innocent little mites through the ugly world?'

A weak smile hovered round his mouth, but his eyes screamed with the unhappiness which was devouring him.

19

On Prinshoop the second and third years passed prosperously. Douw's herd of cattle had increased to forty, and Ruth's hens cackled and scratched all over the yard. Only the sheep would not thrive in the sour veld, or were caught by leopards. But the garden and the fair wheat-field made them self-supporting, so that only once did Douw have to go down the mountain with a load to barter for coffee and other groceries at Murray's shop in Mossel Bay. At the same time he drove three oxen along to pay his yearly quit-rent. The great rains of 1801 provided them with an exceptional wheat-crop, loaded fruit trees and fat pumpkins. In addition the house, with its stone oven and wagonshed, was completed at last. Prinshoop was the proud result of hard labour; a settled farm that was second to few of the older ones belonging to white farmers down in the Keurbooms valley.

On New Year's Day, 1802, Ruth's second child was born, a daughter she herself called Katrientjie, little Katryn. Ouma Katryn, often confined to her bed since Lena had gone away so abruptly, doted on this great-grandchild, more than on Samuel who became two in the winter of that year and was already toddling through the world on two independent fat legs.

Little Samie's brown eyes and inquisitive hands were already reaching out to the big world outside his home.

One morning, when the sky was as blue as his father's shirt, he rode in front on the big horse to where they could look down a deep precipice full of folds, like the dough which Mama kneaded, only much greater. Below were houses, much too small to live in, and also a little thing like an upright ant crawling along a brown snake. A man on a horse, his father explained. But when he asked why Papa did not make the big horse ride down to where the houses and the road were, his Papa said it was time to go home.

'Was I naughty, Papa?' he asked a little later.

His father's face was very funny, like when one did not want to sneeze, only quieter. He said: 'No, Samie, it's because white people live down there.'

His father only said Samie when he had to try to be good, but on top of a horse everything was different, so Samie at once asked: 'Like Ouma, heh, Papa?'

'No, my boy, white people are even whiter than Ouma.'

When Samie wanted to speak again, his father added: 'The white people don't like us. We are brown people. Keep quiet now, and I'll let Pronk gallop nice and fast.'

That evening after prayers Douw discussed his answer to his son with his grandmother and Ruth. 'What should I have said?' he asked.

Ruth, whose life was so full these days that she had no time to think about things too far away, was glad that he felt able to discuss this with them. But it was Ouma Katryn who considered the challenge and then nodded seriously: 'A child has to learn everything. He can learn well. He can learn badly.'

'And what is to learn badly?'

'If a child learns to hate.'

This made Douw flare up: 'Damn it, and why do we have to go on being little angels if the Dutchmen keep on casting us off?'

'Then they are the sinners.'

Ouma Katryn stared at the flame of the candle while the wrinkles around her mouth indented deeper still. Then she nodded again, determinedly: 'Yes, one should never stop trying, never stop striving for love. Otherwise you sin against your Maker's greatest command.'

Ouma Katryn looked like a big grey owl surprised by the wonder of light. Now her voice rose, trembling with sincere conviction:

A Man Apart

'Douw, my boy, do you remember what the Word tells us: blessed are the meek, for they shall inherit the earth? Well, I tell you it's the truth. It's not the rich masters, it's not the hot-headed murderers who form this country, it's the sweat and blood of the poor and the humble that build our future.'

Douw jerked his eyes away from the candle flame, stood up so that he could feel the weight and strength of his body on his two legs, and said with emphasis: 'The Lord's my witness, I'll see to it that my son grows up in such a way that he won't have to be ashamed before anybody, and never crawl before another man.'

Then Ruth said something Douw was to remember long after: 'Samie will never have to be ashamed of his father.' He turned to her and saw only how she rocked Katrientjie on her lap, a tiny bundle of flesh of an indeterminate reddish colour that could soften the heart of a mother and even a father with urgent little hiccups and pipis and wetly sucking lips.

Douw left his farm as little as possible, especially since he had heard that Thomas Muller had fled back from the frontier districts and was staying with his parents-in-law in the Keurbooms valley. The laws controlling hunting and the felling of timber had been abolished by the new deputy-governor, so he did not even need to go and get permits from the Postholder. Whenever he did go down the mountain, he went straight to Tielman Roux and Johan Giese at their new saw-mill on the estuary of the Keurbooms River.

Tielman had moved from Stellenbosch when the great drought had finished and immediately put up a wooden hut to provide his wife and baby with a temporary roof. Because stones could be broken from the steep sea-cliff nearby he started laying the foundations of a stone house; a house that could not be burnt down. His partner's house and the saw-mill itself were being built on the other side of the deep, quiet, beer-brown water of the river, and for that they had to build a flat-bottomed boat, later to be replaced by a pontoon on a cable. Oh yes, Roux and Giese had great plans! Douw went down for several days and helped get the most urgent things done. It was enjoyable work when done in company. He got on well with Giese, too, a tough, lean man with an enterprising spirit, from a part of the country where a hard-working man did not always have to shout at his helpers.

When the saw-mill, too, had some kind of roof and two long-saws were humming in their pits, Sannie Roux's second child was born. Ouma Katryn had to be brought down by wagon in time to help with the confinement, and Ruth came down with her. Douw had to return to Prinshoop, but stayed a short while with Tielman. The men were hopelessly in the way, and could think of nothing to do except row across to the saw-mill and help Giese saw yellow-wood planks. In the afternoon Tielman rode some of the way with Douw. 'Man, you'd better turn back,' Douw stopped him after a while, 'don't you have to go and help catch the little baboon, chop off his tail, and scrape him clean?' They laughed at each other, two young fathers. Days later, after Sannie had become richer by a daughter, the proud father took Ouma Katryn, Ruth and her children back home.

The road through the valley crossed the farmyard of the Kritzingers, the parents of Anna Muller. When they stopped and Tielman went to help the small team-leader with the heavy wooden gate between the garden and the kraal, Anna unexpectedly came towards them, her little boy's hand in hers and her younger boy on her arm. She went straight to the old woman to say 'Good morning' and explained that she had only come to show how big little Hennie had grown. Ouma Katryn and Ruth admired her younger child, Tommie, as blond a child as Hennie. Then Anna smiled no longer, her face becoming quiet in the cool shade of her bonnet.

'And Ouma Katryn,' she said, soft and hurried, 'I saw Hettie at Bosberg. All's going well with her. I don't suppose she's with Karel's family any more, she was to marry a frontier farmer in February. A young widower with three children, called Durandt.'

Anna knew!

Ruth's eyes widened, then swam full of hot tears. Anna knew, she had come to give news of her sister-in-law Hettie, she had called Ouma Katryn grandmother, she had come to show Ouma Katryn her great-grandchildren!

The women were so moved that they could not speak; Anna

Muller, too, with her quiet, modest face that made it seem as if she had learnt the hard way to keep sorrows to herself. Then the old woman stammered with deep emotion: 'Anna, my child, I am thankful and so glad. Thank you for telling me. God bless you, my child, God bless you.' She leant over to the small blonde woman to embrace her. They held each other for only a moment, then Anna tore herself loose with a smothered sob and turned back home. Her husband need not know. Whip in hand, Tielman stood deeply moved, though he could not have said what it was which moved him.

The whole way back Ouma Katryn's old, tired face was radiant, and Ruth's tears kept on joyfully returning. For had love not obtained a victory?

*   *   *   *   *

One afternoon, in the early spring, a woman came walking along from Plettenberg Bay, a pack-ox on a lead-rope behind her. It was Lena. She simply came home as if she had not been away for two whole years, unloaded her possessions, and drove the ox into the kraal. When the surprised Ruth came hurrying up from the stream with Katrientjie on her arm, her cousin merely said: 'I'm back.' And she started unpacking, a present for everybody, a brooch for Ruth, a head cloth for Ouma Katryn, warm clothes for the children, and even something for the menfolk.

Ruth was astounded by the change in Lena. She now looked straight at one, but indifferently, without her old smouldering sullenness, without a hungry mouth. She had experienced much, that was evident. She readily answered Ruth's questions. No, the butcher's agent had abandoned her in Cape Town. Then she just went with any man who wanted her, mostly transport riders who could avoid gossip along the road and were only too glad to get an eager worker without pay. There had also been the discharged official who had started his own farm in isolated country beyond the mouth of the Gouritz River. She had helped him build his first wattle-and-daub hut. But when it was time for him to fetch his wife-to-be, he had asked her to go away and stay away. That was where she came from now, he had given her this pack-ox at least. Oh, she knew the wearers of pants by now, many kinds of heroes in pants, and she said, no thank you—rather a spinster than be the slave of a man.

This was not yet the end of the story which she told so calmly. In her bundle, wrapped around the pincushion of red satin, were also baby clothes.

What about these? Ruth wanted to know.

These? Oh, she had had a child, too, but it had died at birth because nobody had been around to help her. One cold night on a trek.

The warmhearted Ruth was so aghast that she put Katrientjie down and threw her arms round Lena. But Lena slowly freed herself and said, as if it was she who wanted to console Ruth: 'Don't worry, I'm past it now. You don't have to pity me. It's done me good to get out into the world. Now Kromdraai is behind me. For ever.'

She rolled up her bundle and looked at Ruth with a sideways smile: 'In any case, I'm pregnant again. Three months.'

Only after a while did Ruth regain her voice and whisper: 'Whatever Ouma may say, you can stay here with us. Or do you want to go on?'

'I don't know.'

'You probably want to wash and rest,' Ruth whispered, because by now she was upset about Ouma Katryn lying ill in the sitting-room, possibly asleep. It would break Ouma Katryn's heart if she had to hear all these terrible things.

But the old woman had heard already. When the two young women turned round, Ouma Katryn stood on the threshold, her face nearly as grey as her hair. She looked and looked at her grand-daughter.

'Oh, my child,' she mumbled at last, 'to think that I went to fetch you from Kromdraai and deliver you to the evil world. To think that I wanted to help you, and that I only helped create a child of sin.' Her voice rose to a piercing lament: 'A daughter of Babylon, a whore along the public roads of the world, blood of my blood. You, Lena!'

Unmoved, Lena looked at her grandmother's raised arms

trembling ever more helplessly. Then the old woman fell silent, shrinking. Before their eyes she wrinkled smaller in her worn black dress. Then it was as if she stood slightly more erect. In a softer, nearly entreating voice she asked: 'Did you . . . love one of . . . them?'

'I . . . I don't know, Ouma.'

Suddenly the big yellow woman's body jerked and she panted once more: 'I don't know, Ouma!'

Blindly she stuck out her arms till they touched her grandmother and could hold on to her. Now she sobbed, and Ruth with her. In the clear mountain light in front of the house the three women mourned in a communal grace of tears.

When Douw returned for lunch, he was told only what he had to know. Lena was already wearing her coarse working-dress and said: 'I'll work for my keep. I'll see to a wagon-load of soap, butter and honey.'

Douw looked sour, but he was actually glad to have the use of her strong arms. These last days old Speelman had become as slight and trembly as a feather.

Days later Lena asked Ruth if they had heard anything of Hettie. When she heard that Hettie had married a white man, her face stayed closed, as if in future it would be indifferent to her what happened to her sister. Hettie was now completely of the past, though this was only to be seen by the absence of her former jealous hate. Ruth did not like the way in which Lena now sometimes looked at her. Had she used to look like that at Hettie?

At the end of September, when the wild chestnut on the edge of the forest stood adorned in purple bridal dress, they also got news of Mynheer Lindstrom. Jan Karieka unexpectedly arrived at Prinshoop and stayed the night. He told them of the Swedish savant's great journey from Kaffirland in the east up to the Griquas and the black Bechuanas' country far to the north and then down along the Great River and the arid west coast back to Cape Town. Lindstrom had sent a memento to Tielman, his spyglass, as well as something for Douw and his people: a brand-new hymn book with a leather cover.

When they opened it, they read on the fly-leaf: *In memory of*

A Man Apart

Ouma Katryn and Ruth who woke me each morning with such lovely singing, and of Douw who chose to be a man, even though it would mean loneliness. In grateful memory.

In the morning Jan Karieka returned to the Keurbooms estuary where he had become foreman in Roux's saw-mill. Before leaving, the Hottentot made sure his gun was loaded, and looked intently down the valley for signs of smoke.

'One never knows,' he said gloomily, 'Stuurman and Slambie are said to be planning another war-dance together. Every single rascal big enough to murder or steal cattle is coming through the Tzitzikamma. The Keurbooms people want to form a new laager or flee to the other side of the Kaaimans.'

'But the last I heard was that the commando was cleaning up the Sundays valley,' Douw said, surprised.

'Your place is too isolated. Haven't you heard how Commandant Van der Walt was killed and all the burghers went home? Man, now there's nothing to stop these hell-raisers. Except praying, if that'll help!' Karieka exclaimed mockingly, as he swung on to his horse.

That night Douw bolted the doors and the wooden shutters. But nothing happened then or on the following nights. They heard no distant gunfire. The horizon showed no signs of burning farms. The spring days were so serene and lovely that they began to dismiss Karieka's news as wild talk perhaps meant to scare them. Who could anticipate a disaster in days so filled with peace and quiet happiness?

The following Saturday, before she went to bed, Ruth shifted the wooden pegs of the calendar to the holes opposite October 10, 1802. In a wooden bowl in the corner, a fowl lay plucked and cleaned for next day's dinner.

They had hardly lain down in the sweetish odour of snuffed candles, when the dogs began to growl outside the house. Then the growling became a furious barking. Somebody knocked on the kitchen door; loudly, much too loudly and impatiently.

Quickly Douw dressed, lit the candle and stood, gun in hand, beside the door.

'Open up,' a voice said.

'Who's there?'

'A Christian.'

The voice sounded more dissembling than honest. Now the dogs were really furious, as if more than one stranger was in the dark farmyard.

'What's your name? What do you want?'

A pause, and then: 'Hans Jacobs. Open up! I'm looking for some Christian hospitality!'

Douw did not move. What kind of Christian talk was this? Behind him the shadows of the five other people in the house slid across the door.

'Where do you come from so late at night?'

Suddenly the dogs let out horrible howls and yelps which became softer and died away into whimpers. A deathly silence followed.

'Open up, man, your damned dogs are chewing me up,' the voice now insisted, even more impatiently.

Douw grimly shook his head. He would not open the door.

The man knocked again, and at last kicked at the door. Then came a new sound of breathing and many feet just outside the wood and clay wall of the kitchen, a shuffling sound that mounted higher, over the outside oven, on to the roof of the house. A heavy object suddenly tumbled down the chimney on to the hearth. A dead dog, covered in soot and blood. Waaksaam. At the same time the voice jeered outside the door:

'Lickspittle of the whites, that's what happens to dogs! If you don't want to open up, we'll open your house ourselves!'

Now they could hear the breaking of wood and a soft hissing against the side wall. It became louder. Fire! The scum were trying to burn down the house. And the wood in the walls would soon catch light.

Douw licked his dry lips, avoiding the others' anxious eyes. Whatever the price, he had to stay a man, even though a paralysed man who could think no thought, move no muscle.

Outside, the black night now contained many voices, and the laughter of many men; a mixture of Dutch and Hottentot and slower, more sonorous voices with occasional clicking sounds.

Kaffir language. And a lighter, sharper, up-and-down voice they knew. Lafleur's voice! Lafleur, the traitor who would not forgive or forget. Yes, this was Dawid Stuurman's gang come to settle accounts with him.

He felt Ruth's body against his, heard from far away her desperate whisper: 'Don't open, Douw. Let us rather all burn to death in the house. Together, Douw, together.'

Now the fire crackled louder, and somewhere the glint of orange was starting to filter through. In the bedroom the children had started crying.

Suddenly Douw turned round, got the candle and ran to the bedroom. There he twisted his gun, powderhorn and bullet-bag into an old rag, shifted the bed aside, swiftly dug a hole in the earth floor with his knife, buried his weapons in it, trampled the ground hard on top, and pushed the bed back to its former position. He hardly gave himself time to bend over the bed, to press Samie's little fists in his, and kiss Katrientjie's tear-stained cheeks. 'Douw, Douw,' nagged Ruth's voice near him.

'I must,' he panted; and, avoiding her, ran back to the kitchen yelling: 'Put out the fire! I'm coming out!'

The three women stood around him, wet eyes and lips caught in flickering hollows of darkness. Old Speelman crouched, his bow aimed at the door. Tkanna glared over the dead dog which he kept pressed against his chest. The voice called impatiently:

'What are you waiting for?'

'Oh, my children, let me talk to them,' whispered Ouma Katryn; when nobody listened to her, she started praying in a high, firm voice: 'Heavenly Father, be merciful to us, poor sinners. Have mercy on us in this night. . .' Ruth now stood motionless beside Douw, her eyes continually on him. She groaned softly when he pressed her to him for a single moment, and her hand lifted weakly to touch his cheek. Then he gestured to Lena that she should ram the bolt swiftly home, as soon as he was outside.

Now, quickly, before he could become a screaming coward.

His hands grasped, yanked open the door. The instant that he jumped out, he saw an arm holding up a firebrand; next moment a heavy, slack blow struck him in the face. A ball of wet, black clay from Prinshoop's earth blinded him. In a turmoil of fists, legs and arms he tumbled over backwards; the door behind him bursting open once again.

When he could next open his eyes, the kitchen was full of wild men, and he had been pushed down against the bag of flour in the corner. His hands were bound behind him. Ruth knelt sponging his face. Then a man pushed her aside—Lafleur, he managed to see—and he saw Dawid Stuurman sitting importantly on a chair, his hands stretched out to the big fire burning on the hearth. The Hottentot chief ignored Douw; his orders were for the women:

'Haitsa, where's your hospitality? Stick that chicken on to a spit! At once! Bring coffee, much coffee, bring bread and meat, bring everything you have. We've come a long way, my men are hungry and tired. Damnation, hurry up, you spook faces! I won't speak a second time!' When Ouma Katryn came up to him and asked if he had never had a mother, he chased her off to the bedroom: 'Old woman, you go and silence those bawling babies. Or do you want them silenced for ever?'

With leisurely gestures Stuurman took out his pipe and tinder-box from the knapsack at his side, blowing satisfying clouds of smoke before he deigned to look at Douw: 'You were seen in Tzitzikamma and in the Longkloof. You rode with the burgher commandos. You deserve to die.'

'I'm fighting nobody's war. I only wanted to get back my stolen horse and gun.'

Douw saw an ostrich plume nod lower as a Gonaqua bent down to strike his mouth.

'We do not steal, we take what belongs to us,' Captain Stuurman corrected him, amused. 'If I remember correctly, I said three years ago that I'd like to speak to you again. Yes, we may perhaps make use of you, perhaps not.'

He raised his eyes to the men around the prisoner: 'Take him outside. Fasten him well.'

Douw was jerked to his feet and pushed outside the house. The wagon had been moved and now stood outside the wagon-shed. A great fire burnt in front of it, and all around swarmed black warriors in war-dress who had taken over the wagon-shed as their sleeping quarters. With one eye he saw a pack of young men pulling down one of his oxen and cutting off huge strips of live meat with their assegais. The ox bellowed and strained to get away. He was pushed up to the hind wheel of the wagon and his ankles and wrists tied to the spokes. To improve his thinking during the night, a dead dog was thrown at his feet.

As years before, half a lifetime before, he stood tied to a wagon wheel, sleepless, delivered over to the old humiliation more compelling than any mere fear for his life. Then it had been white hands that had bound him, now they were brown and black. Sometimes he desolately strained against his bonds, but the thongs had been too mercilessly tightened. Later, when it became quiet in the house and around the fire, he no longer fought against his bladder, and felt the liquid flow down warm inside his leather trousers. It was a long time before the chill wet dried.

Part Four

20

At dark of night, when stars stippled the black water as brightly
as the black sky above, Jan Karieka became aware of danger.
He had heard splashing on the lagoon side of the drift and had
gone out to see whether it was water birds or springer fish. When
he reached the water-side, he noticed that the flat-bottomed boat
was missing.

Across the water it was dark in Giese's house, as well as in the
saw-mill. They would have known if Giese had taken the boat.
No, something was wrong.

Without waiting any longer, he turned to get his gun. Then he
hurried to Tielman: 'Dark doings are evil doings. Baas Tielman,
I tell you, tonight we have to sleep inside the stone house. All of
us.'

Alarmed, the young burgher nodded. 'And we must warn
Giese. They must come across at once. They can wade through
now, the tide's been going down since sundown. Will you go,
or I?'

'I'll go. Baas can get all the others into the stone house. But
hurry, Baas.'

Tielman saw the trusty Hottentot raise his gun above his head
as he started to wade as noiselessly as possible through the dark
river. Then he hurried to his own gun, and to get his wife, small
children and some water and food inside the stone walls of the
half-completed house. There he stood guard, uncertain if they
had been unnecessarily silly or if death really threatened.

The night was so windlessly quiet that he and Sannie whispered
when they spoke to each other. The only sounds they heard were
across the drift and, then, down by the water. Johan and his
people coming, he hoped. He saw the vague figures approaching:
Karieka, Johan Giese and his wife, the black slave, Moos, and his

wife with the children. Their teeth chattered from the cold water. The women and children were at once wrapped in blankets, but the four men stayed in the doorway to await developments.

'Baas, I think it's a waste of time to go and call Windvoel and Sarel,' was Karieka's opinion. 'I've had my doubts about those two for quite a time, above all about Sarel. It's they who stole the boat. Or else they're so scared they've run away.'

After a silence Tielman asked something he would not have considered before: 'Jan, tell me honestly, have you never felt like joining Stuurman and his people?'

'Never, Baas,' the Hottentot answered at once, 'with those rascals one is never sure of one's life.'

'Why not?'

'They have no respect for any man alive, that's why. Not even for their friends.'

The word respect lingered between them till Giese thought with a sigh: Whatever happens, it would be best for all of us to sleep here tonight.

The practical Giese also thought of carrying logs inside so that they could strengthen the door. Tielman went to get more mattresses, blankets and food; he also carried over the two chests with their best clothing and his wife's linen. No one made any move without his gun by his side. Jan and Tielman kept the first watch. They had long ago been prepared for such an emergency and had cast enough bullets; they were ready for the Kaffirs or whoever the attackers might be. The house was strong. It had no roof as yet, but the stone walls were nine feet high and the back door and window openings were closed up with flat stones, leaving only small loopholes in their centres. It would take hours before the solid front door took fire, and for that they had a barrel of water.

Half an hour passed while the night became pitch black. Jan Karieka had the best eyes, it was he who pointed at the temporary wooden house fifty yards from where they crouched, at shadows moving so silently that the dog only started barking when the first ones reached the stoep. A fierce whisper, and Giese and Moos had joined them.

'They think you're sleeping inside,' Giese whispered.

'Shall we remain silent so they think we fled?'

Across the river flames started licking at the darkness: the saw-mill and Giese's house were burning.

'No!'

The fierce answer was followed by a streak of fire and a thunderous roar. From the darkness opposite a voice bellowed with pain, a Kaffir's voice followed by vague, furtive sounds around the wooden house. The dog yelped. Then a long silence followed from which crackling and hissing sounds were born: fire causing misshapen shadows and smoke-smothered gleams of light to dance against the dark walls of the night. Tielman's wooden house was burning too. While the light grew brighter in the farmyard, as well as on the walls of the stone house, the four men moved deeper into the shadow of their doorway.

'They're going to rush us,' Giese whispered. 'From behind,' Karieka added, for he heard crackling noises from the kraal behind the stone house. Moos and Tielman crouched before the loopholes in the back windows; they told the women and children to sit together against the wall, holding a mattress over their heads in case assegais were thrown over.

Beyond the yard the house was now burning like a mighty bonfire spewing vortexes of orange and sulphurous yellow from all its holes. Then many things happened nearly simultaneously.

They had misjudged Windvoel, for all at once there were the anxious footfalls of someone running for dear life and Windvoel came tearing round the corner.

'Baas Tielman!' he shouted, waving when he saw a gun-muzzle lifting from the dark doorway. 'Don't shoot, it's Windvoel, I'm coming in!'

Uncertain whether this was betrayal and the start of the rush, Giese did not lower his gun. At that moment a streak of fire flashed from the trees to the left, aimed at the running Hottentot, for he stumbled down a few yards from the doorway, though still managing to crawl forward. Karieka dashed forward and dragged him into safety.

Simultaneously more shots thundered and the enemy started

charging from all sides, from in front, from around the corners, from behind, where another tumult arose from stampeding animals crashing through the kraal fence. Giese got in only one shot at a figure rushing black as night against the firelight, then had to slam the door and ram home the heavy bolt. At the back windows several shots thundered. Assegais came whistling over, clattering against the stone walls.

'Now watch out above us! Above us!' Giese yelled.

Mercifully it was light outside, and every hand or head appearing above the walls was clearly delineated. The wounded Windvoel grabbed a pole, banging furiously at a pair of black hands clawing for a hold above him. A warrior loomed up screaming, then tumbled over backwards. Swiftly the defenders ducked down to the loopholes, to aim at bodies appearing in their narrow field of vision, before straightening up once more to hit or fire upwards. Instant followed insane instant, in the choking gunpowder smoke, in the accelerated chaos of fear and noise.

As swiftly as it had begun, the attack stopped. Outside the walls of their fort groaning wounded were being carried away. A Hottentot's voice yelled wrathfully in Dutch: 'Long-haired baboons, we'll get you and kill you slowly! Just you wait!'

Then it became quiet again; only the women could be heard, soothing the children.

'That cost them dearly,' Tielman panted.

They dressed the bullet-wound in Windvoel's thigh as best they could, as well as a glancing cut from an assegai in Giese's arm. Then they could only wait what was to follow. The buildings on this side and beyond the farm were burning lower, duller. Imperceptibly the stars shifted across the sky; they calculated that daybreak, their possible salvation, would not come for another six or seven hours.

Gradually they became aware of the enemy's new activities: a scraping and clicking and clashing down by the water-side, and to the left against the mountain. It sounded as if dozens of men were busy piling stones together. Hottentot sharpshooters were watching them all the time, for when Giese tried to open the door slightly to see what was happening, a bullet slammed within inches of his head. Later they could clearly hear the besiegers piling up loads of stones all around the stone house. The amount must have been enormous, for more than an hour stone rattled against stone.

'Have they no more assegais left?' Karieka tried to joke.

Unexpectedly the new attack started. Simultaneously, from all sides, the square of heaven above their heads started to rain down stones. An iron-hard deluge clattered and ricocheted down, bruising their soft bodies. In vain they tried to duck away, holding their arms over their heads. Huddling together under an umbrella of mattresses, the women and children could endure it, but the men had to stand guard with no more than blankets over their heads.

The dark, merciless rain went on and on and still the enemy did not charge. The men packed some of the flattest stones like small platforms against the side so they could see across when the moment came. It was no use shrinking away from the tormenting hail, they had to endure it as best they could. The stone bottom rose over their ankles, reaching as high as their knees. All the time it clattered and clanged around them as if the sky was made of crazy, flying stone. And all the time the enemy stayed their charge.

Suddenly Giese panted: 'God help us, they're trying to fill up the house! That's their plan! As soon as it's filled up as high as the walls, they've got us at their mercy!'

Stupefied the men looked at each other. The cunning devils! They looked to see how high the bottom had risen already. The floor space was not too big, within a few hours their tortured bodies would be offered up on a stone altar to assegais and gunfire. A woman, peering out from underneath a mattress, was hit in the face; the children could no longer be kept quiet and worsened the awful din.

Like a madman Tielman, then Karieka and Windvoel too, started clawing up stones to throw them upwards, back over the walls. Giese and Moos still stood guard with their guns, but later they, too, ceaselessly threw back stones at the sky whence they came. It became a competition of five against an unknown multitude. A race against the night for, with the coming of dawn, the enemy would have to stop or retreat. However much their bodies were bruised and pounded, the two young women, Sannie and Jacoba, came to help too. All the time the stone bottom rose beneath their staggering legs.

While stones could pound them at any time from any side, their bleeding hands found it impossible to keep up the pace. They had to take it in turns, for at least one man had to stand with his gun at the ready. They thanked God that it was mainly round river stones and not sharp-pointed horrors that could rend a man.

But how long could flesh and blood endure such a ceaseless punishment, such an accumulation of exhaustion? Windvoel fell and remained lying, and after him Jacoba, once more hit in the face; Moos's wife, arms curled all round the children, half buried under stones, had to be dug up and seated at a higher level. Would there never be an end to this godforsaken night?

Once the attackers yelled to know if they wanted to surrender. They would promise to let the women go unhurt. Only Jan Karieka answered, with hoarse curses. All the time they went on, bending down, grabbing and blindly aiming at the sky, grabbing and throwing, staggering as they grabbed and threw, without thinking or ducking or shrinking away when another iron fist hit at them.

When the pile of stones inside the walls had risen so high that they had to stoop slightly so as not to show their heads over the top, Sannie sank to her knees. Her head hung, sinking ever lower. Tielman went to help her, but his arms were so powerless that he sagged down unable to rise. Utterly exhausted the other men stopped their throwing, too; only Giese still stood guard with his gun's butt convulsively clamped to his shoulder. If the enemy had rushed them then, it would have been the last of the defenders. All the time stones still came clattering overhead, with sometimes a duller sound as a body was hit. But less of them. All at once Karieka gasped: 'They're finished too! Look! Look, they're throwing slower now!'

'Ready, men.'

A Man Apart

The men scrambled to their legs but there was no attack. The hail of stones had indeed slowed down, the attackers possibly were exhausted too. Another hour or so went past while they once more bent down and threw, bent down and threw, and the stars moved past on high in serene glory. Unexpectedly another attack came, more assegais rained down, guns barked, dark bodies once more strained from outside against the high battlements. When it was past, Moos remained sitting with an assegai in his shoulder and Karieka wiped blood from his eyes. Without any will-power the defenders leaned against the walls, too stupefied to realise that the rain of stones had not been resumed, that it had become silent outside. And, that together with the incredible, blissful silence, a silvery down was growing over their faces and over the mountain of stones on which they stood. The first paling of dawn was showing on the eastern horizon. The day was breaking. They were saved.

But when one of them said it, the others slumped down to remain lying, to fall asleep. Only one man still stood guard, later to wake a groaning, ghost-faced comrade to take his place. In the obscurity before dawn the enemy had driven a great herd of stolen livestock across the drift, and disappeared into the hairy steeps of the Tzitzikamma. In the gleaming morning a boat drifted past on the unrippled surface of the lagoon.

The sun was burning down when the weeping of the children woke the women. With haggard faces the men, too, arose to survey their wounds and the scene of desolation. They had lost everything except their lives. Now a new terror grew: they had to get away, they could not survive another night like that. There was no sign of the enemy and, in the night's confusion, some of the draught-animals had been overlooked: lower down the lagoon oxen still grazed, as well as a horse. They could get away, for Tielman's light wagon in the shed had not caught fire. Most of them were incapable of walking but they could still ride.

Before they clambered down the wall, Jan Karieka looked at the monstrous heap of stones. With the indestructible humour typical of his race, he shook his head: 'As true as gospel, I'll never, never again touch a stone.'

'Good gracious me, and what about my chests of linen and cutlery lying buried underneath all this?' Sannie protested.

'Yes, do you hear?' Tielman irritably rejoined, 'we'll have to empty the whole house. Every stone'll have to go out.'

'Aie, man alive!'

They looked at each other, bent with pain, black and blue and smeared with blood, and suddenly the nightmare of the stones became so funny that they burst into laughter, unable to stop. But the terror returned.

After the men had harnessed the half-dozen oxen to the wagon, the women and children were handed down the wall. They rode along the bank of the lagoon towards Plettenberg Bay. Tielman rode Vonk bare-back, stiff and sleepy, with a body feeling as if it had gone through a mincing-machine. In the jolting wagon the three women, four children and two wounded men lay like dead, a slack pile of bodies, black, brown and white.

An hour later their miserable trek reached the Government Post. Here Postholder Meeding and his sons had heard the shooting, and had set to work dragging beams from the shed and strengthening the doors and windows of the house.

The refugees from Keurbooms estuary were revived with coffee and bread, and the barrels of their guns hastily rinsed with warm water. But then they had to go on; at the Meedings' place safety of numbers was not to be found. They continued over the hill, to Fieldcornet Van der Wath's old fortress farm where other farmers of the neighbourhood were also fleeing. On their way they saw columns of smoke in the direction of Wittedrift and farther inland: other farmhouses burning.

At the farm terror and confusion reigned. Most of the people higher up the valley had by this time fled to the Olifants River and the Longkloof, where the countryside was open and one could see an enemy approaching from far away. There, too, Commandant Botha's commando was busy driving the barbarians away, while the poor inhabitants of the coastal areas were left to their fate. Unlike three years ago, there were few wagons on Van der Wath's farm, and the majority spoke of fleeing farther, across the Kaaimans to where the commandos from

Swellendam and Stellenbosch could strengthen the defence. The wildest rumours sped from mouth to mouth: not only Congwa's Kaffirs were streaming to the west to murder and plunder, but also King Gaika's tens of thousands of warriors. And the worst rumour added that the five or six hundred Pandours, trained as mounted soldiers, had deserted as one man from their English officers, to join the Hottentots. Where else did Stuurman's vultures get this new courage to terrorise the country in broad daylight? This time they seemed very sure of themselves.

Tielman heard the people speaking about another event earlier that day which had aggravated their fears. The Hottentot half-caste, Douw Prins, living up in the mountain—who was not one to worry much about a white man's misfortune—had arrived shortly before noon on his horse without a gun or saddle, grey from fear. His story had been that Dawid Stuurman was occupying the mountain heights beyond Paardekop with a multitude of fighting men. The robbers had raided his farm where they had slaughtered his cattle and insulted his womenfolk. They had tied him to a wagon wheel and manhandled him badly. He had only been able to save his life by wriggling out of his bonds, jumping bare-back on to his horse and galloping away. For some time he had scouted around and had then ridden straight down to warn the people. Stuurman's gangs were going to sweep every single Christian from the Keurbooms area. After giving this news the Hottentot half-caste had ridden madly away to warn the people on the other side of the Keurbooms estuary, from where smoke had smudged the sky all morning long.

Tielman was too exhausted to add much to the debate: whether to stay where they were, or to flee towards Kaaimans. While the women nursed the severely wounded Windvoel and Moos, as well as Giese's arm wound, a gunshot was heard and whips lashed. Some men grabbed their guns and went to escort the new arrivals to safety. It was Hendrik Heynse and his trek who had forded the Bietou in the nick of time and had been so frightened out of their wits that they were determined to continue in the morning to Kaaimans River. This was the intention of many others as well: to get away as soon and as far as possible from the hell-raisers. Hadn't the Hottentot half-caste said that Stuurman's gangs were murdering along the upper Keurbooms today, and tomorrow would tackle the area down here?

Early next morning, when Tielman awoke from a heavy sleep, five wagons stood harnessed before the farm. A single herdsman was trying to keep his animals together where the Cape wagon road left the farm. Old Botha implored the other men in a tearful voice to escort them as far as Melkhoutkraal, for the sake of the women and the innocent children. Lindenbaum volunteered, and Tielman as well. So that Thomas Muller could hear, he explained out loud: 'If Douw Prins could risk his life to warn us, then I, too, can do something for my fellow-men.'

Good trek-oxen were rare by now, with the result that a number of untrained young oxen hampered their progress. The morning stage took them only as far as a clearing in the forest near Die Poort. There they hastily made coffee and roasted salt meat. Then whips cracked once more, not too loud, for even if sounds were hushed between the two walls of trees along the road, they did not want to attract too much attention.

The wagon road gradually mounted the watershed, keeping between steep hills covered with dense forest, through a kind of passage that had provided it with its name, Die Poort, the portal. As the five wagons entered this narrow passage, gunfire broke out from both sides. The team-leader in front of the first wagon, the freed slave, Israel, fell dead.

The ambush had surprised the trekkers so completely that everything was immediately one desperate confusion. Oxen milled and struck out with their horns, women and children screamed with terror, as the men grabbed their guns and blindly, without any cover, tried to return the fire. They had no chance against the assassins. Hidden in the surrounding forest, these could pick them off at their ease. Clouds of smoke puffed from both sides into the clearing between the walls of foliage, a hollow billowing with the deadly blue of gunpowder smoke. Heynse crumpled up, then young Cornelis Botha and Wolfaardt, too. On the edge of the bush, the enemy were jumping to their feet, shouting with triumph.

Lindenbaum and Roux owed their salvation to the fact that their horses got out of control in the general panic, and were no easy targets. There was nothing to do but race away, back the way they had come. Bent low Tielman urged his horse through the stampeding cattle, in passing grabbing the halter of another saddle-horse that had torn loose. With one eye he saw a girl come running round the last wagon; he galloped up to her, drew Vonk up with ploughing hoofs, jumped down and helped the girl, Botha's youngest daughter he now saw, on to the saddle-horse's back. 'Follow me!' It all happened too swiftly to be afraid or to think. Once more the hooves thundered, while they lay flat, pressed into the manes of their steeds, racing away from the place of murder.

Only hours later did five mounted burghers dare to enter Die Poort cautiously from the eastern side; Tielman Roux and four other young men who had the stomach for such a risky venture. This time Thomas Muller, too, had come.

As they had expected, they came too late. But they had not been prepared for such a grisly scene of murder. Between the plundered wagons Heynse lay with his stomach slit open and his guts pushed down his throat. He must still have been alive when they tortured him like that. Some way beyond, near the dead body of Israel, lay a corpse so unrecognisably cut up and mutilated that they had to guess it was Wolfaardt's. Young Botha's genitals only had been disfigured; he must have died instantly. All four of the corpses lay naked in clouds of buzzing flies. The wagons had been plundered and all the oxen and sheep driven away. The old patriarch, Botha Senior, the women and children and the two servants were nowhere to be seen. The assassins must have abducted them. The thought of the fate possibly awaiting the women replaced fear and horror with anger.

'Though they haven't assaulted women up till now,' one of the men said, without much conviction.

With cold, hating eyes they watched the forest around them and searched for tell-tale tracks. Pieces of clothing, a saddle-cloth, and a bloody kerchief beside a trodden bank of earth, were indications that the murderers had retreated deeper into the forest towards the north. They were too few to dare think of pursuit, but as soon as the promised reinforcement from Stellenbosch or from the Longkloof arrived they would track down the evil scum and exterminate them to a man.

First the dead had to be properly buried. While they were carrying the corpses to a pool of shade beside the road, Tielman stood erect, his eyes wide. Behind them, beyond the plundered wagons, a horseman had come riding from the forest. He had just dismounted and stood looking around him, as if stupefied at the scene of ruin. It was a man with a dark, yellowish face. Douw Prins.

Beside Tielman a man drew in his breath with a hiss, causing the others to turn around, too, and jerk up their guns.

'Don't shoot!' Tielman called. 'He's not armed!'

Ninety yards away the Hottentot half-caste turned his head to look at them. Tielman yanked down the gun-muzzle of the man nearest to him, but he could not stop the others' instinctive reaction of suspicion and wrath. A shot went off, and another. Ahead of them it seemed as if the coloured man was swaying unsteadily on his legs. Then he swiftly bounded on to his roan's back and lay flat as he raced away through the trees.

'Are you crazy?' Tielman shouted. 'Can't you see it's Douw Prins?'

The other men remained silent, perhaps embarrassed by their rashness, but Thomas Muller, busy reloading his smoking gun, scornfully declared: 'Yes, Douw Prins. The lying sneak who came to scare us with the story that Stuurman would attack from the north. And when people tried to flee this way the scum ambushed them. Exactly here. Do you think it was mere coincidence that he himself came riding this way? Was it not to see how his evil work had succeeded? Heh, you who're such a friend of the Hottentots?'

The injustice of this accusation made Tielman feel as if the earth had opened under his feet, so that he could merely stutter: 'Are you . . . are you mad? Do you count Douw with Stuurman's murderers?'

'How else? I'll never again trust a non-white. They're all false traitors waiting to stab us in the back as soon as they get a chance. From now on I shoot before I talk.'

The other men remained silent, their faces morose and closed, their hearts too pained for reason.

'The Lord hears me,' Tielman said with outraged conviction, 'but I've fought side by side with Bastaards and Hottentots and slaves of all colours. I owe my life to them many times over. Douw, Jan Karieka, Windvoel, Moos . . . And Israel?' He pointed to the dead freed slave lying in front of them. 'Did Israel betray us?'

To the swarthy young man from Graaff-Reinet hate was all that counted. His eyes hardly slipping down to the dead brown man, a grimace like a convulsive laugh twisting his mouth, he said:

'Israel had a master who could keep him in his place.'

21

He must have slumbered after all, for when he looked around again it was nearly dawn and he was hanging sideways over the back wheel, his neck stiff, his head propped between the rim and the wagon frame. Blood pounded painfully in his ankles and wrists. With difficulty he shifted his position till his bonds felt looser and he once more stood on his legs. He saw the poor watchdog lying with rigid legs outstretched, his muzzle only inches away from Douw's shoes, as if he had wanted to sniff a last time at his master. Douw looked away. Smoke was curling up from the chimney. Inside the house people were awake. Ruth and Lena were probably scurrying around to serve Stuurman and his henchmen. The night . . . No, he did not want to think of the night, he wanted to retain his self-control for whatever lay ahead.

Wherever he looked, the fruit of three years' labour and dreams surrounded him, his Prinshoop where he had learnt no longer to flee from other people and had found the calm of happiness with a woman. Dear, faithful Ruth. Did he now have to bid farewell to all this? Why? Why? How had he sinned? Desperately he clenched his eyes shut, but he still heard the red cock crowing, the old red cock who could stretch his neck so high, so cheekily, as if the whole world belonged to him, so comically. A sudden, nameless pain made him struggle against weakness, his eyes once more opened wide.

Somewhat later bitter wood-smoke billowed over from the wagon-shed: the blacks were also rising, stretching and yawning. Old Speelman and Tkanna came past to milk, their eyes on the ground. At the back door of the house appeared three or four Hottentots to make water, and then Lafleur as well. The latter, walking jauntily and with a broad smile, came over to the wagon. Douw looked him in the face, bitterly asking himself why this man, who had once worked for him, took such a delight in his humiliation.

'Why do you hate me so, heh, Lafleur?'

Lafleur, who had said: You're like a white man. But, more than hidden envy or inferiority, the reason was clear from the difference between their two faces: that of Douw, narrower and more upright, with the dignity and self-control of a man who had painfully created order in his life; compared with the Hottentot's, sloping and sneering, his dissipated features eloquent of unbridled indulgence of any passion or lust, so that the spirit behind the slit eyes wanted only to break down everything which stood proudly erect. Lafleur who turned his degeneracy into hatred so that he could still feel he was a man filled with passionate life.

'I just piss on you, that's it.'

Nor did he wait to do it, underlining the joke further by making water not on Douw, but on the dog at his feet. His loud laughter made other men approach, blacks from curiosity, Hottentots for communal enjoyment.

Douw waited till he was finished and the fun snickered down: 'Aren't you ashamed of yourself, Lafleur?'

The latter grinned with scornful bravado: 'I am a free man. I can do what I like.'

'How can you be free if you have no respect for yourself or for your fellow-men?'

This was above Lafleur's head, so he growled: 'Just listen who's talking! Lickspittle of the whites that you are!'

'You forget soon, Lafleur. You forget that I never crawled before anyone, while you were the snake in the grass. Flat on your belly, until you saw your chance to bite from the back.'

'Arrogant son of a bitch! You've got a big mouth, heh? Wait, I'll show you who's the boss!'

Furiously Lafleur made the other Gonaquas help him untie Douw's thongs.

'Take off your clothes! All of them! Bare-arse!'

Douw's body tensed with the blind desire to burst from his circle of mockers and run into the forest before they could reach their arms. But the thought of the women and children who would then be delivered into the hands of these men, made him undress till he stood naked. While they once more tied him to the wheel, his face remained expressionless, like the black warriors standing around leaning on their bundles of kieries and assegais. The Hottentot rebels who, in their actions against the Christians, often seemed to whip themselves up as if they were violating themselves, leeringly watched him, eager for any sign of weakness or mortified pride. One handed Lafleur a sjambok. Then fiery pain snaked over his cheeks and mouth.

'And keep your mouth shut till you're asked to speak!'

Douw's eyes stared at the faces before him, as if they still could not comprehend why it was not white men who were torturing him; but inside him everything contracted around a dizzying certainty: You can only respect yourself if you do not do violence to another. You are only free when you do not do violence to another. Lafleur is not a free man. I am free.

When the words were repeated a second time, he heard a new voice speaking: 'Douw Prins, I said I'd spare your life if you were useful. I'm going to give you a chance.'

He saw that Dawid Stuurman was standing before him, a showy, much-too-big swallow-tail coat hanging below the bend of his knees, a blue silk cloth around his top-hat on which a circle of ostrich plumes nodded. Captain Stuurman took a leisurely sip from a bowl of hot milk, before he continued: 'I want to know if you will take a message to the Dutchmen down at Fieldcornet Van der Wath's. You'll be welcome down there. My men won't.'

The Hottentot leader had sharp, prying eyes. Were they hiding a sly gleam?

'What message?' Douw asked, with swollen lips.

Unexpectedly there was a stir among the men to his left; somebody came pressing through and a brown hand held a bowl of milk to his lips. Ruth, he saw, Ruth, not in the least defiant or fearfully aware of his naked humiliation, but smiling with brave love. I and the children are safe, her love-filled eyes said, we are not ashamed of our husband and father. Her eyes stayed on his face and her hands did not tremble. While he drank, it was as if he drank mother's milk, as if strength from the earth itself was flowing through him.

'Thank you, Ruth,' he said out loud.

She did not linger, but left at once with the empty bowl.

Somebody cursed obscenely, and then Dawid Stuurman spoke once more. They were going to wipe the whole neighbourhood clean of the baboon-haired whites. They were going to start with the farms in the upper Keurbooms valley and burn everything, then over Wittedrift, Plettenberg Bay, Knysna and farther, right across the whole Outeniqua country. Detachments of his men had started the night before. But he, Dawid Stuurman, wanted to avoid unnecessary bloodshed, and exposing women and children to unnecessary danger. So a messenger had to go and warn the whites to leave at once. This time there would be no mercy. Everyone who tried to cling to his farm would be exterminated without exception; women and children as well. He and the men with him would leave in a quarter of an hour. Could they make use of Douw? Would he depart at once to Van der Wath and the other farms in that area?

His head high and still, Douw answered: 'I am naked and tied like a dog. Can one trust the answer of a dog?'

Irritably Stuurman indicated that his body should be untied.

Somebody threw his clothes to him. Only when he was dressed did Douw ask: 'So you want me to go and scare the whites?'

'We're so little scared of them that they may as well know our plans,' Stuurman laughed. Why did his face twitch so mockingly? Douw hesitated, then asked what he would have to ask in any case if he wanted to live: 'Captain Stuurman, will your people leave my people alone?'

'Yes.' Stuurman snapped his fingers for Pronk, standing knee-haltered amongst the other horses, to be brought nearer.

'You'll ride without a gun or a saddle, for that is how you got away from us. Hurry up. When the sun rises, you have to be far from here.'

Douw's arms and legs were so cramped that he had trouble getting on to the roan's back. Then he lay forwards, with his arms around Pronk's neck, and dug in his heels. 'Go well, my beauty,' he whispered.

He did not look round. Ruth; dear, faithful Ruth. Could he trust these evil-doers? What were Stuurman's plans really? But what could be wrong in warning the poor people down in the valley? He rode non-stop to just beyond the pass on the seaward side of Paardekop. He looked at ease but his eyes kept darting around for signs of Stuurman's scouts and he was on the alert when he dismounted and walked back to just behind the rise where he could look back unseen.

Yes, Stuurman's commando of horsemen was riding north-wards around the deep ravine, a tail of Kaffirs trotting behind. It really seemed that he had told the truth. Douw counted twenty-seven horsemen and at least as many warriors on foot. Might the Lord keep them from molesting Prinshoop any more. Minutes later he raced down the green slopes, as fast as he could without saddle and bridle. He must go and warn Tielman, too. In his feverish thoughts Tielman became the only reason why he was racing so swiftly through the spring morning.

He hardly recognised the white faces pouring from the wagons on Van der Wath's yard, or dropping their work on the fortress wall to come and listen. Then he rode on once more, northwards, towards pillars of smoke against the blue sky, past a fleeing colonist's trek, and later past charred and still smouldering ruins. Once someone shot at him. At that distance he could not see if it was Christian or Hottentot; after all, everybody wore Christian clothing, and now everyone would suspect everyone else. He turned and followed the woodmen's road down to the estuary of the Keurbooms River.

The wooden houses and the saw-mill across the drift were pitiful skeletons; to the left, in the forest, the fire was still smouldering. The strange circle of stones round the unfinished house drew his attention. He dismounted and went to look; at last clambering to the top of the half-filled house, where he could surmise what had happened. Here and there the heap of stones was stained with blood.

For the first time he felt direct anger against the Kaffirs and their Hottentot allies. These people had dwelled peacefully in this place, only to be surprised in this treacherous way. And murdered? Tielman murdered, too? He knew the heathens never buried their victims, and he saw no trace of corpses. He stood listlessly, the prey of a strange, dull bewilderment. Tielman, the only man with whom he had managed to share the exuberance of youth. Had Tielman escaped?

At last he forded the river to search Giese's house on the opposite side. Dejected and overwhelmed by exhaustion he knee-haltered Pronk and lay down under a bush to sleep.

*   *   *   *   *

It had not started at any given moment, possibly it had always been there: this cool, clear light glowing over everything, this nameless longing urging him ever onwards. He soared over an earth consisting entirely of stones—white, greyish, brown and black—an endless pile of stones beneath him. As he soared, he searched, for what he knew not—for Tielman, for a human being, for a great golden sun in his heart. There were whisperings around him, and every time he soared lower, it seemed that lips opened and closed among the stones, sly whisperings he had heard before: 'I suppose we all run away . . . A man, even though it made you choose loneliness . . . as bad as a white man . . .

Scared of people . . . We Bastaards do not belong anywhere . . .'
A vague fear made him strain to escape faster across the stony
earth. To the front soared a figure, a woman, a young woman in a
blood-red dress. He could not see her face, but he knew her arms
were spread wide in her search for him, her mouth and eyes
radiant with love in the cool, shining light. Wings of sunlight
kicked his heart full of gladness. 'Ruth!' he wanted to call, 'Is
that you, Ruth?' But he had no voice, and however he yearned,
he could not approach her. 'Wait for me!' he tried to call, waving
with arms that did not move. The longing swelled in him, because
in front of him the young woman was turning round. But now
her dress was sombre; and when she looked at him, she did not
have Ruth's face, but the wrinkled features of an ancient woman,
a night-black shawl over her hair. She beckoned to him, she
beckoned. Anxiety filled him, for it became dark. He could see
nothing in the night-black darkness and the world rustled as
stones rained on him from all sides. There was no stability, no
deliverance anywhere. Then Tielman's clear voice called from
somewhere to the front of him: 'Douw! Douw! The track comes
out here on the other side!' With all his might he strained to reach
the voice, but in the pitch-black dark he could not move, could
not advance. It was unbearable . . .

Trembling he woke from the dream to find the cool evening
reflecting silvery white on the black water. For long moments,
without comprehending, he watched a boat slowly drifting past.
What was the matter with him? He must ride to Prinshoop at
once, and see to the safety of Ruth and the others.

But when he rose, he felt so dizzy from hunger that he realised
he first had to eat something. The boat, he thought. He could go
and stun springer fish as he and Tielman had done before. At
once he waded out to the boat, brought it to the bank, and went to
find dry reeds and branches to fashion a torch. Minutes later he
stood in the front of the slowly drifting boat, the burning torch
held high to lure the fish, a stick for striking in his other hand.
Soon afterwards slender, silvery fish were roasting on a fire.

He spoke to the mosquitoes which were pestering him and
argued with himself about the burning streak from the sjambok

blow across his cheek. He massaged his sore haunches, he exaggerated his hunger, he cherished his body before the fire's heat. The dream had faded away, and all that remained was an urgent awareness of himself, lonely as the only man on earth. He rode off in the wake of the evening star. Prinshoop. To Prinshoop!

The going was not too bad along the woodmen's road, on the level, riding without a saddle, precariously, in the thick dark where fireflies provided the only light and stars now and then reflected in the lake to his left. Where Wittedrift's steep hills closed round the valley, he suddenly checked his horse. Somewhere in the dark ahead of him he could smell smoke, and hear men's voices. Peering forward he distinguished a fire glowing on the trees, and guessed at the presence of a big herd of cattle. Fear overwhelmed him so that he did not go any closer but dismounted and led his horse sharply to the right, up the hill-side. For nearly an hour he struggled through whipping branches up the dense slope, too scared to look for the path, with only one desire, to continue in as straight a line as possible towards Prinshoop.

I am a coward, he told himself as he reached the open plateau between the two rivers. A coward, small and miserable under the stars, and yet filled with contentment that he did not need to be a fearless hero, alone where nobody could see him. A bird precipitately whirring up from a bush made him cold with fear, urging on his horse until he tumbled into a patch of vines. 'Pronk, shame on you, old Pronk,' he soothed his horse, his arms round its neck, giggling with fun because he was like a frightened child, with no thought for anything but flight. Prinshoop is too far, he decided at last, so he fastened Pronk to a tree and lay down to sleep, a little bundle of man curled around his own warmth.

Late next morning, when he reached the top of the Paardekop heights and his house was no longer far away, he heard a volley of gunshots, far to the south. The wind blew from the sea, and he could hear clearly that it came from the Cape wagon-road, somewhere near Die Poort. There was a furious volley that lasted for quite a while, then silence.

A paralysing fear stole over him as he sat on his horse, staring south over the undulating forest. Now he understood why Dawid Stuurman had sent him to scare the burghers. It was so that he could ambush the fugitives down south at Die Poort. Had he himself guessed this before, but suppressed it so as to save his own life? The idea paralysed his mind. One thing was certain: the burghers would consider him a Judas. Tielman, too, if Tielman still lived.

He pulled the roan round and raced to the footpath through the thickets above Die Poort. What had happened? Perhaps the attack had been beaten off. Perhaps. Perhaps. May the Lord have mercy on them. On him.

The forest was an evil maze that left no room for purposeful paths; even the rare woodmen's tracks ended at abandoned huts, piles of mouldering logs, or impenetrable whorls of trees. What might have been a pleasant journey of exploration was torture to a man in a hurry. It was hours before he reached the Cape wagon road not far from Die Poort. He skirted the deep wagon-tracks and kept to the edge of the forest, cautiously, until he saw what he had feared to see—the plundered wagons with their torn canvas tents and, over there, four bodies on the ground. Nearby horses stood coupled together and a small group of men; armed burghers, among them Thomas Muller and, thank God, Tielman.

Shaky from simultaneous horror and relief, he got off and stood beside his horse. What should he do now? Go nearer? Sympathise half guiltily? His uncertainty was brutally ended when the men noticed him and, without more ado, fired at him. His paralysis became a blind flight, away, into the forest as he had come. What had happened was irrevocable.

Somewhere he came upon the broad, trampled spoor of cattle, horses and people. Too depressed to have any objective, he followed it for a while below a high hill on which he noticed a sentinel. Stealthily he edged around a clearing where knee-haltered horses grazed by two woodmen's huts. Where would the captured cattle be by now? He could not see too well but heard loud, quarrelsome voices; there must have been liquor on the wagons, too. Then there was the sound of a child's crying, followed by a woman's voice. Two women's voices. Horrified he listened as the murderous gang's drunken squabbling rose and fell. Unarmed as he was, he could not hope to help the poor women. No, first he had to get his own people away from Prinshoop, before Stuurman's bullies could do them more harm. And if Stuurman had already broken his word about Ruth and Lena . . . ?

In the twilight, when he neared Prinshoop, he saw no traces of the enemy. He was already pushing at the kitchen door, when the whole world seemed crazily turned upside down, for Ruth called from inside: 'Take care, Douw! Lena's got the gun! She'll shoot you!'

22

Not long after the trampling of horses outside the house had died down, old uncle Speelman had come limping back at a run, so angry that the wings of his nostrils had trouble drawing in air between the deep valleys of his cheeks.

'They're coming back! Dawid Stuurman's adders are coming back over the hill!'

'Oh, Heavenly Father, they're up to no good!'

Ruth hurried to do everything at once, to hide the boiled milk and the half-cooked meat in the bedroom, as well as the piece of bread she had managed to save from the gluttons, and grab the children's soft blanket which Lafleur had appropriated the night before. With one eye she saw Lena washing the kitchen knife in the tub before taking it with her into the bedroom. When she closed the inner door and pushed the bench against it, uncle Speelman called anxiously, 'Do I have to stay in the kitchen?'

'Don't take any notice of them. Play some music. Do something.'

The outrageousness of these words at a moment when she

herself was hiding away from the approaching calamity, escaped her because, as soon as the door was closed, she started trying to think of Stuurman's reason for pretending that he was riding somewhere, and then returning. Was he trying to hoodwink Douw. If so, why?

Then she heard horses, men's gruff voices and laughter. They laughed like men enjoying a huge joke. It was not long before they were stamping around the kitchen, shouting at poor old Speelman. Where had the herdboy hidden the cattle? Why weren't the women fulfilling their duty towards visitors? Damnation! The bellies of warriors must be filled! Somebody wrenched at the bedroom door. Now that Douw was no longer there to be so miserably maltreated, Ruth had the courage to call: 'We're not coming out!'

This made the man laugh; he could easily have scaled the partition wall, or broken down the wooden latch. Yet he left.

Ruth took little Katrien on to her lap to let her drink, and to calm herself. She had to carry on as if these violent men were not there. Ouma Katryn's neck twitched again as she leant with closed eyes against the top of the bed. Lena sat sullen and wordless, looking at nothing in particular, but deciding at last to unravel the tucks on her old dress and carefully wind up the thread for later use. A fierce squabbling over at the wagon-shed was followed by more sounds of violence as the fowls were caught one by one and their necks wrung. Little Samie pushed closer to her.

'Mummy, are they white people?' he whispered.

'No, no, my little one, they're only bad people. Hush now.'

Now Ruth had to rely on her ears to know what was happening outside the house. From sheer destructiveness they tore down the garden fence to make a fire on which to roast the rest of yesterday's ox. Someone, probably a messenger, came galloping up to the house; after that Stuurman gave orders and soon afterwards a number of men set off in the same direction as Douw, towards Plettenberg Bay. Ruth's heart beat so loudly that she could hear even less what they were saying. But she made out the word 'womenfolk,' followed by laughter.

A little later some men came through the sitting-room to the bedroom door; three or four, she guessed. There was a shuffling noise, and then a loud bang. The bench rolled over and the latch sprang loose before the force of the beam which the men had used as a battering ram. With a self-satisfied smile making the corners of his mouth curl up like little pigs' tails, Lafleur entered, followed by two other smirking Hottentots and the yellowish Kaffir who understood Dutch.

'Captain Stuurman said we had to keep the heifers in the kraal. We must keep you busy so that you can't tell tales.'

'Tell what tales? What do we know about your plans?' Ruth feigned stupidity and then indignation when Lafleur came to sit beside her on the bed, pawing at her.

'The other men are taking a rest, but not us. Heh, my little sugar bush? Pretending to be thorny? Today is the day, today we take out your honey.'

His sugary voice turned husky. When she resisted, he knocked little Samie away from her. Her baby landed on the floor. Little Samie hit with his tiny fists at the ugly man, Ouma Katryn came wrathfully to her feet and Lena strained away from the men grabbing at her, to Ruth's side. The room was suddenly filled with their panting struggle.

'In God's name, not before the children!' Ruth wailed as she felt her dress give way before two pairs of hands. Then a man exclaimed from pain and the room became quiet. Lena stood with the kitchen knife in her hand and Lafleur held on to his cheek: a white jag across it swiftly filling with blood. 'You poisonous bitch!' yelled the furious Hottentot. Spattering drops of blood, he rushed forward to help the others pinion Lena's arms. Desperately Ruth thought of the gun under the bed, but knew that it would only end up in the hands of these villains. Lena was strong but suddenly she no longer resisted, and looking at Lafleur with his bleeding face, she scornfully said: 'Take me, and leave her alone. Take me next door and do what you want with me. But I swear that if you come back into this room with the children and her, then I'll kill you!'

Lena's eyes glowed with passion, and for the first time she

looked beautiful, a big, beautiful woman awakened to passion for the first time in her life.

The other men mumbled in agreement; their eyes had already been avoiding the children and the grey-haired old grandmother who remained lying where she had been pushed. Somebody tore a piece of a sheet from the bed and gave it to Lena to dress Lafleur's cheek. One of them even tried to close the bedroom door as best he could.

Ruth helped Ouma Katryn to bed, cooled her temples, and threw a blanket over her. Then she soothed the children in her arms till they were quiet, hushing and crooning over them so that they could not hear the sounds from the room next door: 'Sleep, mummy's little bokkie, sweet, sweet bokkie ... sleepy, sleepy now ...' But it was impossible, and however much she tried to think that they were merely men of flesh and blood who had been away from their own wives for a long time, she could not check the loathing within her as she listened to the animal panting, and the laughter when Lena moaned from pain or shame.

She only took in the other sound when Ouma Katryn sat bolt upright and haltingly started to pray, her eyes still devoutly closed: 'Thank You, Lord, for Speelman's music. Ach, my Lord, I know he is an old heathen, but I thank You that You use him as an instrument to remind us of Your mercy and grace ...'

Old Speelman played his fiddle just outside their window shutters; shrill and loudly and without stopping he played all the tunes he could remember. Ruth's eyes filled with tears as she lay listening to this music, denying ugly reality with its own striving towards beauty.

Old Speelman's music only became silent when there was new movement around the farm. Already the sun threw vertical shadows on the window-sill behind the shutter. Dawid Stuurman's men were preparing to leave for another scene of violence. It was quiet in the room next door, but now she thought of Douw.

When the trampling of hooves died away, she heard Lena go outside, to the river, to wash. By now the children were asleep in her arms, and she herself felt so weak and exhausted that she was still lying on the bed when Lena returned. Lena did not look at her, but sat down on the bench before the cupboard and collected her spilled needle-work. She put the pin-cushion of red satin beside the other things and kept on looking at it, with lifeless eyes.

'Lena,' Ruth whispered at last, 'oh, Lena, I'm terribly sorry, how can I ever thank you?'

When the big yellow woman did not stir, Ruth rose and put her arms round her, sobbing.

Then only did Lena look as if she could see and hear. A curious frown on her forehead, she looked for a long while at Ruth and then at the children on the bed. Slowly she lifted her hand to stroke Ruth's hair and said, in a queer voice:

'Hettie. Don't worry, Hettie. It won't happen again.'

Ruth drew in her breath when Lena continued in the same monotonous voice: 'Ma tried to hide it from us in vain. All men are filth. But, Hettie, the Lord hears me, this is enough! I'll kill the first man who tries to enter this house.'

Suddenly she pushed the needle-work away and stood up.

'But, Lena, I'm not Hettie! I'm Ruth!'

Lena's frown only became deeper as she came forward and pushed the bed aside with her strong arms. The gun. She wanted to take out Douw's gun. She saw how Lena had looked at her children, and swiftly cold comprehension grasped at her heart. She sprang between the big woman and the children on the bed.

'Douw would not want us to take out his gun,' she tried to stop Lena.

Lena seemed not to hear; she knelt, clearing away the soil, taking out the rag-wrapped bundle and shifting the bed back to its old position. Then she hung the powderhorn and bullet-pouch around her shoulders and looked to see if the gun was loaded and primed.

At her wits' end Ruth stood before the bed. Had her terrible experience made Lena go out of her mind? She seemed so calm. Ruth started with relief when Ouma Katryn sat up, looked at her grand-daughter and asked in a strange, distant voice:

'Lena, my child, my poor child, how do you know how Hettie is? How do you know she has really found love?'

Without even looking at her grandmother, Lena silenced her:

'You with your eternal pious talk about love this and love that. You're an old woman with one foot in the grave. What do you know?'

She walked out. The others heard her close the window shutters and the outer door and bolt the kitchen door. She stayed outside. sitting down, ready to keep any man away from Hettie. And she would shoot, Ruth knew. Even though it might be Douw returning home. Ouma Katryn once more lay on her back, her mouth and eyes closed in her waxen face which already looked like a death-mask. Ruth felt that she would become crazy herself if she did not at once plunge into the daily chores. The house had to be cleaned, the children to be fed, she had to boil water to wash away the blood stains, much boiling water . . .

Lena sat in the kitchen and took no notice of Ruth's bustling. If Ruth said something, she answered curtly. Once Lena asked: 'The man I cut with the knife, what's his name? He sounded as if he knew you.'

'Lafleur. It's he who worked with us before, and who . . .' But Lena knew the whole history of Lafleur, why should she tell it again? And then, Ruth wondered, how would Lena fit Lafleur into her crazy idea that she was Hettie?

'Why do you ask?'

But Lena sat dull and brooding as before, the gun laid menacingly across her lap. She took as little notice of old Speelman's shrill voice.

The whole afternoon and evening Ruth worked hard to get the house to look as it had before the calamity had struck them. Whenever she went outside, Lena stood guard at the corner of the house; whenever Katrientjie cried or little Samie was naughty, she hastened to silence them.

Ouma Katryn was too weak to rise and evening prayers had to be held around the bed in the bedroom. Ruth did not know what Ouma Katryn was reading from the Bible or what she prayed for in so stammering a voice, for all the time she herself was praying that Douw might come back in the night while Lena slept. The greater part of the night she lay awake. She saw no possibility of stealing the gun as it lay beside Lena in her bed; she was too ignorant of fire-arms and Lena was so much stronger than she. The Heavenly Father would have to help her at the last moment, that was all she could hope for.

It became morning, forenoon, and it remained quiet around the house. Once there was a far-off booming, as if giant waves were tumbling wildly against the coast. The house was closed and dark so that if Ruth wanted to see if anybody was approaching, she had to do some kind of chore outside. She became ever more anxious because Douw stayed away so long. Had that been shooting some while ago? Oh God, watch over him, please bring him back safe and sound . . .

In the bedroom Ouma Katryn read the Bible the whole day long. In his corner of the kitchen old uncle Speelman lay staring at Lena with his fever-yellow eyes, even more scared of her than Ruth was.

Shortly before noon Ruth went to rinse the baby's nappies and other clothes in the washing pool. She noticed a wild sweet pea shiver higher up the marsh, as she raised her head she saw Tkanna come towards her at a stealthy run. The Bushman's bright black eyes darted over her to the farm where Lena stood like a pillar of salt with the gun over her shoulder. Eagerly Tkanna wanted to know where baas Douw was; he had looked after the cattle well and had driven them beyond Spitskop where he had hidden them in a bushy hollow. Stuurman's gluttons had only managed to get the lamed heifer which the snake had bitten. Proudly Tkanna boasted how he had saved Douw's livestock.

Ruth pressed him to her heart, grateful that there was another normal person on earth and, what was more, one who loved Douw. She told him that they were waiting for Douw, and asked him to walk homewards by her side. Lena did not seem to regard Tkanna as a man and Ruth was able to take him into the kitchen and let him eat his fill. He left as soon as he had explained at great length to old uncle Speelman where and how the cattle were hidden.

Afternoon became early evening. The flies in the closed house exhausted Ruth, and little Samie became completely unmanageable. Now that all the housework had been done and old Speelman had chopped the necessary firewood, Lena dragged her chair to the kitchen door so that nobody could leave again.

Worn-out from the strain of waiting, Ruth went to sit down. Suddenly she heard a light, hurried step come round the corner of the house, a step that made her jump to her feet. Douw! she knew without question. This was how he walked, erect, with quick, neat steps. The footsteps came straight to the back door. And then, while Lena, too, got to her feet, and stood slightly bent beside the door holding the long muzzle-loader, she saw his hand raised to the top half of the door.

'Take care, Douw!' she cried. 'Lena's got the gun! She'll shoot you!'

There was a silence outside. Then his voice came tiredly: 'What's the matter with you all?'

Ruth heard Ouma Katryn and Speelman approaching; now all her attention was on the big yellow woman and the moment when she would have to jump at her and hold her fast.

'Put down the gun, Lena. Don't you hear, it's Douw, it's Douw!'

Lena's mouth was clenched so that she no longer had lips.

'Lena, in God's name!' Ruth moaned hysterically.

Then suddenly everything became simple.

Ouma Katryn's face twisted in a heartrending way while she put out her trembling arms to hold on to her grand-daughter. 'Forgive me, Lena, my child,' she panted between dry sobs. 'I tried to be a good grandmother to you all. But I'm a stupid old woman, as helpless as you are in this evil world. Oh, Lena, my child, forgive me . . .'

Lena strained rigidly backwards while she supported the old woman so that she could not fall; then the sinews of her neck and the corners of her mouth began to tremble. Suddenly the gun clattered to the ground, and she was moaning, holding on to her grandmother. Ruth's hand flew to the gun on the floor and, almost simultaneously, towards the bolt. Douw stood on the threshold, dismayed by the scene facing him and by the tears which Ruth, too, let flow as soon as he held the gun and she was in his arms.

A Man Apart

When Ruth could see again, Lena was still supporting Ouma Katryn, like a child for whom she was sorry, whom she had to hold erect with passionate solicitousness. Neither was able to speak and Ruth had to explain hurriedly to Douw.

Her news made Douw's features stand out more sharply still, and yet it was as if he hardly heard. Only now did Ruth notice how he shrank back, as timidly as before but with a softer bewilderment or tiredness which he did not try to hide. Frowning, he tried to say something to poor Lena, then announced in a hard, hurried voice: 'Pack only essentials. As soon as it's dark, we must get away. I don't want to live on the charity of others so pack enough food.'

Only then did he tell them of the massacre at Die Poort, and the women and children held as hostages in the forest hideout.

'Aren't you coming with us?' Ruth anxiously wanted to know.

'No. I'm going to Kransbos to try and help the women and children. Perhaps I may get them out.'

Even more than his words, his haggard face made Ruth cold with fear. What had he left out in the telling? He gave her no chance for further questions: their most valuable possessions which they could not take with them had to be packed into the flour-chest and other containers and buried or hidden in the forest behind the house. One never knew whether Stuurman's henchmen might not come to burn this house down, too.

Half an hour later the women still ran around struggling to fit a last indispensable something into their bundles; loads that could be no bigger than the horse or they themselves could carry. Lena's bundle was the smallest: she had lost her interest in earthly possessions, and cared only for helping her grandmother. The old woman was the last to come out into the darkening evening, the heavy Bible pressed to her chest. Sternly she looked at her grandson as he stood tying bundles to Pronk's back: 'We should leave everything rather than the Book. It is the holy command of our Saviour that distinguishes us from the heathens. Bring out the benches, Douw.'

So they prayed for the last time, in the dusk that slowly engulfed the known, loved objects on Prinshoop's farmyard. The leave-taking was so sad that all involuntarily hurried to get away, before it was too dark. Douw carried little Samie and Lena led the old woman; completely different towards her grandmother, as if she were now the older and stronger who had to console the other. As soon as she caught up with him, Ruth asked, softly so that the others should not hear: 'My husband, why do we have to go? To escape all these horrors? So that Stuurman and his men can no longer humiliate us?'

'Yes, Ruth. It's better if they have no more hold on me or on you. I . . .' And then he told her wretchedly: 'When I arrived at the place where the murder had taken place, Thomas Muller and another burgher shot at me. They think it's my doing that Wolfaardt and the others were ambushed. Tielman was with them . . . he wanted to stop them . . . I . . . I rode away as fast as I could.'

In her consternation Ruth's legs failed her. So this was Stuurman's joke! Now Douw's honour was at stake. He would try to save the women and children so as to show that he was not one of the assassins. He would have to.

'Oh, Douw, Douw!' She felt so paralysed with fear that she wanted only to hold on to him.

'Douw,' she whispered, 'it's terribly dangerous! Why do you have to go there; why do we have to go down the mountain; why can't we just flee deeper into the mountains, farther away? We've still got the oxen and the wagon.'

Without answering, he walked on. Stumbling over the uneven ground in the dark, she kept up with him, her hand clenched in his—but how much assurance and love could a desperate hand offer? She was right, fleeing would solve nothing. Yet, before they caught up with the others, she begged in a whisper: 'As you wish, Douw, but come back, my husband, come back to me and Samie and Katrientjie. And to little Douw who still has to be born . . .'

This time he stopped. He stood stiffly erect, afraid of touching her. 'Ruth,' he said hoarsely, 'you once said Samie need not be ashamed of his father. I don't want to make you a liar.'

They walked on. What use were words?

A Man Apart

By now it was completely dark, and their steps were unsure. When they came round Paardekop's slope, they saw red gleams from the dark lowlands reflected against the sky. Somewhere near Wittedrift, and to the south-west, too, behind the hills.

'It's the Melkhoutkraal and the Knysna farms burning down there,' Douw pointed. 'The scum must have pressed on there today.' Ruth remembered Melkhoutkraal, a paradise with orchards and fences laden with rambler roses, red and white ones with pollen-drunk hearts . . .

They were hardly allowed time to rest before Douw hurried them on once more. Plettenberg was far and they had to be close before dawn. Lower down the valley Douw once more pointed to the right. Down there, in the dense thickets was where Stuurman's gang had their hideout, where Douw had to go to endanger his life. It was after this that Ouma Katryn's strength gave in completely. Lena started carrying her but Douw stopped her. They could make room for Ouma on the horse's back.

Now that she no longer had to support the old woman, Lena stood with empty hands not knowing what to do. Speed had deserted her. It was clear that poor Lena had supported her grandmother so as to be able to keep going herself.

'Come on,' Douw curtly hurried her on.

Her eyes swept over him so vehemently that he recoiled.

At their next resting-place, they discovered that Lena had left them, bundle and all. However much they called, softly so as to attract no enemies, no answer came. It would be fruitless to go to look for her in the dark, above all if she had left them of her own accord. Douw lost all patience: 'She knows her way hereabouts, she can't get lost unless she wants to.' He silenced the others and made them move on again. They became so tired that they had no more strength to talk. Right through the night they stumbled on. They had to be as close as possible to the fortress farm by the break of day, for there Douw would leave them.

In the pale light of dawn his only order to the old Bushman was to go back and help Tkanna with the cattle. If something happened or if Prinshoop was burnt down, he must come and tell the women. The leave-taking from Ruth, his grandmother and the children was merely a short embrace. Then he disappeared into the dark forest, alone, on foot.

In this way the little group of fugitives came disconsolately round the last turning of the road: Ruth with the two children in front, then Ouma Katryn who was walking again since Douw's pack had been loaded on to the horse, and lastly old Speelman leading the horse. Just short of the farm a very suspicious sentry stopped them. Douw Prins's people? Why didn't they go and join up with Dawid Stuurman's nest of vipers? To their misery was added this furious interrogation as if they, too, were riff-raff who could not be trusted and hardly had the right even to a hut of matting alongside the cattle kraals. The roan stallion was commandeered at once, even though old Speelman insisted that Douw had sent it for Tielman Roux, in case Tielman had lost his horses at Keurbooms estuary.

It was an upsetting experience for Ruth, the enmity and suspicion of those in the laager against coloured people coming from outside. It was as if the murders and the destruction of their farms had brought madness into the white people, so that they, like Lena, refused to listen to reason. Not everybody's eyes smouldered with hate like Thomas Muller's whenever he passed near them, but nobody showed any sympathy. People who had formerly shown good-will towards them now turned away or were absent; young Botha was dead, and Tielman was away on patrol trying to head off herds of stolen cattle.

Douw was in danger. Ruth did not rest until she stood before the fieldcornet and told him how they had been surprised and maltreated by Stuurman's gang, how the murderers were now hiding behind Kransbos, and how her husband had gone to try to free the hostages. The fieldcornet looked as if he did not believe her story, and his eyes mistrusted her account of Douw's queer actions. However, he did not openly accuse Douw of being a traitor, so poor Ruth was denied even a chance passionately to affirm her husband's innocence. Soon he told her to go, he was busy.

All that day the small number of able-bodied men were busy preparing for the moment when they would be numerous enough to ride out as a punitive commando. Then they would take a bloody revenge. There were as many half-castes and Hottentots as white Christians carrying guns, but all spoke with equal vehemence of the barbaric Children of Ham who had to be quelled for once and for all. Shortly before noon a rider brought the news that six burghers from the Longkloof had arrived at the Government Post in the bay, with extra ammunition. As soon as Tielman's patrol returned they were sent out again, to see if the thirty men of the Stellenbosch commando had already arrived along the coastal road.

That night Ruth's eyes remained dry. There would be no time for tears until Douw had returned safely. Tonight her only refuge was the Bible; when Ouma Katryn's voice tired of spelling out the words, she begged her grandmother to read some more, more of the solemn, sonorous sentences comforting by their wisdom. And yet she was incapable of comfort while Douw still wandered outside in the treacherous night. And poor Lena? Where was she tonight? Involuntarily she put her hands on her belly where she felt the new child stir, the child who had to be a son and to carry Douw's name.

When the twilight became too deep and her grandmother's voice struggled into final silence, Ruth built a small nest for the children inside the shelter of branches and matting, a miserable home for a woman used to a walled house. They had brought candles, but all light had been expressly forbidden. Old Speelman, who had been threatened with death if he were to leave the farm without permission, lay curled around the tiny fire's last embers. Wrapped in her blanket, the old woman remained sitting in front of the shelter. Restlessly the young woman moved around outside.

She stood watching the night grow dense over the laager where violence smouldered in the hearts of people, and thought of another laager deep in the forest where other violent men were lurking. She thought of the man wandering between, the estranged, proud Douw abhorring the violence of both and yet able to be destroyed by both. She who was usually so meek, tonight felt his proud revolt kindle a response in her, so that she stopped walking and raised her face to the sky to mutter: 'You are a much better man than all of them.'

She said it again, louder, defiant, with his bitterness: 'Douw is a better man than all of you!'

Slowly, with a dry rustle, the old woman came to her feet and stood behind her, taller and bigger than Ruth. She uttered no pious words of rebuke, instead, as she threw her shawl over Ruth's head, she said gently: 'The night will be long and cold.'

The young woman bent her head as the shawl covered her hair and temples and fell in long black trails down her shoulders.

23

Patches of sunlight and shade flecked over him as he crawled to where the rivulet lisped under its umbrella of ferns. He lay flat before the pure goodness of water and drank enough to stay his thirst for a long while. Then he crawled back to the clearing in the forest, opposite the woodmen's huts, to a young yellow-wood tree, low and branched like a shrub. Now he knew where the two sentries were stationed, one on the koppie, the other on the forest track to the bay: he was pretty sure that the great majority of the gang had gone to murder and plunder somewhere else, leaving only a handful of men behind. Half a dozen Kaffirs and three Hottentots, including Lafleur who lay sleeping, a hat over his eyes and a red-stained cloth around his cheeks. His immediate problem was Lena, sitting in front of the nearest hut in which the prisoners were locked up.

Had they taken her prisoner somewhere or had she come of her own accord? What could possess her? She did not look like a prisoner or out of her mind. She sat at her ease in the shade of the hut, busy with needle-work. Sometimes her hands stopped, to stroke the cloth slackly and aimlessly. She was only thirty yards away and when Douw looked closely he could see that she was mending a man's torn shirt. He had to suppress a hysterical desire to laugh; had she, after her experiences, come to play housewife for these villains? For one of them? For that rotten Lafleur who now lay sleeping out his drunken debauch? If so, it might be dangerous to try to attract her attention.

In discouraged uncertainty Douw once more studied the camp. It was clear that wild roistering had taken place the night before. A wine-cask, empty flasks, clothes, linen, a flour-chest, a bag of raisins, and dirty plates and pots lay strewn around the ash-heap in the centre of the clearing, all things seized from the fleeing burghers at Die Poort; things which the robbers in their greed had not wanted to leave behind. The group of Kaffirs sat leaning against tree-trunks, to one side as was their custom. The two Hottentots with guns over their knees did not look too sober either. The only sounds came from the prisoners' hut which now stood in full sunlight. Inside it must be unbearably stuffy: tired mothers were continuously trying to soothe their crying or whimpering children. Abruptly there was movement at the one tiny pane-less window; a white woman's haggard face peered out.

'Water,' she said.

She had asked Lena and had to ask again before Lena took the trouble to rise and fill a leather bag from a wooden pail.

With a heavy heart Douw realised that Lena was acting as a kind of prison warder for the imprisoned women and children. That meant that she was doing it with the approval of the assassins. He pushed himself up on one arm and tried to wave with the other, to attract the white woman's attention. But her dull eyes stared emptily before her, she did not see him. Then Lena returned with the water, and he had to duck down once more.

What should he do now? Try to attract Lena's attention? He was nearly certain that that would be dangerous. Even though he was a close relation of hers, she would sound the alarm. And even if he rushed up now to unbolt the door, how on earth would the exhausted women and children escape from nine, no, eleven armed men? No, he would wait till it was dark, and hope for the chaos of a new drinking-bout when the rest of Stuurman's gang returned.

The afternoon sun shifted much too slowly across the leafy roof. While Douw wondered if he should not move deeper back into the forest he saw Lena get up and busy herself by the fire. She poured sweet tea-water into a flowered bowl and carried it and the kettle of warm water to Lafleur. She knelt down by his side and loosened the cloth around his face to sponge the wound. Lovingly her hands nursed the wound which she herself had administered. Lafleur put up with it; he pushed her aside only once to take a heroic draught from the bowl. When she was finished, he gave a great lazy yawn and pinched her on her thigh so that she jumped up shrieking with laughter. It shocked Douw to the depths of his soul, the loud, vulgar, laughing voice of the big woman ringing out over the camp. It was Lafleur's shirt she was mending, no doubt of that. Had she lost all feelings of shame that she could so fling herself at this dirty swine? So extravagantly vulgar?

He could no longer bear to watch her and crept back into the forest till he could once more stand on his legs as befitted a man. Where ferns completely covered the rivulet's deep stone bed, he filled a hollow with mouldy wood and leaves. A tired man was not worth much. The best course would be to sleep till it was dark.

He awoke when red light flickered on the trunks of the trees around him. A big fire was burning in the camp and the tumult of many voices told him that Stuurman's robbers had returned with new booty from which drink was not lacking. Become completely drunk, he thought contemptuously, as he heard Lena's voice screeching as loud as any. Now the false creature was singing a silly song, followed by coarse laughter at some joke or other, most likely at her own expense.

He forced himself to think of something else, and took the bread and dried meat from his knapsack, to eat something and wash it down with clean water. He thought with dismay that Lena's joining up with these villains boded no good for him: young Botha's widow at least knew that Lena was his kin and would put her collusion at his door. So as not to have to think, he listened intently and tried to guess where the sentries could now be posted. The big fire and the reckless noise surprised him: Hottentots easily became rash, but did even crafty Dawid Stuurman reckon that every white man in the world was now fleeing to the Cape, too scared to hit back? If he knew the colonists they would not rest till they had exacted vengeance to the full.

Lena nagged at his thoughts once more. He took his gun, checked the charge, and crept cautiously to his old place opposite the prisoners' hut. Now there was light in the second hut. Through the open door he could see a candle on a corner plank casting light on a chair with leather upholstery, a fine chair which some housewife must have flatly refused to leave at home. Around the campfire bellowing voices were clashing in Dutch and Xhosa: a Hottentot and a Kaffir must have come to blows. Stuurman had probably gone over there to assert his authority. The only guards he saw were two black figures standing listening between the fire and the hut. This was his chance. First he had to get as far as the hut, to whisper to the prisoners that they had to be ready to escape.

Just as he rose on his knees, he heard a shuffling sound behind him. Somebody was stalking him, a clumsy stalker who breathed heavily and made a lot of noise. Somebody who knew he was lying there? He shrank back, gun reversed so that he could hit swiftly with the stock. Even before he recognised the crawling figure and made out pale thighs above a tucked-up dress, he knew it was Lena. She knew he would be here.

In anger that was even more loathing, he lay still till she reached him and peered into his face. He smelt her wine-drenched breath when she started to laugh with panting gasps. He had never heard a human being laugh in such a way, so desperately and yet so obscenely. Disgust and fear rose in him too violently for pity.

'Quiet,' he hissed. 'Have you no longer any respect for another's life?'

Her panting laughter slowly subsided, before she mumbled in a dead voice: 'Everything can go to hell.'

Somewhere in him Douw remembered how this woman had searched for love and had found only the humiliation of the body, but the immediacy of his tongue and jaws recalled only his harsh exclusion of her, the brutal question: 'What do you want?'

Perhaps she did not know herself, or no longer cared for words, for once again she laughed in that obscene way.

Then, unexpectedly, she threw herself forward to grab with all her weight and force at the gun in his hands. Douw was so taken off his guard that he was trying to stop her even as the shot went off with a thunderous roar, scorchingly close. Then only was he able to jerk loose the gun, beat her with the stock so that she fell over backwards, and jump aside, staring fearfully in every direction.

The camp was in an uproar. Men fell flat, milled around, ran for their weapons. Gnashing his teeth with indecision, Douw stood wondering whether he should flee. If he did, his attempt at saving the hostages might have been in vain.

Irrelevantly and absurdly his ears were intent on an innocent sound audible above the stealthy hush in the camp, the high throaty croak of a frog in the ferny dell. Escape in that direction? No, a branch crackled. Before he could get away, they would fire at him. Without having consciously decided he swung the gun over his shoulder and walked forwards to the bright light of the camp fire; leisurely, in peace, even when two black warriors bounded at him with assegais raised above their shields.

'Captain Stuurman,' he said firmly. 'Take me to Captain Stuurman.'

The two men hesitated, before flanking him and pushing him forward towards the fire. A Hottentot barred his way with levelled gun and snarling mouth.

'Crazy Lena tried to turn me back,' he reassured the latter, 'and the gun went off. I'm coming to talk with Captain Stuurman.'

Only when the men were convinced it was a false alarm, was Douw escorted towards Stuurman's hut. His gun was inspected to see if it had indeed been fired recently and then stacked against the wall amongst a dozen others. Captain Stuurman made him wait. Outside, the drunken carousing started up again. At last three more people entered the hut: Lafleur, another of the leading henchmen, and lastly Stuurman, who showed no interest before

he had taken his seat on the Captain's chair. Then he put a flask
of brandy on the shelf beside the candle, preparatory to inspecting
Douw with narrowed eyes. Slowly a grin spread over his face.

'The farmers' guns made you run, heh?'

This wisecrack made Lafleur and the others roar with laughter.

'Oh yes, my men's eyes are everywhere. They were watching,
too, when you took your womenfolk to the Dutchman's laager,
but were too scared to show your own face. Now you're sneaking
around our laager like a jackal's cub. You nearly shoot your own
cousin and then knock her out. You're a busy fellow, Prins.'

He took a leisurely swallow from the flask and let it do the
round of the two Hottentots and the two black men standing
behind Douw. Once it was back in his hand he suddenly narrowed
his eyes:

'Why, Prins?'

Douw looked him straight in the eyes.

'Captain Stuurman, you said yourself you did not want to spill
innocent blood. I have come to propose that I take the prisoners
back to Van der Wath's farm and to ask ransom for old Botha,
if he still lives.' For the first time his tongue stumbled over his
teeth: 'For you it may be dangerous to . . .'

'Dangerous? The only danger to us is a spy like you.'

'I'm no spy for the Dutchmen, Captain. This is not my war.'

Involuntarily the words had come out stiffly. The Hottentot
chief turned his head sideways and his words became slower,
slyer: 'If you're not siding with the Dutchmen, you could easily
join up with us. Isn't that why you came?'

Douw swallowed, shook his head.

'I came to help the defenceless women and children.'

Dawid Stuurman looked at him.

'Why, Prins?'

Douw remained silent.

'I'll tell you why. The farmers don't trust you. Now you're
trying to curry favour by bringing their womenfolk back to
them.' Stuurman took another sip, and laughed scornfully: 'It's
not your war, heh? You only want to have clean hands, heh?'

'Yes, you grovelling coward!' Lafleur added brutally.

Douw's jaws clenched paler as he fought to control himself till he could answer calmly: 'Would a coward be standing here tonight?'

Without replying, Stuurman held out the flask of peach brandy. 'Drink. You need it.'

He held it out till Douw took it and drank a little. Then he told the other four men: 'Go. I want to talk alone with him. The fewer ears the better.'

When the door closed behind them, Stuurman settled the tails of his swallow-tail coat more neatly behind him, and let his chin rest pensively on his palm.

'You're not fond of your life. Now who would have thought that.'

A vague fear took hold of Douw and made his tongue crawl thick and sluggish inside his mouth. Stuurman felt like talking, and no good could come from a conversation with this man. Stuurman watched him, and then slowly stretched out his foot to push a sawn-off stump against the back wall.

'There, sit down. Be comfortable. I'm worried about you, Prins. I heard you ask Lafleur how he could be a free man if he had no respect for others. But tell me now, do you think the Dutch people respect their coloured fellow-men? Do you think they really and truly count us as their equals? Heh, Prins?'

Douw shook his head, but immediately afterwards a fierce loyalty to white people like Tielman and Lindstrom made him add: 'Not easily.'

Now vehement himself, the Hottentot chief continued: 'Man, I tell you there's no place for another man beside a white man. They call me a malevolent rebel and murderer. They lie, I'm fighting for freedom for myself and my people. Do you think I would have taken up arms if they had shown me sincere respect, if they had not always snarled at me like at a dog? Do you think I would have joined up with the Kaffirs without good reason. Do you think I like fighting beside them?'

Douw only got a chance to nod, for Stuurman bounded to his feet and marched around in his excitement.

'Damnation, what man, who *is* a man, can bear to grovel for

ever before a white-skinned baas, sniffing up dust like a slave?
Haitsa, I say no! A man must rise and kill, even if with his bare
hands! But we are not bare-handed, Prins! We don't have to be
the underdog! Look here!' And he kicked the stack of guns so
that they fell to the floor with a clatter. 'I have weapons galore.
Tomorrow morning I'll give you a good gun and a trusty horse
with a saddle and bridle, and you'll ride out with us, a free man.
What do you say?'

Douw's mouth remained closed, and now the drunken din
around the fire crashed into the small room with its soft candle-
light. Dawid Stuurman stood before Douw, the flask of brandy
in his hand, his eyes narrow and sharp like knives. He waited.

'Captain, I came to fetch the women and children.'

Stuurman jerked up the flask to take a deep draught. Then he
held it out once more, imperiously. Feeling the need somehow to
meet the man half-way, Douw again wetted his tongue. The
paralysing spot of fear had sagged down to his stomach; though
it was not yet clear in his mind he already felt that Stuurman
wanted more from him than a mere yes, Stuurman was seeking
honour.

'Drink like a man!'

When Douw obeyed, Stuurman sat down once more on his
plundered chair, a short, bow-legged figure with fiery, darting
eyes, grotesque and yet dignified, a vain man of violence and yet
a chief imposing authority.

'Look, Prins,' he said heavily, 'I said just now that you did not
seem fond of your life. Tell me now, what does a man have to
put above all else? Freedom? Love? Or what?'

Words and concepts milled through Douw's brain while he
pressed his hands to his eyes in his bewilderment. What did the
cruel devil want? Was freedom enough for Damon? Faith?
Love? Did he put Ruth above all else in his life? What shall it
profit a man's soul, if he loved those who loved him? You ran
away, a shaming voice called, followed by Ouma Katryn's soft
rebuke: It's the sweat and blood of the poor and humble which
build our future.

'I don't know,' he groaned, and forced his eyes wide open,

fixed on Stuurman who now grinned mockingly. 'Or wait!' He felt suddenly tranquil, as if he were coming home.

'Captain, it's more than honour or what one receives from others. It's . . . it's respect for yourself.'

'And what is respect for yourself?'

'It's . . . it's to be free.'

This made Stuurman sneer: 'And if, here and now, you have respect for me, are you a free man? Heh, Prins?' Now his eyes were unflickering, unmoving.

Douw knew that it would be better if he sprang up at once and tried to escape into the dark. Yet he did not, he went on sitting before the robber chief as if the latter's eyes were not standing guard like a beast of prey, as if he, Douw, once more tied to a wagon wheel, was cringing away from a sjambok, inescapably committed to resist everything which he was not and did not want to be. Stuurman held the flask like a whip.

'It's . . . as if you are not being forced, by yourself, or by others . . .'

His voice hurried, becoming firmer: 'It's to refuse violence.'

Douw could not turn his eyes from the face before him.

Stuurman's tongue licked convulsively over his lips, then shot out the question: 'I am a captain of fighting men. I fight for freedom. I use violence. Do I then have no respect for myself?'

Douw knew that here was the hell-fire in Stuurman of which he had been afraid, here a raging snake had risen to strike. Desperately he remained silent, turning his eyes to the ground.

'Son of a bitch, I'm asking you a question!' Stuurman bellowed as he sprang to his feet in uncontrollable fury. Adore me! Honour me! Purify me with praise! his eyes screamed, or else I turn the world to a heap of dung on which I vomit!

His neck stiff, Douw looked up.

'I don't think so, Captain,' he said as frankly as ever before in his life. 'Otherwise you would not have asked me.'

Stuurman tilted the flask down his throat, flung it against the wall, and burst into choking laughter which ended abruptly.

'You miserable dog,' he spat out, 'you run this way and that, but all your clever talk only means that you're crawling on your belly, shit scared that I'll raise my hand against you! And you, who think your hands are so clean, not so long ago you rode with the whites to attack my people! Sies, I'm wasting my breath on you!'

It was true. Douw's eyes sank. Now Stuurman was choking with laughter: 'Didn't you yourself say that if you have no respect for another, you're not a free man? Heh?'

Douw did not even raise his eyes when Stuurman called in his guards and snarled at them. 'Take him out and tie him up! Naked!'

Humiliatingly aware that he had not only insulted Stuurman but also disappointed him, Douw did not resist.

Outside the hut his wrists and ankles were strapped together behind his back and the end of the thong tied round the trunk of a tree. Then they forgot him for four nights.

*　　*　　*　　*　　*

The first night somebody was sorry enough for him to throw a sheepskin blanket over his nakedness. When he rolled on to his other side and strained his head up, he saw Lena walking away against the red glow of the embers. Not that he, in his dull dismay, cared much: it was as if he had to learn to think all over again as he lay curled backwards in his humiliation.

For three long days he endured his cramped position, now on one, then on the other side, deaf to the drunken racket regularly recommencing, impervious to the feet which stumbled over him. Only the flies settled on the sjambok wound on his face sometimes made him furiously shake his head. A shallow wooden bowl like a dog's dish was later put down beside his face. In it was water which he could lap. When the sun dried it, Lena brought more water, as well as a piece of meat which she cut into cubes and maternally pushed into his mouth. He could no longer ignore her, and had to glare at her and mutter: 'I'm not Lafleur.'

She took no notice of the rancorous turning away of his mouth, except to wait till she could feed him again, her fingers slack and mechanical as if it did not matter much to her. Douw had to eat to get rid of her; she seemed sorry for him and his aversion to her became a vague kind of pity as well.

A Man Apart

Slowly his thoughts made a fresh start. His pride had been too selfish, he had not been humble enough. Yes, it had been selfishness that had driven him to take Tkanna into his service and to try to save the women and children. It was selfishness that had estranged him for so long from Ruth. All his thoughts now went back to Ruth and the children: Katrientjie who now was nine months old, babbling her first sounds, Samie, that small bundle of energy, talking his whole world awake, Ruth's arms reaching out in the warm caress of the hearth towards pots of food, or swinging the baby from one hip to the other, her lips swelling rounder whenever she looked at him . . . Yearningly he reproached himself for never having been good enough to them, for never having allowed himself enough time to love them. For now he knew that self-respect was more than pride or honour, that it had to be built on love as well. Now he knew what he should have told Stuurman: You do not respect yourself, because you hate.

He could never completely ban Stuurman from his thoughts. It was like a sore which he wanted to scratch till it disappeared.

It was no wish to flee that drove him to try to loosen his bonds; he merely wanted to escape from his thoughts by taking an interest in things outside himself. By then he knew the tiny space of earth around him well. The clods of black-brown earth belonging to diligent ants, the dozens of blades of grass he had already tried to count, the shrubby patch of 'Hottentot bedding,' and the tattered bushes at the edge of the thicket where tree trunks began. Also the sultry and heavy smell of earth and his own urine. His excrement he had regularly managed to bury by painfully digging oblong trenches with his toes and then kicking earth back over them. To get his naked body back under the skin blanket once he had emerged from it, was a challenge which he mastered ever more easily. Obstinately the need to create order around him was reborn, even here.

He also began to take more interest in what was happening in the camp around him. Stuurman and his horsemen once more rode out on a plundering expedition, to return after two days with new loot: livestock, clothes, household objects and drink

S

that caused tedious quarrels before they managed to divide it. After that they once more abandoned themselves to a wild night of guzzling and drinking. From the men's talk he realised that one of the Hottentots, called Hans Afrika, had been sent to the Christians' fortified farm to demand a huge ransom for the prisoners. Hans had not come back. The third afternoon a spy returned and great excitement followed. The Christians had detained Hans and, after they had interrogated him and found a bloody kerchief and an ivory tinder-box on his person, they had shot him for complicity in the murder at Die Poort. At this Dawid Stuurman announced with awful curses that the prisoners were to get no more food or water.

That afternoon Douw tried to attract Lena's attention. She was still guardian of the prisoners, but she was now less loud and vulgar than before, and often she merely sat staring at Lafleur, an eternal maudlin smile on her lips, her hands for ever busied with nothing in particular. That afternoon she was interested in the stolen clothes which the plunderers had brought along and which made the camp look like a rich household's Monday wash. The lot included some lovely gowns and after Lena had collected them in one place and tenderly felt them all, she threw one over her head. Two or three of the biggest, most colourful dresses she put on over her own clothes, the topmost one a satin gown with fine lace tucks. Then she wandered, grand and stately, around the camp, deaf to the men's coarse jokes.

When she passed near Douw he whispered: 'Lena. Untie me. Tonight in the dark. Lena!'

She stopped, standing slightly bent like an old person. He once again noticed her hands, her big, strong hands that ceaselessly wriggled and wandered around in the air and on her clothes.

'Damn it, I say untie me,' he whispered, after a while, 'tonight, in the dark.'

She did not nod or respond in any way, she merely bent still more while her fingers clutched at the fragile lace collar round her neck and started tugging at it. Ever more fiercely her hands tore till lace and blue satin fell in shreds around her.

Douw had to turn away his face as from an abyss, but it was

after this that his thoughts became clear and he again felt he was a man.

No, he now argued further with Stuurman, no, I do not belong here. No, it is not that you use violence, it is that you love violence, that you take pleasure in humiliating and destroying people. No, I should simply have said no to you. I should have said that I have respect for Tielman. I belong with Christians like Tielman who are capable of compassion.

That night Douw nearly succeeded in wriggling out of his bonds.

Exhausted and with raw wrists he only managed to fall asleep about dawn; it seemed immediately afterwards that he was rudely awakened.

Black tree crests were sawing at the fish-pale sky, and two men were untying him, cursing because the knots had tightened so much. Then he was yanked to his feet and told to get back the circulation of his blood. Stiff-legged he stumbled and fell as, like a child, he learnt all over again how to walk. Then clothes were flung to him and he had to put them on, the jacket and shoes too big and the trousers so long that they hung over his ankles. Now that he was back on his own legs, he could look the grinning villains around him in the eyes.

He had to stay standing at the fire-place and was given a piece of cold meat to choke down. Dawid Stuurman, who for three days had not once deigned to glance at him as he lay bound hand and foot, at last came up to him.

'Now you look fine,' the Hottentot chief nodded with a sarcastic smile. 'Feathers make the man, don't they? Now your self-respect is safe, heh?'

He looked at Douw from hooded slit eyes, while his right hand jerkily played with a sjambok.

'Look, Prins, the women and their brats are eating up our food. I thought of burning them up, hut and all, but then I remembered that you had come to be their saviour. Well, take them back. Just tell Van der Wath that I'm doubling old Botha's ransom. I now want two men's equipment for him, two horses, with their saddles, two guns with their ammunition. I'm sending horsemen with you, to protect you in case the Dutchmen take it into their heads to fire at you.' He laughed at his own joke. If there were some other kind of venom or evil intent in him, he hid it well.

But this man hates me, Douw thought with wonderment, what does this change of mind mean? He had little time for further reflection, for the women and children arrived in a stumbling group. Behind them, from the hut, came the pathetic cries of the old Patriarch, Botha Senior, who would have to remain behind alone. Some of the Hottentots were already mounted on horses urgently trampling and rearing around the camp.

There were six women with haggard faces and crumpled dresses, four white and two brown, and about twelve children, some still so small that they had to be carried. When Heynse's wife passed Lena, her face became convulsed and she spat at the yellow half-caste. The latter remained indifferent but Captain Stuurman strode forward with a hard laugh.

'She's going with them! Bring her bundle!' he ordered. At this he turned on Douw: 'Don't forget your family!'

A horrid scene followed. When Lena realised that she had to go with the others, that she was being sent away, she threw herself flat on the ground, shudderingly trying to cling to it. Now the men loudly mocked Lafleur on whom rested the onus of getting her away. In the end he was obliged to tie a thong with a noose round her middle and the other end attached to a horseman's saddle. Lena was dragged some distance before she stood up and followed by herself. Douw ran forward and helped her rise. At that moment he knew that his place would be in the punitive commando beside the burghers.

The last he saw of the robbers' hideout was Stuurman standing with his hands on his hips, laughing at him; destroyer where love's honour was lacking.

*   *   *   *   *

Later the sun rose and changed the landscape into a blue roof above a green earth. In the heat their progress was slow. The women and children were so weak after their privations that by noon they had only reached an upper branch of the Bietou on the near side of the wagon road. Although they had shown no open revulsion from him, and perhaps even were confused by his presence, it was clear that their suspicion of Lena clung to Douw, too. When he noticed with what horror Wolfaardt's widow looked at his clothes, he found the courage to say: 'Mrs. Wolfaardt, I'm sorry if I'm wearing clothes belonging to your loved ones. But Stuurman took my clothes and made me wear these.' After that he remained to one side away from them as well as from their Hottentot escort. Still more did he avoid crazy Lena who followed, dumb as a stone, at the end of her thong. Now he knew why Stuurman was sending him, why Stuurman had laughed.

Too proud to talk to anyone, even to explain to the women how he had become their guide, he kept on arguing as he walked, not with Stuurman now but with the whole world. Self-respect meant that you had continually to accept the risks, the dangers of life in all its possibilities. You yourself, even if you were alone. As long as you did what you had to do, because you believed it to be right ... I swore I would bring back the women, and isn't that what I am doing? Yes, I know I'm risking my life; I know I'm selfishly worried about my own life, but what about it, what man would not be? Yes, I know I'm being mocked. But who are you to laugh, or threaten with guns or rant about Whiteskin, or Hottentot, long-haired Baboons, or Half-Breed this or Bastaard that? Do I have to grovel to the other side when a hand of another colour holds the whip? Do I always have to run away from the white man's high and mighty self-righteousness? Can't a man stand fast, and say: Here I am, let us stand together? Yes, I may be afraid of them, but I should try. I should try and help to end that kind of violence. I should try to be a man so that Samie can become a man.

In the exaltation of his senses objects along the road took on more passionate colours and shapes, as if leaves had veins of green blood and flowers at his approach became fluttering butterflies, as if everything had become part of him, irradiated with the same fiery elevation. He was not a Hottentot half-caste in the clothes of a murdered man, he was Douw Prins who could only preserve his self-respect if he tried to save the poor women and children. Was he not himself a father and a husband? Did Ruth not wait for him, did his whole being not yearn and reach out to her, with whom he had learnt what love was?

It became unbearable to him to see Lena walking, tied like an animal, and he hurried to catch up with her and to ask: 'Will you stay with us? Do you promise?' When she nodded, he talked the Hottentot rider into stopping, so that the thong could be untied. After that he walked a long while beside her, met by her dumb silence, incapable of reaching her. He could only turn back to the exhausted women and offer to carry a little girl who could hardly walk. The child shrank from him, yet allowed him to put her on his shoulders.

Again he walked beside Lena and spoke to her, without getting any answer. Lena had been demolished beyond words, alive only at the single moments when her hands could caress or break: in between lay long deserts. Now he understood Lafleur and Stuurman better: they only desired the chaos of violence, the evil lust to destroy. But how could compassion survive before the rearing stallion of one's own terror?

Their last resting-place was beside a stream where they could drink water and rest long enough for the men to smoke a pipe. Then they went on again. In his sympathy for the women he no longer saw their eyes. Young Botha's widow fell and lay moaning; zealously he went to revive and console her. Then on again. About a mile before they reached the fortress farm, the Hottentot horsemen reined in their steeds. Grinning, their leader indicated that Douw should lead on his flock alone.

'Pleasant journey!' They shook in their saddles from laughter.

The afternoon sun burnt down on the road. Douw walked ahead, followed by the women and children, with Lena at their heels.

His shadow walked ahead of him, his fear walked ahead of him, but he no longer noticed the shadow or the road; it was as if nothing mattered except this strange, feverish silence that grew in him; nothing was true if it was not inside him, did not become this certainty of himself. He, Douw, a man walking with firm steps inside himself.

Round the last bend the house with its white circlet of wagons and tents came into view. They were close to the camp before they were noticed. Then people swarmed out as if from an antheap; running or racing towards them on horseback. Armed horsemen spread out, prepared for an ambush. A moment later the survivors could experience the joyful, sobbing moment of return.

Someone plucked the little girl from Douw's arms. People milled past him, past the open space around him. Then he saw Ruth come with flying dress, felt her falling against his chest, felt the quiet exaltation flowing into his hands and lips. There was no time for words of love; immediately she raised her panic-stricken eyes and whispered:

'Oh, Douw, be careful; they suspect you. They shot Hans. They don't want to listen, they . . .'

'Hush,' he silenced her, and quickly told her of Lena's betrayal and what had happened to him. Over her red bonnet he saw that a circle of silence had formed around them, the weeping women and children were being led away by other women and the men now stood looking at him and Lena. There was no time for love: he pushed Ruth gently aside and walked up to Fieldcornet Van der Wath.

'Fieldcornet,' he spoke as calmly as he could, 'I have brought back the women and children as I said I would. They maltreated me and tied me up for four nights. But Stuurman found the prisoners too much of an encumbrance. I think he wants to shift his camp before the Stellenbosch commando arrives. And so, this morning, he allowed me to take the women and children away. But he asked a double ransom for old Botha; two horses with their saddles, two guns with their ammunition. And, Fieldcornet, I'm coming to help punish the murderers.'

Heavy and broad of body the fieldcornet stood before him, silent.

It was another man who asked with hostility: 'Is that all you have to say?'

And from behind the men a woman called hysterically: 'He's not even ashamed to wear a murdered man's clothes!'

'Stuurman took my clothes,' Douw explained. 'He wanted to make fun of me.'

'Stuurman hates us since Douw had been with you on commando!' Ruth called with passionate indignation. 'He set his men on to us women, he . . .'

'Let the women remain silent!' the fieldcornet suddenly growled. 'This is a matter for men. Let us go to one side. Bring the yellow Bastaard woman too.'

As he turned away with the group of men to the kraal wall, Douw was particularly conscious of some faces, of Ruth being pushed aside and grasping imploringly at Tielman Roux's arm, of Thomas Muller's face swinging behind other faces as Lena came past, of tense chins, hard eyes, and grim, twitching lips in the other faces over which his eyes swept. His intense perception ceased to take account of externals, but was replaced by a heightened vigilance inside him which allowed him to walk forward, one step like the other, his gaze as frank as heretofore. I am no criminal, I have come to help you as I am. As I am.

The fieldcornet walked ahead to the empty milking kraal beside the pen for the calves. The old, familiar smell of cattle dung came to his nostrils, then the men stood in a semi-circle around him, the majority with their guns still over their shoulders. The fieldcornet came to the point at once:

'Look, Prins, your role in this whole business is not clear to us. You brought false reports about where the enemy was supposed to attack. Then you were seen at the scene of murder, and when the men fired at you, you rode away. Now you arrive here, supposedly as the saviour of the hostages, and yet you act on the orders of Stuurman. He sent you here, like he sent you the first time, without any longer demanding ransom for the women and children. A jackal like him can only think and plot like a jackal. I tell you, if you are the traitor we think you are, you may as well say your prayers straight away.'

Resolutely Douw looked into the unwinking eyes which hid their grief and hatred behind stern authority; briefly he explained what had happened and how Stuurman had hoodwinked him. When he stopped, the fieldcornet said, chill as ever: 'We threatened his first spy, the Hottentot, Hans, to make him talk. Hans said that you would bring the women and children for ransom. When we asked him about you, he answered that Stuurman considered you to be his best spy because the Christians did not mistrust you.'

'That's a lie! Stuurman was angry because I did not want to join up with him, and so he tried to slander me.'

'Can you prove that Hans lied?'

The world shrank around Douw; his throat started to contract so that he had to raise his voice. But he would not grovel, he would not beg for mercy, he would remain standing firmly erect and answer like a man:

'I can only give you my word, Fieldcornet. My word of honour that I am no villain, that I only wanted to help and . . .'

'A Child of Ham has no word of honour!' a man interrupted him, hoarse with passion. 'We do not need help from a Child of Ham!'

As if he had been slapped, Douw's head jerked back, suddenly uncontrollably flung once more into the old, loathsome defilement of Thomas's racial hatred. From the corner of his eye he saw that Tielman came forward to his side, but even before he could feel grateful for this, the fieldcornet repeated his inexorable question: 'Can you prove it?'

Reluctantly Douw turned to where Lena had stood with head down cast.

'Lena was there. She's not right in her head since those rascals violated her, but she knows I'm speaking the truth.'

But the big yellow woman did not hear him and no longer stood there. When she heard Thomas's voice, she raised her head and began walking forward with gleaming eyes towards him; towards her brother, who could no longer avoid her without taking to his heels. 'Tommy,' she lisped like a little girl, as if taken back to the last time she had seen him when he had left the house, a downy-bearded youth. Her hands reached out to touch and stroke his face, and her face took on life with a consuming curiosity. Her brother leant rigidly backwards; then he jerked the gun strap from his shoulder, grabbed his gun and fiercely beat away her hands. 'Stay away from me, damn it!' he panted. His sister's face slowly died once more as she retreated, her eyes still fixed on him.

In paralysed incomprehension Douw stopped her: 'Lena, you were with the Stuurman gang. Tell the fieldcornet how I hid in the forest and how they caught me.'

Her face had returned to a loveless desert, she hardly looked at him. When he grabbed her shoulder, she pulled loose with a grunt which sounded like a disgusted laugh. Her hands went up to her face, and from behind her convulsively wandering fingers she kept on peering at her brother.

At this moment, while Douw stood open-mouthed in the sudden realisation of what Thomas Muller was to Lena and to him, Tielman Roux got a chance to speak, no longer embarrassed as in the past when he had had to defend Douw, but resolute with indignation: 'Fieldcornet, I have the utmost faith in Douw Prins's words. I know him. He is an honest man. He is an innocent man. Look at the mark on his face where he has been beaten up. Look at his wrists to see how he has been tied up. Fieldcornet, there's far too much suspicion against people who are our friends and allies. The vermin hiding over there in Kransbos, they're the murderers and it's them on whom we should take revenge. If there had not been men here who wanted to sit like cowards waiting till the day we could march out with a mighty commando, we would have gone to smoke out the robbers' nest long ago. Fieldcornet, this man went back all alone to Kransbos to try and do something, and on his return the would-be heroes who stayed at home want to smell out enemies amongst our friends. I say that it's a great shame, Fieldcornet. I say, let us do nothing hasty. I'll answer for Douw. Doesn't he say clearly that he is coming to fight beside us now, like last time? Heh, men, don't you agree?'

Tielman had looked at Thomas Muller while he spoke, but now he looked around at the others, who shifted their feet uncomfortably or nodded in agreement. The tension in the circle of men was noticeably less, until Muller sprang into the centre beside the fieldcornet, his eyes wildly searching the faces of the burghers around him but avoiding Lena's slanted, peering face. Suddenly the yellow woman laughed once more, grating and spiteful, and as if to drown her voice, Thomas shouted: 'There's too much talking here, and too little doing! Get away there!' Dementedly he clawed at his powderhorn to throw a pinch of gunpowder into the pan of his gun.

Lightning-swift, Douw's world shrank to its last, inviolable possession, his dignity, his clear, straight gaze. He was simultaneously aware of many things: of the restraining hand his friend now raised while the men closer to Thomas did not seem to do anything to stop him; of an intense determination not to run or to scream; of animal fear trying to choke his throat; of amazed disbelief that his cousin could put such a high price on being a white man, that he could let evil powers take possession of his soul in such a way; and, farther away, of footfalls at the kraal gate where Ruth was leading Ouma Katryn nearer in all speed. Simultaneously, everything receded, he became free from everything, even consciousness of himself shrank to an all-encompassing compassion for the man before him, to the utterance of one single word: 'Ruth,' a thunderous truth.

The shot hit Douw from so close that the bullet knocked him over backwards and his knees folded as he fell. Foam flecked Thomas's lips when Tielman knocked him stumbling across the kraal dung, to remain crouched some distance away, retching.

The men turned their eyes away from Ruth who came desperately running, her arms spread wide as if to ward off death, her mouth open to the one, continuous gasping moan of his name: 'Douwww . . . !' Douwww . . . !' Even before she reached him where he lay with a tiny hole in his forehead, the unborn Douw in her womb kicked black pain over her eyes so that she sank down into a swoon.

The old woman came alone to the corpse. Her head sank before Douw; then the sinews of her neck jerked up again as her grief-blinded eyes searched for Thomas, for Lena, for her daughter-in-law Ruth, for the shamed circle of men. Her black shawl spread shudderingly over her arms as she raised them high, as if to curse where a family's bonds of love had been so dreadfully broken. Her wrinkled lips shuddered, but when at last words came, it was the supplication with which the Almighty himself had led the people in prayer:

'Our father which art in heaven, Hallowed be Thy name. Thy Kingdom come. Thy will be done in earth, as it is in heaven . . .'

24

Early in the year 1803 Bengt Lindstrom stood on the deck of the *Goude Leeuw*, watching the white city recede. The mountain had once again put on its white wig, for the trade wind was roaring from the south-east. It was a majestic spectacle, the high table rising sheer from the sea, covered with a cloud that poured white and endless across it like a waterfall without ever reaching the houses below on the beach. While the mad wind made the sails above his head bulge and flap, Lindstrom stood watching the Town of the Cape disappear while the mountain, too, gradually sank away farther and smaller behind the foam-churned waves. For him it meant farewell to a country in which he had spent more than four years. With a heavy yet thankful heart he recalled landscapes, faces, unexpected hospitality, camp fires across the length and breadth of the wide southern land which he had learned to love so much; so much so that during the past few weeks, he had come to share the inhabitants' relief at the ending of the frontier war and at the return of the Cape of Good Hope to the Dutch authorities. Four years. Yes, he had been here long enough. In the hold of the ship he had more than enough botanical material to keep him busy for many years. And yet his heart felt heavy, something still felt incomplete.

An officer had to come twice to call him to his meal. As soon as he could, he left to go to his cabin and take his journal from his trunk. His thoughts urgently needed the clarification which he could only achieve pen in hand. The ship lurched creaking over the infamous Cape rollers; he hesitated long before he began to write:

'If I want to be honest, I have to admit that I undertook my journey to the southern tip of Africa, not only to examine the country's fantastic wealth in plants, but also to satisfy an inherent and probably depressive tendency to loneliness far away from Europe's over-filled cities. I found both: the botanical riches, as well as the lonely, unspoilt spaces where a man may still breathe freely without coming up against some regulation or other, or bumping into his neighbour's washing lines. But I also have to admit that the Cape of Good Hope has surprised me with something else: its motley variety of peoples such as occurs in no single country of Europe. Yes, a botanist like myself had to come to this enigmatic country to become interested in people.

'To put it differently: I return with love and deep concern for the inhabitants of this land. I say "concern" because here a new people is being born, and because any scientific observer of such a process must note the ingredients in the crucible and seek to predict the viability of the end product. Compared with my fatherland's relatively homogeneous population, we have here an unequalled number of racial groups from Asia, Africa and Europe, irrevocably thrown together; their success or failure in becoming one will determine their future. Either a totally new nation will come into being, or a Babylonian madhouse that will finally produce a tragedy *sans pareil*.

'To my mind, until now the former has been happening. Admittedly there were great class differences based on cultural or religious distinctions, but these did not always coincide with differences in the colour of people's skins. There was growing up a new people in which more than a thousand self-supporting half-caste and "free black" men had been listed on the roll of the burghers. Except for the Dutch Afrikaners in the Town of the Cape who still tried to speak pure Dutch, I found all over the country that the descendants of the whites more and more spoke the same simplified Cape Dutch as the Afrikaners of mixed blood, the Hottentots and their slave servants. The same history, cultural standards or clothing, as well as the same Christian moulding,

penetrated everywhere. The white Christians' success in main-
taining their initial superiority over the former barbarians could
not last for ever.

'However, in the last decade or two, this process has been
radically checked. This comes from the clash with the migratory
waves of black Negro races from the north-east, races which do
not want to relinquish their own languages, traditions, culture
and national pride, and therefore are not assimilable. There is once
more peace on the eastern frontier, but this peace will never last
long, for the two nations, the two imperialisms will remain in-
compatible and irreconcilable. On this dangerous meeting-ground
a new condition has been created: a fear of a race, of the dark
race, has been born; fear which easily turns into enmity towards
all who are not of pure white descent. For understandable reasons
frontier dwellers are more exclusive and less tolerant. And it is
exactly these frontiersmen who will more and more determine
national policy as land-hungry colonists, from the areas settled
since 1652, trek increasingly into the interior. These men will
gradually forget their origin in the "Boland," and thus come also
to forget the coloured Afrikaners or to treat them like a foreign
race.

'I can still remember my sadness when I received Tielman
Roux's letter in which he told of the tragic death of Douw Prins.
I can imagine no greater failure or diminishing of human values,
than a situation where even blood-relationship can no longer
prevail against colour-prejudice. Thus we obtain a divided house
doomed to destroy itself.

'It does not become me to try and play the prophet, for prophets
are seldom optimistic. And if I say that I cannot imagine how a
nation can be born without trying to unite all its elements so as
to lay firm foundations for itself, then I must add that the Cape-
Dutch nation derived from such heterogeneous elements, is
bound to have a birth which is difficult, sadly drawn-out and
unpredictable in its outcome. I, a mere outsider, have the right
to say only this: though I now return to my fatherland, my sincere
blessings will remain with these people of the Cape, with many
persons of many racial groups whom I have learnt to know. It is

my fervent hope that their future will not be without happiness for themselves, nor without meaning for others.'

For a while Lindstrom sat silent, then added a footnote:

'How little I know about love. What, for example, is the essential difference between the love of two people for each other, and love for one's fellow-men in general?'

He mused some time more before he went back on deck. By now Table Mountain was a tiny white cloud, and the African coastline a fragile tracery, sometimes disappearing behind the swells. In the cool wind blowing flecks of foam into his face, the clean wind which the people of the Cape call the Cape Doctor, he felt his old, patient calm return. What is man without the glad certainty of hope?

CAPE TOWN, 1966